VAQUERO

An SOBs Novel

IRISH WINTERS

WINDY DAYS
PRESS

Vaquero, An SOBs Novel, #3
Copyright ©2020 by Irish Winters
All rights reserved

First Edition

Cover design: Letitia Hasser, Romantic Book Design
Interior book design: Bob Houston, eBook Formatting
Editor: Linda Clarkson, Black Opal Editing

ISBN Paperback: 978-1-942895-91-6
ISBN eBook: 978-1-942895-90-9
Library of Congress Control Number: 2020905096

Irish Winter's websites: http://www.irishwinters.com and irishwinters.blogspot.com

Vaquero

An SOBs novel

Angel – Chance's story
Assassin – Pagan's story
Vaquero – Julio's story

Coming soon:

Damned – Kruze's story

You can find Irish Winters

On Facebook
https://www.facebook.com/IrishWintersAuthor/
&
On Twitter
https://twitter.com/irishwinters1

Sign up for Irish Winters' Newsletter at:
http://www.irishwinters.com/newsletter.html

For more information about all Irish Winters' books,
visit:
http://www.irishwinters.com.

Prologue

Julio Juarez currently attached to an elite, former military group of covert presidential watchdogs, watched and waited in the trees. He wouldn't move until Pagan Sinclair lifted the woman he loved, Julio's sister, into his arms and carried her into her poor excuse of a house. It had taken Pagan nearly two years to track his woman down. They had a lot of catching up to do.

The hut Paloma called home was insufficient by United States standards, but she was happy here. She'd made a life for herself in this humble Mexican village. Better yet, the people had accepted her. Julio had checked. Everyone thought highly of her. They might not be rich or famous, but it was obvious they considered her part of their *familia*. That was all Julio wanted for his baby sister, that she finally had what she'd been searching for.

Whether Pagan actually stayed in this part of Mexico for long remained to be seen. Julio suspected not. The Sinclairs all had bigger-than-life, winner-takes-all personas. He and his brothers, Chance and Kruze were meant for better things than the simple, unobtrusive, backward ways of village life. Pagan was one of those Chris Kyle types, a former Navy SEAL still out to save the world. He'd been born for more than happily-ever-after in a wooden hut. That'd never be enough for him.

But the Sin Boys were not Julio's problem, and he'd interfered in his sister's life enough. "What do you say, *amigo*?" he asked the sniper fidgeting at his side. "Have you seen enough? Are we done here?"

"Yeah. He's got what he's always wanted. Let's move." Kruze grunted as his fingertips toyed with the cigarette he had yet to light. Whether they realized it or not, snipers who smoked had a death wish. If tobacco didn't kill them, their target would once he or she caught a whiff off that cancer stick. Kruze was in desperate need of a nicotine fix. It was time to move before Pagan realized he'd been followed.

Julio faced west. The Pacific lay beyond the sandy, grass-covered berm, so close he could smell the salt in the water and the seaweed on shore.

Paloma had chosen her hideaway well. Southeast of the Baja Peninsula and north of Guadalajara, she could've lived out the rest of her days here if she wanted. Maybe she would, but Julio doubted that also.

Now that Pagan had come for her, it was easier to leave. Julio had a date with the ocean. One he couldn't break. That was where he was headed. To the Pacific and his dead wife, Bianca.

"Where to?" he asked his *compadre*.

Kruze hooked a thumb over one shoulder. "Back to Sonora." Which meant he'd soon cross the border from Sonora into Tucson, where he'd catch a ride home to Montana.

Julio had never understood this recalcitrant Sinclair brother. Of the three, Kruze was the tight-lipped one, caught forever between Chance, his domineering older brother, and Pagan, the razor-sharp baby of the three. Surrounded by a good strong family, Kruze still didn't seem to appreciate the richness of having two brothers who loved him the way Chance and Pagan did. If anything, Julio got the impression Kruze avoided his brothers, which was just plain sad. *Familia* meant everything to Julio. He'd give his soul to have his back.

But that day was gone. During the past two years, Julio had lost everything. With a sigh, he offered his hand. "Then this is adios, *amigo*."

Kruze squeezed harder than Julio expected. But no problem. Everything with Kruze seemed to be a contest of wills or strengths. As if he needed to prove he was tougher, he stared Julio down and held on for a fraction of a second too long.

Wincing, Julio let his friend think he'd won. What did it matter? In the end, they were all losers.

"I'll see you around, won't I?" Kruze asked, suddenly more perceptive than Julio had given him credit for.

Playing along, he lifted his shoulders. "Of course. Why wouldn't you?"

"Hell, I don't know," Kruze muttered, as he let go and ran his fingers over his head. "Just thought maybe you were tired or something. Maybe sick and tired. Like me."

"We are all sick and tired, my friend." Wasn't that the truth? "But there's someone else I need to visit before I leave. Be at peace, brother." Then he lied and said, "If you need me, call. I will always come."

Kruze's head nod said he believed his friend. "Later then," he said, as he faded into the fronds and tall grasses that grew along this stretch of the beach.

Breathing a sigh he hadn't realized he'd been holding, Julio set a steady pace away from Paloma and toward the pounding surf. This stretch of the Pacific wasn't the exact location he'd planned on, but it was the same ocean Bianca had once sought out, and that was good enough.

He ran his palms over the tips of thigh-high grasses that clung to the sandy shoreline, letting them tickle what was left of the shredded husband and father in him. Which wasn't much. But Bianca would've loved this beach and this view. So would Tomas. Which was why Julio was here.

The tide was in. The tremendously huge rollers pounded the surf, demanding to be heard perhaps even miles away. Anyone might slip and fall to their death. It was possible, especially if they were foolish enough to be caught on those massive rock fingers that broke through the sand and reached for the ocean. That took the beating the surf dished out. That waited for him.

Gulls hovered overhead, caught in the brisk breeze like living kites. They squawked. Their silvery gray wings flapped. They screeched and they called. And once again, Julio heard Bianca's sweet siren call in the wind.

'Come with me,' she begged again. Just like she'd begged that last day.

Yes. This stretch of the Pacific would work just fine. He would leave the earth here. He could float away and finally be done with the lies all survivors told their well-meaning friends and neighbors. Because, no. He was not okay, and he would never be okay again. The pain had to stop. This was the only way.

The greatest regret Julio carried was that he hadn't gone with Bianca that day eighteen months ago. Her depression had grown more stifling over the three months since she'd been found. But sweet battered Tomas had cried non-stop the night before. It wasn't until early morning that he'd finally fallen asleep from exhaustion. Their son hadn't been right since Julio rescued them from Domingo Zapata's hellish, Brazilian home. But worse, Julio hadn't understood how Bianca could want to run away to the beach when her only child needed her so desperately.

So he'd held Tomas, while Bianca left the two of them behind. She'd always told him that sitting near the ocean gave her hope. Like a fool, he'd believed her. But hope was not what she'd gone to find that day. Only relief from the demons Zapata's cruelty had embedded deep in her soul. Only the final peace of never having to wake again.

Ironically, a SEAL had pulled her lifeless body out of the ocean just off Coronado that morning. A SEAL like Julio could've been, had Zapata not broken his life and ripped his family away. This guy had simply been swimming with his girlfriend when he'd spotted Bianca. But he'd never resuscitated her. Hadn't even tried. There was no need. No reason. You can't bring a woman who'd slashed her forearms from wrists to elbows back to life.

Bianca finally had what she'd wanted. A way out.

As for poor sweet Tomas? Julio swiped at the bitterness stinging the corners of his eyes. He hadn't been able to save his son, either. The two people in the world he treasured most were gone. In the end, Zapata had taken everything. Even Tomas' will to live.

The breeze off the ocean was stiff once Julio crested the berm, and at last, the dazzling Pacific stretched wide and long, deep and turquoise-blue ahead of him. He could almost feel its tender, cold embrace wrapping around him. Holding him down. His greatest fear at this pivotal point in time was that he'd struggle when the final moment came. That his body's natural instinct to survive would kick in and sabotage everything. That he'd be forced to live without Bianca and Tomas.

Like his wife, Julio needed the pain to end. His soul begged for relief. Julio steeled his courage. It must not fail in this, his final endeavor.

An old man tottered along the shore at Julio's left while a black dog scampered into the waves, chasing sandpipers or fish. Julio no longer cared what the man saw or who the dog belonged with. He truly cared about so few things these days. Now that Paloma was in Pagan's good hands, he had one less reason to worry or live.

With one hand, he tugged his shirt over his head, tossed it to the sand, and began jogging along the shore. That way the old man and the dog wouldn't think it suspicious when he dove into the surf. They might think he was crazy. They might try to rescue him. But by then, Julio's powerful strokes would've taken him beyond their reach. He was an excellent swimmer. Every SEAL, even the ones who rang out, knew how to swim. He'd give it his best until he tired, then he'd roll onto his back and float. He'd close his eyes and pray, until the Pacific took him under the way it had taken Bianca.

He was deep in the shallows when a buzz in his rear pocket told him he had an incoming call. Julio's heart kicked an odd beat and a half. He stopped short of the beckoning waves. "No," he told himself with conviction. "It's too late. I'm not answering."

But yes. His dutiful fingers had already maneuvered the cell into his palm, and...

Okay, fine. One last call. This won't take long.

"Hello?" he asked, as he turned aside from the breeze to better hear his caller.

"McQueen here. Got a minute?" Sullivan asked, as in Senator McQueen Sullivan, the force behind the darkest black ops team in the United States. Sullivan was a devil in his own right.

Julio let his gaze scan the distant western horizon where Bianca waited and whispered, *'Come with me. I'm waiting.'* "Actually, sir, I'm in the middle of something important. Can I call you back?"

"No," McQueen bit out, his cheery Texas twang gone, and his I-am-the-boss, do-you-want-a-piece-of-me persona radiating loud, clear, and nasty over the connection.

Automatically, Julio snapped to attention. His shoulders squared. His gut sucked in like it had been trained to. His brain cleared enough that his mouth replied, "Yes, sir. What can I do for you?"

"I've got trouble in Brazil. A former Army corporal. Duncan's his name. Runs an orphanage. Claims he and his kids need immediate evac. Didn't ask why, because I don't care when kids are involved. Can you do it or not?" Sullivan might make it sound like a question, but Julio knew an order when he heard one.

"But sir, isn't that *Dia de Muertos* territory?"

Like the *Sin Boys*, the *Dia de Muertos* were another of McQueen's deep, dark, black ops teams. He managed several. The Sinclairs handled terrorist troubles in the Middle East. The *Lone Wolves,* a covert team of former Army Rangers known to frequent the inner workings of Russia and China, operated out of central Wyoming. *The Panthers,* an elusive group of former CIA agents, worked deep in the Everglades, as well as both Atlantic and Gulf sides of the Florida panhandle. Former FBI agents, who'd seen too much and felt like they'd done too little, comprised The *Night Shadows.* They resolved American terrorist issues in general, from sea to shining sea.

But the grief caused by South American despots and tyrants, belonged to the deadly *Dia de Muertos,* headquartered out of New Mexico. Comprised of an elite team of three former USA border guards, they were the ones who should handle this assignment. Not a guy on his way to meet his dead wife, who even now called to him with a hushed but persuasive, nearly irresistible, *'Come, Julio. Please, come to me. Join me. I've missed you.'*

"No go, Juarez," McQueen replied tersely. "Lost two of those agents last night. Firefight outside of Tegucigalpa, Honduras. I'm in trouble. I need you."

Julio's heart sank at the thought of his brothers' deaths. "Which agents, sir?"

"Diego and Seb. Santiago's bringing their bodies home today. They'll be at Dover before nightfall, and I'll meet them there. Can you do it or not, damn it? This is urgent. I can't wait."

This was another unexpected blow. A loss for the world, not just the States. Julio had known Diego Cortez and Sebastian Torres from his Navy days. They hadn't rung out, and had gone on to become decorated SEALs. Diego signed up to work for Sullivan as team leader of the ruthless *Dia de Muertos*. "But I work directly for the President, sir. Have you cleared it with—"

"Yes, Goddamnit. President Adams is on board. Did you hear what I said? Kids are involved. Orphans, damn it. The world's lost enough of its next generation. Are you with me or not?"

Julio cast one last longing look toward the ocean.

"Talk to me, Juarez. Someone's got to replace Diego. I need an answer, ASAP."

"You want me to lead *Dia de Muertos*?" *Unbelievable.* "Now?" *When I have nothing to live for?* "Why me?"

"Yes, now, damn it. Because more than any man on this team, I trust you. Sign up with me once and for all. Be the leader I know you are. Say yes."

Julio could actually hear McQueen's fingertips drumming his desk over the line.

"No," he replied evenly. He didn't want anything but out of the highly secret, super-covert world. Not only no, but Hell no. He'd lost too much already. He was done with too much death and not enough family.

Only now that he thought about it... Kids were involved? Orphans? Innocents like Tomas?

Julio glanced one last time at the Pacific with its cold, endless embrace. Bianca wasn't really out there, was she? The only part left of the beautiful body he'd had cremated, according to her last wishes, were ashes. Even those he'd let loose on the outgoing tide of a different shore of this same ocean. The mighty Pacific had done what it did best. It'd diluted her earthly remains and dispersed what was left, so far and so wide not a trace could ever be found.

The voice he'd thought he'd heard wasn't hers, either. It was just the wind moaning over the waves, luring his broken heart with the only thing it had to offer. Cold and final death. Like Bianca's. Like Tomas'. That was all. In her passive-aggressive way, she'd reached behind her and she'd taken the tiny boy Julio still loved with her.

Dulce Madre de Dios! This was a hard decision. Stay and die? Leave the only family he had left behind? Paloma and Pagan. The men who called him brother. Chance and Kruze Sinclair. McQueen Sullivan. Rick Santiago. Or live, when he couldn't seem to find any reason to. Rescue other poor, defenseless children. Find a way to breathe around the hole in his heart.

Julio cast a lingering glance over his shoulder, back to where Paloma's humble little home stood beyond the sandy berm and those gently waving grasses. Back to where she and Pagan were no doubt happily getting busy. Back to where another life might just be starting, if Pagan finally had his way. Julio hoped he did. The man wanted a family more than any man Julio had ever known. Except for him. Only Julio wanted his family back.

But that wasn't going to happen, was it? He'd lost the right to ever be called lover again.

Husband.

Daddy.

Then Sullivan made it worse. "It's Oz, Goddamn it. Oz is hunting Duncan and those kids while we're wasting time talking. You go in now, you secure Duncan and his orphans. Then you wipe Oz's ugly ass off the face of the earth once and for all. You hear me? With extreme prejudice, by hell."

Oz.

With that one word, the Earth stopped spinning. The tumultuous waves of the great Pacific ceased crashing. Even the seagulls overhead held their peace. All creation sucked in a combined breath, waiting on Julio's answer.

He'd frozen, but not in terror. Julio wasn't afraid, not of Oz, nicknamed after the *'great and terrible'* deceiver from the movie, *"Wizard of Oz"*. Oz, as in Orlando Zapata, the sadistic baby brother of Domingo Zapata, the diabolical spawn from Hell who'd kidnapped and tormented Bianca and Tomas until they'd broke.

If anyone needed to die, it was Oz. Domingo Zapata, too. But, for the moment, he was untouchable, locked away in a top-secret private facility north of Deadhorse, Alaska, alongside the former governor of Oregon, Mick Tennyson. It had taken every last shred of Julio's restraint not to kill Zapata back then. It would've been easy, and he would have done it. No one would have blamed him.

But the memory of his son had stopped him from exacting righteous judgment on Domingo. Pure, sweet Tomas hadn't asked for the life sentence he'd been given. Neither he nor his father could've foreseen the trials he'd had to endure. Julio refused to add the burden of a revenge killing on that small soul's shoulders. He'd strived to be an honorable father. Had even accompanied Zapata the day he'd been locked forever away.

A man could die in there. Julio hoped Domingo would. Then, and only then, could the need to strangle Zapata with his bare hands until his ugly face turned red, then blue, fade away. Julio's fingers clenched tight at the thought of that bastard's black eyes rolling back in his head when he gasped his last wicked breath.

It was hard to breathe. Even now, Domingo Zapata was still killing him.

"I'll do it," Julio blurted before he gave himself more time to think.

"Well, good," McQueen replied, as if he'd known what Julio's answer would be all along. "Check your email. I sent an encrypted file with what details I know now. You'll fly out of Houston. Be there by seven tomorrow morning. Locate and hook-up with former US Army Corporal Duncan as soon as you can. I'll send coordinates where to find him."

"Sir, may I ask how Duncan knew to call you?"

"He didn't. Duncan sent word to an Army Ranger I know. Asked for help. Said Oz is after his kids. Don't know how many. Only know Oz is behind the disappearance of hundreds of adults and children in Minas Gerais, Brazil. He forces them to work his mines. Kills those who refuse. He's a bastard. Keep your sat phone charged. I'll forward more info as I dig it up. Be safe."

The connection ended. Julio sucked in a lungful of the contrary winds blowing off the Pacific. Swallowing hard, he pocketed his cell. Bianca would have to wait.

Chapter One

Meg ran with her six reclaimed stolen ducklings following close on her heels, all of them panting from the relentless pace she'd set since she'd broken them out of Oz's clutches. Not a one of them complained. At all. Children tended to be fiercely obedient when monsters like Orlando Zapata were after them. They knew from experience what he'd do if he caught them again. Oz was a monster of Godzilla proportions. Maybe not in stature, but most definitely in character. Or lack thereof.

"Hurry, kids," she urged, as she tried to catch her breath between the pounding heartbeats climbing up her throat. Running wasn't easy for someone who'd suffered a mild stroke a couple years ago, a stroke that even now, threatened to expose her for who she was. A fool who'd thought she could save these children and their world. Ha. Zapata had shot that dream to hell.

She'd slung her nearly empty backpack, now carrying empty water bottles and a box of ammo, over one aching shoulder because she needed both hands to swat branches and grasses out of her way. The lack of an actual trail hindered her, as much as her partially paralyzed left side. Her feet worked better on solid, flatter footing. It was easier to keep her balance when she didn't have to dodge roots, carpet vines, or all these bushes. Or when she didn't have to hurry and hide. But Oz and his men would follow the trails. They had Jeeps and trucks. Meg had six hungry, hairless, frightened children.

Doctors had told her she might fully recover one day. Chances were good she'd regain full mobility. With enough physical therapy, she might even walk like everyone else. Couldn't this please be that day?

"We'll rest as soon as we get to the big banyan tree by the river. We can hide there. You know the one."

"Sim," sweet Maria murmured Portuguese for yes. Wiping the sweat dripping into her eyes away and blinking hard because the tall stinging grasses and low hanging vines kept whipping all their faces, she hung tightly to Joachim's hand.

Joachim was smaller than Maria, but like a big sister, she'd taken charge of him. That was what good kids did, and all Meg's kids were the best.

"Just a little farther," she promised even as she prayed, *'Please, God. He can't have them back. Don't let him win. Not these children, too. They're Yours, and they're mine, and no. Just no.'*

Oz had taken too many of the local villagers' children and most hadn't been seen again. He owned several mines in the state, and he ran his like the dictator he wanted so much to be. With cruelty and absolute power. Public whippings and worse. Hangings. He'd left the poor bodies of adult men and women to rot in village squares until the tendons that held their arm and knee-bones together finally disintegrated in the humid heat. In other words, darned near forever. He treated children no better, not in this destitute, mountainous district of Brazil where law and order was miles away. If Oz caught up with these little ones...

Meg steeled her soul at what she knew he'd do to her and her kids. But stealing innocents from certain death in one of his dark, dank mines was the least she could've done. She couldn't go to the village, not anymore. The villagers wouldn't hide these babies. They were kind, but they were also afraid of Oz and what he'd do to them and their children if he knew they'd helped her. She needed to get these kids to her new camp by Giant's Toes, the villagers' name for an unusual granite outcropping rising out of a nearby forest. Oz would never suspect she'd go there.

A treacherous root across the path snared her slower, sluggish left foot, nearly tripping her. If not for stalwart Pepe running at her side, she'd have face-planted.

"Thanks," she murmured, her fear of Oz catching her children a living, breathing snake circling her windpipe like an invisible noose. He'd hang her. But first, he'd make her watch while he tortured, then killed these kids. Her kids.

"Is okay. I help you walk, too," Pepe replied, his one hand cradling her elbow beneath her sarape, the other holding onto five-year-old Pedro.

Meg wasn't dumb enough to refuse Pepe's gentlemanly offer. On a good day, she needed her cane just to walk. Running was another agony all together. But here she was, running for her children's lives.

Sweating like the rest of them, this ten-year-old boy had faced the challenge of saving the kids who'd been kidnapped with him like a man. Never once had Pepe argued in the mine. Instead, he'd simply gathered Maria onto his back, told her to hang on tight, and proceeded to shepherd the others. Encouraging them. Promising them freedom. All those things these little ones needed so desperately to believe as they'd all followed Meg.

She cast a longing glance over her shoulder. Man, she loved them like they were hers. All her shorn little ones. But their hair would grow back. And they would smile again. She'd make certain of that.

Regret warred with anger. Someone needed to end Oz, damn it. Or soon, there'd be no children left in the district. He was a murderer, plain and simple. His mines were all underground. The adults and children he kidnapped were forced to work long hours in dark, stone tunnels with little food or water. The smallest kids had no protection against the bigger, meaner kids.

It was a wicked survival test, pitting the strength of babies against the worst kind of bullies. It was genocide, pure and simple. What he was doing to the poor people of this state, was genocide.

At last, she caught sight of the fifty or so tree trunks ahead. All comprised one living tree that ruled this side of the riverbank. One magnificent, stately, humongous tree. The poor thing's highest branches had been scorched by the latest lumber company to clear-cut the hillside across the river. When they left, they'd set fire to the heap of scrap lumber they'd left behind. That fire had grown so hot and leaped so high, it jumped the river and spread among the tree tops for miles until it ran out.

This beautiful tree, bare of its usual glossy green leaves at the top, looked as shorn as Meg and her kids. But life steadfastly endured in rainforest climates when uninterrupted by man or nature. Even now, the wide, long stand of trunks that comprised this single tree had set down an arsenal of new, aerial prop roots from its scorched, higher branches overhead. The inadvertent damage those loggers caused had merely pruned the tree. Those prop roots had already created a thicker, deeper wall of new growth. These green, grasping roots would eventually dip their fingertips into the riverbank. Others would engulf every living branch, twig, or bush they encountered on their way down.

The banyan tree itself was a fast-growing parasite, an epiphyte that had originally attached to other plants. In doing so, it had strangled its hosts. Now, more like a forest than one, single tree, it had dropped enough aerial roots that it spread horizontally for much of this section of river. Gangs of monkeys and swarms of wasps took over these trees when its fruit ripened. But this wasn't the season of fruit, and this tree was where Meg intended to hide her children. Right out in the open.

"This is it," she told her anxious charges. "Maria, climb up as high as you can go. Hurry. Joachim, you're next. Maria, give him a hand once you're settled. Make sure he's got a good hold and won't fall. Thank you, sweetie. Then you, Phillipe. Take it easy but quickly, please. Climb high and stay out of sight, all of you. Be very quiet. Don't let anyone see you. We don't have much time."

The children were as silent, obedient, and as quick as little monkeys. Ah, to be so young and so agile again. Meg would've settled for being able to walk without limping. But watching these kids scramble up into the thick, green cover overhead, then disappear entirely from sight, gave her hope they would all survive what was coming.

Now for her and baby Dom, the barely-breathing man-child tucked inside Meg's shirt. He'd barely stirred even in the sweaty warmth of her sarape. That was how small he was, so feeble that he fit easily inside her shirt. Despite the tropical heat, he'd been cold when she'd found him. If there were one thing, two things in this case, that Meg had in abundance, it was her warm, sweaty breasts.

Which was why she'd worn a sarape most of the time. Wearing a blanket might make her sweat, but men tended to stare at those jugs, and the last thing she needed in this backward, poverty-stricken part of Brazil, was pretend-romance from some randy Romeo with a glib tongue and a quick eye. Not happening. Not ever. She was an aid-worker, and she'd come to this country because children like Dom—not grown men— needed her.

Poor little guy hadn't made a peep when she'd pulled him off the ground and into her arms, and asked him why he was there instead of in the cage with the others. She worried she'd arrived too late. The tiny guy was listless and his will to live was nearly gone. But if he were to die, at least with her, he would die surrounded by dignity and love. Not tossed away like garbage on a scrap heap, left for wild animals. She could barely contain her rage at what this sweet little guy had suffered. Damn Oz to Hell!

"Now, you," Pepe ordered. "Please, my friend. Come up with us." Hanging nearly upside down from the branch he clung to by one hand, he offered Meg his other. His black eyes were bright and encouraging. His fingers fluttered for her to take hold. That was Pepe for you, always brave, and so much a man despite his tender ten years.

She shook her head. "I'm too heavy for anyone to lift, and it's better if I stay down here. Hide yourself where no one can see you. Tell the others to be very, very quiet. One small sound will give us away."

His fingers fluttered urgently. "No, no, *Senhorita*. Please. I can pull you to safety. I am strong like Papa. I can save you. Come with me."

Ah, she loved this young boy so, so much. Like the rest of her kids, Pepe spoke Portuguese, the official national language of Brazil, but he was fluent in English as well. Somewhere in his past, he'd been educated and loved. He was not only gallant, but intelligent and a quick learner. Like the rest of these kids, she would die for him.

The day Oz and his men raided her orphanage while she'd been in town begging scraps and supplies, might just prove that bastard's undoing. Because now Meg was mad. Not only for herself, but for kind and gentle boys like Pepe who still honored a man he might never see again. The papa Pepe spoke of had disappeared two years ago. His mother died of tuberculosis soon after. Pepe had no other family and nowhere to go, which was why he'd ended up on the streets, then in the orphanage. Like every last one of her kids, he was worth everything to Meg. She would save these children, damn it. They were hers. Not Zapata's.

"Hide yourself, Pepe," she ordered sternly. "Please, do it now. Trust me. I know what I'm doing."

"Are you certain?" he asked, his large expressively dark eyes begging her to climb into the safety of the high branches with him and the others.

Too late. The air filled with noise and the ground rumbled. Scores of armed men in camouflaged uniforms, red bandanas tied at their necks like tribal/gang colors, and dirty black boots, broke through the trees like a dirty wave. Oz's army had found them.

"Hide!" she hissed, as she ducked back in the shadows of that same tree. Pepe's skinny arm disappeared up into the abundant foliage overhead. Barely in time. A dirty, rusted, topless Jeep roared into view, crashing over the bushes, saplings, and vines, bouncing over the same path Meg and her kids had walked just moments ago.

Oz himself was here. *The ass.* Only he didn't ride seated like most men. That would've marked him a mere mortal. No. He stood in the front of the Jeep even as it bounced over roots and uneven ground, holding onto the windshield like a pompous peacock. Swearing and bellowing in colorful Portuguese with every jolt.

Oz was not a big man, not even six-feet tall. His driver was much larger and could've killed Oz easily with his hands alone. But what Oz lacked in height, he'd made up for in cruelty. That was how he commanded, with sheer brutality, some leveled against his soldiers' families.

Dressed in rip-off ACUs, he wore dark glasses beneath his cap and the same garish bandana at his neck as his men. Meg wore a bandana, too, only hers was black, like the shadows she'd melted into. The last time she'd put on Army utilities, she'd been a real soldier, not terrorists like these guys. But hey. That red rag they all wore worked for her. It made every last one of them a target. Told a good sniper precisely where to shoot. Straight at all those bulls-eyes.

And her without her rifle...

Oz bellowed, demanding to know why his men couldn't find one woman and a few kids. What were they, *"Idiotas?!"* He denigrated them again and again, but didn't give anyone time to answer. His diatribe escalated from insults to threats of bloody punishments if she weren't captured and hanging in his *"quartos do general"* by the time the sun set.

Meg's blood ran hot at the image of her dangling like a piece of meat anywhere, certainly not in Oz's headquarters. No doubt stripped and bloodied. Possibly dead. Or raped and about to be dead. Oz was no respecter of women, any more than men, children, or animals. People, his army included, were just things to be used and discarded on his way to fame and glory.

That this runty little twerp thought he could handle her? Not on his best day.

Where Oz pointed and bellowed, his muscle-bound driver cranked the wheel to go. They'd have to travel around the banyan's impressive columnar trunks and roots, though. The tree blocked a long portion of the bank. Meg wished she'd told her kids to cling to the riverside of this tree. Surely Oz wouldn't be able to spot them there.

Frightened now, she leaned deeper into the hollow of her hiding place while the rest of Oz's army tromped by. She held her breath, making sure her backpack and sarape were tucked in tightly beside her.

This was no professional army. Bronze-skinned, many of the men weren't wearing complete uniforms or boots. Each soldier looked weary. All were dirty and slick with sweat. Which made Meg smile. She'd outsmarted every last one of these men and their tyrannical leader. So far...

Some carried rifles on their shoulders while others gripped their weapons like shopping bags at their side. Many didn't have rifles at all, only backpacks. Which might contain ammunition, food, maybe water. Other soldiers, most barefooted, walked the periphery of the main group, swinging scythes, hacking at the thick grasses and shrubbery along their route. Which now snaked around the far side of the tree instead of close to the river. *Thank heavens.*

Meg held her breath even as her poor heart jackhammered like a beast. But she hadn't stayed on the ground to become a decoy or a bag of meat. Never. The large, dangling aerial roots dropped long ago from overhead branches of this tree had created hollowed-out depressions in these wall-like trunks. Backed tightly into one of those hollows, Meg prayed that every one of her children listened and obeyed. That no one slipped from those high branches. That no one had climbed too high to come back down safely. That no one cried out in terror if another child fell and was caught. Or killed...

Cradling Dom under her chin to comfort the silent child, she prayed, *Oh, Jesus, please help my babies hang onto the branches of this tree. It's a blessing from You. I know it, and thank You for it. Please keep Oz and his men blind to us. Let them search the riverbank beyond us, not the trees.*

She hadn't needed to worry. In minutes, Oz's noisy army passed by, his Jeep leading the way, and leaving puffs of black diesel smoke thick in the air. Meg waited only as long as it took for the dust and smoke to settle and the din to subside. Then she whispered, "Come down, children. Hurry fast. We need to run away from here before they come back."

Pepe dropped out of the tree to his feet first, then turned to help Pedro, Phillipe, and Joachim. Lithe Maria plopped to the ground all by herself. Pepe offered his hand and she climbed up his leg, her brown eyes wide, as she hugged his neck and laid her cheek to his sweaty back.

"Where to? The Giant's Toes? Are you sure?" he asked breathlessly, his arms now crossed behind him, cradling Maria's bottom. "Tell me. What do we do?"

Meg shifted the collar of her sarape enough that she was able to kiss the top of Dom's sweaty head. Her backpack went up on her shoulder. Her determination never flagged. "Now, we run for our lives, children. Run. Run!"

Chapter Two

Corporal Duncan wasn't here. No one was. By the looks of the burned-out buildings and the few upright timbers still standing, the total destruction, Duncan hadn't been around this out-of-the-way village for a week or more. He may not even be alive. Creeping vines had already invaded the scorched wreckage of what might have been an orphanage. In forests like these in Brazil, invasive plant life could take over anything in its path within days.

Julio found the bomb craters interesting, though. This level of destruction hadn't been caused by ordinary fire. Duncan could've been killed in whatever battle had gone down here. The orphans he'd wanted exfils for, too. Who would've caused this level of destruction? Who was evil enough to try to kill motherless kids?

As if Julio didn't know. Standing in the middle of what should've been an active, thriving orphanage, he cast an evil glare in the direction he'd just come from, to OZ Metallurgy Mining, Inc. Orlando Zapata and his army of local thugs, mercenaries, and renegades. That was who'd done this despicable damage, to an orphanage, for hell's sake. To children and aid-workers.

After finally making it to this part of Minas Gerais, Brazil, and before reaching out to Duncan, Julio had paid OZ Mining, an odd name for a black, colorless scar on the land, a visit. He'd planned to set up a sniper hide and wait the bastard out. Zapata was Julio's number one priority. Until now, locating Duncan had been an extra, when-I-get-around-to-it duty. An add-on, something any operator would do, but only *if or when* he or she were able to during the completion of their primary goal.

But it hadn't been difficult getting close to, then into, OZ Mining. When he'd stopped there earlier, both Orlando Zapata's impressively large wrought-iron gates had been propped open instead of locked-up tight. Julio had even talked with the single guard at the entrance. A. Single. Guard. Who couldn't have stopped anything if Oz's enslaved workforce would've attempted a coup.

As it was, Julio had nearly walked past the lazy oaf sitting on the hood of a derelict Jeep in the shade. Said guard's teeth had been discolored and crooked. Like his eyes. Judging by his dilated pupils and slurred speech, he'd been smoking something that was not tobacco.

Julio had simply walked up to him and asked to speak with his boss, Orlando Zapata.

"He ain't here," the guard mumbled.

"Do you know when he'll return?" Julio used his best manners.

"I own't know. Maybe tomorrow. Maybe next week..." He stared off into the nearby trees as if he needed somewhere to nap. Or to take a leak.

"Where'd he go? Maybe I can meet him there," Julio offered cordially. It never hurt to ask.

"Doubt it. He's hunting. Him and his guys. Took all of 'em. Never know when he'll be back when he takes everyone like he done."

"How long has he been gone?"

"Couple weeks. Err..." The guy rolled his eyes. Thinking seemed to be difficult for him.

"No matter. What's he hunting this time of year? Jaguars? Monkeys?"

"Rats-s-s-s-s-s," the idiot hissed. *"Just rats-s-s-s-s-s."*

Which meant Oz was hunting either runaway slaves or troublesome foreign aid-workers. Still, Julio prodded. *"I thought this place was a thriving business. Looks deserted."*

The guy grunted. *"Ain't you the genius? For your information..."* He'd actually puffed out his chest like he had something important to share. *"This place is deserted. For now. Might not reopen for business."*

Julio had read the 'Eyes Only' brief Sullivan had sent, but the object of Orlando Zapata's greed hadn't *stuck in Julio's mind. Might be gold. Might be a hundred different types of precious gemstones for all Julio cared. Whatever Oz mined, it would still only be fool's gold in Julio's book. Familia was all that truly mattered. But a bastard like Zapata could never comprehend a simple truth like that.*

"A strike then?" Julio packed as much disbelief into the question as he could.

The guard guffawed. "Them slaves? Strike? Hell, no. The ore's run out. Don't need workers when there ain't nothing in the ground."

"So everyone's gone but you?"

"Yeah, but he'll be back soon. Maybe in a couple days-s-s-s-s. Maybe weeks-s-s-s-s-s... Just you wait. He'll bring everyone back, 'less he kills 'em first."

And there, intelligence gathering had stalled. With a quick goodbye, Julio'd left the guard sitting on his Jeep in the middle of nowhere. Turning into the same trees the quirky guy had been staring off into, Julio had beelined for the coordinates of Duncan's orphanage.

Which was where he stood now. Only Oz wasn't here, and he'd definitely struck the orphanage with fury. Even the leaves on the highest branches overhead were scorched or missing all together. Had Corporal Duncan gone down fighting Zapata's army?

Except for the over-abundance of fifty-caliber brass littering the rutted ground, the ruined camp certainly looked like it. There were more expended shells than one man could've fired. If he'd thought he could protect children while fending off Oz's army at the same time, with just a fifty cal, Duncan was a fool. He should've run.

At least there weren't any bodies. Small consolation, that. Julio worried. A two-week hunting trip, huh? The timeline fit what appeared to have taken place here. Vining tendrils were already creeping through the ash and debris. Leaves from scorched branches overhead had fallen onto the firepit and onto ruined tents, into the ruts.

Julio slapped the annoying insect stinging the back of his neck. The forests of Minas Gerais weren't as lush nor as formidable as the rainforests up north. The waterways of the Amazon River didn't reach this far south. The entire state lay within the hilly, mineral-rich Brazilian Highlands, where elevations reached as high as twenty-eight hundred feet.

But the blessing and curse of Minas Gerais had always been its wealth. First the Portuguese raped the country and its indigenous peoples for its minerals and gold. Then the English. Now slash-and-burn farming, open-pit mining, and the double-edged sword of civilization were doing the same. The once proud indigenous tribes of Brazil had been reduced to mere handfuls, all now living on government reservations. Slavery was no stranger to Minas Gerais. Neither were ruthless men like Domingo and Orlando Zapata.

There was nothing left of the orphanage worth saving. Julio would know. Back in his Navy days, he'd seen absolute destruction like this in Iraq and Bosnia, then Afghanistan. Back when he had something and someone to come home to. Still...

Two ragged marks declared something had been dragged around the scattered stones of the firepit and into the forest. Too short and jagged, too irregular to be tire treads, the tracks told him that something heavy had been moved. Perhaps a travois like the early American Indians used when they'd moved their villages? A sled like that could've hauled whatever valuables hadn't been burned by the fire. Or children. Possibly bodies. Which meant someone had survived. Or a looter had been here. Either way, Julio needed to know where Oz was now, and what had happened to Corporal Duncan.

Leaving the destroyed orphanage behind, he set a quick, but silent pace, following those tracks through the thick woods and shrubs that comprised this part of Brazil.

Man, this day just wouldn't quit. It had already been damned long. In the middle of last night, he'd touched down at Rio de Janeiro's international airport after an hours-long flight out of Houston. Then, because there was no choice, he'd risked his life on an independently-owned puddle-jumper to Pampulha in Brazil's highland state of Minas Gerais. The short, bumpy flight in a prehistoric Cessna had landed Julio at an out-of-the-way jungle runway that looked like something drug runners used.

But the harrowing flight had still left him short about fifty miles from OZ Metallurgy Mining, Inc. By ten the next morning, he was exhausted, grimy, and sweaty, but he had located a bus going in that direction. By noon he was onboard, holding the ragged, grimy suicide strap inside an over-crowded and frighteningly dilapidated form of what Brazilians called transportation. He shared that leg of his journey with a couple dozen locals, several tattooed men from one of the four indigenous tribes in the state, chickens, two pigs, and a baby goat that left stinky little goat-pellets wherever it bounced.

And away he went. Past a collection of colonial towns, all loaded with remnants from the state's phenomenal Baroque history. Away from the elegant stretches of manicured lawns and red-tile-roofed mansions. Past the patchwork quilt of rich, green cornfields intermingled with banana orchards and fields full of cattle. Away from civilization with its order and decorum. Into the rural heartland of Mina Gerais with its forests full of tamarin monkeys, snakes, and roving bands of wanna be guerillas.

Once the bus left the pavement behind, it took excruciatingly long hours traversing the sometimes there, sometimes not there, sometimes imaginary, steep, back roads. The last time its bald tires ground to a squeaky stop, which had been in the middle of nowhere to let the woman with five live chickens shoved into her brightly woven basket off, Julio had simply climbed out with her and melted into the forest. He couldn't take anymore.

Julio was now following tracks that would, hopefully, lead him to the aid-worker's latest attempt to hide. Though why anyone in their right mind located a home for parentless children near one of Oz's mines was beyond Julio's comprehension. Duncan had to be as crazy as Oz.

After Duncan was out of the way, Julio intended to backtrack and establish a sniper hide near OZ Mining. Ending Orlando Zapata wouldn't take long. Eventually, he'd return to his home base, and when he did, Oz would never hear the round that would, most assuredly, end his reign of terror.

But for now, Julio had a missing aid-worker to corral. And he was tired. He'd brought a smaller gear bag with him instead of his usual LBE, a hefty pack that normally carried his *load bearing equipment*. For this excursion, he'd only brought a couple bottles of sports drink and his blow-out kit. Toilet paper. Fingerless gloves. Beef jerky. Protein bars. Plenty of ammo for the pistols now sheltered beneath his button-up shirt. He wasn't here to make friends, and he didn't care if he lived or died. He'd only come to Brazil to stab at the heart of an enemy he couldn't reach. Nothing more.

The simple exercise of tracking what had turned out to be three, maybe four people pulling some kind of travois through trees as thick as those in the forest, was therapeutic for a hardened operator. Julio honestly liked Brazil. It was an easy country to fall in love with, and he'd come to care for its wide diversity of people.

Whether of Portuguese, African, or European descent, or one of the hundreds of native tribes still holding onto their way of life, Brazilians were no different than others. They wanted to be left alone to raise their families. They wanted jobs and national security. That was what mattered to all peoples of the world. Until greedy men like Domingo and Orlando Zapata came along and ruined those simple wants and needs for everyone.

Julio had spent years in Brazil during one of his past lives. Back then, he'd been an undercover operator, posing as security for the boss of a drug cartel who'd foolishly decided he could move his bloody business into Northwest America, as in Portland, Oregon. It hadn't worked out so well. What was left of that drug lord's carcass now rested in an unmarked grave on a tiny island off the coast of Costa Rica. Julio was the operator who'd ended the bizarre alliance of the three criminals: Viktor Patrone, Mitchel Franks, and Benito Garcia. All murderers. All psychotic. Each as despicable as the other. He'd set the explosive that literally rocked Franks' island off its foundation. And he'd do it again.

Personally, Julio found it blasphemous the way most drug pushers wanted, no, needed, to be called drug *lords*. As if they, the scum of the Earth, were better than their victims? Than the grieving parents and families their victims left behind? The arrogance of greedy men and women the world over never ceased to surprise Julio. He'd seen too much of it in his short thirty-three years.

He kept his eye on the ruts and broken grasses, branches, and other tells marking his path. Walking and tracking. Finally, something he could do.

Yet even the sacred number of his age bothered Julio now. It irked him. At thirty-three, Christ, the real Lord, had suffered and died for mankind. He'd laid down his life. Or so the priests said. But even they'd eventually besmirched the purity of the gospel they'd all claimed the Lord had died for. All those pedophile priests... All those liars and accomplices to the worst crimes imaginable, pedophilia and rape. Deceit.

Julio still hadn't forgiven the church for its crimes against so many children or for the priests they'd shielded from justice for far too long. Didn't know if he ever could. No father should.

The point behind Julio's vast well of angst was merely that Christ had accomplished much more than him during His short thirty-three years. He'd saved the world. What had Julio accomplished with the same amount of time? Nothing. If anything, he'd digressed since Domingo Zapata kidnapped his family. He'd sinned. He'd rung out of his one and only chance to be a Navy SEAL. After that, he'd deserted his buddies, even Kruze, who'd always seemed more of a brother than just a friend. *Who does that?* What kind of man turns his back on his brothers?

As if those sins weren't enough, Julio had been a piss poor husband. Any man who'd lost his poor wife to depression, then suicide, proved that in spades. Then Tomas, the son he still loved with every fiber of his broken, shattered heart, the son he still cried for, had died from, of all things, failure to thrive. As if Julio hadn't slept with that sweet boy laying on his chest every single night since he'd rescued his family from Zapata. As if Julio hadn't been a good enough man for even tiny Tomas. A good enough father. Failure to thrive? Jesus Christ, what man could bear that diagnosis, much less live with it after he'd given all to save his son?

Julio kicked at the roots lacing the animal path ahead of him, waiting to trip him. Talk about heartache. He would've gladly given his life to save Tomas. His love alone should've been enough to keep Tomas alive. But the morning came when that sweet, dark-haired boy sleeping on Julio's chest didn't wake up. He hadn't been a baby then, not really. He'd been six. But in Julio's mind, Tomas would always be his baby boy.

His throat tightened remembering the terror that had rocked him when he'd realized Tomas wasn't breathing. He'd eased his son to his back on the floor and started chest compressions. He did everything he could to resuscitate his boy. He was trained in saving lives. He'd been so sure that, if anyone could save Tomas, he could.

But it was too late. His baby son had already been limp and cold and—gone.

What made everything worse was that Tomas had finally smiled—then—after he'd died. His sweet sad face had relaxed. He'd looked pure and holy and childlike again, as if he'd found the happiness in death that he couldn't find in the arms of the father who loved him still. Who grieved every waking hour of every day for him. Whose arms physically ached to hold that sweet boy again. Just one more time. Only Julio knew better. Once more would never be enough.

A bitter salty tear stung the corner of his eye, but he dashed it away. He knew his son had loved him as much as a little boy could, after what he'd lived through. Domingo Zapata had gotten what he'd wanted. He'd succeeded in breaking Bianca and Tomas. Maybe not physically, that was true enough. Zapata had not raped, beaten, or even touched either of them. But he had threatened to do those things, and worse. They'd heard terrible things while trapped in his prison. He'd kept them locked inside a windowless, secret bunker—his idea of home. He'd tormented them with isolation and so many lies that neither Bianca nor Tomas had known what to believe by the time Julio had finally rescued them. They'd been traumatized too long.

And sometimes, those broken pieces of a person's soul, well, they never quite fit together again. Verbal abuse was every bit as damming as physical torture. Every bit as cruel. The mind was a hard organ to heal.

It was never that Julio wasn't a good enough father for Tomas, because he knew damned well that he was. It was just the fickle finger of fate that had upended his life, that made sure he understood every single day that some men were born to be heroes. Not Julio. Hell, he hadn't even been able to kill himself when he'd truly wanted to.

Or had he? Wanted to, that is? This was where Julio stalled every time he thought about his last moment on that windy Pacific shore. Had he really intended to go through with his last act of—cowardice? It irked him now, the very real fact that he was a coward, and that he'd sabotaged himself by answering McQueen's phone call instead of marching into the ocean to finally be at peace with Bianca. Was the universe trying to tell him something? Was that why he'd pulled his cell out of his pocket? Had his thumb acted on some subconscious command of his when it pressed TALK? Was that why he'd wasted no time telling Sullivan yes once he'd understood who really needed to die.

Try as he might, Julio could not deny the rightness of his being here in South America. Unfortunately, Domingo Zapata was untouchable. But if Julio couldn't locate Corporal Duncan soon, he meant to return to OZ Mining and end Orlando Zapata. That would hurt Domingo. His baby brother's death would shatter that stone-cold heart of his, and, God willing, the bastard would scream until he vomited his guts out of his worthless, soulless body.

Even someone made of stone ought to feel that kind of pain. Wouldn't they?

Julio prayed so. He deeply, passionately wanted Domingo to suffer the rest of his life, just as Julio had. And he wanted it. No, Julio ached for it, every waking hour of every heartbreakingly long endurance test of his days. Only then, when Domingo had finally offed himself in that concrete box of a cell he was forced to live in, when he killed himself out of despair, would Julio know peace again. Only then, when they scraped Zapata's blood and gore off the concrete floors and disinfected the tiled walls for the next criminal occupant, would justice truly be served.

Someone had once said that vengeance was a dish best served cold.

Domingo could count on it.

*****

"We're going back toward Oz's mine," Meg told Pepe, "but before we get there, we'll turn left and head to Giant's Toes. That's where our new camp is. You know where I mean?"

Giant's Toes was simply a strange rock formation that jutted upward and out of the forest like a giant's leg. The five boulders clustered at its base gave it the name. For some reason, no vines or parasitic creepers fancied the monolithic stone, most likely because of some poisonous element embedded in the deeply veined rock. At least, that was Meg's uneducated guess. The locals claimed the column was all that remained of an ancient, evil shaman. A witch doctor. That was why no living thing dared touch it. Oddly, in Brazil, that made sense, too.

She'd needed the cover of the forest, and the legends surrounding Giant's Toes to keep close enough to Oz's despicable mine in order to rescue her kids, yet far enough away to keep her other children safe. That location had given her time to scout the edges of his vast empire while she kept her children hidden in plain sight. It was an old Army Ranger trick she'd learned from a good friend.

"You are not taking us back to your place?" Pepe asked fearfully.

My place. She loved that he called the orphanage her place.

"No. I'm sorry, but Oz destroyed it after he kidnapped you kids. Marta and Craig stood up to him, and that made him mad. They escaped when his army overran everything, but for now, everyone's hiding out near Giant's Toes. We'll be okay there, Pepe. It's a really good hideaway, and no, it's not haunted like everyone says. Trust me. You'll be okay there. We all will. Fernando and Joseph are there. Marta and Craig will be waiting for you kids."

Fernando and Joseph Alcaldo were local brothers who'd started the orphanage several years back. They should've been priests, the way they nurtured and tended the children in their care.

Marta and Craig Brunner were married German missionaries out to save the world. Driven by a relentless work ethic, they firmly believed in twenty-four-hour days, God bless them. These four caretakes each gave so much back to the kids. Almost made Meg tear up thinking about all they'd done.

But then there were the older kids, which meant any child over nine. They buckled in to help care for the smaller ones as well. This group of big and little brothers and sisters had become Meg's family away from home. She'd die for any one of them.

"But he will hunt Marta and Craig now," Pepe murmured. "He will kill them."

Meg nodded. "Honey, Oz will kill all of us if he catches us. It's up to you and me to make sure that doesn't happen. Are you up for it?"

Good morale always focused on commitment. That was what Pepe needed now, the internal commitment and willpower to overcome assholes like Orlando Zapata in his life. He wasn't the first and he wouldn't be the last. Something warm and fragile passed between Meg and her valiant ten-year-old warrior then. Something she hoped would eventually turn permanent if she had her way. She'd adopt all of these kids if she could.

"Then I will lead the others to our new home," Pepe declared resolutely, his eyes bright with what Meg knew was a childish crush on her.

"Thank you. Kids? Please follow Pepe and be quiet. But be fast, too." *Because you are not going back into those mines. Not a one of you. Never again. And somehow, I will find a way to kill that son of a bitch Orlando Zapata if I have to do it myself.*

The kids were so dirty, and their clothes had been reduced to rags over the weeks they'd been stuck inside Oz's mines. It had taken Meg way too long to locate them. By then, she was as dirty and hungry as they were, and there was no time for anything but running. Like the best little soldiers ever, they stuck to Pepe while she brought up the rear.

What a sight, her dear, sweet family marching toward what she hoped was their freedom. A month ago, she'd placed a call to an old Army friend for exfil of these kids out of Brazil. Still active duty, Corporal Zabrina Pisoni had promised she'd pass Meg's SOS along. But then Oz struck, and Meg had no way of knowing whether Zabrina followed through or not. Even if she had, everything was different now. The orphanage was gone. The remaining kids were relocated with Marta and Craig. And Meg had gone off the reservation to find her babies. If the Army had sent an assist, which they might not have since Brazilian officials might not have appreciated USA interference, would the Army have searched long enough to have been any help?

Wasn't that the question of the hour?

A weak cough rattled the tiny body tucked against her heart.

"Hey," she crooned to Dom. Peeling the sarape over one shoulder, she unbuttoned her blouse's top two buttons and peered down at him. "How you doing, big guy?"

He smiled! This darling little soldier smiled up at her. It was a feeble effort at best, but it was a ghost of an authentic smile nonetheless. He was going to live, damn it. He had to.

Meg eased the last of her water up from her backpack. Carefully, she set the pack at her feet, then pressed the nearly empty plastic bottle inside her shirt, angling it so she didn't drown this precious boy. "Drink slowly," she whispered as he took a sip, having come to a full stop by now. "Pepe," she called out as quietly as she could. "Hold up. Dom needs a break. Let's all rest for a—"

Of course, Pepe obeyed so quickly that little Joachim ran into him, crushing poor Maria, who was on Pepe's back, between the two boys. Air whooshed out of the little girl. She drew in a deep breath, then choked back the tears gathering in her pretty eyes. But that wasn't what Meg focused on. She'd spotted the dark, hulking shadow just ahead of Pepe, hiding on the animal trail they'd been following back to camp.

"Break time's over, kids," Meg ordered gently, as she tucked Dom back where he'd be safest. The bottled water went back in her pack. Her voice stayed low and certain. "Stay here, Pepe. Keep everyone quiet. Don't make a peep. I'll be right back."

Once beyond their view, she reached under her sarape and unleashed the Army service revolver from its holster in the back of her pants. She had work to do. If Oz was out there, he wouldn't last long. Not today, damn him.

Chapter Three

A quiet, stealthy sound ahead brought Julio's morbid musings to a full stop. He crouched low in the brush he'd been marching through. But whoever he'd heard must've heard him, too. He'd been loud enough. Might be Oz himself, the bastard. Instantly, the pistol in Julio's left holster sprang to his right palm, already cocked and loaded, pointed at what could very well be one of Oz's soldiers or, just as easily, a wild animal of the forest, maybe a leopard. There was no need to thumb the safety off. His pistols bore no such cautionary devices. That'd take too long. At moments like this, when death was close, every precious millisecond had to count.

He steadied his breathing, his sniper senses already kicked in to do what he did best. Kill, if needed. Apprehend, if not. Didn't matter who or what was out there. They weren't getting past him.

Until the quiet cough of what sounded like a very little girl caught his ear.

Then a more masculine, boyish, "Shhhhh, Maria. Be quiet. She said she'll be right back."

Children? Here? She? She who? He'd honestly thought the orphanage would've been closer to the village. Julio lifted his head just high enough to see past the brush between him and those kids when—

"Drop your weapon, asshole," a scratchy but very stern, feminine voice demanded from behind him. At the same time, something that felt very much like the deadly business end of a rifle dug into the back of his skull.

Shit. He'd been caught by a woman. An American woman if his ears hadn't lied. Not like that meant anything, but who was she and who were those kids? The orphans he'd been sent to rescue? *Dulce Madre de Dios!* How many were there? And where was Corporal Duncan?

Pursing his lips, Julio lifted both hands, his pistol now barrel-up. This cocky woman would have to take it if she wanted it. Let her try. "At least, tell me your name."

"You're American?" The disbelief in her tone was a good thing. "Who sent you? Why?"

"Answer my question and maybe I'll answer yours," he bargained.

The tip of her weapon dug deeper. "My kids, my rules, Bucko. Did Orlando send you? Do you work for him?" Interestingly, she'd punctuated every demand with the end of that weapon, which he now suspected was a pistol, judging by how close she'd gotten. Close enough he could smell the sweet scent of feminine sweat wafting off her. A rifle would've kept them farther apart. But if she hissed any harder, she'd soon be spitting nails into his skull.

Julio shook his head in pretend defeat and decided to let her think she'd won. Maybe it was the soft Southern twang to her voice or those lost children out here in the middle of nowhere that did it. He passed his pistol over his left shoulder to his captor and told her what she'd demanded.

"I'm Julio Juarez, Special Agent to Senator McQueen Sullivan, United States Senator. Texas." Then he added, "At your service, ma'am."

Quickly, she divested him of his piece, but damn. The woman was smart. "I know you've got two. I want both of them," she ordered.

There went the pointy end of her weapon again. By the time this ordeal was over, he might have a tunnel drilled into his skull.

"Do you have to keep stabbing me with your gun?" he asked, testing her for military service.

"It's a pistol, you idiot, not a gun," she hissed. "You must be Air Force, or you'd know better. But I'm not telling you again. Your other damned weapon. Hand it over. Nice and easy."

That was the first lesson most grunts learned in boot camp. Drill sergeants loved to explain how a gun was that brainless thing in their pants, while the pistol in their hands was a weapon, firearm, handgun, piece, hardware—anything but a G.U.N. And that dig at him being Air Force was spot on. Most services called Air Force members Chair Force, since they weren't usually boots-on-the-ground like Marines, soldiers, or SEALs. Also, since they were always quartered in nicer digs, like actual hotel rooms with A/C when they traveled.

She was absolutely former military.

And enough. Julio might give up one pistol. Never two. He cocked his left elbow, and in one swift move, punched backward, aiming for her windpipe. When he connected, she gasped and stumbled away. But not before he reached over his shoulder and grabbed hold of the business end of her weapon to ensure she didn't get a lucky shot off and into his head.

Yup. His quick fingers had latched onto an Army service pistol. Beretta M9. Semi-automatic. Nine-millimeter. One in the chamber. Just like he carried. Julio liked her instantly.

Almost made him sorry he'd elbowed her. But then the black bandana perched on her head slipped, revealing a nearly hairless scalp, and reddening waves of shock registered across her creamy complexion. Julio couldn't have been more surprised.

Until a sweaty cannonball hit him in the back. A short, frantic cannonball with hard-hitting fists, who screamed, "Let her go! *Ela é minha amiga! Seu porco vagabundo!*" And a slew of other Portuguese vitriol Julio hadn't heard since his days standing guard for his cartel boss during Rio's Carnaval.

"Stop," he growled, as he tried capturing the kid's flailing fists. "I'm not hurting her. I'm here to help."

"I kill you, *porco*!" the young man screamed, his face red, his hair wet with sweat, and his temper out of control. "You hurt her already! She's crying!"

Which made Julio look over his shoulder at the woman—who was *not* crying—but who was now pointing her pistol, and his, at him. This woman was not the boy's mother, and she most certainly didn't work for Oz.

At last, he snagged the kid's wrists with one hand and held them high enough the kid had to cease kicking to avoid falling. Julio reached into his pocket with his other.

"Don't make me shoot you," the woman hissed, both pistols on target. "Hands where I can see them. Both of them. Now!"

Whoever she was, she had the perfect stance to take those shots, one foot positioned slightly ahead of the other and her legs spread, but not too wide. Just enough to support the kinetic energy from her weapons once, or if, she pressed those triggers.

"Only reaching for my sat phone, ma'am," he answered, dodging the kid's attempt to kick him. "Press one," he said as he held the phone out to her. "Talk to Senator Sullivan yourself. Ask anything you need to confirm that I'm Special Agent Julio Juarez, that I'm here to help."

Something he said got her attention. "I heard. Let Pepe go," she snapped instead of taking the phone.

Julio obeyed. He would've spoken to the boy, but the woman interrupted with, "Pepe, thanks for coming to my rescue, but I'm okay. Really. Go tell the others not to worry. This won't take long."

Why not? Julio thought. *Are you going to kill me? Here? In front of your children?*

"Who's Maria?" Julio asked.

Cords flexed in the woman's neck as she swallowed hard. She was a tiny, but fierce thing. Creamy complexion and exotically beautiful, but nearly bald. He could tell by the way that bandana slipped over her skull when she'd straightened it back into place. No stray tendrils snaked out from under it, either. Anywhere.

She wore grimy jeans that looked like they'd been slept in beneath that gray and black sarape. But she was overheated, and sarapes were made for cooler weather, not for traipsing around in jungles. Was she sick?

Oh, damn. "Cancer?" he asked softly. That would explain her hair loss and the sarape.

Her perfect brows clashed together like twin crimson streaks of lightning. What was most likely a very lovely face when she wasn't pissed off, scrunched into absolute insolence. Her head cocked nearly onto her shoulder like she thought he was stupid. "What did you say?"

He let his gaze wander to the top of her head, answering with his eyes.

She answered back with her chin and two, lush, mauve lips that pursed tight with disdain. "Lice, you moron. Or are you blind and stupid, too? Didn't you notice Pepe's as bald as I am? That none of us have much hair?!"

See? Fierce. But Julio couldn't answer, because she was right. He hadn't noticed Pepe's or the children's lack of locks. Only hers. Maybe because she still had two weapons pointed at him?

She sent him another evil eye that, oddly, he was beginning to enjoy. "We all had to shave our heads. You ever had lice? If not, then shut the hell up."

"That explains it," he offered lamely, his hands raised again until she decided to either call Sullivan or step back and maybe return his pistol. That'd be a nice gesture.

She seemed undecided. Breathing hard, her nostrils flared with every puff. She blinked like she was afraid, though. Shooting a man was not something she did lightly, and that helped Julio decide to trust her. Ever so slowly, he lowered his left hand, watching her closely while she tracked the descent of his hand to the weapon still sitting loose and ready in his right holster cup.

"Do you want this pistol, too? You might as well take it. I can't help you and your children if you won't let me."

Her lips thinned and her nostrils flared again. "Why should I?"

With his second weapon still holstered under his arm, he played his ace in the hole. "Because I'm here to end Orlando Zapata, and I need your help to do it."

The Beretta in her hand dropped to her side like she'd lowered her toll gate. "Honest? You're going after Oz?" she asked breathlessly, handing his piece back without further hesitation.

Lowering his arms, he took it gingerly by the grip and snugged both weapons back where they belonged. "I never lie," he stated unequivocally. "How can I help?"

Her lips pinched inward then, turning her into a sight for sore eyes. Whoever she was, she had the prettiest, thickest lashes. Burnished red, but not scarlet. More like the color of Monarch butterfly wings in November, they curled soft and lush against the apple of her cheeks, both burned either by the sun or embarrassment. He couldn't tell if her natural hair color was brownish-red or deep, rich mahogany. Not that he cared either way. But the combination of colors warming the creamy palette of her skin declared an innate beauty to the woman wearing that stark, black bandana.

It was a rare thing to admit, but Julio liked looking at her. She radiated something—he wasn't sure what— that had been missing in his life until now. She had guts to be out here alone with a bunch of kids. Maybe that was it. Her courage.

"Really? You're here to help us?" she whispered, her take-command tone gone soft and faint, like she didn't dare believe him.

"Yes, ma'am, but precisely who is us? How many children are with you? Are there others?"

The strange compulsion to gather her into his arms stormed Julio's good sense like a rogue wave out on the wild, capricious Pacific. The kind that came out of nowhere, and heralded tsunamis at the end of the world. It struck him so hard and so furiously, he stiffened his spine before he did something stupid, like act on that urge. He hadn't come here to comfort strangers. Not that this woman was undeserving of comfort. More because she was quite a good-looking woman, even wearing a sarape that disguised her figure.

They said beauty was in the eye of the beholder, but the great, wise, unknown *they* were wrong. Beauty lay within the subject's eyes, not the person looking at her. This woman's eyes were two deep, green wells of camouflaged secrets he wished he had time to dive into. Because she was definitely hiding something. He could tell by the way she kept cocking her head at him, as if she couldn't believe anything he said. The left side of her mouth seemed perpetually twisted with disgust. Or maybe disdain. He couldn't decide. Did she think he was lying?

Now it was his turn to swallow hard. He'd come a long way with no sleep since the flight out of Houston two mornings ago. Six thousand miles of jetlag made a man dizzy and unbalanced. He was tired and dirty; his mind was foggy. Yet there he stood, flummoxed, a warrior ready to drop to his knees in front of the most unlikely angel he'd ever met. And he'd met a few. Only most of them were already married. Or dead. Which didn't give this chance meeting much hope, did it?

"I've got six beautiful, amazing kids with me, Special Agent," she answered tightly. "They're the ones Oz kidnapped. That's where I've been, at his stinking mine. I had to get them back before I lost them forever. Are you really here to help?"

Her question irked Julio. Why did she find that so hard to believe? He was here, wasn't he? But... "You went into Oz's mine? You kidnapped these children back from him? All by yourself?" Inconceivable. The nerve of this woman.

"Well, yeah, of course. He hadn't chained them together or dragged them into one of his tunnels yet. Most of them were still in cages. What was I supposed to do? Leave them because I was too scared?" She shot that accusation like a spear, with plenty of swagger, and Julio was pretty sure lightning had just stabbed the ground between his feet. Hot, green lightning. "For your information, bucko. I don't ever leave anyone behind! Now tell me again, Juarez." Again with that sarcastic, cocky dare in her tone. "Are you going to help me save these kids or not?"

"Yes," he replied quickly, wishing he could sit down before he fell down. "I'm here to exfil you and the children out of Brazil as soon as we get everyone ready. How many more?"

Her head jerked a short quick affirmative, like she might have just appreciated his answer. "Seven back at camp. Four adults. Three more kids."

Fourteen, total. That was doable. He nodded back. "Then let's move."

"Well, okay." She hesitated, her hands rummaging under that uncomfortable sarape. "But first..." She pulled a bulky package from beneath that confounded blanket she wore. No wonder she was sweating. She held that package for Julio to hurry up and take it as she ordered, "I've got to round up everyone else. Can you hold onto...?"

He reached both hands to accept whatever she offered, but—

Madre de Dios. She'd just handed Julio the tiniest child he'd ever seen. "What... what do you want me to do with this? Err, him?" he asked, his hands trembling under the weight of a one or two-year-old, very thin, very sick little boy.

"Sit down, for one thing," she ordered. "Don't drop him. Put him inside your shirt. Skin to skin. He's sweaty and he's sick. He'll get a chill. Hurry for Pete's sake, Juarez. He needs your body's heat to keep him warm."

I can do that. If there were one thing Julio knew how to do, it was to obey orders. Quickly. Unbuttoning the top buttons of his cotton shirt, he very gently maneuvered the emaciated body against his broad chest, extra carefully, so he didn't bend the boy's arms or legs or hurt him in the process of hiding him. *But he needs me? Are you sure?*

"What's wrong with him? What's his name?" Names were important. They breached barriers when spoken. They created bonds when heard. They gave people back their identities, and this little guy looked like he very much needed to be recognized. To be seen.

"That's Dominic, Dom for short," she called across the way where she was now checking the other children, speaking softly to them, and telling them they'd be okay. "He's always been small for his age, and he's been sick all his life. Might have worms or some other parasite, the local doctor's not sure. But being in Oz's possession the last couple weeks didn't do him any good."

"How old is he?" The kid was no baby. But he was so, so small.

"Three. You gonna be okay, tough guy?" she asked, her tone laced with sarcasm.

Man, this woman gave no quarter. Push. Push. Push.

"Yes, ma'am." *I can do this. I can help this boy.* Julio folded his legs and sat. He wanted to ask if Dom was dying. How long had he been in the orphanage, and why, *Dios!* Why had Oz taken one so small?

But the woman was over-the-top caustic, and none of those things mattered. Julio'd already made up his mind. Dominic wasn't going to die. Not on Julio's watch. Not worms or parasites, hell, not even Orlando

Zapata would end this boy's life. Not anymore. Oz might think he could, damn him, but Julio had a bullet with the bastard's name on it. Just let him try.

The little guy's lashes fluttered. His eyes opened, and Julio fell into two pools of the weakest, watered-down coffee he'd ever seen. If color were an indicator of one's life force, this little guy's was ebbing. "Hey there," Julio whispered extra-softly so he didn't frighten Dominic. "Want to go for a ride back to your place? With me? It would be my pleasure, and I'll be very careful nothing happens to you."

Dom never made a sound. Just closed his eyes and relaxed, his cheek pressed against Julio's skin. So relaxed and so still, for a second Julio's heart skidded to a stop. "Please live," he breathed into the baby's dirty, weary face. "Don't give up, Dom. I can save you this time. I know I can, but you have to want to live. Please. Choose life." *Don't be like Bianca or Tomas. Please fight. Give me another chance. Let me do this one thing.*

The floodgate of awful, fragile memories crashed open. Sweet vignettes of Bianca holding Tomas when he'd been a wiggling, wet newborn. When he'd woken during thunderstorms at night and cried for his daddy as a one-year-old. He'd always been so little and helpless. So fragile. So much more like his high-strung mother instead of his headstrong Navy father. So much like this dainty, feeble boy whose chest, even now, lifted and lowered as if each breath were his last. As if living were too, too hard.

"Promise me, little one. Promise me that you will try," Julio murmured, his heart breaking all over again for the treasure and curse now laying against it. He swallowed hard. Could this child be what had brought him to this part of the world? Could God be that cruel? That wise? Was Dom the reason Julio still lived? But what if he failed this time, too? What if he'd sinned too much and couldn't save Tomas this time, either? *Err, Dominic.* Julio meant Dominic, not Tomas. Was he losing his mind?

Lord... Padre... Enough! Forgive me already! Julio cried silently. *I'm not like You. I'm not good enough.* When he lowered his sweaty head, he found himself surrounded by five more children, all brown-skinned like him. All silently studying him with wide-eyed curiosity. All except brave Pepe. His fingers were still fisted and his back was stiff.

He's just like me. He holds a grudge.

Julio dashed his free hand over his eyes, steeled his softer side, and gave the woman standing behind the kids his best Navy stare. "What?" he asked as if she hadn't caught him in the middle of a private, pity party. As if she weren't looking at him with the same wonder as her kids.

She offered a firm handshake over the head of a skinny, dark-haired, little girl. "I'm Meg, by the way. Good to meet you, Julio Juarez. And no, I don't have to call any senator to put my faith in you. I trust you. You former Army?"

Damn, she had the most expressive green eyes. The color itself signified life, and life was good, and... shit. His mind seemed incapable of mustering up anything since the sick little boy she'd handed off had molded his feverish body against Julio's belly and chest. Julio didn't dare square his shoulders for fear that that might stretch his shirt too tight and upset the fragile peace of this uniquely painful, but tender, moment. It'd been so long since he'd held a child in his arms, but to have this tiny body snuggled against his heart, precisely where Tomas had once lain, was the toughest best thing that had happened to Julio in a long time.

"No, ma'am. Navy." He gave her hand a firm, albeit quick squeeze before he dropped his hand and cupped the tiny bottom of the child inside his shirt. Dom's backside was more bones that buttocks. What was wrong with him? "You wouldn't happen to know where Corporal Duncan is, or if he survived the fight back at the orphanage, would you? Did you work with him?" *What kind of jerk is he to leave you out here alone with a bunch of helpless little ones?*

Julio was on unfamiliar territory. Emotional territory. It had to stop. He was only here to save Duncan, this woman, and everyone associated with the orphanage, not to father these kids, any of them. Though he very much wanted to care for Dom. This was all he'd ever wanted, *familia.*

But this was just one of many black op missions. When it was done, there'd be others. Other people to save. Other demons to end. He'd never see these kids again.

Eyes on the mission, Juarez. Only the mission. Save the kids. Save the girl. Get the hell out of these woods and find a way to end Oz. He's the goal. Not this brash woman and not some former Army nobody who obviously has no problem deserting women and children.

Yet, even as Julio schooled his judgment, an irrepressible charm lit Meg's face like sunrise in the middle of the day. Tremendously vibrant laugh lines bracketed her brilliant green eyes. For the first time in years, sunlight, so bright that it hurt, broke through the shadows in Julio's dark, ravaged soul. Or maybe that radiant glow arcing over the forest was just a rainbow. The illusion that the sun was brighter could've been caused by clouds clearing the sky. That had to be why the forest seemed somehow greener. Only it wasn't. The glow warming his insides definitely emanated from this woman.

"That's me! I'm Duncan!" she squealed with all the enthusiasm of a kid at Christmas, as she stabbed a thumb into her chest. "Used to be Corporal Meg Duncan. Not Megan. Sure as heck not Nutmeg. Just Meg. You're here to save me! How do you like them apples, Juarez?"

¡Ay, caramba! Julio could barely catch a breath. This ferocious woman was Corporal Duncan? Somehow, that changed everything.

"Julio," he dared to breathe. "Please. Call me Julio."

Chapter Four

Meg had never felt better in her life. Never! Help had really come. She and her babies were saved. Orlando could have this part of Brazil, because she was on her way back to the land of milk and honey. Streets of gold. The good old US of A. And somehow, she was taking these kids with her. *Thank you, Jesus!* She felt like dancing. Or singing. But that'd make too much noise, and they weren't on North American soil yet. But soon. Oh, baby, soon!

"He hurt you," Pepe grumbled. They'd taken a spot and were sitting a way from Mr. Juarez. "And you like him better than me."

"Oh, sweetheart, no, he didn't hurt me at all. And I don't like him better. I would never," Meg assured her handsome, albeit too-young and very jealous suitor, even as she glanced surreptitiously at the badassed man in question. "I'm just happy to see another American. But I also believe what Mr. Juarez said. He is here to help us, and he's one of the good guys. I can tell. But you know I'll always love you." To prove it, she tugged Pepe close enough to hip-check him, even sitting like they were. "I've known you lots longer than that grumpy guy over there. Trust me. You're my main squeeze."

Pepe's handsome face brightened as he wiggled his skinny backside enough to hip-check her in return. "I kind of like him, too. Sort of," he admitted, his gaze drifting over his shoulder to the man in question, who was now staring at the way he'd come. Back to the land of Oz. "He is taking good care of Dominic. I can see that, but he is so ugly. No wonder he is a soldier. People must scream in fright and run away to hide when they see him coming."

That made Meg chuckle. Mr. Juarez, make that Julio, did look fierce and scary, with those masculine brows knotted like ropes drawn too tight across his forehead. They all but shadowed the upper portion of his face. And that perpetual scowl. He seemed not to know how to smile, maybe because he'd seen too much on his tours with the Navy? That seemed a plausible deduction.

There were no laugh lines at the corners of his beautiful, deep brown eyes, either. Which was unfortunate. Those grumpy eyes were fringed in black, his lashes so thick, they could have passed for brushes—or wings.

He was an enigma. One moment a kickass warrior, leading with that scowl and military, take-charge attitude. The next, as humble as a Boy Scout, calling her ma'am, and trying to please. But darkness hovered over him. Or was it just his all-black attire, dark as sin button-up shirt and tactical pants that gave Meg that impression? Maybe. But she'd seen past that harder-than-nails masculine façade when she'd forced this big, tough guy to take Dom.

There was a sadness lurking inside this man, a need. She was sure of it. If not, he would've quickly handed Dom back and grouched that he wasn't a nursemaid, or something just as heartless. He would've acted offended that she'd challenged his masculinity. Most men would have.

But Julio hadn't. Not even for a second. If anything, he'd immediately secured that frail little body inside his shirt and tucked Dom against his chest. He looked more like he'd latched onto a lifeline instead of an unwanted duty. The stoic, hard-core look on his grumpy face had even brightened for a few seconds with unabashed wonder, or something equally as bright. That was the word that fit best what Meg had witnessed inside her rescuer. Bright. Julio's countenance had changed the moment he'd looked at Dom and realized he was holding a little boy. For some reason, he needed this sickly little guy, and Dom sure as heck needed him.

"I think Mr. Juarez is handsome," Meg replied, keeping her tone level so none of her emotions showed. Julio wasn't just handsome. Uh uh. Grown men with the kind of emotion emanating from his dark eyes, with such an intense feeling for a motherless child, were hot as hell in her little black book. Not that she had a little black book. Her dating days ended the day she'd woken in the ER after her stroke. But she could dream, couldn't she? And when she dreamed of her future white knight, there was always a real man in that suit of armor. Not some slacker who tolerated 'babysitting' his own children. But a kind, gentle guy who truly wanted to be a good father. Who truly loved his wife and children.

"When a person risks their life to save yours, they change into the most beautiful creature on earth," she told Pepe. Julio Juarez was beautiful. No doubt about that.

Not that she'd found him unattractive before he'd proven he had a tender heart. Not at all. If anything, Juarez was a sturdy bulwark of a man, his body compact and built like a bull's. A very handsome bull. Yes, that fit him, too. He was a beast of burden, but a workhorse maybe, instead of a bull. Not Hollywood tall or handsome in that vain and shallow, look-at-me, I'm-somebody-important-and-you're-not kind of way. Not one of those prissy, high-strung thoroughbreds. But definitely noticeable. Maybe even eye-catching if a woman knew what to look for.

Meg knew as surely as she was sitting there that something traumatic had happened to this noble creature. It was a wild guess after spending so little time with Julio, but Meg was a decent judge of characters, and she knew trauma. Her diagnosis of this strange, tender warrior felt right. This big fierce draft horse needed the tiny life tucked so carefully against his heart.

Yet, somehow in their first meeting, Mr. Juarez had also ended up being in command, and that was disconcerting. Meg was not a pushover. Despite her handicap, which was getting better every day, she excelled at everything she put her hand to. She, a single woman and a dedicated foreign aid-worker, was here in the Highlands, wasn't she? She had rescued and saved her kids from a fate worse than death, hadn't she? And she'd done that alone. Well, almost alone until he'd shown up. So why was she arguing with herself? She didn't need to convince anyone that she would, by hell, overcome the ridiculous limitation the Lord had 'blessed' her with. But she was, and she knew it, and that was just plain aggravating. Attitude. She needed to change her attitude. Julio was not in charge. She was.

Yet look at him. He sat there cross-legged with his free hand on his knee, the other cupping Dom's scrawny backside. There was something incredibly tender about the way he cradled the boy while they rested before completing the walk into camp. Julio wasn't holding the boy like most men would. Like a football. Casually.

Uh uh. Julio was holding Dom like he'd been entrusted with a gift he didn't want to drop. He hadn't stopped murmuring to the boy or kissing the top of Dom's head through the space he'd left unbuttoned in his shirt. Which made Meg cringe, because that little guy's head had to reek of sweat and filth by now. Lord, all these kids desperately needed baths. But Julio didn't seem to notice. And her crack about worms and parasites? That hadn't stopped him from kissing Dom's head for a second.

Julio's chin came up suddenly. He didn't blink, but man, he glared as if he'd read Meg's mind. As if he wanted her to stop thinking he was some kind of hero. Too bad. That boat had already sailed. He was a hero, at least, for today.

"It's time to leave this place, ma'am," he said respectfully. "Oz will have scouts out looking for you."

She nodded back at him, unable to stop thinking and wondering about him. Not even going to try. "Yes, you're right. We've already run into them. And him. Pack up, kids. Let's go home."

Like they had anything to pack. But brave Pepe assumed his position as a mule for Maria, crossing his arms behind his back to cradle her skinny backside once she'd climbed up his body again. Joachim took hold of Pedro's and Phillipe's hands, and they were moving again.

Meg led the way, while Julio hung back, making certain no one followed. Make that, as he and Dom followed. Because there were two warriors guarding this tiny flock of ducklings now.

"There it is, *Senhorita*. Look," Pepe said, pointing excitedly at the stone monolith peeking through the branches and leaves of the wide green canopy overhead.

"Madre de Dios!" Julio murmured as his gaze drifted higher and higher until he was nearly looking straight up. "What is that?"

"I see it. I see it," Maria whispered. "Is that our new home?"

"It's a geological formation called Giant's Toes," Meg explained. "Yes, Maria. We'll stay here for now. Circle the toes, Pepe, but be cautious. We won't go into camp until we're sure the way is clear."

By then, Julio had advanced to the front of the group and rested his big hand on Pepe's shoulder. "Are you a brave man?" he asked the boy quietly.

Pepe's head bobbed. "Yes. I am brave like my Papa, and I am strong, too. See?" He flexed his bicep like any excited ten-year-old boy would.

Julio gave him a quick, appreciative nod like a man gave his equal. Then he squeezed the barely there bump on proud Pepe's bicep. "I see. You have been working out. That is good. Then we will go into camp together, *amigo.* You and I will make absolutely sure it is safe before we let the women and children enter."

Meg couldn't believe her ears. This man seemed to know precisely how to speak to little boys.

Julio's dark eyes sparkled when he lifted sweet Dominic out of his shirt and, cradling his head so, so carefully, handed him over the heads of the other children to Meg. "Please hold my baby, *Senorita,* but just until I return."

"Your baby?" Meg cocked her head at this incredible man. And he knew the difference between the Spanish version of *Senorita* and the Portuguese, *Senhorita*. "You... you want him back?"

He gave her the same curt nod he'd given Pepe, then asked Pepe, "Are you ready, *compadre*?"

"Yes, *Senhor* Juarez. I am ready." Pepe puffed out his skinny chest. Ah, this boy was in such a hurry to grow up.

"Wait," Meg whispered as she shifted her sarape and shirt to accommodate toasty warm Dom. "Pepe's only ten. He's too young. I should be the one going with you."

"Not so. This is men's work. Trust us. We'll take good care of each other. Right, *amigo*?"

Of course, Pepe's hard, proud, little head bobbed like a cork on a fishing line with a ten-pound trout on the other end. He was trying so hard to be like his father.

"Don't let anything happen to him." Meg laced that command with the promise of a painful death if Julio didn't return with her boy.

Oddly, it was Pepe who answered with, "Do not worry, *Senhorita*. I will take especially good care of *Senhor Juarez*."

"I meant—"

The barest hint of pride tweaked the corners of *Senhor* Juarez's lips. Enough that it stopped Meg from correcting Pepe. Julio nodded at her, *message received*. He knew something she was just beginning to realize. Pepe was already a man.

She sent them on their way with a fervent, "Be safe, guys."

Then she sat with the others in the shade of the monolith called Giant's Toes and waited for the worst to happen. For gunfire and screaming. For mayhem and death to break out.

For all of five minutes. Until Pepe ran back to her, sweating, grinning, and proud like the sweet kid he truly was. "Come quickly, *Senhorita*. Hurry!" he whispered. "Marta made stew! There is enough for all of us, and Craig has bread, real bread! Come fast, children!"

He scooped Maria high onto his shoulders, and the kids all but danced into camp while Meg held back, holding sweet Dom to her overly fluffy, warm breasts. He seemed to like it there, and she loved holding him.

By the time she rounded the Giant's final toe, she could see clearly into camp, and that Marta and Craig had salvaged quite a few supplies. A couple boxes of their precious bottled water. Canned items like milk and meat. One of the ten tents they'd used when they'd called themselves an orphanage. Someone had fashioned a table from a long wooden plank and two tree trunks. It was scorched on one end and crooked, but for now, a buffet of soup and bread awaited.

Julio, Fernando, Joseph, and Craig stood at the end of that table with their heads together like conspirators. Kindly Marta *oooh'd* and *ahhh'd* over each child in turn. Hugging them. Telling them they had to be quiet. Yet declaring how much they'd grown while they'd been gone, when they had done anything but. Crying over Maria, Joachim, and Pedro as they sobbed their relief and fears into her ample arms.

Family. This family meant so, so much to Meg. Hurriedly, she swiped the stray droplets sparkling at the corners of her eyes away. No one needed to see how deeply this miraculous reunion affected her. By all rights, these children should've never been seen again, not after Oz had them. Orlando wasn't a man of leniency, kindness, or courage. He was one of many bullies who ruled this portion of the globe.

Someone needed to stand up to him, and she wanted to be that person. But a woman with partial paralysis was no match for a brutal warlord, cartel lord, or whatever the hell he wanted to be called today. But there had to be a way to end his reign of terror, once and for all.

"Let's eat," she whispered with as much cheer as she could muster quietly. "Kids, grab a bowl. Marta, did you manage to salvage any utensils? You gentlemen, come and eat. Make it quick. My kids are hungry." She directed that stern, but hushed order, at the clustered group of too-serious males still huddled in conference. All four looked across camp at her, but it was Julio's dark, nearly black eyes, that skewered hers. In three long strides, he was at her side.

"I can take him," he offered, his hands splayed for Dom and his voice an urgent murmur.

"But you should eat," she replied. "Eat first, then I'll—"

"No. I'll hold him while you eat. The kids need you. Go."

And you need this little angel, don't you? Meg acquiesced instead of arguing who was hungrier or tougher. "Well, if you're sure," she said to make it sound like giving Dom back was no big deal, when it was obviously a very big deal for Julio.

He fluttered his fingers. Manly fingers. Not long or elegant, but sturdy and compact like the rest of him. Trimmed nails. No ring. Not like she cared. But, yeah. No ring. Not even a white line around his finger where one might have recently been. That was worth noticing.

Once again, Meg maneuvered Dom out from under her shirt and the sarape. When she extended her arms, Julio's hands slid under hers. Over hers. Skin to skin, touching her to make certain there was no way Dom could fall.

The air shimmered between them for a second. Not long. But something extraordinary sizzled. It was gone as quickly as this big, tough special agent returned Dom to what had to be heaven beneath his black button-up shirt. One big hand now cupped the boy's little butt, making sure Dom was securely supported.

Meg forced a swallow, her heart fluttering like a hummingbird in her throat, and her mouth suddenly dry. Was that not the sexiest thing she'd ever seen? A man who genuinely knew how to handle a strange, sick, dirty, little boy. Who wanted him back, and who actually wanted to comfort him?

She took a step back before she reached into Julio's shirt and put a hand over his heart. Or before she did something even more foolish. Like thank him. Hug him. Kiss the bejesus out of him. Man, what a rush just looking at him was. She forced another spitless swallow, sure she was making a complete fool of herself, but unable to stop watching.

Good grief, Duncan. Get a grip.

Unnerved by the electricity sizzling between them, she bowed her head and retreated to the makeshift table, took a bowl, and sat down on the sturdy log that now served as a bench.

Lucky her, she'd grown up in a family of one girl and four boys, all older brothers. Which had alternately turned her into the spoiled brat of the Duncan family and one toady little tomboy who adored her brothers. When the oldest, Trevor, joined the Army, the twins, Dallas and Ash, followed suit by enlisting early in the Air Force. Colt, the fourth in line, opted for the Navy when it came his turn. Which would've left Meg behind. But was she content to stay home, write letters to her valiant brothers, and wait while they served their country and saw the world? Not on your life.

As soon as she could, Meg took the ASVAB, Armed Services Vocational Aptitude Battery, scored high enough to get into the MOS, Military Occupational Specialty, she'd wanted, Communications. Then she'd followed Trevor into the Army. Which was why she was in Brazil today.

After torrential downpours hit Brazil two years ago, when the São Paulo overflowed its banks and flooded Rio de Janeiro, American-aid came in the form of US Army troops, supplies, and financial-aid packages. That was when Meg fell in love with this country and the hardworking Brazilians. She'd stood side-by-side with armies of volunteers, sandbagging, digging victims out of their mud-encased homes, and just generally doing everything and anything that was needed. Right then and there, she knew she'd be back. She'd found her niche in the world, and it was service.

Little did she know then the condition she'd return under, however. After that exhausting humanitarian mission, she'd taken two weeks leave. She was married by then. Ted Jeurgen, her dashing blond husband of seven months, one week, and three days, met her at DFW, Dallas-Fort Worth airport. They'd had four days to spend alone before they'd go home to Big Springs, Texas, and reconnect with family and friends. It was supposed to have been their second honeymoon, and the perfect break for Meg after an incredibly difficult, but satisfying, deployment. Trevor, her oldest brother, happened to be on leave from the Army at the same time. He was supposed to have been home by the time she'd arrived.

Until the second day into her leave, when Meg collapsed in the hotel shower. Stroke. She'd had a damned stroke. Her. At the ridiculously young age of twenty-three. She'd come to in some DFW emergency room with an overzealous doctor shining a bright light into her bleary, aching eyes. He'd kept asking questions that didn't make sense. It would've helped if he'd spoken English. Which he had, but which her damaged brain could no longer process.

When he'd forced her into a sitting position by raising the bed, her nose started bleeding. That was when she'd figured things were serious. All that red blood had literally poured out of her head, like a river she couldn't stop. But what she remembered most vividly was Ted standing behind the ER doctor and the horrified shock on his pale face. The way disgust curled his upper lip. The rejection in his headshake. The revulsion in his eyes.

He didn't offer one word of encouragement. Never once made a move to hold or console her or—anything. He'd turned into stone, the invisible husband, all because she'd had a stroke. Like that was her fault? She'd loved his pale blue eyes until the day they'd stopped seeing his wife as the perky, take-all-comers, sassy Corporal he'd married. He'd never said a word. Not 'I love you, we're going to fight this stroke together.' Not 'go to hell. It's been fun. Buh-bye'. He'd just turned his back while she lay bleeding like a stuck pig, and he'd walked out of her life.

Two hours later, Trevor slammed the door to her hospital room open and bellowed, "Where's my little sister?"

She'd burst out bawling like a baby then. Someone still loved her. Might not be the guy who'd taken marriage vows with her, but Trevor made sure she knew she was not only going to make it, she was going to do better than ever before. She could and she would! She was not a pariah. Damn Ted for making her feel like one!

Trevor, bless his heart, had comforted her through the first days and weeks of the paralysis. He was the one who'd taken her back to her old room in their parents' home, and he was the one who held her upright while she learned to stand again. When she couldn't hold a spoon, he did it for her. He made her laugh, told her she looked like a baby orangutan when she was all lips and couldn't get anything on her soft-food diet to stay inside her mouth. Trevor made her human again. He made her believe in herself. God, she adored her big brother.

Not Ted, the man she'd thought she'd love forever. He'd already deployed to Afghanistan by the time she went home. Had the nerve to write one last letter, though. Thoughtful jerk. What'd they call them? Dear Jane letters? He'd kept it short, Meg had to give him that. The man knew how to end things. Short, but not sweet or painless.

She'd cried for weeks, her emotions strung tighter because of the stroke. It took months before she could process information correctly again. Her speech returned around the same time. Muscle coordination on her left side was the problem. She still tired easily.

But what she lacked in physical prowess, she'd made up for in sheer willpower and good old Army determination, by hell. Trevor taught her that. *'She was an Army of one, damn it,'* he'd say when he helped her into the swimming pool at the gym. And Meg chose to believe him. It was either that or turn into a weeping, sniveling recluse. A victim. Not her. Trevor said she was better than that. So she was.

Meg didn't blame Ted for ditching her. She couldn't. Some guys just didn't have the capacity to nurture their partially-paralyzed wife—the same woman they'd vowed to love through sickness and health, til death us do part—back to health. And that was okay. It was better to have loved and lost, and all that crap. But mostly, she thanked her lucky stars they hadn't had children. Ted would never have made a good father. He didn't have the balls.

Chapter Five

He couldn't stop watching Meg Duncan. Eying the emerald glint in her pretty eyes. Wishing she'd smile at him instead of sneering. She'd taken a bowl and sat alongside Pepe on that wobbly log, but she wasn't eating. Not that Julio wanted her to hurry up and wolf down her stew. He could wait, and besides, she needed more rest and food than he did. That was apparent.

Meg had grown pale since they'd arrived in this poor excuse for a camp. Her limp was more pronounced. He'd like to know how she'd gotten injured, but he'd never ask. He wasn't staying much longer. The end of this journey lay elsewhere.

But why'd she keep glaring at him? He was no monster. Did she have blisters or something? Had she twisted her ankle? Was that why she limped? That actually made sense. She'd rescued these kids from the mine. Was she hurt and too stubborn to ask for help?

Mrs. Brunner seemed friendly enough. Everyone was, even Pepe now that Julio had made it clear he was a valued team member. That was all it took to get the kid on his side. Trust. It might seem like an insignificant thing to most leaders, but Julio had seen intangibles like courage and trust move mountains and save lives. He'd seen it dash across minefields to rescue brothers and sisters caught in enemy crossfire. He'd seen it drop out of the sky with a K-9 working dog strapped to its chest and land in the middle of unholy hellfire and brimstone. He'd seen it work miracles, on the field and off. So why didn't Duncan trust him?

Julio was not the bad guy here. How could she not understand that?

"Thought you could use something to eat. You're a big man. You must be hungry," Craig said as he offered a tin bowl filled to the brim with steaming stew from the aluminum stockpot balanced on rocks that formed the firepit. "Hold this while I make a table for you and bring some bread. I'm the official baker around here, you know."

Julio would've offered some trite comment about the weather, but Craig was gone and back before he knew it. The table ended up being nothing more than a plastic tray Craig balanced on two thick, round branches he laid parallel to each other on the ground nearest Julio. It might not be perfect, but it worked, and it wasn't wobbly. Then he retrieved a tall plastic mug of something that resembled orange juice from the dining area and scooped two thick slices of buttered bread from his wife's tin plate as he passed by. Taking the bowl from Julio, he set it where Julio could easily ladle a hefty spoonful of stew up to his mouth without spilling it.

"Thank you, sir," Julio said respectfully, not wanting to disturb baby Dom, but growing more concerned that the little guy was sleeping too much. He needed to wake up and eat. Even just a spoonful. At least take a sip of that orange drink. But Dom seemed content to sleep his life away.

Folding his long legs, Craig took up a spot on the ground near Julio, both men facing the children, Marta, and Meg. Fernando and Joseph were the quiet ones. Both Brazilians, they kept to themselves, sitting away from the others while they ate and conversed in low tones of Portuguese. Julio knew they were worried that Oz and his men would soon track them down and destroy this camp as well as everyone in it. That was the first thing they'd asked him in broken English when he'd arrived. Craig had interpreted for them. How quickly would USA resources arrive? Would they come by helicopter or on land? Why was he the only one here now?

But now Julio wondered why Oz's mine was deserted? What had he done to the slaves he'd kidnapped, the adults and children? Were they all in danger? If so, Julio was going to require more than a lightning-quick exfil. He'd need boots on the ground. SEALs.

"She does well for a recovering stroke patient, doesn't she?" Craig asked with the slightest German accent coloring his question, but with plenty of pride.

He and Marta were the old couple in the nursery rhyme, Jack Sprat, come to life. Craig stood around six feet tall and was as thin as a rail, while Marta didn't look like she'd missed many meals. Not that Julio would ever voice his opinion. There was a saying among SEALs that opinions were like assholes. Everyone had one, but no one needed to see it. Or hear it.

"Your wife's a hard worker," Julio agreed, patting the little soldier beneath his shirt, wishing Dom would wake up before Julio was forced to wake him. The boy needed nourishment.

"Not Marta. Miss Duncan. It's her I am speaking of."

"Meg?" *She had a stroke?*

Craig nodded, his eyes still set on the ladies. "Yes, I'm sorry to say. Working in the orphanage was hard for her when she first arrived. She had two canes then. Had a hard time making it through a full day. I thought for sure she'd give up and go back to the States. Good hell, man. Where are my manners? That's what she's missing. Her cane. *Scheisse!* It must've burned in the fire."

"When?" Julio asked, studying Meg differently now. A stroke would certainly explain why the left side of her face drooped the tiniest bit. Not bad, though, just enough for him to have misjudged her for thinking she scowled, when she might not have done that at all.

Yet, as he glanced at her now, it was clear to see how some facial paralysis limited her smile. It wasn't as wide or deep on her left side. When she buttered a slice of bread, she seemed to have difficulty getting the fingers on her left hand to cooperate and lift the slice off the flat tabletop to hand it to Maria. Yet she'd never asked for help nor drawn attention to her limitation. She kept on keeping on. Might sound insignificant, but that can-do attitude made the difference between guys who rang out of BUD/S and those who wore the trident.

"A year before she showed up here. I think, anyway. You'll have to ask Marta. She has a better memory for personal details than I do. I just know Meg took charge the second she showed up."

"When was that?" Julio asked, keeping his voice low and emotionless.

"'Bout a year ago. I remember the day she marched into camp. The kids loved her on sight, and she loved them. Meg can make a friend out of a rock, I swear. But she was still having trouble walking then. She needed more rest, not that she didn't do more than her share. Not Meg. Despite her handicap, she set to organizing learning games for the little ones the day after she arrived. In the next couple weeks, she taught them to fish with nothing but a string, and how to clean and cook what they caught. Taught the older ones how to shoot. Even showed them how to make something called a tandoori oven out of clay pots. You ever heard of such a thing? I sat in on that lesson. Had to. She was making these kids smarter than me." Craig chuckled loudly at that, the sound of his mirth a pleasant distraction that woke Dom. The little guy stirred.

"Hey there," Julio said softly as he peeled his shirt back to check on his new little buddy.

Dom stared up at him, as weak as ever, but finally acting interested instead of simply lethargic. No smile. Just bleary-eyed curiosity.

"You need to eat something, buddy," Julio murmured, keeping his voice soft and low.

Dom had the too-big eyes, the hollowed cheeks, and the long arms and legs of a starving child. Like the rest of the children, his head had been shaved.

Craig handed a bit of the buttered bread over Julio's arm. "For the tyke. It's fresh. Churned the butter myself."

"Where did you get the cream?" Julio needed to know.

Craig's voice lowered to a whisper. "It's like this. I sneak into the castle at night and I milk the king's cows while no one's looking."

Julio had nothing to say to that wild story.

Craig guffawed and slapped his thigh. "You should see the look on your face. Ha! No. Look over there." He pointed to the far side of the camp, where, behind the sheet of canvas stretched between two trees, one long-horned red and white cow stood quietly chewing its cud.

Okay. That made better sense. "You have a cow," Julio said flatly.

"Had two before Oz ran us out. Bought the first from a farmer in the village. This one was a stray. Found her over on the next hillside. Couldn't just leave her there, could I?"

Julio lowered the bread inside his shirt to Dom's lips. "No. These kids need her. Good thinking."

"The Lord provides in times of need," Craig answered on a sigh. "Marta and I just go where He tells us to go."

Craig made living sound easy. Julio wished it were.

"It's magic bread," Julio whispered to Dom, teasing the boy's dry lips with the buttery morsel. "It'll make you grow strong like... like Meg. You want to be like her, don't you?"

The little guy nodded. Not vehemently. Just barely.

"Aw, will you look at that. I think he likes you," Craig murmured, peering over Julio's shoulder and into his shirt at Dom.

"Feel like sitting up? It might be easier to eat," Julio asked.

Again with the barely perceptible nod of agreement. This time, the tip of Dom's tongue passed over his lower lip. He was hungry. Julio could tell.

He handed the piece of bread back to Craig. "I think he's thirsty. Would you please dip the end of this bread into my juice? Maybe he'll take it that way."

After Craig did as asked, Julio tried again, maneuvering that moistened piece of bread inside his shirt to the little guy's dry lips. "Here you go. Suck on this for a second. See if—"

It worked. Dom craned his skinny neck forward, latched onto that crust, and slurped and moaned and...

Tears sprang to Julio's eyes. Damn it. He was bawling over nothing. Dom wasn't out of the woods by a long shot. He needed much more than one crust of bread to live, but... He. Was. Eating!

"These kids all had rickets when we arrived," Craig muttered confidentially. "That's why the orange drink. It's fortified with calcium and vitamin D, lots of other good things. Your American Aid society sees that we get a shipment of supplies every month. All we have to do is go into town to pick it up. But with Oz's army patrolling the roads lately, we haven't been able to. We're on our last box."

Could that be all that troubled Dominic? Rickets? Julio knew the symptoms. Tenderness in joints, bones, muscles. Deformed and missing teeth. Bowlegs. Diminished growth. Shortness in stature. Stunted growth that could make a five-year-old look like a two-year-old.

"Did Dom drink it before Oz kidnapped him?" Julio needed to know.

"He was supposed to. They all got their fair share. I know. I measured it out every morning."

But that didn't mean this little guy had actually drunk his fair share. But he would from now on. And what about the other children Oz had enslaved and kept in the dark tunnels of his mines? Where were they? Had they succumbed to the effects of the lack of sunlight, which was how most people's bodies took in sufficient daily doses of vitamin D?

Julio stuck his tongue out at the child in his arm, slurping the soggy bread, needing Dominic to crack another smile. Some of the orange juice trickled around the little fellow's lips to Julio's belly. But, for the first time in a long, long time, something deep inside his chest cracked open. Not a broken rib. More like a broken heart. This right here, this little boy trying to stay alive, was all Julio had ever wanted with Tomas. A little hope. The smallest smile. Another chance to prove a father's love.

Julio stifled the long-denied tenderness washing over him now. He didn't want to break down and cry. It might frighten Dom, and Julio couldn't stand the thought of hurting this tiny prizefighter. He'd been through too much. But how Julio dared anyone to tell him Dominic couldn't make it.

As if he could read Julio's mind, the kindly gentleman sitting beside him wrapped a firm arm around his shoulder. "You go ahead and cry if you want, son," Craig murmured huskily. "It isn't often we see our prayers answered, is it?"

Julio stiffened at the fatherly touch. But SEALs did not break down. They just didn't. They stood brave and strong at all times. They were America's strongest, meanest, and toughest warriors. The absolute best America had to offer. Only Julio wasn't a SEAL. He'd rung out.

He blinked rapidly to dispel the notion that a good cry solved everything. Too bad Julio looked down at the baby boy tucked inside his shirt then. Dominic's eyes were opened wide. He'd stretched one skinny arm and extended one finger, pointing up at Julio.

"You need something, little man?" Julio asked extra quietly, so he didn't draw any more attention than he was already getting. Meg sure was keeping a close watch on him.

Dom nodded. Just once. Still pointing up at Julio.

"I think he wants you," Craig whispered. "You want this big guy, Dom? Is he who you want?"

Damned if Dom didn't nod and—

Cue the tears. Julio lost it. He had no choice but to bury his face into his shirt and hope he lived long enough to give this brave little guy a fighting chance. One crust of bread wasn't enough. But love was.

Chapter Six

Meg eyed the two men across from her. Craig and Julio were awfully quiet. Too serious. Her heart thudded to a full stop. Those were tears in Julio's eyes. No. Had Dom died? Was that why Julio looked like he was—

She jumped to her feet, her heart pounding. No child in her care had ever died. Dom wasn't the first, was he? *Oh, please, no. Not my sweet little baby.*

Stumbling in her haste to get to him, she bumped someone's drink when she grabbed onto the end of the table to keep from falling. Liquid flew everywhere. She went down to her hands and knees anyway.

"Craig. Julio," she called out. "Is he…? Is Dom…?" She couldn't say it. Couldn't bear to think it. *No, no, no. He's too little, too sweet to die.*

Julio's head jerked up. His eyes were red. Those were definitely tears streaking his sad, dirty face. He looked away, as if he couldn't bear to tell her. Damn it.

Dom was gone. It had finally happened. That sweet little guy had died and she hadn't been with him.

"No," she ground out as she crawled to her baby's side. Her heart was ripped apart, yet it urged her to run to him when it knew damned well that was the last thing she could do.

"Meg, my good heavens, let me help you up," Marta called out as she eased Maria off her lap.

But by then Craig had lifted to his feet and was headed Meg's way. "Up you go," he said as he took hold of her elbow and held her steady, allowing her enough time to shift her weight onto her right foot and catch her balance.

Finally on both feet, she asked Julio, "Is he...?" She couldn't bear to say the word. "Did he...?" *Please, just read my mind and say no.*

"He's eating," Julio murmured very quietly. "Dom's finally awake and eating, Meg. You did it. You saved him."

"He also seems to like the guy you brought home with you," Craig announced, slapping Julio's broad back with a resounding smack. "Guess I'd better make more bread."

Julio never flinched, but his lips thinned as if there were more he wanted to tell her.

"Then why are you crying?" she yelled at this stoic, emotionless man. "How could you do this to me?" By then she was on the ground next to him and all but sitting on his lap, her need to see Dominic so strong she could've torn Julio's shirt off to get at that boy. "I th-thought..." She choked, her poor heart still recovering from what might've been. "You guys were so quiet, and I thought—" Her words caught in her heart.

Julio shook his head, the tender light in his eyes gone as hard as flint. "Don't even think it, Meg. Dom's a prizefighter. He's tough and he is going to live, damn it. Say it with me. Dominic will live. I damned well know that he will."

She burst into tears. "Dominic will live," she repeated, then said it again. "Dominic will live. He's going to make it. Right?"

Nodding, Julio parted his unbuttoned shirt and peeled one side of it back. "See for yourself."

Aww, there he was, her tiniest orphan, laying comfortable against Julio's taut, but orange-stained belly. Looked like Julio had given him some bread dipped in that sticky breakfast drink. There were orange crumbs stuck in one corner of his lips and his chin.

Dom blinked up fiercely, trying to see Meg against the blinding light of the first day of the rest of his life. He didn't say anything, and he looked like he still had a long recovery ahead of him. But he'd eaten, and he looked better, somehow. Or maybe it was the magnificent wall of muscle his tiny palm rested against. Or the smattering of crisp, black chest hairs beneath his head.

Meg couldn't help but breathe in the masculine scent cocooning her youngest child. Was that what made a difference in Dom, all those wonderful alpha-male pheromones surrounding him? They were working on her.

She drew in another deep breath, then reached into that protected hideaway and let her hands melt all over that smiling baby boy's body. And Julio's. She kind of melted all over him, too. But he didn't seem to mind when her fingernails scraped his skin as she lifted Dom to her lips and kissed his forehead.

Julio's arm snaked solidly around her, his other still carefully holding Dom steady while she fell apart and cried.

Something sparked between Julio and Meg then. They were so close. Too close.

Somehow, her hungry mouth found Julio's. Lightning sizzled. Thunder flared. That strong arm held onto her as Julio lowered his head and kissed the bejesus out of her. All lips. No tongue. But her heart screamed with fire for more. For everything!

Everyone else and the kids were still gathered out there somewhere, but right here in this moment, in this intimate bubble, there was only one strong man, a very frightened, but eternally thankful woman, and her littlest angel.

"Dominic is going to live," she mumbled through her tears and around Julio's warm, sensual, but tightly sealed lips.

He took a breath and whispered back, "Dominic *will* live. Say it again."

So she did. Like a couple of idiots, they told each other again and again that, "Dominic *will* live."

Finally spent, she bowed her head and broke the tender connection with a guy she didn't really know. What just happened? It was hard to swallow or catch her breath. Something was stuck in her throat. Felt a lot like her heart.

"I'm sorry," she whispered for his ears only. "I... I..." Why couldn't she form intelligent words around this man? "I don't know why I did that."

When he didn't say anything back, she lifted her chin. How embarrassing. She could see Craig over Julio's shoulder, and the man was grinning from ear to ear. The shy Alcaldo brothers were watching too, when—

The baby mashed between Meg and Julio murmured, "Mum."

"Dom's talking," sweet Maria announced brightly. "Quiet everybody! Dom's got something to say. Go ahead, baby," she crooned. "We're listening."

My goodness, she'd been kneeling on the ground right beside Meg all this time. She'd seen everything. Even that hotter than hell, chaste kiss.

Meg covered her mouth with one hand as, sure enough, Dom whispered, "Mum," again.

"No, honey. Not mom. Meg," she explained, her voice inexplicably hoarse. Obviously, Dom was still a little confused, and she was a little bit flustered. If only her heart would stop throbbing like a beast brought suddenly back to life.

"No, Meg. Mum," Julio said quietly but sternly. "He needs a mother, and he just picked you out of everyone here. Say it with me. Mmmm-uuuu-mmmm."

Funny guy. A smile had almost breached his unhappy lips when he'd exaggerated that perfect word.

Something very much like a hysterical laugh bubbled out of Meg at the mountain of restraint and humility behind this ruggedly handsome guy. He could've chosen to be slighted when Dom chose her instead of him. A lot of silly men would've had their egos bruised. Not Julio.

Instead of selfishness, there was a definite aura of sorrow about him. She could feel it. Almost see it. For a reason she couldn't understand, she wanted to comfort this stranger. Her hand lifted automatically to his face.

He let her touch him, but there was no sense of acceptance coming from him. No invitation to draw closer. He didn't close his eyes. He was simply allowing the contact, not embracing it. Even his kiss had been measured. Dry. Distant. Which meant he was probably married.

Well, darn. And here Meg was letting her emotions build this moment into something it would never be. Which made her the world's biggest idiot. Flustered, she let her hand drop. Everyone here had watched her kiss this stranger. They'd also watched him keep that kiss chaste and pure and... Yeah. Unwelcome.

Well, okay then. Brushing a hand over her head to make sure her bandana hadn't slipped and embarrassed her more, she swallowed her pride, and pulled her eyes off Julio's breathtakingly handsome face. Honestly, she should've known he'd be married. The man had strength of character stamped all over his proud Hispanic features. His heart was taken. Well, so was hers. She'd given it to these orphans. So there.

Pulling Dom away from Julio, she put an end to her foolish schoolgirl expectations and locked her heart again.

The grand illusion of being Dom's *m-m-mother* was a frighteningly dizzying, yet awesome, concept to accept. She'd tossed all hope of ever achieving that sacred title after her stroke left her partially paralyzed. By then, Trevor had been deployed to some unknown valley in Afghanistan on a humanitarian mission. Ted? No one in her family would tell her where he'd gone.

She'd gotten his divorce papers in the mail, though. The coward. She couldn't blame him for not having the guts to face her. He didn't have the emotional depth to truly care for another person, either. But Meg blamed him plenty for being a chicken-shit and bailing on their marriage before they'd even hit their one-year anniversary. What'd he think marriage was meant to be, romance and sex every day?

But okay, that was then, and this was now, and things had changed. She'd moved on. She was still going strong, and Dom had called her Mum. Seemed simple enough. She could most certainly handle that role until a better, more physically-sound mother came along. She could do Mum. She'd been doing it for a year now.

Marta stood close by, fanning herself with an empty tin plate. "Praise Jesus, this man is the miracle we've all been praying for."

Meg shot her a look. Jesus might have sent Julio, but she was quite sure He wouldn't have if Julio hadn't been a worthy soldier in the first place. Praise the Lord all you want. He still only sent honorable men to do His work. Which told her why Teddy-Boy wasn't there and Julio—

BOOM!

One massively loud explosion sent an ear-splitting shockwave through camp. Trees leaned and saplings bent under the sheer force of the reverberation from the blast. Parrots and monkeys in the branches overhead squealed, chirped, shrieked, and scattered. The kids cried. Meg found herself pulled tightly against Julio, his hand over her one ear, her other ear plastered against his heart. Sweet baby Dom was soundly mashed between Julio and her. *What just happened?*

"Earthquake!" Marta shrieked. "It's an earthquake. Run! We'll all be crushed! We must run before that giant rock falls on us!"

"No!" the usually placid Joseph bellowed over the din of crying children and the hysterical German woman. "Explosion. Not earthquake."

My gosh, his ears were bleeding. Meg looked to her kids, all of them crying as they ran to her and Julio. Their ears were bleeding, too.

"Come here," she called out, waving them forward but not sure they could hear. "Explosion?" she asked Julio perhaps a little too loudly.

"Joseph is right," he answered, shaking the effects of the shockwave off. "Oz must have other mines nearby."

"There's one in the quarry," Meg replied as she looked straight into Julio's eyes. There was sadness there, but she also saw the strength of a man who'd come prepared for combat.

Simultaneously, they both said, "That's where the kidnapped villagers are."

Chapter Seven

Still on the ground, Julio eased away from Meg and Dom. The little guy would make it now. He was certainly in good hands. "I have to leave. Stay here," he told Meg even as he fingered both ears to make sure his weren't bleeding. Fortunately, no. He'd been deafened, but he'd be fine.

'Wait for me' begged to be spoken, but this was not just another deployment, and Meg was not the woman he needed to beg forgiveness from. She was a foreign aid-worker, not his wife. Not even a girlfriend. All she needed from him was a way back to the States for her kids.

He shouldn't have kissed her, though. Like Meg, he didn't know what came over him. Other than he'd been alone for too long, and lonely men tended to lose their souls after too many years of solitude and suffering.

But that was a warrior's lot in life, and he'd accepted his fate long ago. There'd been no one in his life to come home to for years now. Even when Julio'd succeeded in rescuing the woman he'd loved from Domingo Zapata, she'd still chosen suicide over living with him and Tomas. That bitter pill lay lodged in Julio's throat. As much as Bianca's death had broken his heart, her final act of selfishness pissed him off more.

He'd been to counseling to come to grips with that last slap in his face. Too bad it hadn't helped. The anger never went away. Neither did the loss of his only child.

The only thing all that counseling changed was understanding that healing took time. With every step Julio walked now, he began to realize that Bianca had deserted Tomas when they'd been imprisoned by Zapata. That was why Tomas died. He'd needed someone to hold him and shield him then, but Bianca had readily confessed she'd been so frightened of Zapata's vitriol, that she'd thought nothing of her son. Only of herself.

Which at first, made sense, and Julio had accepted everything she'd said as truth. She had been traumatized. But so had Tomas. How could a mother be too frightened to acknowledge her baby son's emotional needs? That was what Julio couldn't comprehend. Bianca had been the only one with Tomas, yet she'd been too scared for herself to comfort her only child? Her one-year-old baby?

Madre de Dios! That was what ate at Julio now. He couldn't understand how any woman could betray her child like that. The thought of sweet Tomas all alone in that damp, dark bunker where Julio had finally found them... *Dulce Madre de Dios!* The terror Tomas must have endured. The loneliness! Despair for things he couldn't change consumed Julio as he began to truly understand the shallow depths of the woman he'd thought he'd loved. The thought of that baby crying himself to sleep, maybe crying for his Daddy...

Dios! Had Bianca ever loved either of the men in her life? And here he'd been willing to follow her into the unforgiving Pacific. "Why?" he railed at the heavens now. "How blind was I?"

Simple answer. He'd been blind like a lovesick fool. And he knew it. Only Bianca hadn't really loved him. Or his son. Only herself...

The relentless assassin called Heartache that had religiously tracked him these last five years breathed its cold, rotten breath down the back of his neck today. He was a marked man. Someday, Heartache would get him killed. Not that he was afraid of dying. Not now that he'd lost Tomas and finally understood his wife. A man with nothing to lose became a different kind of warrior. Bottom line, Julio refused to invite Meg any deeper into his life. She didn't need the heartache.

But instead of meek compliance and a poor-me sigh of perceived feminine martyrdom from her, he got, "Like hell, you're leaving. I'm going with you."

Julio would've argued, but he'd been hit with a full dose of the emerald fire in Meg's bright eyes. Took his breath and stopped his heart. Made him realize that she was not passively aggressive. She didn't play games like his wife had. Meg said what she wanted, when she wanted. She might even be good in bed.

In bed? Angrily, he shoved that stupid notion right out of his head, not sure where it came from. He wasn't looking at Meg through any romantic lens. She wasn't his type, and she didn't need to see what he meant to do to Zapata and his men, either. This was a day of reckoning. Domingo's baby brother was going to die. So would anyone who got in Julio's way.

"I need you to stay here, Meg," he told her sincerely, hoping she'd at least hear him out. "When this is over, I'll be bringing other children back with me. They'll need food and water, baths, maybe doctoring. They'll be scared. Someone who cares about them has to be waiting for them, ready to comfort them." He wanted to say, 'For Tomas' sake.' But he didn't.

"You don't think I know that?" she bit out, glancing across the camp at Craig and Marta, Joseph and Fernando, no doubt mentally assigning that chore to them.

Julio didn't dare suggest that she couldn't possibly handle two difficult rescues in the same day. He knew that, despite her physical condition, Meg would fight to get the villagers' kidnapped children back just as hard as she'd fought for hers. Remembering her down on her hands and knees, crawling to get to Dom a moment ago, confirmed her determination. But Julio didn't need a physically challenged soldier on this operation, either, especially Meg. He wouldn't be able to stop worrying about her.

"I see your heart, Meg Duncan," he told her honestly. "I do. Just like Dominic sees your heart. But he needs you more, Mum. Please, let me do this dirty job for you and your kids. Stay here and fortify the camp while I'm gone. Arm as many as you can. Be prepared in all things."

Man, he wanted so badly to kiss her again and do it properly this time. But he didn't. Julio pulled back, once and for all. Their one kiss was their last. To end Zapata, he had to get moving. Jerking his sat phone up from the compact ammo bag at his belt, he thumb dialed Sullivan.

Meg glanced away, probably mad at him because she thought she'd been dismissed.

"Sullivan," McQueen bit out. "About time you checked in. How's Mr. Zapata?"

"Still breathing, sir," Julio replied evenly. "Transportation is different here, but I've finally made contact with Former Army Corporal Meg Duncan."

"Meg? He's a woman?"

Julio nodded though Sullivan couldn't see him. Yes, Meg was all woman. *And how.* "Yes, sir, Corporal Duncan is female. Requesting immediate airlift for five adults, nine children. Possibly more by the end of the day. Oz knows I'm here. He's already moved his operation. I suspect he's burying evidence." Evidence, as in bodies.

Meg shot him a look as Sullivan promised, "On its way. When do you anticipate initial contact?"

Julio looked to the columns of gray ash and smoke still lifting heavenward. "Soon. He just set off an explosion near my location. I'm on my way to end him now."

"Good. Have Duncan get everyone ready to travel while you're gone. They'll need to move fast once the bird shows. I'm sending Night Stalkers. They'll deliver a team of Rangers to your location. This'll be quick and dirty."

Exfils on the run usually were. That Sullivan could tap resources like the US Army's 160th Special Operations Aviation Regiment, declared the man's incredible influence at the Pentagon.

Humbled, Julio sincerely offered, "Night Stalkers. Helos. Yes, sir."

"Can you suggest a nearby LZ?" Landing zone.

"The flatlands north of the southernmost cliffs of the São Francisco River. It's less than a mile from our location. They'll know where to touchdown once they see the smoke."

"I'll relay that intel. Watch the skies. You know what to do."

"Copy that." Julio secured his sat phone and turned back to Meg. There was no reason to pretend she hadn't heard. Sullivan's voice carried. "I need someone qualified to supervise these aid-workers and get these children to the landing zone. He's sending Night

Stalkers. Sullivan's team will touch down in the flatlands."

"I heard." She nodded curtly. Just once. But then she murmured, "I didn't think he'd come."

Julio cocked his head. "Who? Senator Sullivan?"

"No, my Army Ranger friend, Charlie Brown. It has to be him on that helo. Don't you see? He works closely with the Night Stalkers. The village tavern, Mamacita's, has a phone, so I called in a favor and asked Charlie to help get my kids out of Oz's territory. Only by the time I got back to camp, Oz had already taken most of them." She smoothed a hand over her sweat-stained bandana. "But wow. Charlie's really on his way? That's awesome."

For some reason, her confidence in this Charlie Brown fellow irritated Julio. "How do you know he's coming? Maybe he's not on that helo."

Her eyes brightened. "Of course he's coming. I called him, didn't I?"

As if that answered everything, Julio replied, "Yes, ma'am."

Leaving would be easier now. Meg had a real hero coming to save her.

Chapter Eight

Meg watched Julio steel his heart along with that firm, stern chin of his. The warm spark hidden deep inside his melted dark-chocolate eyes went flat, then cold. It was as if all life had been sucked out of him. At the mention of Charlie Brown coming with the Night Stalkers, he'd turned from the tender man who'd brought sweet Dominic back from the grave into the emotionless automaton she'd met at first contact. Once again, Julio reeked of the despair she'd been familiar with not long ago. The one called death wish.

That was what had first brought her to Brazil, her own private death wish. The sure knowledge that a disabled American woman alone in the Highlands of Brazil might not last long. That, at least somehow, she could go down fighting for something worth dying for, instead of wallowing in a puddle of self-pity back in that tidy home on Walnut Street, USA.

That was all she'd wanted then. To feel alive one more time. To live like she had on her last deployment, the only time she'd been in combat. There was no better high on earth than the high of covering her brothers' and sisters' backsides when all hell broke loose. Neither were there any better friends than the family who fought shoulder to shoulder with you. She'd wanted to be that fierce woman again.

They'd been tracking a small ISIL team of murderers that day. Turned a corner and ran into fifty more armed terrorists. Meg's RTO, her radio man, requested immediate Air Force cover. But until that A-10 Warthog showed up with its lethal 'brrrrt-t-t-t-t', Meg and her squad had been trapped in the fight of their lives.

Two friends died that day. But her squad had made certain ISIL paid for it. Killed dozens of Mohammed Whoever's bloodthirsty, *wanna-die-and-go-to-Allah-so-I-can-fuck-all-those-virgins* soldiers. But that single battle stood as the worst and best of her entire life. Fighting for something bigger and nobler than one's self tended to change a soldier's perspective. She would've given her life to save her squad that day. She'd do the same for these orphans now.

And for Julio.

Meg refused to let this seemingly emotionless man simply pass through her life like the São Francisco River passed through Minas Gerais. Now that she'd tasted his lips, she wanted the rest of him. Julio might have kept his tongue sealed behind that veritable wall of solitude he packed with him, but she'd felt more than just anguished heat behind that chaste kiss. His body had most definitely responded, and she'd sensed a gentle man beneath that stoic mask. Whatever had happened in his life, it must have been wickedly tragic. But everyone deserved a second chance at happiness. She intended to make sure he got one.

Even now, facing this stubborn man with his back turned to her like a wall, she saw him for who he was. Alone. Arrogant enough to think he didn't need anyone. Sullen. Over-confident, too. But before he walked out of her life, she meant him to know he'd made a difference. That what he'd done by coming alone to face Zapata on his turf, counted. That whatever Julio did next, she would be waiting for him when he returned.

"I need to talk with you before you leave," she told those heavily muscled shoulders and the stubborn shaved neck holding up one damned hard head.

He tossed a look over his shoulder. "Me?"

"You see anyone else around?" She gave him her chin, signaling this was not a request.

Their eyes locked, just like she'd meant them to. He blinked, but shook her demand off. The stubborn man swung his bag up on his shoulder.

"I don't have time," he told her simply. Quietly. Too quietly for a man leaving on what could very well be a suicide mission.

That was what irked Meg the most. Everything Julio did was so damned deliberate and steady. Except for that kiss, not once had he over-reacted or gotten angry. In fact, he had yet to express any emotion other than stoicism sprinkled with intermittent tenderness for Dom.

Julio seemed to be made of steel and stone, but she knew better. There was a heart beating in that magnificent chest. She'd heard it when the explosion ripped over them, when he'd pressed her ear to said chest. He hadn't had to do that. She was just some foreign aid-worker. She meant nothing to him.

Yet he'd reached for her, and that simple act had spoken volumes. He'd known darned well the damage a concussive sound wave caused a person's eardrums. It might've been an automatic reaction on his part, but it had given her an unexpected insight. The steady *kerthump* of the humble man's heart had been louder than Oz's attempt at violent destruction—if that's what that explosion was.

Yet this taciturn, steadfast, stubborn warrior was even now prepared to go into combat, to kill and possibly die for his country. For her. Alone. Darn his noble ass.

She refused to let him walk away. Not from Meg Duncan. She'd lost enough friends in her short Army career. This hard-headed man would not be another.

Climbing to her feet, she ordered, "Make time, Juarez. This is important. Marta, please take Dom for me. See if he'll eat more bread, but dip it in orange juice first. He seems to like that."

"It's easier for him to swallow," Julio explained quietly, as usual.

"Come here, little one. Sweet baby of mine," Marta crooned as she settled Dom against her shoulder. "I will feed you, but I cannot give you a bath until we are out of here. You'll have to be stinky a little while longer, ya?"

Julio faced Meg by then. She stuck her chin at him and ground out, "Privately. Now."

He shrugged indifferently. "You've got two minutes."

That'd work. Wriggling out of her sarape, Meg tossed it back onto the table, then walked past Julio on her way to the five boulders that made up Giant's Toes. They'd have privacy in the bushes between here and there.

"I'll be right back, Marta," she called over her shoulder. "Check everyone's ears, Craig. Please make sure our kids are ready to travel when I get back."

"Aye, aye, captain," he replied with customary cheerfulness.

Joseph and Fernando were already attending to the kids. This wouldn't take long.

It took seconds to walk out of sight. Another second for Meg to make sure no one could see her when she spun on the balls of her feet, holding her arms out to catch herself in case she fell down. Recovering stroke patients were not known for agility or speed. She allowed one more second to make sure she was balanced.

Julio had gone stock still by then, probably wondering what she was doing.

Meg clapped both hands on the shoulders of this big, gruff, too-quiet man.

He cocked his head.

She'd startled him. Well, good. Surprise was a better look in those dark chocolate eyes than that damned stoicism. Thank goodness, there was a tree behind him. Putting all her weight into it, she shoved Julio backward against the sturdy trunk.

He let out a manly "oomph," but Meg wasn't offering any quarter, not until he knew precisely how she felt about him. In for a penny, in for a pound. Jerking his shirt up out of his pants, she let her fingers smooth up his belly, then to his chest before he could tell her to stop.

Julio seemed flummoxed, but he was breathing hard and his belly quivered under her touch. Her heart took flight. She'd seen enough of his physique to know he was built like a toned, sculpted Clydesdale.

The desperate beating of butterfly wings fluttered low in her belly. She'd never done anything so brazen. What had seemed like the perfect sneak attack, took her breath now.

But she wanted more.

Rubbing her palms up the warm ridges of taut, hard muscle under that shirt took a lot of nerve. This was no little boy Meg was playing with. Julio was all man, his belly and chest carved from a slab of warm marble. The valley between his pecs felt more like a steep precipice than a slope. This guy was ripped, but his flat, male nipples sprang to life at her touch.

So did hers. Heat coiled in her breasts at the testosterone pouring off Julio. Her entire body flushed with the fire she'd intentionally set. And she was falling.

Before he could open his mouth to argue, she covered his lips and swallowed his words. Then purposefully ran her tongue over the damned seam he'd pressed so tightly into place. Darn this foolish, stubborn man. He groaned, yet even that sounded more of restraint than pleasure. Worse, he refused to let her in.

Wanting more from this suppressed warrior than refusal, she pressed her belly to the zipper of his tactical pants, nudging the gear bag dangling off his shoulder and out of her way. This man had quite the impressive bulge behind that zipper. Wasn't that a surprise?

Kiss me, damn it. Really kiss me. I know you want to.

One hand went possessively to the back of his neck. Her thumb came to rest at the base of his skull. Her nostrils flared at the heady scent of the aroused male in her arms. Part sweat and part musk, the subtle hint of men's cologne or aftershave enhanced both odors, turning them into aphrodisiacs. She had him right where she wanted him now.

If only he'd do something besides stand there and take it. But he didn't lift his arms to hold her or to push her away. Meg really wanted that stoic act to mean something more than goodbye. But after licking his lips and growling her frustration at him, she had to admit, this was a mistake.

Julio didn't want her. He was a one-track kind of guy. But, unlike most other males, that one track had nothing to do with sex. Or her. Or what she very much wanted to do to him.

Sucking in a deep breath of what-the-hell-have-I-done, she forced her capricious wild side to stand down. Swallowing hard, she stepped back. She'd come to her senses. If any guy had done what she'd just done, it would've been termed attempted rape. At the very least, assault.

Meg licked her own lips, suddenly dry with embarrassment. Her lashes fell, hiding what she should've guessed all along. Handicapped people were buzz-kills. This all-American, red-blooded male could have any woman. Why would Julio ever settle for a nearly hairless, scrawny woman with big boobs? Even when she'd all but molested him and... Yeah. That.

She got it. Hell, she'd suspected it before. Now he'd confirmed it. If this wasn't about her handicap, then, for sure, despite wearing no ring, Julio was married. He belonged to that rare breed of men. He was a faithful man, err, husband. Damn. Whoever the lady in his life was, she was lucky. And Meg was a fool.

It sure would've helped if he'd worn a ring. Married men should do that. But she should've asked, too. He'd just seemed so sad, and the feminine loser in Meg had interpreted that male sadness into a solvable puzzle she could've deciphered with enough time, comfort, kindness, and... yes. A healthy dose of lust. At least a kiss that meant something besides goodbye.

"I, ah..." Crap, it was hard to talk with her heart pounding in her throat. "I'm sorry. Won't do that again. Did I, umm, hurt you?" As if that were even remotely possible.

A warm male finger settled under her chin, forcing her head up. Humiliated, she focused her gaze on the hollow of his tanned neck, instead of meeting his eyes. This guy was ruggedly scrumptious on so many levels. Even his neck was all male. Strong. Resolute. Clean shaven. Lickable...

But yeah, no. She'd read Julio wrong. That mistake was on her, not him. He was the good guy here. She was the village idiot. Now she knew how guys felt when they took a chance and got turned down by the lady they thought they loved. Only Julio hadn't turned her down. Yet.

But he would.

"Look at me, Meg," he murmured, his voice as rough as sandpaper over her flaming raw shame. "Please?"

She shook her head. "Nah. Already said I was sorry." *I've humiliated myself enough for one day.* "Guess it's really time for you to go. Bye. See you around." *But probably not. You're too honorable.*

Gently, his hands went to both sides of her hard head. Man, this day just kept getting worse. What man on earth wanted a bald woman in his bed?

He cupped her jaw, his thumbs on her cheeks, holding her still. His breath drifted into her face. He'd gotten too close.

Meg squeezed her eyes to forestall the tears. If this was his way of saying goodbye, it wasn't fair. He was breaking her heart. "Please. Just leave, Juarez. I'll make sure the kids—"

He kissed her then. His lips fell soft and warm—on her forehead. The manly scrape of his scruff over her skin brought the sweetest, saddest knowledge to her hopeful heart. This was his way of leaving. Treat her like a kid instead of a woman. Deny the only gift she had to offer. She'd never see him again. He meant to disappear into the history books. The story of her life.

Meg reached for his wrists then, needing that small physical contact to keep from falling apart. Okay, so maybe the puzzle she'd been supposed to unscramble had been her, not him. But ever since Ted's utter betrayal... Ever since that damned stroke... She'd tried so hard to be an attractive woman again. Not just any woman, but a sensual, loving female who could catch some worthy male's eye. Maybe turn his head. Make him look twice. Or something. Anything but this wretched goodbye scene.

Was this chaste, brotherly kiss all she'd ever have? *Guess so.*

The first tears escaped down her cheek. *Damn, damn, damn.*

"We just met, Meg Duncan," he breathed against her forehead.

"I know," she whispered to his scruffy chin, trying to sound stronger than she felt. Her eyes were still closed and her heart was still breaking.

"I can't promise I'll be back."

She nodded. "Yeah. I get it. I know that, too." *So, leave already. Don't make this harder than I've already made it. Man, I'm so stupid.*

"But I'd like to stay in touch," he murmured, kissing her forehead again. Unexpectedly, his hot lips turned that desperate moment into a sweet and tender anointing instead of the brush-off she'd thought it was.

Her eyes flashed open. "You do? With me?" she asked that strong chin even as she tipped forward and kissed it.

Julio bowed his forehead to hers then, and she was blinking hard to maintain eye contact. The warmth in those dark chocolates reached into her Doubting Thomas soul, melting Meg's heart.

"You really want to video chat or text or write or something? With me?" And now she was babbling.

His lips pinched for just a second, like maybe they'd forgotten how to smile. "Yes, Corporal Duncan. With you. If we both survive this day, I will be in touch."

"But I don't know where in the States I'll be by then." *Or if I'll even be in the States.* How could she tell him she still lived with her parents? "And I don't have a phone."

Julio pulled her flush against his hard body then, her legs tucked between his knees, letting her feel his raging desire. Hip to hip and belly to belly, she breathed the life of him back into her. This was all she'd wanted, a gentle man who truly cared.

He made it better then. Cupping her jaw, his eyes wide open, he closed the distance between them and kissed her mouth. Fighting for control, she offered nothing more than the same sealed kiss he had. Only now, his tongue slid over her lips with the gentlest, silky caress.

Cinnamon. She tasted the barest hint of cinnamon. And she was on fire. When he urged her to open, she let him into her mouth and her heart, maybe even her soul. This man was thorough, his tongue sweeping over hers like he already owned her. Their lips locked as their tongues tangled.

When she arched into him, his grip on her shoulders tightened. Like the alpha male he was, Julio canted her head just enough to gain better, more thorough, access. So, so good. He seemed determined to make a meal of her, their teeth bumping, his tongue claiming every dip, fold, and taste bud. His breath became hers. His tongue, a scorching heatwave she swallowed. She moaned, thrilled Julio had finally shared a part of himself. She would've given him everything, right then and there. *This. Just. This. I don't need roses or diamonds, just this man. Just this moment.*

"Now we're even," he finally whispered into her open mouth. "I shouldn't have done that, either."

Meg held on fast. He was breathing as hard as she was, but she hadn't been this dizzy in years. Not since her stroke.

"But I have to go." His tone hardened, and Julio released his grip.

Suddenly on her own again, Meg wobbled a tiny bit to the left, her weaker side. Instantly, Julio caught her elbow. Good thing. Face-planting after a kiss like that might hurt his feelings. And her nose.

"You're dizzy. Why? What happened? Do you need to sit down?" he asked, his voice as soft as melted butter.

Some men would've assumed her lack of balance was due to their terrific kissing skills. Not Julio. That was authentic worry deepening his already dark chocolate eyes.

"Stroke," she told him, melting into a puddle at his feet. Still, there was no need to skirt the obvious. He needed to know. "I'm still recovering from a minor stroke." *And that incredible kiss.*

"Craig told me it was fairly recent. Why aren't you home recovering in America instead of working here in the Highlands of Brazil?"

"Because I'm still alive, Special Agent, and because I'm better off working my ass off here with my orphans than I ever was feeling sorry for myself in Texas. That orphanage back there," she stuck her chin at the scene over his shoulder, "I mean what's left of it, used to care for more than thirty children before I arrived. Now we're down to nine, all because of Oz. I have to stop him."

"*I* will stop him," Julio corrected. "Your job is to get your children to safety. Understood?"

Meg wanted to argue, but, deep down, she knew her paralysis made her a liability, and the last thing she wanted was to endanger Julio's mission. "Yes, but do you understand that you'd better come back to me?"

Man, it'd be nice if he'd smiled. Maybe Meg would've believed him then. But all Julio offered was a non-committal nod that declared more dismissal than agreement. Then he made it worse. He dug into his pocket and handed his phone over. "Remember. Press one to connect with Senator Sullivan."

She shook her head. "I can't take your phone. You'll need it."

"But you need it more to coordinate the exfil once the Night Stalkers arrive," he insisted, his hand outstretched.

Meg shivered. His eyes were so dark and compelling. This guy was all kinds of dark magic, and she could not keep her eyes from straying up his wrist to the bunched muscles under his shirt. From there, her gaze hopped, skipped, and jumped to his shoulder, then to his neck and chin. His mouth. Once again vertigo struck, and she was falling.

"Take it," he ordered quietly.

Nodding because she couldn't think straight, she complied. "I wish I could call you once you leave."

That earned her the tiniest curl at the corners of his mouth. Until he said, "Goodbye, Corporal Duncan."

Chapter Nine

'You did it now,' Julio thought once he'd left Meg behind. He'd kissed her. Not just kissed her, but he'd tongued her good and proper. Like a man should with a no-holds-barred woman like Meg. Hell, he would've stripped her bare and plunged into her sweet, warm body if he'd had more time. If he'd been any other man. If he'd been smart. She'd be absolutely certain how much he wanted her then. Only Julio didn't just want someone like her. He wanted her.

His tongue ran a slow lap around his lips. She'd tasted incredibly sweet. Meg was not what he'd expected in an aid-worker. Marta was, but Meg was young and vibrant and...

Julio growled at the way his entire body had hardened with blood during that kiss. He'd been dead for so long, and here in the middle of Nowhere, Brazil, she'd brought him back to life. Piece by piece and part by part, his body was remembering how to hold little children and how to hold—her. It was remembering how good it was to eat. How starved he'd been.

His long, sturdy legs ate up the ground between him and the site of the explosion. Gravel pit, huh? This part of Brazil was rich in gold, as well as gemstones. Precisely what precious gems or mineral was Oz mining? Hematite? Tourmaline? The most prized imperial topaz? The gravel pit itself was man-made, the gravel used for roadbeds and damming rivers. Had Oz hit a vein of gold there? Seemed logical. Gold had turned enough weak-minded men into greedy bastards before.

Like a heat-seeking missile, Julio's mind zeroed back to Meg. Acknowledging that he had feelings for a woman other than his wife was an astounding new development all by itself. He'd been living on heartache for so long. But everything had changed the second Meg dropped that sweet little boy into Julio's hands. When she'd badgered him into securing the sickly child inside his shirt... Skin to skin... Against his heart...

The sweetest, bitterest memories of his short time with Tomas sprang back to life. It was as if the love he'd had for his son had jumpstarted Julio's heart again. Holding Dom had only hurt because loving and losing Tomas was still stuck in his chest like a living, writhing knife. Only now, he felt more than just the bittersweet agony of loss. The sweetness to life that Julio'd thought he'd lost, was suddenly found again. He could breathe. Better yet, he actually wanted to breathe. It'd been a long time coming, this simple act of allowing oxygen to fill his lungs and his being. His mind cleared as, with every breath, his belly expanded. *Dios,* it felt good to be drinking in the oxygen-rich breath of the forest. All because of Meg.

It had taken her brassy way of ordering him around, as if he were nothing but a raw recruit, for Julio to realize that, although Bianca and Tomas were gone, he was still here. There was still purpose in living. In getting up every day. There was still work worth doing. Enemies still to fight. Love to be made...

From the first sight of her with those little kids around her, Meg had brought color back into his depressed, weary life. Now she'd awakened his soul. Better still, Julio wanted to live again. He wanted that elusive one more chance.

Because Meg was different. While Bianca had always said what she'd thought Julio wanted to hear, Meg did not. She knew what she wanted, and she had no trouble telling him what that was or going after it. But who would've thought she'd ever want him? That scene against the tree back there? Downright erotic, and precisely the stimulation he'd needed to wake the hell up and stop grieving. To start living. For the first time in years, Julio had a spring in his step.

She loved children, too. Didn't that make his heart skip a beat? Most women these days were career-minded and driven to succeed the world over. Somewhere along the line, the traditional motherly role of bearing children and raising those little ones to productive adulthood had taken a backseat to industrial promotions and professional notoriety.

During his short stint in the Navy, he'd seen enough Navy wives to know exactly who ruled their husbands' careers and what little downtime they had. The divorce rate among SEALs alone exceeded all other military departmental divorces at a whopping ninety percent. Suicide among military spouses in general was another dilemma all together.

Yet even as he walked away from her, there was no doubt in Julio's mind that Meg was made of stronger stuff. Bianca had never supported his decision to apply for BUD/S, Basic Underwater Demolition/SEAL training. He had a feeling Meg would have. She might've argued like hell, but in the end, she would've understood why becoming a SEAL had been important to Julio.

What would she be like in bed? Julio had to wonder. Then he had to knock off wondering because a man with a hard-on couldn't walk to save his life. The oddest sound croaked out of his throat. Almost a laugh. At himself. At the fiery sensations of lust surging through his blood. It made him believe that today would end well. That he was a man again. Not just a shadow.

But first, Julio had a job to do. Schooling his tender feelings for Meg in order to negate the surge of blood in his nether parts, Julio changed back into the special operator he was. Oz would die screaming today. Then

Julio meant to return to Meg, and he'd save her like she'd saved him. Piece by piece.

*****

"Where is Pepe?" Meg asked no one in particular.

Fernando and Joseph had the children ready to go. Each child shouldered a small backpack with two bottled waters stuck in the mesh side-pockets. No doubt those bags were stuffed with food, what few medical supplies had been salvaged from the orphanage, and whatever necessities were needed on a helicopter flight. Marta and Craig carried much larger backpacks. Fernando and Joseph did, too.

"He was just here," Marta said as she turned around in a full circle. "Craig? Do you see him?"

Craig was a foot taller than his wife. "No, and I haven't seen him since you and the kids arrived. I thought he was helping Phillipe or Maria like he usually does. Pepe!" he called out. "We're ready to leave. Time to get going, son. Where are you?"

But no Pepe came running breathlessly into camp. No pounding footsteps sounded from the forest beyond. Panic flared up Meg's spine. "Where could he have gone?" She directed this question at Craig, yet feared she already knew the answer.

"Either he went after Mr. Juarez or—"

"But Julio just barely left. If you haven't seen him since we arrived... My God." Meg's heart stopped. "He's gone after Oz." That would be just like Pepe, to think he had to protect the younger children, and yes,

Meg. Pepe had a crush on her. Of course. He wanted to be a man. He had to be hunting Orlando.

The eyes of the children gathered around her zeroed on Meg like a target.

"We can't leave Pepe here," Maria said.

"I don't intend to," Meg replied.

"He has to be close by," Marta argued. "That boy was just here. He wouldn't just leave. I know it."

But Meg knew different. Marta had been preoccupied with the smaller ones, and more than anything, Pepe wanted to be like his father. Which meant he was right now on his way to confront the man who'd undoubtedly murdered that father. And he had a head start.

Meg whipped Julio's sat phone out of her pocket and pressed one.

"Sullivan."

"Senator Sullivan, you don't know me, but I need your help, and I need it right damned now," she barked.

"You must be Corporal Duncan. What can I do for you, and where the hell's Julio?"

"He's on his way to confront Orlando Zapata, but one of my children is missing. A ten-year-old boy, Pepe. I can't leave without him. I won't."

"Then you'd better find him. My men are in transit. ETA in eight minutes."

He'd no more than said that, when the steady whump-whump-whump of heavy-duty rotor blades echoed from far away. Eight minutes wasn't enough.

"Sir, he's gone after Oz. I'm sure of it. Respectfully requesting enough men to assist in search—"

"I didn't send a damned army, Duncan. This is an illegal infil, don't you get it? The USA military is non-grata in Brazil. There are five men on that Blackhawk, and one of them pilots the bird. That leaves four. Their mission is only to retrieve you and your children. Find. That. Kid."

"Then you need to change your mission, damn it. I don't leave anyone behind! Especially not a child!" That earned her a snort. Like Meg cared if she'd pissed off a snooty US Senator. Not on her best day. She'd never put pompous politicians' opinions above the lives of her troops. "Is Charlie Brown on that chopper? Let me talk to him."

"Hold, goddamn it."

She held for thirty achingly-long seconds before Sullivan came back with, "Yes, your boyfriend's on board. He says he can spare two men, but you've only got ten minutes after they land, Duncan. Then you're on your own."

"Yes, sir," she shot back at him. "Find Pepe or you'll leave without me and without that little boy." *Like the powerful asshole that you are.* "Copy that. Understood."

The line clicked. Either she'd lost the connection, or Sullivan had hung up on her. Either way, it didn't matter. Everything was up to her now. She'd found Pepe before. She could do it again.

Turning to the Brazilian family she loved with every beat of her heart, she said, "A chopper's already coming for us. It's close. You can hear its rotor slap if you listen. It'll touch down in the flatlands by the river gorge. You'll have to run," she told them as evenly as she could. Sullivan had made her mad, damn him. Would he leave a woman and a little boy behind? Undoubtedly. The ass.

"Will it be large enough for all of us?" Fernando asked, his eyes wide with worry.

"It's a Blackhawk, people. So, yeah. It can handle thirteen passengers easily." More when needed.

"You're not coming with us?" Joseph asked.

She shook her head. "Can't. I'm going after Pepe. Hurry. You can't miss this ride out of here."

"Will I ever see you again?" Maria asked softly.

Meg dropped to one knee and hugged the only girl in this rag-tag family of orphans. "You'd better believe it, sweetheart. Now run as fast as you can. Marta and Craig, Fernando and Joseph? Thanks for everything you've done for me and these kids. I'll catch up with you all as soon as I find Pepe."

Marta's eyes glimmered with emotion. "*Ja.* We will see you soon."

"Plan on it," Meg lied.

There would be no chopper waiting when she found Pepe this time. If she found him. Not even Charlie Brown would break Army protocol during an illegal op. He'd give Meg ten minutes tops, then like it or not, he'd hightail it out of here before the Brazilian government realized a US Blackhawk had breached their airspace. Charlie was smart. He'd put the children first. But when push came to shove, he'd follow orders. He'd leave.

"Keep this," Craig said as he tossed his personal service revolver across the space between them. He'd been a police officer in Germany. Marta had worked as a dispatcher at his precinct. That was how they'd met.

Meg easily captured the weapon. "But you might need it." There was still nearly a mile to the LZ. She didn't want to take his only means of defense.

"But you *will* need it," Craig said, his tone grave. "Take care of it. I want it back."

"Promise," she answered, wishing she could keep the promise, but pretty sure that her living through this day would be a miracle. She had to find Pepe. Then she had to end Orlando. Or die trying. Securing the revolver in the back of her pants, she told the family she'd come to love, "Don't worry about me. Get to that chopper! Run!"

Meg went the opposite direction. Into the forest. Tracking Pepe. All the way to Oz.

Chapter Ten

Casting his humanity aside, Julio allowed the darkness inside him to rise. He might not have a SEAL team at his six, but since Zapata came into his life, he'd become as ruthless as one. As lethal. The first armed idiot wearing Oz's red bandana, died swiftly. Silently.

He let the limp body fall into the bushes, then stooped one knee to the ground and cleaned his blade on a patch of dried sphagnum moss. The gravel pit lay beyond the fringe of honey locust trees up ahead. Advancing, he stopped in the shadows of those trees to plot an azimuth. In and out. That was how this infiltration would go down. The fewer men who died between here and there, the better. Especially the enslaved, whose lives had now taken front and center of Julio's plan. He couldn't end Oz if it meant endangering the men, women, and children he'd kidnapped.

But then...Damn. Everything went from bad to worse. This wasn't just another one of Oz's mines dug into the middle of some gravel pit. This was an armed camp, and that explosion hadn't created a tunnel. It was the beginning of a well where, even now, a team of men were gathered around a drilling rig, complete with twenty-foot high boom and hydraulic hoist.

Julio tugged his micro-binocs up from one of the many pockets in his tactical pants, needing to verify what he was seeing. *Madre de Dios!* Were those missiles on the backs of those three flatbeds? Were those mobile launchers, not just flatbeds?

His heart fluttered to a full suffocating stop in the back of his throat. Those weren't just missiles. They were Russian intercontinental ballistic missiles. ICBMs. Designation: RS-24 YARS. Range: close to seventy-five hundred miles. Warheads: nuclear. Weight: nearly fifty-thousand-kilograms per warhead. Three-stage solid-fueled rockets powered these missiles. They were mobile launch capable. And sitting right goddamned here in the middle of fuckin' Brazil.

Julio faded back into the shadowy oblivion offered by the setting sun, and crossed himself with a fervent, "Padre, Hijo y Esporitu Santo." *Father, Son, and Holy Ghost.* Of all the stupid things, he'd left his sat phone with Meg. There was no way to call Sullivan to warn him, and Oz meant for these warheads to strike America. Those weren't wells he was digging. They were missile silos. With well-digging equipment, maybe, but the man meant to dig missile silos nonetheless. That miscalculation alone offered Julio the single spark of hope he desperately needed. His mission became crystal clear. Orlando Zapata had to die before he brought in more efficient equipment. As in tonight. Every last one of his Russian friends, too.

But where were the Brazilian people he'd enslaved? Where were the children he'd stolen?

Julio needed to know. Intensely alert and focused now, he adjusted the binocs, needing to absorb every last detail below. A hard man made impossible decisions. Life and death decisions. Right now, Julio was faced with one helluva dilemma. If the Russians and Oz meant to strike at America, how many lives could he save by striking them first, here? Tonight? How many American lives would end horribly, painfully, if he did nothing? At what cost? Who was more worth saving? American lives at the expense of these few enslaved Brazilians? Or did he focus on the here and now, save these slaves—if there were any—and hope that another chance to stop Orlando Zapata just, somehow, came along? What about the poor people, men, women, and children he had yet to locate? Were they below in some tunnel, working their guts out? Or were they already dead?

Julio rethought what had previously seemed a simple hit.

"Russians," he breathed. Sullivan needed to know. Now. Yet Sullivan wasn't here, and Julio had no way to reach him.

"Shit," he hissed out loud, pissed at his arrogant stupidity. This was his fault. Yet even as he cussed, he knew he'd give his sat phone to Meg all over again. No regrets. No do-overs. She was the genuine lifesaver and Dom's choice for a mom. But Julio was just Uncle Sam's hitman. Expendable. Not even worth a footnote in the annuls of history.

But a sniper in the right place, at the right time, could save the world. His heroes Navy SEALs Chris Kyle, Adam Brown, and Eddie Gallagher had proven that. As had many others.

Okay then. New plan. Better plan.

Julio steeled his heart. There wasn't enough room in it now for thoughts of Meg, Tomas, or Bianca. There was only now, and the filthy job that had to be done. Decisions to be made. He would end Orlando Zapata. But before he neutralized that bastard, he'd save every last one of Zapata's slaves. And America. By all that was holy, he'd save America.

The decision made, Julio stepped back to the edge of the quarry. It was time to get real.

A couple guards were still visible, silhouetted along the upper rim, both armed and looking as enthused as the guard Julio had run into earlier at Oz's mine. Below, razor wire coiled on top the fence that protected the missiles and launchers. Four armed guards kept watch there, but even they lazed against the fence posts as if the nuclear missiles behind them were no big deal.

He didn't blame them. At its best, Brazil was hot and humid. They were out in the open with no cover, and the heat captured in the pit had to be intense. Plus, they were uneducated muscle. Not trained Navy SEALs. Probably hadn't any formal education.

Wiping the sweat out of his eyes, he focused on the quarry layout. Several sloping paths and two gravel roads led to ground level. They'd make infil easy. Several boulders and large rocks dotted the edges of those paths and roads, another plus in Julio's favor. They'd provide solid cover during exfil for the slaves Julio had yet to locate. Plain and simple, this was a suicide mission. Oz had an army. Who knew what resources the Russians had? But with one hot round, Julio intended to turn this pit into Armageddon. All he had to do was locate the missing Brazilians first.

He worked faster now. Studied everything twice. Quickly. At his right, two fuel pumps. Both diesel. Dump trucks, pickups, flat-bed trailers, and automobiles were parked nearby.

Two rows of three tents had each been set up farther south. Both rows faced each other. Had to be where the guards slept. The walkway between the tents led to a single wooden cabin, the rear of it built into the southern wall.

Julio sharpened the focus on his binocs, going for distance. There were two caves in the opposite wall to the east, across from where he stood. Both opened at ground level. A dozen uniformed, armed men stood guard there. Some were smoking, some scooping food off tin plates and into their mouths. Others stood ready with rifles in hand, actually guarding. But guarding what?

The big guy with a rifle slung over his back seemed to be in charge. All the others straightened when he started gesturing, talking, and pointing at the caves. Looked like a drill sergeant giving orders. Three of the other guards disappeared into one of the tunnels. The left one. Not the right. Interesting.

At Julio's left, two more tents faced the center of the quarry, only these were a bright white. Not dingy gray like the others. Possibly the Russians? Hard to know for sure. Interesting layout, though, with Oz's cabin tucked in the shade and the Russian tents positioned where they stood in the sun all day. Looked more like a camp of opposing forces instead of friendly allies. It reminded Julio of a line from one of the nonsensical rhymes his grandmother used to sing to him and his sister. '*...back to back, they faced each other... drew their swords and shot each other...*'

The scene definitely declared a shaky alliance between Zapata and his Russian friends. They didn't trust each other. Julio intended to use that to his advantage.

Cautiously, he left the cover of the trees and made his way around the lip of the quarry, needing to understand the entire scene before he ventured down. In the process, he neutralized another guard. This one had a walkie talkie Velcroed to his shirt. Which meant

Oz expected a sitrep. Also meant Julio's time was running out.

But he'd expected that when he'd ended the first guard. Pocketing the walkie-talkie, he settled into his belly at the edge of the east wall, above the caves' entrances for another thorough sweep of the quarry before he engaged Oz's army.

Smoke and ash from the previous explosion still hung heavy overhead. As it drifted downward, the air grew drier, and drier air made breathing harder. Julio pulled his full canteen out of his gear bag and swallowed just enough to keep from coughing.

The view across from him revealed a long, wooden lean-to against the west wall. Topped with corrugated metal roofing, the building extended the length of the wall, though what it was for, Julio couldn't decide. Might be an equipment or supply shed. That actually made sense given its location.

Yet, it didn't. There were no visible access points into the lean-to. No windows. No garage doors. No doors at all. Which was odd. Why build something that couldn't accommodate vehicles from all sides? He shrugged the puzzle of the day off. It didn't matter what Oz built. He'd be dead soon. So would his Russian friends and every other terrorist down there. But where were the slaves?

When two more guards below Julio's position took off at a dead run into one of the tunnels, still the most northern tunnel, he backtracked to his previous location. There'd been no sign of actual mining or slaves yet. He needed confirmation those Brazilians were still alive. He had a fuel dump to torch. Human collateral was unacceptable. Except Oz and his army. They didn't count.

The sun had barely begun to set, turning the sky beyond the quarry a majestic blue, and tinging the universe overhead with gathering purples to the east. Brilliant oranges flamed to the west even as inky black fingers stretched across the forest around the quarry. Sunsets came early on the west side of mountain ranges, even earlier for those in valleys. Or gravel pits.

Julio inhaled deeply of what he now knew would be the end of a life well spent. And that was okay. Saving others was a good way to die.

*****

By the time Meg made it to the southern edge of the gravel pit, her backside was dragging. So were her arms. Her ten minutes to locate Pepe had come and gone hours ago. As were Charlie Brown and his Blackhawk, her aid-workers, and every last one of her children. She'd heard the bird lift off. She'd seen it fly away from the gravel pit. It had actually brought a tear to her eye knowing her children were now safely beyond Oz's grasp. Not once had she regretted her decision to stay.

Finally, Dom and the kids would receive the care and medical attention they deserved. Army medics were the best in the world, and a lot of them were fathers with hearts as big and soft as hers. They'd spoil these orphans like they spoiled all the children they'd been called in to rescue over the years. She had no idea where they'd take her kids, though. Most likely, the chopper would head straight for a US aircraft carrier somewhere off the coast in international waters. While the Brazilian government accommodated most adoptions, they probably wouldn't appreciate US interference inside their country, even if it meant saving kids.

Meg didn't really care what Brazil's officials thought, as long her children were safe. Let Sullivan work out the foreign relations nightmare this extraction would surely create. Let him face political assassination for the undisclosed covert exfil. That was his job. Hers was to save one little boy from himself. *Pepe, where are you?*

If only she could find him. If only she'd thought to bring her backpack when she'd charged out of camp. Then she'd at least have bottled water. But she'd been tired and...

Aww, who was she kidding? She'd run away because she couldn't handle all those tear-jerking goodbyes. Man, she was going to miss her kids. Mostly Dom. He'd needed her the most, and she'd fallen in love with him the first time she'd seen him. That poor little guy needed a chance to live to a ripe old age. Now, maybe he could.

Something warm trickled down her grimy cheek. *Knock it off, Duncan. Stop crying! You've got a runaway child-hero to find, and an asshole to kill.*

Buck up, or back off and quit. Your choice. Winner or loser. Who you gonna be today? Trevor's tough, tender encouragement assailed her. Just what she needed.

"Winner," she told him in no uncertain terms, wiping a finger under her nose in defiance. Okay, so Trevor couldn't hear or see her show of attitude, but maybe he could. They'd always had an unbreakable bond. Wherever he was, he was probably smiling. That was all the incentive Meg needed. *Okay, then. Find Pepe. Stop Oz's heart. Run like hell.*

Almost sounded easy.

Yet there she stood like a lump at the edge of a forest, overlooking what resembled an armed camp instead of a mine down deep in Oz's gravel pit. Sheer granite walls, broken only by a couple steep footpaths and a sturdy, wide, gravel road, dropped to the level floor of the pit. The sun had just set, making it difficult to see. Nights in the forest were exceedingly dark. And dangerous. Not a sign of Julio or Pepe. Was she a complete idiot to think she could ever hook up with either of them? In these woods? Maybe...

She folded, ending on the ground with her hands on her knees and her heart in her throat. What the hell had she been thinking, that someone like her could ever save another missing child? Her? An exhausted stroke victim who'd been running on empty for too many days now? Who'd been stupid enough to taunt Orlando Zapata by stealing her kids back from under his nose? What a fool.

When a spotlight flashed on below, the quiet rustlings of birds and small forest animals quieted behind her. She leaned forward to see exactly what she was up against. Another set of bright lights, an array actually, cast light farther over and into the camp. Lots of trucks. Heavy digging equipment. A few tents. What might be an office. Oz had certainly turned this pit into an organized headquarters. What was he thinking, of moving OZ Metallurgy Mining, Inc. down there? Sure as heck looked like it.

Well, okay then. She hadn't spotted any children, but Pepe had to be down there somewhere. Maybe Julio too. That'd be nice, to work with him again. Not likely, but yeah. Nice.

Meg made her move, inching forward to the trail she'd glimpsed before the sun set. But twilight was not her friend, not as tired as she was. Inching along only helped her avoid the worst pitfalls and vines. Didn't help her tired, grit-filled eyes distinguish between the dark and a sturdy branch pointing straight at her, the one that stabbed her hard in the chest when she hit it head-on.

An unintentional "Oomph!" breathed out of her on impact. She dropped to her butt, rubbing what felt like a hole drilled in the center of her sternum. Damned pointy finger of God. But okay then. *If at first you don't succeed…*

Slower now and breathing hard, she lifted to her feet and began again. At least, there was no moon tonight. Made it easier to stay out of sight. But it didn't do much good for walking. The glaring beams from those floodlights cast eerie black shadows across her path, blurring the way forward. More than once, she landed on her rear end, then scooted along when moving forward that way seemed easier. Also kept her low to the ground and out of sight.

Because there were so many more men over by the heavy equipment, and she doubted Pepe would be stupid enough to engage with them first, Meg eventually climbed to her feet and veered toward the cabin at her far right. Oz was either out with the men, or hiding while everyone else did his dirty work. *The ass.* Maybe Pepe would be there, too.

Chapter Eleven

On ground level now, Julio stayed to the shadows, using his binocs to recon the camp. Someone had started a bonfire between the Russians' and Oz's soldiers' tents. Next, a camp stove appeared out of nowhere, then pans and large, white coolers. Camp chairs. Two muscular soldiers carried a giant pig, already skewered on an iron rod, over to the fire. The comradery on the Brazilian side of the camp grew loud and boisterous. This wasn't just dinner. This was a party.

But not on the Russian side. There were six of them, all dressed in matching black coveralls, with Mother Russia's flag emblazoned on their left pecs. They stood together like an attack force, shoulder-to-shoulder and hip-to-hip. Not sprawled on the ground by the fire. Not chatting up the Brazilians. Finally, the tallest Russian, a blond man with a square chin and crewcut, stepped forward. He lifted the large liquor bottle in his hand, probably vodka. He stuck his chin out at someone, and out of the crowd stepped—Orlando Zapata.

Julio hissed at his first sight of Domingo's baby brother. It'd been years since he'd seen this upstart. Orlando and his brother shared many physical traits. Same psychotic need to make their victims bleed. Same short, stocky build. Same ink all over his face, neck, probably on the bald head under his cap, too. Same flat-black eyes beneath soot-black brows.

But while Domingo preferred tattooed sixes, snakes, and Spanish hexes all over his body and scalp, Orlando preferred tattoos of naked females and female body parts. Breasts. Backsides. Mostly eyes. Not the evil-eye symbol thought to reflect evil back onto the person cursing you, though. These eyes were all wide and expressive, the lashes around them lush and intensely feminine. All sad. All in pain. Tears. Orlando liked tears, too. They rained out of those sad, sad feminine, tattooed eyes...

Domingo was also known for his cruelty, but he'd never used guns. He preferred close and personal time with his victims. To that end, he'd used knives, switchblades, and razor-sharp scalpels. He'd also used his teeth, all filed to vicious points intended to tear flesh and muscle. To chew the fingers and toes of the living—and the dead.

Julio'd seen his work before. That time, Domingo had painted his face, neck, and chest with the blood of his victim, a kidnapped French diplomat. A kind, white-haired elderly gentleman, known the world over for his discretion, his negotiating skills, and philanthropy. He'd given millions to charities in Africa. But he hadn't been able to negotiate with the likes of Domingo. Zapata had sent a selfie he'd taken to the diplomat's family once the deed was done. He'd painted his face with the blood of the unfortunate man and used the diplomat's displayed, butchered body for a backdrop.

Cold-blooded killers. Mad dogs. That's all the Zapata brothers were.

But the scene by the firepit was almost comical. A tall, lean foreign mercenary standing over his stubby frenemy. Julio had forgotten how short in stature the Zapata brothers were. How stout. Like Domingo, Orlando stood maybe five-eight, five-nine at the most. Also like his older brother once, he wore the uniform of a wannabe guerilla commander. Camouflage cap. Sweat-stained BDU shirt and dirty trousers. Tan, desert combat boots. Black mustache. Shit-eating attitude. Blatant disregard for everyone. Plenty of ego. A sneer. Probably got the entire get-up off eBay.

The need to strike at the bantam-weight peacock nearly did Julio in. Oz was right there, out in the open. Sure, he was surrounded by his army, but he was still a hard hit to walk away from. One round was all it would take to end this despicable tyrant. Julio's trigger finger twitched to make it so. Why not? Orlando was just standing there. Shaking hands. Making nice with his Russian buddies like he had nothing to worry about.

But all hell would break loose the moment Julio fired, and he'd surely die instead of Zapata. This mission would end before he accomplished what he'd set out to do. What Americans and Brazilians needed him to do. More women and children would die at Oz's filthy hands. Sullivan would be pissed. Julio bowed his head, resigned to a night of patience and thoughtful strategy. He had to find Oz's enslaved workforce first.

The distinct rustle of pebbles sliding over dirt and stone somewhere behind him caught Julio's attention. He glanced over his shoulder. Perhaps one of Oz's guards? Didn't matter. Julio couldn't risk being seen. Thinking fast, he ducked behind the two dozing guards, and into the northernmost tunnel, the same tunnel where Oz's guards had gone earlier. Just that fast, Julio was out of sight, and out of his mind. But possibly, finally on the right track.

A faint light glowed far ahead in the carved stone tunnel. Buttressed at intervals with frameworks of four-by-four timbers, piles of shovels and sledgehammers lay to his left. He'd expected mine carts to haul whatever Oz was mining, but there weren't any. No rail tracks for carts to roll on, either.

Bare electrical wiring stretched from one overhead beam to the next. No light sockets, though, and no lightbulbs. Not yet. The deeper he went, the cooler the air became and the more overpowering the scent of dirt. More and more dust clogged the air. Which meant there had been a recent explosion, but not here. The packed dirt pathway was still too smooth and clear.

He kept going toward the glow at the end of the tunnel, thinking about canaries, the early warning system in American coal mines, with every step. For all he knew, this tunnel could be full of deadly vapors. Ruthless men didn't care if their workers died from carbon monoxide or other toxic gasses, as long as they dug, clawed, or scratched precious gold, gems, and other worthless shit out of the earth. As long as those poor workers made their bosses wealthy at the end of the day.

So Julio ventured onward. As he stepped quietly, he snorted at the utter stupidity of mankind to value rocks—to value anything!—over *familia*. Diamonds. Gold. Didn't matter. They were nothing compared to the one thing he'd never truly had. Made him sick.

Madre de Dios! Familia! Since the day his parents died, all he'd wanted was his family back. But no. His greedy parents destroyed theirs when they'd been shot during their last robbery—of stones! Okay, jewels, according to Mexican *policia* reports. But stones, nonetheless. Rocks. They'd died for a few handfuls of rocks.

Julio'd fled northward into Southern California then. His sister, Paloma had lingered in Mexico with their grandmother. But that hadn't lasted long. Still just a teenager, she'd applied for work in America with the CIA and disappeared into the world of undercover work and espionage. That hadn't worked out for her, either. Which was why she'd fled to Mexico. She'd killed her CIA handler, not that he hadn't had it coming. But, yeah... The Juarez family seemed destined for misery and loneliness.

Then along came Bianca...

Dios! Julio should've known the night he'd proposed to her. The night she'd demanded he prove his love by buying her a bigger diamond. A nicer band.

Do you think I'm easy? What are you, cheap? Don't you care? Don't I deserve the best?

He should've realized then that Bianca had also loved cold, dead stones.

With every step into the unknown, Julio remembered. The dear, sweet wife he'd loved with all he had. Only she'd said she loved him *after* he'd gone into serious debt for the one-carat solitaire she'd adored and absolutely had to have. Then and only then was she so ecstatic she'd screamed with what he'd thought was joy. Now he wondered. Was it joy or was it greed? Had she ever loved him? Or Tomas?

A dark doubt threaded its malicious toehold into Julio's already deep depression. He'd never understood how Domingo Zapata had known where to find Bianca and Tomas. They'd been living in off-base housing near Naval Base San Diego, pending availability of something better. But Bianca had never been happy there. She'd always wanted better, and she'd hated being tied down. She'd insisted they move into a better neighborhood because she'd hated the appearance of their first bungalow on low-income military housing. Said it made her feel inferior to the rich, white celebrities of San Diego. But she hated the other Navy wives too, which was just plain wrong. Those women supported each other while their men were OCONUS, out of the country.

But because of plastic facial surgery she'd insisted she'd needed, elective surgery on her brows, breasts, and buttocks, Julio's debt ratio climbed until they were payment poor. He'd demanded they tighten their belts. Again, Julio had foolishly considered those expenses the cost of loving such a beautiful woman, just another sacrifice to be made for his dearly beloved.

He'd thought he was lucky to have Bianca. Until he thought back on her words. *Always something better. You must work harder. You must use that brain of yours.* So Julio had done anything and everything to keep her happy.

Had she been looking for *someone* better, too? Was that someone Domingo Zapata? The thought of his wife with that inked snake of a man curdled Julio's blood.

At last, the tunnel branched, pulling him back to his mission. The darkened way continued straight ahead as far as Julio could see, but the overhead electrical wiring didn't. He turned left, toward the barest sign of light. This was the glow he'd been tracking. Julio ended in a fully-lit cavern the size of a football stadium. That one electrical wire overhead had now branched into dozens of spotlights, all aimed at hundreds of workers bent over and hard at work. He'd found Oz's enslaved workforce.

None of them had seen him yet. But what a desperate, sorry sight. The workers were filthy, their clothes tattered. Most were barefooted. Most men wore no shirts. The women fared no better. Some were in shorts, others in ratty skirts. Torn blouses. No shoes.

But the children... Julio's heart broke at the tender ages he saw working on their hands and knees. Some were so small and slight, they could only be three, maybe four years old. All kept their eyes down. All were so thin.

The terraced, stone rows lining the cavern climbed down to a rock and boulder-strewn floor, while other rows climbed up the walls to the glistening, stalactite-bedazzled ceiling.

Hundreds. He was looking at hundreds of people who deserved better. "*¡Maldita sea cada Zapata que haya vivido!*" he swore. *God damn every Zapata who'd ever lived!*

All nearest the cavern entrance saw him then. A filthy, young boy burst out of the crowd, screaming, "*Meu soldado! Meu amiga!*" *My soldier! My friend!*

Julio looked twice. "Pepe? What are you doing here?"

Pepe hit Julio like a frightened child. Circling his arms around Julio's waist, he buried his face in Julio's shirt. "I knew you would come," he sobbed, his poor body shaking. "I knew it. Miss Duncan said you were the most beautiful creature on earth. She is right. You came. *Obrigado, meu amiga. Obrigado." Thank you, my friend, Thank you.*

The agony pouring out of this child humbled Julio. Almost made him overlook Pepe saying that Meg had thought Julio the most beautiful creature on earth. But thinking on that choice compliment had to wait. He dropped to one knee to get a better grip on this shivering, ice-cold boy. My God, Pepe's eyes were black and swollen. His bottom lip was split, and there were definite finger-sized bruises on his neck. Dried blood was caked through his scalp.

"Who hurt you?" Julio demanded.

"The... the guards. *Senhor* Zapata. They... they laughed. Said I was a g-g-good sport. A good game."

I will kill them all! Julio promised himself. Yet he had to know, "Why are you here?"

The brave, battered boy leaned back on his heels, scrubbing a hand over his teary eyes. "Because I am a man, *Senhor* Juarez" —he whined like the frightened child he was— "like Papa. I had to do something. I could not let that *porco* hurt Miss Duncan. Or Dom. Or even you."

Julio cupped this brave warrior's jaw. "Yet now you are trapped in his mine with all these other slaves."

Pepe nodded, tears streaking down his dust-encrusted face. "I... I..." His throat worked as he swallowed hard. "I have sinned. I am sorry, but..."

"No, Pepe, you are not a sinner, and I am not a priest." Poor kid needed something to believe in, so Julio whispered in Portuguese, *"Mas você tem a alma de um guerreiro, e os guerreiros não ficam à toa enquanto o mal existe. E agora, você é meu cúmplice."*

But you have the soul of a warrior, and warriors do not stand idly by while evil exists. And now, you are my inside man.

"I... I am?" Pepe stuttered, wiping the tears off his bruised cheeks.

A crowd of workers had gathered around them by then. "Ha. I am warrior, too, but see where... got me," an older man grumbled in broken English.

Pepe whirled on the poor, dirty fellow. "But my friend is a real warrior!" he yelled in perfect English, slapping his skinny chest and on fire with unearned devotion for a man who'd rung out. "He is a warrior of God! Do you hear me? Of God! And he has already saved hundreds! Maybe thousands! He is the miracle you all prayed for! Be thankful! Respect him or God will strike you down!"

Such vehemence. Such hero worship. Julio swallowed hard at the adoration pouring out of this boy's heart. "People," he said quietly. "Talk to me. Is there another way out of this tunnel?"

All heads shook, but the older man answered, "Only way out is the way you got in. What are you, *estúpido*? Didn't you see the armed guards out there?"

Julio didn't need to translate that. The man's disgust permeated every other grimy face here. They'd all lost hope. All except Pepe. His bright eyes hadn't dimmed for a second.

"*Eu não sou estúpido, senhor,*" Julio replied, keeping his answer between him and his antagonist. *I am not stupid, sir.* Then in English and loud enough for all to hear, he said, "I am Julio Juarez, Special Agent to United States Senator McQueen Sullivan. I am here to rescue you."

The old man spat at Julio's boots. "*Apenas um homem? Ainda mais um homem incompetente? Para salvar todos nós?*" *One man? One very stupid man? To save all of us?*

"Your name, Senhor?" Julio asked politely.

His adversary growled, but answered, "Mauricio Contreras."

Julio stuck out his hand. Respect. Despite the humiliating circumstances, this older man deserved Julio's respect. "It is good to meet you, *Senhor* Contreras."

"Are you American SEAL? One of the brave ones?" some feminine voice lost in the back of the crowd asked.

He released Mauricio's firm handshake. There was no sense lying. "No, *Senhorita*, I am not a SEAL," he declared loudly, needing everyone to understand that right here and now. "But I have come to end Orlando Zapata. Are you with me?"

"Yes," Pepe blurted. "I am with you, *Senhor* Juarez, and I'm so sorry I said you were ugly."

Julio let that telling info-byte pass. He might yet have to be damned ugly before this night ended.

Straightening to his feet, he secured Pepe against his hip, keeping his palm between the poor kid's shoulder blades to steady him as much as to warm him. "Will you people join me, or would you rather stay here and die working for Zapata?"

And there it was. A challenge and a dare. Fight to live, or lie down under Zapata's boot. Julio had never understood men or women who preferred safety over freedom. He understood it less in the face of such cruelty.

Pepe lifted his tear-stained face, his neck taut and his head tilted back as he breathed, "I will fight with you, *Senhor* Juarez. This I vow. To the death."

Julio rubbed a circle of warmth over the young man's back. "And I will fight to the death for you, Pepe. But we need an army to win this battle. We need everyone here."

"I will fight with you," that same feminine voice declared among the ocean of grumbles echoing throughout the crowd. When she finally cleared the masses, Julio saw that she was built like a willow, thin and diminutive, but fierce. Brown-eyed. Maybe five foot nothing. A black, curly-haired ponytail hung limp and dirty down her back. Her denim shorts were threadbare and her blouse was torn. Her face and body were covered in dust and sweaty grime, but the fire in her eyes was something else. "I will fight with you and your boy," she told Julio with venom. "Are you the only one?"

"Yes, yes, *Senhorita*," Pepe sputtered enthusiastically, patting Julio's belly. "But he is more than enough for *Senhor* Oz. You will see. My soldier is stronger than even my Papa."

Julio shook his head and looked down at his faithful *compadre*. "No, I'm not, Pepe. No man will ever be stronger than your papa. He loved you with all his heart, and love is all that matters. Never forget that."

"But he left me," Pepe whispered, like he was ashamed. "He left me and he never came back."

"Pepe!" a tired voice boomed from the other side of the cavern. "My son! Is that you? Pepe!"

The sure knowledge of who that voice belonged to shivered up Julio's spine. How was a miracle like that even possible?

As if in answer, Pepe burst off the balls of his bare feet and took off running, pushing people out of his way as he yelled, "Papa? Papa! Papa!"

A skeletal gentleman dressed in nothing but rags stood far off, waving a hand over his head to be seen in this mass of disgruntled slaves. "Here! Son! I am here!"

A murmur lifted through the crowd as they gave way. At last, Pepe crashed into his father's open arms. Sobs of both father and son echoed through the cavern.

Julio stood waiting while the enslaved workers absorbed their new reality. If they needed a miracle to convince them to fight, surely this was it. It had certainly strengthened Julio's resolve to end Zapata tonight. But he had to hurry. He couldn't afford to get trapped inside the cave.

Clearing his throat loudly enough to regain some of the crowd's attention, he called out, "Pepe. I must go. It is time."

"Papa, we have to help *Senhor* Juarez," Pepe told his father earnestly, tugging him toward Julio. "Please. Come. We must fight with my friend, not against him. He is a brave soldier, but he needs our help."

The acoustics in this cave were unreal. Julio could've heard a mouse fart. Instead, a gentle wave of affirmation rolled over the weary Brazilians when Pepe and his father began the climb to the mouth of the cavern, to Julio.

"I am in," a young voice declared.

Right on its heels, several male voices followed with, "We will fight!"

"With what?" Mauricio bellowed. "Our broken fingers and toes? Our broken bodies? Do not forget that we got no weapons." He sing-songed that last word.

Julio lifted his short stock, sniper rifle out of his bag and brandished it over his head for all to see. "With this," he stated evenly, "and with the picks, shovels, and hammers stacked at the cave entrance."

"No. If Oz finds us with shovels..." Mauricio bellowed. "He said he will kill our families, remember? All of our families. He will burn them alive and make us watch. Our tools, too. Only he..." Mauricio's rant ground to a full stop. He cocked his head as if he'd finally heard what Julio had said. "Our shovels and tools? They are still here?"

Julio stared Mauricio down. He was the wise one here. The leader. The one everyone else would follow. But he had to wake up and smell the coffee first. He had to believe.

"He was punishing us," Mauricio continued. "We rebelled when there was no food. We fought back, but we were stupid. His men beat us, but Oz was angry. He took our tools to punish us. He demanded we dig stone with nothing but our bare fingers and hands. Said we did not deserve the right to use his tools until we learned our lesson. That we had to earn those stinking shovels back." Mauricio stopped again, blinking as the truth assailed him now. "Revolução..." he breathed. "We attempted revolução before and we lost. But now...?"

His muttered diatribe ended on a note of hope. The best thing he could've said. *Revolution.*

"Wars have been won with less, *Senhor*," Julio told his new friend earnestly. "A brave North American once said" —he raised his voice above the murmuring crowd— "*The tree of liberty must be refreshed from time to time with the blood of patriots and tyrants.*' My friends, it is time to take back what was yours. Your homes. Your children. Take back who you were. Who you are."

"Thomas Jefferson..." Mauricio murmured. "I have read much of his works. I remember now."

Julio looked twice at the grumpy older man. Mauricio was not who Julio'd thought he was. Not if he knew who Thomas Jefferson was.

"Whatcha gonna do? Shoot your way outta here?" a tired, weary-looking woman sniped, "while us without guns hafta fight hand-to-hand?"

"No, *Senhorita*," Julio said humbly. Quietly. "I intend to put one hot round into Zapata's fuel dump, right next to the Russian nuclear missile. Right before I put another one through his head."

A chorus of anger gasped, "Russians? They've got a missile here? In our country?"

A new energy flared to life in the cavern. The fire of patriotism. The fiercest national pride.

"Who's with me?" Julio asked again, still patiently hoping he could get everyone out of this cave, up the trails, and to safety alive. It seemed an impossible feat, yet he'd done the impossible before. Once or twice.

"I am with the *Norte-Americano*!" the willowy woman bellowed. "Give me a shovel or a gun. Give me a rock! They are the same. I have courage, and I will kill Orlando with my bare hands. He killed my baby!"

The crowd changed from meek and beaten down, to angry and proud.

Julio called out, "Then we fight now!"

"And this time we win!" Pepe's father shouted, one hand clenched in a fist high over his head, with his son sitting high on his shoulder.

Julio locked eyes with Pepe as a wave of all he'd lost crushed him once again. Tomas' eyes would've been as bright as Pepe's, if he'd been here.

Pepe winked then, the same as Tomas had barely learned to do before Domingo took him. With both cheeks scrunched. While he grinned. Same bright brown eyes. Same love of life. Same glowing adoration for his father.

Made Julio stop and think. Had Tomas led him here? Was the glow he'd followed down this dark tunnel called life simply the spirit of his son? Was that what Julio'd been searching for, the missing connection with the son he'd loved and would always love with his whole heart?

It felt true. Perfect and true. And somehow, the image of Tomas' smiling face overlaying Pepe's bright, shining countenance, helped. Julio bowed his head, acknowledging the miracle that he'd also needed. At last he knew. Tomas would always be with him in spirit. Still proud of him. Still very much a part of his life. Still walking beside him. And that was enough.

He lifted his head and stared Mauricio down. "Will you honor me by fighting for these people? At my side?"

Mauricio nodded, finally in step. Drawing in a belly full of freedom, he tilted his face to the ceiling and bellowed, *"Revolução!"*

Chapter Twelve

Just inside the cabin door, Meg froze, letting her eyes grow accustomed to the dark. Her senses flared, searching for the killer she'd come to end. Her nostrils widened to detect sweat, male body odor, or worse. When nothing came back to her, she slid one foot forward, keeping her sole flat to the floorboards to keep from accidentally stepping on anything. Or anyone. With Oz's army outside and their loud, brash voices behind her, the silence inside the cabin became her friend. Like smells, or lack of them, silence encouraged confidence. Orlando Zapata wasn't at home. Which meant he was with his men. That gave her time to locate Pepe. Maybe Julio. Wouldn't he be surprised?

She inched forward, wishing again for her gear bag and the flashlight in it. Or a match. Any light would be better than sneaking along in this inky darkness. Three more cautious, sliding steps forward, brought her shin,

"Ouch," to the bottom rung of a heavy wooden chair. She let her fingertips walk along the edge of the desk that went with the chair. Then the wall behind the chair. The wall. Another door, this one left barely open.

Carefully, she pushed it open. A chilly draft breathed past her. Still no light. No sound. No smells. Well, almost no smells. An unexpected acrid scent that could only be sulfur and cordite mixed with sawdust and gunmetal struck her nostrils. She didn't need light to know she'd located Orlando Zapata's weapons cache.

Working quickly, but still only by touch, she located a wall of stacked, long, wooden crates, most likely rifles. Then metal ammo boxes that climbed twenty high. Bags of brass shells. Rolls upon rolls of coiled dynamite fuse. *Shit. Were these... Yup.* Two open crates of what could only be LAWs. Tank killers. As in sleek, light anti-tank, over-the-shoulder rocket launchers. Most likely M72 equivalents. But her searching fingertips quickly established the launch tubes were hollow and empty. Not loaded. That was good and that was bad. Where were their sixty-six-millimeter warheads that, when fired, could penetrate eight to twelve inches of armor?

Man. What she'd give for a flashlight. Not a match. Not in this room. Just one bright LED flashlight. That would do.

With her heart pounding up high in her throat, Meg searched quickly for those warheads. It would only take one fired in the right place to end Oz. She had to find them. He wouldn't have bought all those launchers without having tried them out. But those open boxes of launchers could only mean—

"What the fuck are you doing here, Corporal Duncan?"

Meg whirled on that tough male voice, but came face to face with a bright stabbing light in her eyes. "Charlie? Charlie Brown?"

With a quick flick, he blocked the light with one hand, his long fingers now glowing pink. "Jesus Christ, are you trying to get yourself killed?"

What a sight for sore eyes! Her friend. Charlie Brown. All six feet, five inches of him. Decked out in tactical gear. Armed to the hilt and loaded. NVGs sat high on his head, and a big shit-eating grin stretching his ruggedly handsome, angular, but round, face.

Blowing out a deep breath of relief, Meg plowed into him. When he tucked her head under his chin, her ear went easily over his generous heart. Man, she loved this guy. "You scared me. Thought you were Oz." Then she pulled back. "Why aren't you on that Blackhawk and out of here?"

The smile she'd grown to love during their single operation together, lit his face. His shaggy hair and the thick scruff on his chin declared he'd been going to or coming back from covert ops in some far-off country when he'd gotten the call to rescue her and her children. Of course he'd obliged. Charlie'd always been a tough guy and a risk-taker. Unmarried the last time they'd talked over drinks, he was a damn handsome man. Blonde and blue-eyed, he was now darkly tanned and as rugged as they came. She'd fallen in love with him at first sight. But like a brother, not a lover. He was another Trevor, always looking out for her like a brother, instead of competing with her like other male soldiers.

For whatever reason, they'd clicked the first time they'd met at Fort Campbell's firing range. He'd been headed for Afghanistan and was testing the latest experimental smart weaponry, the type with a bullet that could actually turn corners. Special ops always got the fun toys first. She'd just come home from a remote assignment in Kore, and had taken to the range to clear her head. But she'd been flat out goo-goo eyed over that experimental rifle. She'd talked him into letting her try it out. So sweet! By the time they were done plinking away, she'd seriously considered applying to work with the Night Stalkers. She couldn't fly those spiffy helicopters, but there had to be some MOS that would get her onto their team.

But then her stroke… Yeah. End of that sweet dream.

"Been following this stubborn-as-shit woman I used to know," he drawled now. "Just wanted to say hi."

Her heart nearly melted. "Hi," she murmured, wishing he were Julio, then embarrassed at her lack of gratitude. "Thanks for coming so fast."

He held a gloved hand to her face. "Hey, slow down. Who said anything about coming fast? I'm usually slow and easy. Like to keep the tension level just right so my lady friend—"

"You clown." His sexual innuendo made her smile. "You're here to help me find Pepe and kill Oz, right?"

He shook that big round head of his, the reason behind his handle. "No, ma'am. Only here to pull you out of this shithole before you start a war. Who the fuck's Pepe?"

"A ten-year-old orphan who came here after Oz to keep the rest of us safe. I think. He ran away from the rest of us. But I'm sure he's here somewhere. He wants so much to be brave like his father."

Charlie shook his head. "You think? But you don't know for sure? Jesus Christ, Duncan. That kid could be anywhere." He lifted his left wrist to his face and squinted at the large watch on his wrist. "We've only got a small window. Get going. We're Oscar Mike."

"No. Not yet." She stepped back, gesturing to the stash behind her. "I haven't located Pepe, but look what I did find."

When the beam from Charlie's light moved over the room, Meg's heart stalled. Stacks, she was looking at stacks, some as high as the earthen ceiling. That was why this cabin had been built into the southern wall, to keep these explosives cool. All wooden crates, the contents of the nearest crates were clearly stenciled. M-16s. Kalashnikovs out of Russia. Bushmasters out of Remington Arms, USA. BR18s out of Singapore. And more.

The labels on the last stack in that cache scared the hell out of her. TNT. Semtex. C4. Oh, there they were. Open crates of warheads that went with those launchers.

A whistle escaped Charlie's lips. "Guess you have been busy, Meg, but no can do. I don't have time to engage Zapata, and these gunrunners are not why I'm here. I just came for the orphans and you. Pack it up, kiddo. Let's go. Move out."

There was a day she would've snapped to, saluted, and followed this man anywhere. But not tonight. She was an ex-pat now, and as committed to her adopted country as she was to the United States. Brazil had enough troubles, what with the Amazon on fire like it was. But the neglected orphans of Brazil didn't need more despots like Zapata. He had to die, and she meant to kill him. Preferably with one of his own warheads. That'd be a nice touch.

"Then go," she told her lanky defender evenly, "but I'm staying. Oz stole my children, and he's killed enough little kids. I'm not leaving until I have Pepe back and Zapata's dead."

"God damn it, woman. Do I have to toss your stubborn butt over my shoulder to get you to listen?" And he would. Charlie Brown was the soldier who'd hauled ass out of the burning UK consulate in Yemen with the female ambassador draped over one shoulder while he shot both mercenaries who'd been trying to kidnap her. That scene had made for macho drama on all the big networks, his big, gloved hand square on her forty-something backside while they'd ducked for cover.

Meg planted her feet, not going anywhere. "No, CB. You have to help me find Pepe while we still have time. These weapons are my only chance. With them, I can finally end Zapata."

"I have to, huh?"

She nodded. Man, she wished she knew Charlie's real name. So she asked. Mostly to distract him from following through with his threat of leaving. "What is your name, your full name? I've always used your handle, but seriously. I'd like to know the real man behind the mask."

His forehead wrinkled. His brows clenched. But he said, "Gregor Jorgensen." Only he pronounced the J with a Y, making it Yorgensen. Which explained the obvious Viking in the man. His height. His striking blue eyes. His everything.

She stuck a hand out. "Well, hello, Gregor Jorgensen. I'm Meg Duncan, and I'm so thankful you're here. You always show up in the darnedest places."

His brows lifted at that, even as he took her hand into his gloved fingers. "Me? I'm not the one standing in the middle of a psychotic guerilla's ammo dump. Come with me, woman. Let's blow this place. Now."

His touch was warm and gentle. She half expected him to lift her hand to his mouth and kiss her knuckles, as carefully as he held onto her.

She wished she knew him better. Yes, he was FMQ, *fully mission qualified*, but was he crew chief yet? She doubted it. There'd always been a somber streak behind those gorgeous blues, one she recognized. Loneliness. Which made sense. Career soldiers tended to be divorced males, getting divorced males, or never married males. Whether because of the steady deployments they sought out or just because of how they were made, she didn't know.

But she did know they went home to empty barracks or off-base quarters when they finally touched down. Yeah, sure, they might party with their buddies, get stinking drunk, and bed a few skanky wannabe-Army-wives. But at the end of the day, no one was waiting for them. There were no home-cooked meals to look forward to. No tender kisses or crushing hugs at their front doors. No *'I-love-you'*. No *'please, don't go'*. Which tugged at her heart where Charlie, aka Gregor, was concerned. He deserved a kind, generous, and devoted someone in his hairy, scary world. That person just wasn't her.

Steeling herself for the task at hand, and the very real possibility she would die before the night ended, Meg told him, "I respectfully decline your offer, Sergeant Jorgensen. I came here on a mission. Like you, I will not fail, and I cannot quit. Not until I know for sure Pepe isn't here and Orlando Zapata is dead. Now go." She fluttered her fingers at him. "Leave me behind. It's okay. I understand. Neither of our missions are authorized, but yours can be forgiven. Mine—" *Will probably get me killed.*

"Shut. The fuck. Up," he growled. Man, this guy was all things rough, ready, and gorgeously masculine. She couldn't quell the thrill zipping up her spine at the wicked gleam in his eyes. But her feminine response to his apex predator vibe was short-lived. Charlie'd never settle down. How many times had he told her that over drinks? Enough to know this was probably the last time she'd ever see him.

She hedged. "You wouldn't happen to have a spare flashlight I could borrow before you head out, would you?"

She could tell that question stunned him. His already icy stare turned downright glacial. Hard as stone. Not a hint of humor in sight. Then, suddenly, a gust of aggravation burst out of him. "What the fuck do you want me to do? This better be good."

"You're staying?" she asked to be sure she was reading him right.

"Yesssss," he hissed. "Why leave now? I'm already AWOL. Going to get my ass reamed for hanging around too long, but since I'm here... Fuck, Meg! Why can't you be like every other woman in the world? Why die here? Huh? Can you answer me that?"

Charlie always did like his f-bombs. She squeezed his hand extra hard before she let him go. "Because I love these kids and so do you. Stop worrying about me, and let's get this done."

"Woman, you drive me fuckin' crazy. You always have to have the last word. You know that, don't you?" Charlie had a funny look in his eye, like maybe he didn't see her the same way she saw him. Like maybe this was the start of something it wasn't.

Any reply would only encourage his line of questioning, so she ducked answering. "Well, then listen up, Charlie Brown. This is the plan..."

Chapter Thirteen

Julio stood at the north tunnel's entrance, the path behind him packed with more than two hundred women, children, and men. In no particular order. During any other rescue, he'd have insisted the women and children go first. Not tonight.

He'd selected the strongest, most able-bodied of the masses, regardless of gender, to lead the way to safety. Because there would be blood, and there would be death. But the men in this weak, little army of survivors had all been told to take care of the injured ones. They knew they had to hurry, and if they had to drag someone out of the tunnel, they'd better do it quickly. Oz's soldiers would retaliate, and they'd strike without mercy.

"Heroes only die once," he'd told his band of survivors, "but I will shoot any of you who puts his or her freedom before the weak or sickly."

And he'd meant it. These starving people needed to exit as quietly and as orderly as they could, or they'd all be caught again. Heaven only knew what Oz would do to them then—if he were still alive.

For now, Mauricio, Pepe, and Pepe's father Rafael, were armed with shovels and pickaxes at Julio's left. Susana Cortes stood at his right, gripping a long, dirty screwdriver she'd found, as well as a short-handled ax. Of all the rebels in this cave, aka the adults Oz had enslaved, she alone had the makings of a decent soldier. Obedience without arguing. A fierce will to live. But Julio had chosen Susana to stand with him purely because she seemed to want Oz dead more than Meg did.

Meg. His lips pinched thinking of her and that foolish, stupid kiss. The kiss he'd loved and would steal again if he had the chance. As torn as he was that he'd betrayed his marriage vows by kissing Meg, Julio still savored the sweet honey of her lips. Her mouth. Her fervor. Both times, she'd kissed him without his permission. But with such passion. Almost frantically, as if she'd needed him. Him, of all the men she could have had. She'd kissed him! And she'd seemed to like it.

Not that he understood why, but his blood warmed anyway, remembering her hands on his belly and chest. Her fingers around his neck. His heart beat faster, like it had a reason to beat again. Like it wanted to live out the rest of its time on earth with Meg. But that was a dream for another man. Not Julio Juarez.

The young man who'd dropped out of college to join the Navy. The sailor who'd rung out of BUD/S. The man who couldn't even save his woman and child.

Shaking the sweet taste of Meg out of his mind and off his tongue, Julio settled for knowing she and her children were safe instead of about to go to war. That would have to be enough.

The muscle in Julio's taut, stern cheek twitched like it thought otherwise. There was a day when he'd smiled easily. His facial muscles seemed determined to relive those days. But there was no reason to smile now. He wasn't happily married, and he wasn't on top of the world. Once he fired the first fifty caliber round tonight, there'd be no going back. And a smart man never smiled back at death.

The crowd pressed anxiously at his back. It was time. But first...

Julio needed to know. "What is in the other tunnel?"

Susana answered, "Gold. Tons of gold. Gold we dug with our bare hands so Oz could steal it from us."

Mauricio nodded. "Did you not know Zapata mined gold?"

Come to think of it, no. Julio hadn't cared enough to ask or research what kind of rocks Zapata had lusted after. But gold made sense. It had blinded enough greedy men before. "The other mine as well? You mined gold there, too?"

"All Zapata ever mines is gold," Pepe said.

"But the vein at OZ Metallurgy Mining is no more," Rafael offered. "He'd always kept a smaller exploratory group of men here, but then, the owner of this quarry found a good-sized nugget. The rock alone would've made him rich, but he made the mistake of bragging to Zapata that he would soon be richer than him. Now, he is blind. He used to work in Zapata's mine with us."

Mauricio nodded sadly. "After he cut his eyes out."

"Where is the rightful owner of this mine now?"

Mauricio's shoulders lifted. "Do not ask us. Ask Orlando Zapata. If you dare."

Which meant the actual owner was undoubtedly dead.

"That must be how Oz paid the Russians for those missiles," Julio murmured. In gold.

"They really have a missile?" Pepe asked.

Julio nodded grimly. "Three. And they are in the beginning stages of excavating missile silos."

"And they have dynamite," Pepe added. "That is what caused the explosion."

Susana growled. "Bastard. I thought the world was ending. This tunnel could've collapsed. He could've buried us alive."

"But they didn't," Julio reminded her and the others near to him. "And that is why you are here with me now. Let us focus, people. Tonight we fight back. Do not leave the tunnel until I create a diversion to hide your escape. Remember what I said. Run away as fast as you can, but take care of each other. All must be saved or all will die."

Murmurs rolled from the desperate people deeper in the tunnel when Julio stepped into the night. Aromas of grilled meats and coffee wafted from the campfire beyond. Good. Oz's army was eating and drinking. Soon they'd tire. It looked like some of his men were already prone, hopefully sleeping.

Mauricio clapped a firm hand onto Julio's shoulder. "Pepe is right," he breathed. "You are the hand of God."

The notion stuck in Julio's throat like a rock. If he were the hand of God, then God was a very poor judge of character. Without answering, Julio dropped to one knee, then settled on his belly in the dirt. There was no need to unroll the mat he used for times like this when dirt was all a guy had to lie on. He didn't intend to stay here long.

With a flick of his thumb, the front legs of his tripod fell into place. He removed the lens cap to his scope. Steadied his aim. Checked windage, distance, and elevation. Took a deep breath. Let his lungs deflate slowly, like a mediation. Which, for him, it was.

Next came his mental prayer heavenward. *Madre de Dios, please pray to your Son for me. Beg Him to guide my hand that I may end the terrible injustice this wicked man has done to your people. Help me save the innocent souls gathered behind me. Bless Meg and her children, wherever they are. Bless Dom especially. And bless me, dulce Madre de María. Please. No matter how this fight ends, bless me to die with honor.*

Another breath. One last thought of Meg and... Julio leaned his eye into his scope and located Domingo's baby brother's ugly, wicked face in his crosshairs. The man seemed to be looking straight at Julio, as if he sensed a predator watching him.

Look at me, Senor Zapata. See me. Know I have come here to kill you for crimes committed against God and mankind. Tonight, you die.

Oz laughed as if he hadn't a care in the world. As if he were untouchable.

Julio's right index finger settled into his rifle's trigger loop, then squeezed the metal loop halfway toward him. Finally. It was time to release the first hound of hell.

Domingo's brother sweetened the deal when he unwittingly stepped between the fuel pumps in the background and the business end of Julio's rifle. Looked like he wanted a picture taken of him with his new Russian friends. Still grinning. Still thinking he was safe.

When that was the last thing Orlando Zapata would ever be again.

*****

Packing one loaded rocket launcher on her right shoulder, with a squeaky-new M16 rifle holstered at her back and two more empty launchers with warheads waiting at her feet, Meg took a knee several yards from the munitions-packed cabin. The night was black, the air still and stifling hot. All the action in the gravel pit seemed to be centered around a pig on the spit in the middle of this hell-hole Orlando Zapata called home. Or whatever he called it. His headquarters. His mine. His gravel pit. Didn't much matter as long as he was dead when the sun came up. And he would be. Meg knew that for sure. Then she could continue her search for Pepe. She had to find him.

The launcher itself was fully extended with the warhead locked in place. Ready to fire. She'd already pulled the warhead's arming pin. She had no intention of changing her mind, and there was no way to telescope the warhead back if she did. Its folded fins were spring-loaded and ready to fly.

Her left elbow rested firm and steady on her left knee. While supporting the launcher with her weaker left hand, she flipped the sight reticule on the launch tube up with her right. She was good to go. The launcher itself was now trapped between her shoulder and her cheek, as if she were talking on a bulky telephone. All she had to do now was line Zapata in her sights, wait on Charlie's signal, and blow that bastard to hell. Didn't even have to target Oz's head to get her part of the job done.

They'd carefully planned a two-pronged attack. Charlie was on top of the cabin roof, ready to snipe the bastard who murdered children. All she had to do was wait for Charlie's signal. Then, while he turned Zapata's head to mist, she'd blow the rest of him, and anyone who got in her way, to Hell.

Check. Check. And double check.

"Arm your weapon, soldier," Charlie ordered from the cabin roof behind her.

Man, he was as bossy as ever. Still, she nodded her compliance, and let him think he was in charge. Holding the launcher firmly, she pulled the arming trigger into ARM position. The only thing left was for her to squeeze the trigger bar. How easy was that? *Okay then*.

She'd reconned enough of the gravel pit to know there were no Brazilian slaves yucking it up with Oz and his guys over there at the barbeque. Only some tall, uniformed, white guys she'd never seen before. Also armed to the teeth, they were most likely more mercenaries come to die in the land of, duh, Oz. What a fun play on words. Oz, as in the *"Wizard of Oz"*, surely wouldn't see the flying monkey coming at him that Meg was about to unleash. But he would melt like the green witch in that old-time movie.

Meg nearly smiled. But killing wasn't funny, and the warhead on her shoulder would leave damned few of Oz's buddies alive. If any. Yet that was her plan and her heart's desire. Kill the man who'd kidnapped her kids and who'd left Dom to die. End anyone who tried to protect him.

Disgust at what Zapata had done to Dom and other children slithered up her spine like a warm, friendly snake. But this snake she liked. The one across the pit from her. The cold-blooded monster, now staring at the tunnel where Meg was certain she'd find the enslaved Brazilians and maybe Pepe. Zapata? That snake had to die. Because, as quiet as those two tunnels were, she wasn't sure she'd find anything alive in them. Even the guards he'd posted outside the nearest tunnel weren't worried. All five were ringside and porking-out on roast pig now. Laughing. Guzzling what had to be nasty, warm beer.

Okay then... Ready. Set.

Only now... She wiped the sheen of sweat dripping off her forehead out of her eyes. This brilliant ambush plan sounded so much easier in the cabin, when they were deciding who would do what. She'd been pumped full of righteous rage then. She'd known she was right, damn it.

But out here in the dark, standing under all those stars in the universe overhead? Finally faced with the full weight of ending a life, even one so despicable? Meg faltered. Every last speck of her almighty self-righteousness had fled the instant she'd shouldered the LAW. Her heart thumped like a living beast, so loud that she could hear it once she'd snuggled the tank killer like a close friend. She couldn't breathe. Couldn't think straight. Didn't feel like rejoicing at what she damned well knew was the right way to end Orlando Zapata's reign of terror.

Yes, he'd be dead, and yes, he deserved the death sentence she was about to send him. But to be his executioner? To be the one taking his life, even a life so foul? Mind numbingly frightening. Overpowering.

She'd never felt so supremely capable or powerful, yet so lost and alone at the same time.

This action was final. He'd never see another sunrise. He'd never breathe the rich bouquet of a new Brazilian morning. Trevor had always said that killing your enemy took a part of your soul. That the more people or animals you killed, the more of your internal light you gave to the devil. It was karma in all its glory. There was always a trade-off. A balance.

All at once, the life and death decision wasn't between her and Oz. It was between her and God. Meg swallowed hard, praying for strength to see this judgment call through. To free the world of one of its worst, brutal aggressors. If that meant she'd have to sacrifice a part of her soul to save children like Dom, she was willing to let it be her. Wasn't she?

Am I?

"Talk to me, Trevor," she whispered to the sleek tube with its deadly cargo beneath her cheek. "If you're so smart, tell me what to do. Do I end him or—?"

"On my count of three." It seemed Charlie Brown, not her brother, Trevor Duncan, was speaking for the Lord tonight. *Okay then...*

With a deep breath, Meg took that as her sign from heaven. She *had* been called to end Zapata. She was the one. She *could* do it.

Leaning her cheek into the launcher, she sighted Orlando Zapata, standing all smug and domineering across the pit, in her reticle. One of his soldiers held a camera to his face. *Oh, look. Oz wants his picture taken with those tall, pasty white guys.*

"One, sugar dumpling."

The soft and low, sweet-southern-boy charm oozing out of the Viking at her six amazed Meg. Charlie didn't seem worried about right or wrong. He wasn't having second thoughts. Then why was she? Zapata had this coming, damn him.

Smile for me, Commander Oz. Prepare to die, you bastard.

"Two, sugar dumpling."

Oh, for hell's sake. Charlie was calling her sugar dumpling, not counting them. Silly, silly, courageous man. Somehow that helped.

Okay then...

More focused. She took one last deep breath. Flexed her fingers. She'd never been more ready to squeeze the trigger bar when—

Pew. A single gunshot rent the air. Then... *BOOM!* Followed swiftly by a thunderous succession of *BOOM! BOOM! BOOM!*

Holy hell! A gigantic explosion rippled through the center of the pit. The earth quivered and shook like popcorn on a wet dog. The ground groaned and heaved. A ring of vicious, roaring fireworks from deep within the pit broadcast zinging shrapnel and flaming wreckage outward. Whole burning trucks sailed into the sky like Tonka toys. Another thunderous explosion followed, shaking the earth. Then another!

Smoking hot debris rained down, trailing smoke and ash like monstrous fireworks out of the now glowing night sky. My God! The entire center of the gravel pit was one horrific belching ball of fire. Like a hungry dragon, it had engulfed every soldier in sight. There was no one left standing. Even Oz was gone. Those foreigners. All the vehicles. Tents. Equipment. Everything. The raging fire sucked everything into its cavernous jaws.

Only the three trailers parked way across the pit, near the farthest wall, were left. Wait. Were those missile launchers? *Oh. My. God!* They were. What the hell had Oz done? She blinked, not believing what her eyes were telling her when a blistering shockwave tipped Meg back on her heels. She turned sideways to escape the stifling, suffocating heat roaring over her, her skin already tender and no doubt burned. Armageddon had come to Brazil.

"You ass!" she bellowed over her shoulder at the big tough guy who supposedly had her six. Her eyes teared. "Damn it, CB! Why'd you fire prematurely? You hit some kind of ammo dump. You were supposed to—"

"No, ma'am! I didn't fire! Was not me," he yelled back, his grim face tinted orange by the sky-high flames reaching into the sky.

The ground shuddered again. Then again. Meg planted her feet to keep from toppling over. If Charlie hadn't fired, who--? Oh, my God, Julio? She was sure she'd heard a gunshot. Her gaze arrowed to the tunnels

Oz had been watching. Had Julio taken that shot? Was he here?

"You need to launch that warhead, soldier. Do it now, Goddamnit!" Charlie ordered, "before it detonates in your face."

Okay then... She didn't need to aim at Zapata now. Close. She only had to be close. Squeezing the trigger bar, she immediately felt the whoosh as the two-stage sixty-six-millimeter warhead launched. Mesmerized by the power at her hands, she watched the charge she'd lit simply by pressing the trigger bar, hurl the rocket from the tube and send it straight into the fireball. That was the rocket she'd intended to blow Zapata apart with. Damn, this was too easy. He deserved pain and suffering. Dismemberment. Torture! Not instantaneous death by a fire she hadn't started. So who the hell had? Could Julio have finally ended this monster? God, Meg hoped so.

"Holy fuck!" Charlie bellowed. "Who is that guy? You see him?"

"I don't see anyone, damn it," she muttered under her breath, wiping her face again. The heat from the fire was so hot that tiny blisters had formed along her hairline and her eyes kept tearing.

Meg stepped back against the cabin. She heard it then. The distinct rat-a-tat-tat of a room broom, aka the Heckler and Koch MP7. Way over there. It was him! At the farthest tunnel entrance. A single man stood dark and brave, his stocky profile lit from behind by an orange wall of fire. *Julio!*

Her heart leaped into her throat. What was he thinking? He was in danger. He needed to duck and cover. At least, drop flat into the dirt, so he made less of a target. There were at least a dozen guards pouring out of the one tunnel. As much as they were firing at him, he should've been dead by now. At least, wounded and staggering. Bleeding.

Yet Julio walked deliberately into their line of attack like he was invincible. He didn't falter. Didn't slow down. Just kept advancing, while he sent a steady strobe-light of death their way. One fell, then two more.

Oz's men didn't stand a chance. They should've turned and run. Julio might have let them live. But they kept shooting. And he kept giving them what they were asking for. Death without mercy.

When another guard appeared out of nowhere behind him, he pivoted, turning a shoulder to the few guards still standing. Still firing.

No! Meg's heart stopped. Julio was caught in a crossfire. He'd die. One against so many stood no chance of surviving.

"You know that ass?" Charlie asked, suddenly standing at her side.

She nodded, biting her lip, her gaze riveted to the death struggle across the way. "Yes, I do," she breathed. "That's Special Agent Julio Juarez. And he's not an ass." *He's my hero.*

Charlie leveled his rifle and fired three deadly rounds. Three guards nearest Julio fell. The others turned away, aware they had trouble at their rear. Big mistake.

While Charlie neutralized two more attackers, Julio took down the usurper at his rear. Man, he moved as if he were performing a deadly ballet. In the middle of a jump, he'd made a perfect half twist. With the ball of one foot still on the ground, he swung the top of his body around and leveled the compact rifle in his shoulder at his would-be assassin.

No hesitation.

No mercy.

Fire flashed again and no one was left standing when the room broom finished sweeping.

"Looks like he found the folks you came to save. Look at the hill behind your friend, Meg. You see that?" Charlie growled and fired again. "God, how fuckin' many guards did Oz hide in that son of a bitchin' tunnel?"

She saw them then, all those kidnapped villagers on the steep dirt path behind Julio. A steady flood of men, women, and children, some carrying others. Many children were secured to adults' backs or shoulders.

"He saved them," she said, straining to see Pepe in that fleeing line of survivors. But they were too far away. She couldn't make out faces.

"You might want to save his ass then, too," Charlie quipped, his eyes still fastened to his scope. "These guys just keep coming. You've got two warheads left.

Think you can send one into that tunnel without killing your boyfriend?"

Yes, I can, Meg thought determinedly even as she replied, "He's not my boyfriend."

Steadier now and with calm conviction, she cast the expended launch tube in her hand aside, grabbed another, and loaded the rocket. This time she knew precisely what she was doing.

Everything went smoothly. She sighted her target in the launch reticle. Only this time, she was saving Julio's life. That damned man would probably walk straight into death tonight if she didn't put an end to Oz's guys. What a crazy, brave, wonderful, hell of an idiot Julio was.

"Not tonight, Agent Juarez," she breathed as she snugged her deadly weapon into the crook of her neck. "You owe me another kiss." With the taste of his mouth in mind, she fired the warhead without a single twinge of conscience. And... *WHOOSH!*

It never wavered, just flew straight into the yawing mouth of Oz's tunnel. Straight into the stream of armed guards. When the warhead exploded, it was deep inside the tunnel. A brilliant blast of orange fire, brimstone, and twisted bodies belched out of the tunnel and into the already burning pit. Finally. The last of Oz's army had fallen.

"Way to go, Duncan!" Charlie cheered over the sizzling din.

"Thank God, I didn't kill him," Meg breathed as she let the expended tube drop and pulled another into position. She'd done it. She'd saved Julio's life. The ground hadn't even quivered, but the immediate shockwave from her blast had knocked him to his ass. Climbing to his feet, he turned toward her.

Even as far apart as they were, she felt his eyes zero hungrily in on hers. Meg lowered the second launch tube and waved, straining to see him more clearly. She wanted so much to run to him. To kiss the hell out of that badass warrior. Her badass warrior.

But the sudden updraft of a chopper overhead incited a whirlwind of dirt, dust, and leaves, blinding her. Ducking her head, she cupped one hand to her eyes. Where was he? One minute, she'd thought he might've smiled at her. But the next—

"What the hell?" she yelled at Charlie as she pointed to the sky. "Your guys?"

"We've got to leave, Meg. Now," Charlie yelled, his arm a manacle around her waist, while he carried her to what he thought was safety.

"I can't just leave him," she yelled over the roar of the rotor's blades. "That's Julio Juarez. He's one of Senator Sullivan's agents. He came here to save me."

Charlie shook his head. "No, babe. I came to save you. He came to end Zapata. Looks like both our jobs are done. Move it."

"No way!" Meg elbowed out of Charlie's tight grip. "I don't leave anyone behind, Jorgensen, and neither do you. We have to go get him!"

Charlie glared down at her, his eyes dark, and his jaw set. "He's gone, Duncan. See for yourself."

Disbelieving, Meg peered past Charlie's big bicep. He was right. Julio wasn't standing where she'd last seen him. He wasn't standing anywhere. How could he just walk away? He'd seen her. She'd felt his eyes on her. Hadn't she?

"He can't be gone," she muttered, even as her eyes declared there was no Julio to be seen.

"Brazilian army will be here soon, kiddo," Charlie urged. "Let's get out of here. If your boyfriend's one of Sullivan's agents, he'll be okay. Trust me. This is what guys like him do for a living. They strike hard and fast. They end the bad guys. Then they disappear. He belongs to the shadows. Let him go."

"But..." Her heart fluttered like the wings of a gut-shot dove plummeting to earth. "But I haven't found Pepe yet. And I won't, I can't just walk away and leave Julio!"

"He means something to you?" Charlie asked as he hefted her up backward into the Blackhawk's open side door.

"Yes," she breathed, sitting on the edge of never seeing Julio again, her eyes still frantically searching the trail where the last of Oz's now-freed slaves walked away. He had to be there with them. That's why he couldn't run to her. He was still on the job. *Wasn't he?*

Some of the people fleeing kept looking over their shoulders as if they expected to be followed. They looked fearful. Desperate. Pepe had to be with them. *Didn't he?* If not, where could he be? How would she ever find him?

Meg kept hoping Julio would jump up from somewhere. Maybe turn back and wave at her, just to let her know he'd seen her. That he cared. But no one jumped to their feet and no one waved. There wasn't a man or child in the group marching away that resembled him or Pepe. They were so, so thin. Ragged.

Charlie tossed his gear on board, then pulled himself up beside her. He joked with one of the operators, then made sure Meg was strapped securely into a safety harness. Like the macho guy he was and would always be, Charlie snaked one arm around her shoulders when the bird lifted off. Another hurricane of dust and dirt billowed around them. But even as hard as Meg looked for Julio, even as often as she quartered the scene below, there was no sign of him.

This time, he really was gone.

So was Pepe...

Chapter Fourteen

Julio lay flat in the weeds, his face to the dirt and his weapon beneath him, making sure no reflection from the blazing fire showed off his scope. He'd been hit. Upper arm. Nothing serious. But Meg Duncan's warrior friend had finally arrived, and they were flying off together. That was the best way for this nightmare day to end. She'd spoken of her buddy with some degree of tenderness. She'd probably worked with Charlie Brown enough to know what kind of man he was. Julio had to respect that. Meg deserved someone who'd fight for her. She deserved a hero. Looked like she had one now.

Wasn't that a kick in the heart? When the Blackhawk lifted off, just before it veered north, Julio lifted his chin and stole one last look, but only to make certain she was aboard the bird this time. Then he wished he hadn't. There they sat together, Meg and her hero, their legs dangling off the side, his big arm around her shoulders, and her leaning into him like a lover. At least like his best friend. He had his lips on the side of her head, over her bandana. Looked like he was kissing her.

Something ripped deep inside Julio, in that dark, isolated corner where a single ray of Meg's brightness had so briefly shone. Felt like a sucking black hole had cut through his chest like the São Francisco River cut through Minas Gerais. Stole his breath like he'd taken a sucker punch to his solar plexus. He couldn't breathe. Couldn't swallow. Didn't want to think about what Charlie Brown might be telling Meg up there in that chopper. Probably sweet nothings. Or lies. She might even be peering up at him and believing him. Thanking him. Promising him God knew what.

Julio ran his fingers through his short, wiry hair, remorseful at how things had turned out. But thankful Meg was finally on her way to safety. She never should've been in these Highlands in the first place, given her partial paralysis. But watching her leave with some bigshot Ranger named Charlie Brown? *Madre de Dios!* It hurt just the same.

Instead of bouncing to his knees once the chopper's running lights disappeared into the night, Julio took it slow and careful, lifting up and out of the dirt. Like it or not, he was injured. He took a quick moment to take care of his bleeding bicep. He'd been grazed. No big deal. Jerking his blow-out kit from his pocket, he tied his wound off with the belt that worked as his tourniquet. He'd clean that wound later. If he lived.

Right now, Senator Sullivan expected a thorough sitrep, which required absolute assurance the designated target had been neutralized. For that, Julio needed to see the corpse. Not that he expected to find one. Not that he'd file paperwork or take one last photo as proof if he did. Things like that just weren't done in the elite, black ops world Senator Sullivan commanded. The only things Sullivan wanted to hear was two little words: *Job complete.*

Not like Julio could transmit them. Meg still had his phone.

It'd only been a year or so since the SOBs, the name of Sullivan's clandestine workforce, had been created. Sullivan had originally tagged it with a politically correct moniker: Strike Back Force. Only former SEAL Chance Sinclair, Sullivan's first recruit, never liked it. One of three brothers, all former SEALs, Chance had promptly changed the name to Sons of Bitches, aka SOBs. What'd Sullivan expect from a former SEAL? Compliance? He should've known better. When you hired hard men, you got what you asked for. And the Sinclair Boys were some of the toughest.

All SOB teams consisted of three team members and all operated on a strict eyes-only, don't talk, don't tell, protocol. Every last one of them operated outside the law, yet all were comprised of men and women who'd honorably served America, some of the men as spec ops guys while in the military, CIA, or FBI SWAT. Some as hardened Department of Homeland Defense and Border Patrol agents. After continually witnessing man's depravity to man and various nations' failures to protect the common people, everyone Sullivan tagged to work with him pledged their allegiance to make a difference. Their goal was simply to turn the tide of evil in the world while it was still doable. Sounded simple. Was anything but.

Each team had a designated leader and two followers. Made things easier. None took their assignments lightly, and each decision to end a life required a unanimous vote by all team members, then team leaders. Sullivan demanded a unanimous vote to end any target. Once the yays and nays were in, he assigned the job to the most appropriate team. From that point on, the team leader assigned one of his people to perform the actual hit. No reports were filed afterward. No forensic evidence was collected at any scene. Once the selected agent reported back with *Job complete*, Sullivan and the SOBs moved on to the next despot, tyrant, or psychopath killer.

Surprisingly, among men and women who'd seen what most combat-hardened SEALs, Green Berets, Rangers, PJs, and SWAT officers had seen, there tended to be more unanimous votes than not. Discussions, when they surfaced, were brief, punctuated with rapid-fire acronyms, and buried in code. But decisive and final. Predators existed. The SOBs vowed to end them. One by one, they were getting the hardest jobs done.

Were the SOBs a behind-the-scenes organization created to exact justice for crimes against man and nature? Hell, yeah. Was it legal? Authorized? Moral? In a redacted, change-the-names-to-protect-the-innocent kind of way, maybe. Didn't matter to Julio. He'd already lived through the worst a man could survive. All he knew now was that a man on his own— any man—could still make a difference. At least until his dying day.

But he still had no phone. Guess that call to Sullivan would have to wait.

Not like it mattered. Since Sullivan enlisted Ranger and Nightstalker assistance, good old Charlie Brown would've reported how he'd rescued the orphans and former Corporal Duncan by now. No doubt he wouldn't end his mission with the standard SOB sit rep. He'd brag and provide details, maybe even a written after-action report, like good guys did.

Too bad Sullivan hadn't employed any good guys. Too bad Julio no longer cared. Meg Duncan didn't need him. She never truly had. Their brief interlude had been more about adrenaline than romance. Caring for orphans would fill the holes in her life. Hell, she actually had a life. All Julio had coming at him was another far-off target to eliminate. Another monster to neutralize.

Steady on his feet now and his arm wrapped for the time being, he aimed for the point of detonation. He should hurry. Verifying Zapata's death couldn't be hard. No one could've survived that blast. But Julio's heart was no longer in the assignment. His boots felt heavy, as if he were walking through wet concrete. His spirits were low.

The woman who'd breathed life back into his heart was gone from Brazil and from his life. And with her departure, nature's bright vibrant colors once again dimmed into the customary blacks and grays he'd been used to. The night sky overhead, which he knew was full of stars, seemed darker with the orange flames licking at the heavens like they were. No stars were visible. Even in death, Oz had robbed the night of life. In a way, that blank, black sky was Domingo Zapata all over again. Still protected and alive. Still aching to kill innocent victims with the cruelest violence, to paint himself with their blood. Still sucking the life out of everything good, pure, and holy.

But for a moment today, with Meg, Julio had actually felt alive. Maybe even good. At least better. He'd actually breathed like he wanted to live. His blood had boiled. He'd tasted hope, and it had come from Meg's sweet lips. The honey of her mouth. Her breath.

But no more. Fumes from the latest underground explosions punctuated this godforsaken pit of death and despair.

Shaking his head to clear the regret ringing in his ears, Julio approached the edge of the crater he'd created with that single well-placed shot. Another loud pop from below declared that Oz had stockpiled plenty of fuel below the surface. That explained the successive explosions at first impact. Also explained the burgeoning crater that, even now, swallowed another fiery mouthful. If the ground kept collapsing as quickly as it was, the warheads would soon fall into the burning abyss.

As it was, the mobile launchers were twisted metal carcasses. Two lethal payloads lay loose on the ground between two of the transport vehicles. The third balanced precariously, half-on, half-off its trailer. The three nukes appeared intact, though. Their casings weren't dented, only scorched and scuffed.

He doubted they'd detonate, but they might already be leaking radiation. Therein lay Brazil's next problem. Sullivan needed to get a nuclear safety hazmat team in here soon. But Julio suspected Sullivan already knew that, courtesy of Charlie Brown. The guy was no dummy. He had Meg, didn't he?

Not only had all other vehicles been incinerated, but Oz, his army, and every last one of the Russians had been evaporated as well. There were no bones or bodies anywhere. No blood. Not even a whiff of the barbecued pig. The equipment shed behind the vehicles was gone as well. Only smoking ash and the active fire in the ever-growing hole in the pit remained. Only the odor all dead things left behind...

Julio nodded to himself, satisfied that Oz hadn't survived this hit. He couldn't have, not as quickly as the fuel pumps blew. This job was done. It was time to step back and complete Sullivan's second assignment, organize and lead the deadliest of SOB teams. The *Dia de Muertos.*

But Julio would have to guard these missiles until Sullivan's hazmat team showed. South America was heavy with bands of guerillas, all out for world domination, fame, and glory. If any of them took possession of these nukes, there'd be hell to pay.

Turning his back on the fiery grave, Julio dusted his palms on his thighs and called it a day. Not a great day, but sufficient. It hadn't ended precisely how he'd wanted, but that was life for you. Full of heartache and lost chances. Not fairy tales. Certainly not happy endings.

Sullivan would be at Dover Air Force Base, Delaware, by now. Dover housed the Air Force Mortuary Affairs Operations. It was there the dignified transfers of all military remains were handled, processed, and made ready to go home to their families. Santiago would've accompanied Diego's and Seb's bodies to Dover. Julio needed to know precisely how his friends died. He needed to know who'd killed them and why. He had to get to New Mexico.

But first... He would finish this mission. He'd set up a makeshift camp somewhere above the pit. He'd keep watch over the nukes. He'd fish and he'd hunt the nearby forest until either Sullivan's team or the Brazilian army showed. Then he'd fade to black without anyone ever knowing he'd been there. He'd find a way back to Rio, and from there, to his new responsibility in New Mexico.

Julio crooked his neck and looked up into the night sky. If there were stars there, he couldn't see them, not through the thick veil of smoke and ash in his way. "Adios," he whispered to the woman who'd shot through his life like a falling star. "I'm sorry I lied, but it's best if we don't meet again. I will miss you, but you deserve better. *Vaya con Dios, mi amigo.*"

Go with God, my friend.

Chapter Fifteen

Meg watched the fiery glow from the gravel pit as long as she could see it through the trees, but the Blackhawk cut her view short when it veered north. Charlie still had his big arm wrapped tightly around her. But that was Charlie for you, acting all macho and proprietary in front of his buddies. He probably thought she was some brainless newbie who'd fall out of the chopper or something. But there was no way she could. Her harness held her secure just like his harness did him. They weren't going anywhere. Not falling out of the chopper nor falling in love.

As strange as it seemed, given she'd only met Julio earlier today, she'd recognized something in him. Something she hadn't realized she'd been searching for until now. Whatever it was, it felt stronger than the friendship she shared with the cocky, wanna-be-friends guy beside her. Like other male soldiers she'd deployed with, Charlie'd always been more of an over-protective brother than a lover. But Julio?

She cocked her head trying to figure him out. He said he'd come back to her, and she'd believed him. Yet when the Blackhawk appeared overhead for this exfil, he'd vanished. Which meant he still had work to do. Didn't it? She hoped that was all it meant. Either he intended to follow the workers out of the pit to make sure they were safe, or he'd disappear. To do what, she couldn't imagine. Oz was dead. There was no way anyone could've survived that blast. What else was important enough to stay?

Oh, yeah. Had to be those three missiles. Which made sense. A man like Julio wouldn't leave until the nukes were secured. He was too honorable, and he cared about the Brazilian people too much to let those weapons fall into the wrong hands.

But her heart hurt for Pepe. That was a hard loss to this day. There had to be a way to return, to search for him until she knew for certain what happened to him. *God, please let him stay alive until I can get back to him,* she prayed. *Keep him safe.*

Brushing a hand over her head, she was thankful her bandana was, at least, still hiding her lack of hair. But by then, Meg didn't really care about hair. She had Pepe to worry about, and she sure hadn't come to Brazil to impress Charlie or anyone else. She'd come here to help Brazil's orphans, and she'd already given her heart to Julio. What difference did hair make? None. None at all.

Sliding the grimy square of black fabric off her head, she extended her arm and let the wind take it. If this was to be her last time in Brazil, she wanted to leave something else behind instead of just the bodies of the orphans Oz had taken. Her bandana was all she had to give at the moment. Covered with her sweat, it was her last promise to Brazil. She would return.

The noisy Blackhawk made conversation impossible, and Meg was glad for that. She didn't need Charlie's interpretation of what she'd just done. He tended to minimize what he perceived as foolish, feminine promises, and she didn't want to hear it.

Her gift to Brazil had been hours and sweat well-spent. She liked to think she'd made a difference.

In minutes, they cleared Brazil's coastline and the bird headed out to sea. Pulling the last of her bravado out of her bag of tricks, Meg slapped Charlie's big mitt off her shoulder. "Knock it off, CB. It's not like I haven't flown side-saddle before."

He cast a mischievous glance at her bare head. A big, wide Cheshire cat grin deepened the dimples in both cheeks. "Remember that last op?"

"Sure, yeah. Who could forget?"

"You weren't married then, but you had hair."

"No, but I was engaged, and hair can grow back."

"So, the answer's still no?"

"That depends. What's the question this time?" Like she didn't already know what he was after.

His shoulders lifted.

Charlie, Charlie. Charlie... "God, you never change, do you?"

"Can you blame me? I see something I like, I go after it. And I never quit. You should know that by now. What do you say, Duncan? You and me make a good team. We could go far."

Smiling, she shook her head. Charlie wasn't so bad. He'd make some woman a husband—maybe not a good husband, but a halfway decent husband—someday. "I say the same thing I told you last time, CB. We want different things out of life, and this time around, I'm not willing to settle for less."

He winked. "I can change."

"No, big guy, I don't think you can, and neither will I. When I settle down, I want a houseful of children, and that'll take two adults, as in one mother and one father, who choose to be actively engaged with their marriage and their children every minute of every day. Not once in a while. Not just one harried woman who keeps the home fires burning while her guy goes off to war on the opposite side of the world at the drop of a hat."

Thankfully, the chopper dipped down toward a gray Navy aircraft carrier then, the *Iwo Jima*, and Charlie stopped pushing.

Not as impressive as a Nimitz class supercarrier, the *Iwo Jima* was still a breath of home-sweet-home in the middle of the wide, gray Atlantic. Wasp class carriers were the Navy's amphibious assault ships, the much-touted landing helicopter dock (LHD) for any aircraft from the super cobra attack helicopter to...

Oh, look. Are those F-35 Lightnings? Why yes, six Joint Strike Fighters were parked aft in a tight row with their wheels pegged. Excited now, Meg strained to see the newest bad boys of the sky. These Air Force fighters were designed to support Navy, Army, Marines, and Guard. Talk about firepower. Between the Osprey tiltrotor helicopters, the F-35s, and the mix of other helicopters, some large and some small, parked on deck, this ship had it in spades. Pride blossomed in her chest for the men and women of America's armed forces. There were none better in the world.

She'd no more than jumped off the chopper once it landed—without Charlie's help, thank you very much—when Maria came running out of nowhere, and grabbed onto Meg's leg. She nearly stumbled backward at the tender assault. Her left side kept telling her it needed rest, the sooner the better. But Meg enjoyed the snuggle until she sensed the girl was sobbing. With the noisy flight deck in her ears, she couldn't ask why. Ushering Maria back through the nearest door, she secured it behind her, glad Charlie hadn't tagged along.

"What's wrong?" she asked as she knelt at Maria's level, threading her fingers over the short dark hairs growing back on the girl's shorn head. "Where's everyone else?"

"He's..." Maria hiccupped. "He's really, really sick."

"Who? Dom?"

"Yeah, and that mean man won't let me sing to him and—"

"Ah, there you are!" Craig called out from the end of the passageway, his face red with worry. He'd been running. He was out of breath. "Little Scallywag," he teased once he'd caught up. "Thought I'd lost you. Where's Pepe?" he asked Meg.

She shook her head, heading off upsetting Maria any more, as she picked Maria up and cuddled her. For the first time since she'd been kidnapped, this sweet little girl smelled the way a frilly little girl should smell, of soap and shampoo and squeaky clean hair. "He's still in Brazil, somewhere. How bad is Dom?"

"I really thought you'd find him." Craig made a sad face.

"But Oz is dead. I know that for sure. I saw it with my own eyes. Julio ended him. Pepe will be safe until I can get back." Man, she wanted to believe that.

But Craig's unblinking stare told Meg he didn't believe her. She swallowed hard. She didn't believe it, either. Wherever he was, Pepe was alone, and the Highlands of Minas Gerais was no place for a lost ten-year-old. Damn Charlie for making her leave when she'd still had work to do.

Craig cleared his throat. "Well, it's good to have you back at least. And you're right. Once you rest and get something to eat, I'll see if we can fly back and search for Pepe. But no, Dom is not dying. Yes, he's been in sickbay since we arrived, but that's because he's getting a thorough check-up. He'll need to stay there awhile."

"They're being mean to him," Maria murmured around the fingers in her mouth.

"Ah, little one, the medics aren't being mean to him. They're helping him. Come see." He held out his hand for her to take.

Maria shook her head, content to stay with Meg.

"But they did start him on an IV, didn't they?" he asked. Then to Meg he said, "That's what upset Maria, seeing the Corpsmen insert that needle into his skinny little arm. Poor boy's anemic, plus a couple other things. They've taken blood tests. We never knew."

"I need to see him."

"And you shall, if I can find my way back to sickbay, that is. This place is one giant maze. Sometimes I have to go upstairs to go down a level. It's a crazy boat, but I'm learning Navy life."

"It's a ship," Maria whispered around her soggy fingers.

Meg kissed the girl's cheek, grinning at Craig. "Ship, Craig. The Navy builds ships and carriers, not boats."

He snapped a decent salute at Maria. "Aye, aye, captain."

Finally in sickbay, Meg nearly lost control when she saw two medics leaning over Dom. They were so big and imposing. So male. He was skinny and small. His eyes big, the whites showing. Poor little guy!

She'd barely regained a modicum of restraint when one of them spoke to Dom in fluent Portuguese. Then more, once she heard Dom's soft reply. He didn't sound frightened. The rest of her fears evaporated when she finally caught sight of him staring up at the medic. His eyes were loaded with hero-worship, and his cheeks were pink, but that smile...

"Mum!" he whispered excitedly when she came into view.

Setting Maria to the floor, Meg leaned over the bed and kissed his forehead. He'd been bathed. He smelled as good as Maria. "How do you feel?" she asked in English.

The medic who'd been speaking with Dom instantly translated, which made Dom's eyes sparkle. "My mum," he rasped, stretching his hand to her face as if introducing her.

That was a first. Meg cupped his thin fingers and pressed them to her cheek. Tears glistened like diamonds caught in the corners of her eyes. "I am so happy to see you, my brave, brave boy." *If only I could have saved Pepe...*

Again, the kindly medic translated, and again, Dom's lips curled with a tiny smile.

The other medic offered introductions. "Miss Duncan, I'm Corpsman Giacomo. Assisting me today is SAR Corpsman... Excuse me, I meant to say Search and Rescue Corpsman Daniel Shaw."

"I know how you guys work. I'm former Army," she told him. "So, what's up with my boy?"

Corpsman Giacomo's blue eyes softened. "Your boy has tuberculosis, ma'am. I'm assuming that you, as an American citizen and a foreign-aid worker, have already been inoculated against TB?"

"You bet. I was Army, been inoculated against everything, even anthrax. The TB shot lasts fifteen years, right?"

"Yes, ma'am, it does. Mr. Brunner already shared what little he knows of Dominic's family history. We suspect he came to your orphanage already sick with this disease, meaning a family member, possibly one of his parents or siblings, contaminated him. That might be how he became orphaned. We've already started him on a strong FDC, err, sorry, ma'am. An FDC is a fixed dose combination of the four strongest TB drugs on the market. But this little guy will need constant adult supervision for the next few months. He'll need to be weighed daily, and his health must be closely monitored. Every ounce he gains is a good thing, but as he gains weight, he'll also require stronger doses of drugs. They may even need to be adjusted daily once he starts to fatten up."

She ran a hand over her bare head. "Wow. TB. That's bad." Pepe's mother had also died of tuberculosis, but she knew for a fact Dom and Pepe were not related.

"Yes, but it's not the death sentence it once was. Technology and drugs have come a long way."

Meg nodded, thankful for all modern medicine had done for her when she'd needed it after her stroke.

"He's always been sickly, but the local doctor said he was just small for his age, a runt. That he'd recover and be stronger once he got older. I thought maybe he just had some kind of intestinal parasite, so I've treated him for that."

Corpsman Giacomo had the gentlest brown eyes. He nodded like he understood. "I'm just telling you what we know now. It's possible Dom has parasites, as well as other problems. We won't know until we get all his blood work back. But Captain Dooley will want to know. Where are we taking these children?"

Meg swallowed hard. She didn't know immigration law, and until now, she'd had no other plan than to save these orphans' lives. But she'd hoped. "Aren't they officially on United States property?"

His lips thinned. "Yes, they're aboard a Navy vessel, but that doesn't make them citizens, ma'am."

Oh, damn. "Safe harbor," she shot back at the patient corpsman. "They're orphans, for God's sake. All these kids need is safe harbor for once in their lives." And now she was going to cry.

The other medic kept the children preoccupied, blowing up a surgical glove. He pulled a marker out of his chest pocket and drew a face on the thumb. Dom smiled and Maria giggled. But Meg's heart was sinking.

"Then tell Captain Dooley they need humanitarian protection, ma'am. Regardless what you see in the press, America doesn't turn vulnerable children away. Dooley's a fair man, and he knows people in

Washington. He'll know someone who can help you apply for lawful permanent resident status for them. If it's doable, he might even contact someone to make it happen before we dock."

Her lips pursed with a sigh of relief. "Thank you, umm…"

"Lucas. Corpsman Lucas Giacomo, at your service," he reminded her, tapping a slender finger to his head while he looked at hers. "I'm guessing lice or fleas?"

She nodded, chagrined at her bare, shorn head. It seemed Mother Nature had worked against her at every turn. First the stroke. Then lice. Then Oz stealing her kid. Everything seemed determined to make her unattractive and useless. What could possibly be next? Leprosy? Her nose falling off her face? Worse, her fingers or toes? How could she help any child then? "Yes. Me and the kids. That's why we've all got short, short hair. Not sure why Craig and Marta escaped the infestation, but they did."

He cocked his head at her. "I'm guessing because you're more of a hands-on caregiver."

She shrugged. "Craig and Marta love these kids as much as I do."

"I'm sure they do." Corpsman Giacomo's gaze fell on the frail boy beneath the Navy's warm blankets on the bed. "But the world's damned hard on kids with no parents, and I've noticed you don't have a problem hugging or holding them. You get close and personal with them, and Dominic called you Mom, Miss

Duncan. That tells me a lot. Come on, Danny. Let's let the lady have some time with her kids, her *son*."

Meg stifled the impulse to punch Corpsman Giacomo's muscular bicep playfully, the way he'd emphasized *son*. He was as bad as Trevor, teasing her even as he hit the mark. She did love these kids, all of them. Tears filled her eyes. Even sweet Pepe. Damned if her mother's wise words didn't come back to her now: *A mother is only as happy as her unhappiest child.*

Only Pepe wasn't just unhappy. He was lost and alone and—there had to be a way to get back to him!

"We'll be right outside this cubicle, ma'am," Lucas assured her. "Don't worry if Dom falls asleep. We've got him on extremely low doses of pain meds. But as small as he is, it'll probably knock him out."

Which was correct. She'd no more than gathered Maria up into her arms and taken the chair at Dom's side when he dozed off without speaking another word.

"I still wanna sing him a lullaby," Maria whispered. "He looks so small. You think he can hear me with his eyes closed?"

"Sure," Meg soothed. "Ears still work even when we can't see. Let's both sing to him. The usual?"

Maria's head bobbed. "Ah huh. It's my favorite."

Meg drew in a long slow breath and let her cares drift away for the time being. She still had a missing child to search for, a special agent to track down, and a cocky Army Ranger to deal with. But for now, the little girl in her arms and the child sleeping so peacefully in bed came first. They always would.

The first lines of Maria's favorite carol murmured out of her. *'Silent Night'*. What else? For the first time in this long, harrowing day, all really was calm. A tear wound its way down Meg's cheek. She brushed it off. If only she knew where Pepe was.

Chapter Sixteen

Instead of using one of the tunnels for a hideout, Julio opted for a higher venue, one easier to escape from when needed. Also where the air was fresher and not so hot or stifling. He settled for a quick camp he'd made in the trees above the gravel pit, opposite the trail where Mauricio, Susana, Pepe and his father, Rafael, had gone. But he did some exploring first. Then, Julio spent the rest of the night hauling as much of Oz's cache of weaponry, ammo, and explosives into that camp as he could. It made for one helluva lot of backbreaking trips up that gravel road. A vehicle would've made it easier, but he'd been born for drudgery. Why change now?

It wasn't until he'd made a dozen or so trips into the quarry and back up the trail again that he heard a donkey bray. That stopped him cold, but it was not unexpected. People would've seen and heard the explosion by now. As isolated as this mine was, someone was bound to come looking. Guess that time was now.

Still on the trail, but not far enough to escape discovery, he pulled his pistol and flattened his back to the steep granite wall behind him.

"You still down there, *Senhor*?"

Julio couldn't believe his ears. "*Senhor* Contreras?" he whispered, peering up at the group of tired faces staring down at him.

"Aye, me and Papa, too!" an excited Pepe called out.

"Shhhhh," several voices hissed.

"We must do this quietly and quickly. Come. Let us help our brave defender of the people." That could only be Susana.

What were these foolish, brave people doing? "No. Please take care of yourselves. Go," he argued, his weapon now safely secured in its holster, but his heart on fire. These villagers were all in mortal danger. Surely another guerilla band was on its way to raid Oz's mine. That was how these desperados worked. If they couldn't take over the country, they raided, murdered, and stole from each other.

But there was no arguing, not with the determined band of villagers or the three donkeys ambling down the trail toward him.

"I don't need help," he told them bluntly. Urgently.

But by then, Mauricio and his white donkey were nearly to him. Of all the colors that could blend into this gravel pit and its granite walls, white was not it.

"Is not good to argue with our mayor," Mauricio said gruffly. "When Mayor Rafael Velasquez says 'we go'..." Mauricio shrugged. "We go. And now we are here. What do you have in that heavy pack on your back that my brave Annie can help you carry?"

Annie. His white donkey was named Annie. But Mayor Velasquez? Unbelievable. Pepe was the mayor's son? Why hadn't anyone known that until now?

Julio stopped fighting then. Besides Mauricio, there were a total of twenty men and women here to help. Oz's weaponry had to be moved out of the gravel pit. It took a dozen more trips to get the crated weapons and boxed ammo into the trees. Then another dozen to secure the plastic explosives alongside them. That was not the best location, and Julio was well aware he needed a more secure spot for the mountain of guns and ammo he'd accumulated, but first things first. All of Oz's cache had to be removed from the pit before the fire spread.

While the men and donkeys carried the heaviest loads, Julio handed Susana a paper tablet and a pen from his pack, and assigned her the job of organizing and inventorying every last box and ammo can. Nothing must fall into the wrong hands. Not one bullet. Not one brick of Semtex or C4.

At the first blush of dawn, the last tired donkey plodded out of the pit and into his haphazard camp. By then, Julio had worked non-stop for too damned long. He couldn't remember the last time he'd slept. He was sweating, tired, and worried. This place was utterly indefensible. All he'd done was make Oz's weapons more easily available to the first outlaws that came along. And they would come.

He'd ignored his injured arm until now, but the damned thing ached. He couldn't rest. Not yet. Wiping a quick hand over his brow, he reassessed the growing stockpile.

Susana had done a good job. The wooden crates were divided by type of weaponry, the ammo that went with each rifle, stacked between the crates. She'd organized the LAWs the same way, the warheads stacked neatly alongside the crates of launchers. But what good did that do if it fell into the wrong hands? Now Julio had two problems. Protect this camp above the pit and the ICBMs below. While he lived off the land. While he went without sleep.

Madre de Dios, he would die here.

"I think you have a problem," Rafael said quietly, his hand suddenly on Julio's shoulder, squeezing him the way a father squeezes a friend. "Pepe? Run and get Uncle Ralph. Tell him to bring his truck. His big truck. Our friend is injured."

Julio shook his head. "No, Mayor Velasquez. I'm fine. But I can't put you and your friends in any more danger. You must leave. If necessary, I'll set traps and blow this stockpile before I let anyone take it."

"But we need it," Rafael said just as quietly. "For years, the Zapata brothers have raided these Highlands, and we've had no way to stop them. They've taken our children, and they've raped our women. Our daughters, *Senhor* Juarez. It is time we took from them and defended ourselves."

Julio cocked his head, worried all over again. "How many Zapata brothers are there?" He only knew the two. Please, God, let there be no more.

"Orlando was the younger, but Domingo is much worse."

That was true enough. "Only two then? Any sisters?"

There were no gender-specific boundaries when it came to psychosis. There were just as many cruel women in the world as men, like Catalina Montego, the Cuban woman who had recently terrorized the East Coast of America.

Rafael shook his head. "Trust me. Two were more than enough."

Julio nodded. "Their parents?"

"Both dead."

"Good," Julio replied with a heartfelt sigh. "But *Senhor*, rest easy. Domingo Zapata cannot hurt you anymore. I've already apprehended him."

Susana looked up from where she knelt with her tablet, her eyes bright and hard. "Is he dead? Are you sure? Did you see him die when you killed him?"

"No, but he's in an American high-security prison from which there is no escape. He won't be back."

It irked Julio to no end that Domingo was still alive. He breathed, ate, and slept on the American taxpayer's dime. Did that bastard know yet that his baby brother had died in a ball of fire? Would he ever know? Had someone told him? Had he cried for his baby brother? Had he ranted and raved and scratched his face until his tattoos bled with the news of his brother's violent passing? Was his heart broken yet? Would it ever be?

No, because this mission was so top-secret that no word of it would ever hit American networks. Domingo would never realize all he'd lost—if he even cared about Orlando. In the end, he'd spend the rest of his days in relative peace and safety, in ignorance. Confined, but never truly punished for his crimes against humanity. Against women and helpless children. Little boys...

Where was the justice in that? Julio wanted to be the man who told him. Who watched him suffer until he went insane with grief. Until it ate him from the inside. Like Julio's loss ate at him. Every. Day!

But that was where he and the Zapatas were different. Julio adored his *familia*. But he doubted they even knew what the word meant.

Rafael's big, warm hand squeezed Julio's shoulder, bringing him back from the weary world of revenge. "I'm glad to hear Domingo is in your American prison, my friend. But we can move these munitions to our village. We will make a safe place for them, and for you, too. Please come with us. Let the fire take this pit back to hell. You are worth much; the Zapata brothers were not. They have been nothing but a blight on our land, but you..." Rafael cocked his head, his rich brown eyes speaking straight to Julio's soul. "I think you have seen too much death, *Senhor* Juarez. Come. Be my guest for a while. I do not have much, but my wife will open our home, and you will find rest."

Julio grunted, then regretted his careless response to such a kind offer. But he'd been homeless so long, and the thought of being in this generous man's house with a kind woman who honestly cared for her husband, galled Julio to his core. It'd been hard enough sitting in Chance Sinclair's Montana hideaway with Suede, all those months ago. The love for her man had shone so brightly in her eyes, that Julio had felt the warmth. Chance and Suede were happily married now. Paloma and Pagan would either marry soon, or at least, she'd be with child. Pagan would make sure of that. They were destined for that same kind of bliss and the unconditional adoration Julio had only found in the eyes of his sweet son.

And Meg...

The picture of her hanging off that Blackhawk with Charlie Brown obliterated any foolish notion Julio might have held onto. He hadn't been born lucky like the Sinclair brothers. They'd had a mother who'd adored them. Who'd provided and sacrificed for them. But his and Paloma's parents had always acted like teenagers on a crime spree instead of adults with parental responsibilities. They'd lived for the thrill, for the adrenaline rush. Not for their children. That was what had gotten them killed.

Julio drew in a deep breath that did nothing to assuage the pain in his heart. Not even the tiniest bit.

The sad truth was that Meg was as lost to him as Bianca and Tomas.

Ironically, the only thing he'd ever wanted besides his own *familia* was to be a SEAL. In a way, he was now the same as all those courageous men who hadn't rung out, their success made complete by the overwhelming divorce rate stacked against them. SEALs didn't stay married long. Like him, they were condemned to walk alone. Which was why they stayed in the Navy as long as they could. It was all they had.

A donkey brayed then. A lonely sound. A sad sound. It's loud asthmatic hee-haw jolted Julio back to the world of hard truths and harder facts. Back to his reality. Back to solitude.

Below, the fire still growled, crackled, and burned. Angry black clouds filled the sky. Zapata's enemies and competitors, every lowlife he'd ever stepped on, would arrive soon. They'd crow at the chance to rob their now dead enemy. These weapons could not fall into the wrong hands. Minas Gerais didn't need more bloodshed.

"I am tired," Julio admitted, humbled by the mayor's offer.

"You cannot stop those missiles from exploding," Rafael murmured. "I am not a wealthy man, Agent Juarez, but you are one against the world. Let the rich and the powerful have what they think is so important. Come with me where you'll be safe, brother. Before it is too late."

Rafael didn't understand. It was already too late, and Julio would never be safe.

"Thank you for your kind offer, but no," Julio said quietly. "I have a job to do, *Senhor* Velasquez. It is you and your son, your people, who must leave. Trust me. I know what I'm doing, and I must finish my work." He stuck his hand out. "Take what weapons you want and need, then go. I cannot do what needs to be done until you and your friends are out of harm's way."

Rafael's eyes glistened. "You intend to die here."

Julio's shoulders lifted, but he said nothing. Death would be welcome when it came.

With a soft command, Mayor Velasquez passed Julio's offer to his friends. In short order, several crates and ammunition were loaded back onto the donkeys. Every villager took what they could carry. Susana took one of the Kalashnikovs, a good choice. Even Pepe brandished an empty rocket launcher like a trophy. Which made Julio morose all over again. A world in which little children were well-acquainted with death and killing was a dismal world indeed.

"Goodbye, my friend," Rafael called out as he and the villagers wound their way through the trees and back to their homes. "Until we meet again."

"Goodbye," Julio replied evenly. There would be no meeting again. Rafael hadn't told the people Julio wasn't joining them. Even Pepe had gone ahead with the villagers, thinking all was well.

Which it soon would be. Julio had the motive and means. It wouldn't take much to set a few traps in the pit below. When he was done, Brazil would be rid of more than just Orlando Zapata.

Chapter Seventeen

"We can't just leave Pepe or Agent Juarez," Meg told Charlie. Again.

"Hand it over," he answered, his big, callused hand stretched out, his palm open.

Oh, that. Meg had forgotten. Tugging Julio's sat phone out of her jeans pocket, she gave it to Charlie.

He stuffed the phone into the gear bag slung over his shoulder. "You do realize Sullivan has no way to contact his agent now." Heavy innuendo laced the comment.

"I know. I argued against taking it, but Julio insisted. He did that, so I could hook up with you."

Charlie growled. "That man's going to be the death of me."

That sounded promising. "You're going back for him?" she breathed. "I'm going."

He shook his head. "No way. My op. My rules. You stay with the kids and—"

She let her crusty Army persona loose. "Bullshit. I may be a woman, but I'm capable and you know it. I need to find Pepe. He'll listen to me, but you'll scare him."

Charlie's big chin turned square. "This has nothing to do with gender inequality, and you know that. Damn it, woman, you're a liability." Raising one hand to her face, he ticked the reasons off his fingers. "Can't run. Can't keep up. Can't carry one damned one of us bigger guys if we're unlucky and get injured. Can't even carry half the equipment we carry. Am I right?"

By then her heart had lodged high in her chest. She was breathing heavily. "Yes, but—"

"But what?" Charlie cocked his head, his eyes as hard as a drill sergeant's.

'But I wanna go,' seemed like such a crybaby answer, so Meg swallowed past the rock in her throat instead. The Army didn't care what any one person wanted, not during dangerous operations like this one, and going back into Brazil would be risky. Brazil was no third world country. That day was long past. Their armed forces were the third largest in the Americas and the largest in all Latin America. The current president had to know by now that his airspace had been breached and precisely which county had done it, his pushy neighbor to the north. He aggressively defended his country against foreign threats. There would be diplomatic consequences.

But Meg didn't care. Squaring her shoulders, she said, "I'll stay in the Blackhawk then. I'll be your corpsman." Aka, medic. "You know, in case anyone gets injured. In case you find Pepe. You need me and you know it."

Charlie's eyes narrowed and his nostrils flared. His lips pinched thin and unyielding.

Darn. She could tell by the way he'd shifted his stance, his legs spread wider and his chin stuck forward. She wasn't going. She wouldn't be there if he and his guys found Pepe or Julio. If there were a gunfight, Pepe could be hurt. Julio might already be dead, and she'd never know, never see either of them again.

"This guy means that much to you? That Juarez fellow?"

Meg pursed her lips, not sure precisely what Julio meant to her. She didn't know him, not really. One day in the life of a woman on the run from a psychotic, ruthless killer was not how to meet men. And Julio was so damned timid. No, not timid, but...

She struggled to describe him. Her dad would've said he needed a swift kick in the pants. But Meg thought, hoped, maybe Julio just needed someone like her in his life. Wouldn't that be something, a big, strong, capable man like him needing a damaged woman like her? Her confidence faltered. Maybe this wasn't such a good idea.

"You're right. I'm not any use to you—"

"Damn it, Duncan. That's not what I meant, and it's not what I asked." Charlie leaned down and into her face. "Listen up, Corporal. I know the kid's important to you, but does this Juarez ass mean enough to you that you'd put yourself at risk to save his life, too?"

She nodded, afraid to speak. More afraid to admit to this brash Ranger that she cared for a stranger she'd just met almost as much as she cared for the boy she'd mothered this past year.

Charlie shook his head as if he were shaking off an annoying horsefly. "Grab your gawddamned gear, Duncan. Guess you're going with us."

She couldn't help it. Meg rushed Charlie and hugged him. "Thanks. I won't be any trouble."

He relaxed around her, his chin on her head and his arms a sturdy cage she knew would always protect her. Charlie was like Julio. Born that way.

"I sure hope you know what you're getting yourself into," he murmured into the top of her head.

"I'll bet you said that the first time you jumped out of an airplane."

His chin bobbed against her. "What you feel for this guy feels like that?"

"Yes. It does. I know it's bizarre, but I have to see this through. It's important to find Pepe, but it's also important to help Julio."

"Julio, huh? He's only gonna break your heart, kiddo. Black ops guys don't stick around long enough to make families. They don't play fair with their relationships, because deep down, all they are is ghosts and shadows. You ever think that maybe all this Juarez dude wants is his job? His solitude? That he's happier being left alone?"

Then why did he kiss me like he was starving?

Meg pushed out of Charlie's arms, so she could look him in the eye. If her stroke had taught her anything, it was not to give up hope. True, she'd lost her way for a while a year ago. She'd been despondent and even a touch depressed when she'd left home. But once she'd come to Brazil, she'd been reborn again, and she knew it. As backward as it sounded, she'd found herself the moment she'd given herself away to her work. After she'd fallen in love with her kids.

Meg made a fist and clocked Charlie's shoulder. Of course, he didn't flinch. "Thinking's over-rated, CB. Get that chopper ready. Let's roll."

*****

They came like jackals and snakes. Like devious coyotes. Quietly. Stealthily. But loaded for war and prepared to attack the alpha predator of the region. At least, to take advantage of the tragedy that had befallen Orlando Zapata.

Julio watched from his sniper hide in the dense trees around the gravel pit. He'd studied the local demographics on his long flight to South America. Because Minas Gerais was one of the more populated states in southern Brazil, it had more than its share of lowlifes, troublemakers, and illegal militias. Those local bands of thugs would surely come looking for Oz.

After Rafael and his villagers had left with their share of Zapata's weapons, Julio had hurriedly camouflaged the remaining stockpile beneath thick layers of leathery banana leaves. To make sure none of the remaining cache in the pit survived, he'd set simple explosives to ignite at his command. Then he'd laced the trail into the pit with the same remote-controlled charges. He couldn't chance that a lone child wandering these hills might set off a carelessly set booby trap. Or that a troop of monkeys wouldn't grow curious at the disturbed topography and investigate.

No. The only way to ensure there was no collateral damage was for Julio to stay alert, awake, and ready to detonate those charges.

Which was difficult after the last forty-eight plus hours without sleep. But he'd managed to grab a few combat naps. Now, he drew a bead on the tall, slender Brazilian standing with his hands on his hips, staring into the fire. Smoke still billowed from the cavernous hole. That Zapata had stockpiled enough diesel fuel to stoke this fire so that it had lasted all night and most of this morning, was a unique feat unto itself. But then again, maybe not.

Julio'd witnessed enough despots the world over to know they all thought themselves above man's and God's laws. Yet they were all paranoid, too. Always looking over their shoulders for that knife in the back. Hence, they overcompensated, like Hitler, who'd built so many secret bunkers that myths he still lived abounded yet today.

All hoaxes and conspiracy theories. Julio knew bastards like Hitler. He couldn't have stayed hidden all this time if he'd tried. His ego wouldn't have let him.

Without glancing behind him, the man below waved his arm, and several more men appeared out of the forest and came forward. All were dressed in the same military fashion as Zapata's men, only their neckerchiefs were green instead of red. All were armed, either with rifles, machine guns, or machetes.

In the end, thirteen men lined the edge of the pit above the tunnels. Three more stood across the pit from them. They waved at each other, signaling all clear when it was anything but. These guys hadn't discovered what was left of Zapata's stockpile yet. They were too preoccupied by the three Russian missiles. Too excited.

Julio steadied his rifle stock into his cheek and bided his time. Patience ruled all decent snipers. He waited until he was absolutely sure he could end as many of these men as possible before he was spotted. It'd be a fight for survival after that, yet he'd been in tighter situations. He wasn't worried.

Drawing in a slow, steady breath, he let it ease just as slowly out of his lungs. Tired or not, he would end anyone who tried to control those missiles. It might take the rest of this morning, but those missiles weren't going anywhere.

At last, the leader waved his men forward, and they took the trail at a trot. He led the way, and, sure enough, he skirted the massive crater and marched straight for the twisted missile carriers and their payload.

Sweat dripped into Julio's eyes, stinging, but not enough that he wiped it away. The injury to his bicep throbbed, but he dealt with it. Nothing must come between him and his task. Not now. No sniper moved once his targets had lined up as easily as these guys did. Even the three from the opposite edge of the pit had now joined their fearless leader. Interestingly, no guards stood watch at their backs. That made this ambush easier. The trail was the nearest way out of the pit, and right now, those tough guys were all out in the open.

But greed tended to make even the smartest men stupid.

Julio waited until they'd all surrounded the nearest missile. He watched them stroke it like the prize it was. Then it got interesting. The last three to join the group opened fire on the others, shooting them in the back and killing everyone. Once the assassination ended, they laughed. They yelled. They high-fived each other.

Julio had just witnessed a bloody coup. A massacre. If he had any doubts before, he didn't now. He fired three deadly rounds, ending the assassins' brief powerplay once and for all. Within seconds, the reverberation from his rifle reports grew silent. The jungle stilled.

Good enough. Good plan. Good riddance.

The earth heaved then as another underground explosion belched and obliterated the sixteen bodies. Satisfied, Julio reloaded, then leaned back into the sturdy trunk behind him. He'd chosen well. This tree's wide branches made for a decent place to sit, and its dense growth kept him hidden. A man could easily drift off to sleep here. He couldn't have asked for anything more.

Except for Meg to share this branch with him. That'd be nice.

Chapter Eighteen

Meg leaned into the wind passing through the wide-open Blackhawk's doors. They'd just entered Brazil's air space and were flying at a fast clip over the northern rainforest instead of traveling directly over downtown Rio. This operation needed to be handled as covertly as possible. Hence the helo skimmed low over treetops and dodged flocks of birds to avoid radar detection. There was no sense spitting in the Brazilian president's face.

She now knew Charlie wasn't going back to save Julio or to locate Pepe. Uh uh. This mission was all about the Russian ICBMs, not saving a lost boy or a downed covert operator who might need an emergency exfil. CB was escorting blonde, buxom, and beautiful, Dr. Barbara Hazelton, the over-the-top sexy nuclear engineer from the UK's Proliferation and Nuclear Policy Institute, to the pit. She'd already been on the *Iwo Jima*, called upon to disarm the warheads that neither Washington nor the UK had been able to locate. Seems those two countries had been fully aware of the deal between Orlando Zapata and the Russians for months. They just hadn't known the precise location where that transfer would take place.

By sheer dumb luck, it was Julio who'd stumbled on the Russians and the ICBMs. If not for Meg following him, and for Charlie tracking Meg, these missiles would already be in the wrong hands. She wanted to point that out to her Ranger buddy, but Charlie hadn't yet given Julio credit for taking out Orlando Zapata, much less for locating the warheads.

Meg worried for Julio. Had he been exposed to radiation? Was he sick? Injured? Was he still near the pit, or had he fled with the villagers he'd rescued? Their village was maybe twenty miles from Giant's Toes. Were they in danger from radiation leakage?

Which was why she'd covertly acquired the Glock now tucked in the back of her jeans, from the carrier's munitions locker. Charlie didn't need to know everything, but if push came to shove, she meant to be an actively engaged asset, not a whimpering please-don't-kill-me victim.

Princess Di, aka Dr. Barbara Hazelton, tipped her head back and laughed at something Charlie said. They were both wearing bulky, full-body, heavy radiation suits, complete with TLDs, thermoluminescent dosimeter badges, to monitor exposure, if any, to leaking particle radiation. The suits were comprised of the latest nanotechnology that incorporated radiation-resistant materials into the lead and rubber embedded in the fabric. They'd have to put head covers and face masks on, once—if—those dosimeters registered the slightest alarm.

"Oh, no. It's really quite simple once you understand Russian mindsets. You see," she equivocated loudly in her adorable, clipped British accent. "Disassembly of any nuclear weapon is merely a matter of reverse engineering. What was designed, can always be un-designed. What is assembled can be disassembled. You said there was an explosion near the warheads?"

"Yes, ma'am," Charlie drawled just as loudly. "Zapata was one paranoid motherfucker, so like a dumbass, he stockpiled diesel fuel in the pit. You'll see the black smoke soon enough. That kind of fire could burn for months, maybe years."

Her lush red lips pursed. "I'm afraid that may require an entirely different solution which has more to do with politics than common sense. I suggest we investigate as closely as possible before we offer any reports to our governments. I need eyes-on, not best guesses."

"If you say so, ma'am." Charlie poured on an extra dose of his good old Southern Boy charm.

Meg was sitting across from Charlie and the Princess. The sight of them flirting made her gag. She wanted to throw up in her mouth. He was a slick devil, chatting up this long-legged woman who could easily pass for a movie star, and doing it so soon after he'd all but propositioned Meg. The cocky ass hadn't even strapped in this time, probably because he needed to prove he was invincible. For two cents, she could've shoved him out the chopper door just to prove he couldn't fly. The dog.

Hazelton smiled. Charlie grinned. And once again, Meg swiped a hand over the new, clean bandana she bought onboard the carrier to disguise her substantial lack of hair. Not that she needed to compete with this woman, but just once, it'd be nice to be called beautiful. Not by Charlie though. God, no. He wouldn't know the truth if it bit his big, hairy ass.

"How did you say those fuel tanks exploded?" Princess Di asked Charlie in what Meg thought was totally fake, but loud, innocence.

She cocked a closer look at this gorgeous blond. Had Hazelton just baited the superior macho male like a femme fatale pro? Did she suspect he'd left certain details out of his report? For that matter, had he mentioned Special Agent Julio Juarez at all? Did anyone know Julio was still down there?

The tiny hairs at Meg's nape prickled to attention. How could Princess Di have deduced Charlie's deceit, if that was what it was? Who exactly was this savvy nuclear engineer from the UK's Proliferation and Nuclear Policy Institute? Had anyone checked her credentials?

Just then, the Blackhawk veered sharply to the south, forcing Meg to hang on tighter or risk sliding out of her portion of the molded bench. Her harness dug into her left side, exacerbating the dull ache that spread from her clavicle to her toes.

Doctors said every time her nerves tingled was a good sign. Nerves took a long time to regenerate, years even. But man, she was tired, and not in the mood to project a sense of sparkly positivity to talk herself out of the all-over pain creeping up her left leg. Strokes sucked, damn it. Yes, every little step forward was freaking progress, but why'd they all have to be such tiny baby steps?

Meg squeezed her eyes shut to block the sight of the flirty couple across from her, as much as to block the aching pain she lived with. She thought of her hero, Neil Armstrong, and the famous line he'd uttered when he'd first set foot on the moon: *"That's one small step for man, one giant leap for mankind."*

She could use one of those giant leaps—right damned now. But that wasn't going to happen, and this day might not end how she wanted. She might never see Pepe again, and that hurt her heart more than losing Julio. He was a trained covert operator, but Pepe was just a kid. Brave, yes, but all alone and fending for himself in a warzone.

Tears glimmered at all he might be going through right now. There were wild animals in the Highlands. Jaguars. Feral pigs as big as small horses. Poisonous snakes. Even an occasional harpy eagle. Couldn't this helo fly any faster?!

Plus, Meg hadn't been given a radiation suit. Oh, no, because Charlie had ordered her to stay with the helo, while he and Hazelton did their thing. She couldn't even stand back and watch from afar while they descended into the dangerous pit. She'd have to be satisfied with whatever intel Charlie decided to pass onto his pilot. If Charlie found Pepe, would he rescue the boy? Meg felt certain Charlie wouldn't leave a child behind. He wasn't that heartless. But what would he do with Julio if he spotted him? Would Charlie run to his aid? Would he leave him behind again or—?

No. Just no! Banishing her negative thoughts, Meg cast her gaze forward to the column of thick, oily smoke ahead of the helo. Pepe hadn't been missing that long. He'd know how to take care of himself for a day or two. He'd been forced to do that before, and Julio was too smart to be dead. If anything, Charlie had better worry about himself, not the other way around. Because Julio had been downright magnificent fighting those soldiers. He'd been fearless and brave and bigger than life. A man on a mission, intent on ending anyone stupid enough to stand in his way. And he'd saved all those poor, enslaved men, women, and children.

Her heart skipped a beat remembering. Julio had all but danced through the carnage, the fire backlit behind him, when he'd taken on Oz's remaining guards. She'd never seen such a man before. Such daring.

"You promised," she whispered to the wind. "You said if we both survived this day, you'd be in touch. Well, I survived and so did you." *I hope...*

Meg swallowed hard. She could be wrong. Pepe might have gotten into trouble, and Julio might not have survived. But her heart was too intent on hope to entertain what could very well be the truth. All she had to hold onto was what Julio had said. She clenched her knuckles to her teeth.

He will be in touch. He will!

*****

Thwack. Thwack. Thwack. Not the hefty rotor slap of a Blackhawk helo, but a helicopter nonetheless. Probably stolen or procured off the black market. Mountain guerilla warfare had certainly evolved. These guys had the means to rival any nation's civil defense.

Julio opened his bleary eyes and cocked his head at the sound of a single approaching aircraft. He'd stolen a few minutes of sleep, just enough to keep the dizziness at bay. He was weary of the world of men. It was time to go to war again, and he was sick of it.

Sure enough, a sleek black phantom appeared at the treetops. Hovering, it took position directly above the pit, sending curlicues of diesel smoke wafting away from its blades. Like smoke signals.

Julio kept his back flat against the trunk of his sturdy tree. In the shadows. Watching. Waiting. This helo might very well belong to someone from the media or possibly, a higher up in the Brazilian government. It looked that expensive. Because it was. He'd only seen a Sikorsky S-76++ once before, that

time in England when it transported one of the British
Royal Family to and from some elitist's wedding. The
thing banked at more than thirteen million dollars.
First-class all the way, its darkened windows gave
nothing away. Super light with two turboshaft engines.
Maximum payload: eight passengers. Interesting, but
not surprising. It seemed everyone wanted what Oz
had once ruled.

When its side door slid open, Julio drew the butt
stoke of his rifle under his chin and into position.
Whoever these guys were, they were not Brazilian
army. Not as swiftly as two slender men dressed in
uniforms of black, strapped in and fast-roped to a safe
ledge near the three missiles. Which put them opposite
Julio, but behind the thick curtain of black smoke.

Needing to see better, he secured his rifle into the
holster on his back and climbed down from his perch.
Greed kept no social graces. It knew no limits.
Whoever these guys were, they were definitely here for
the warheads.

Keeping out of sight, but watching the helo, he
circumnavigated the lip of the gravel pit until he was
in a better position to fire. When one of the men below
opened a panel near the tailfin of a missile, it became
obvious these guys knew precisely what they were
doing. The other did the same to the second missile.
Russians maybe? Russian mafia possibly? Julio
couldn't be sure.

One tapped his ear, obviously communicating with the helo. Lifting one arm, he offered a thumbs up. Did that mean the missiles were intact?

While the other guy performed the same examination on the third missile, Julio watched. He'd already taken a knee in the shadows and had the fuel tank of that fancy chopper in his crosshairs. One shot would bring it down. Two more would end the men in the pit below. This could be over in seconds. But he needed to be sure. The world abounded with covert agents. These two could very well be working for legitimate countries with the best intentions.

He saw it then, carefully painted and nearly invisible to the naked eye, but not to his high-powered scope. Back behind the chopper's tail number. The barest black and gray ghost of a cheery, smiling Matryoshka doll. Am evil nesting doll.

He made a quick sign of the cross. *Madre de Dios!* The Matryoshka Dolls were comprised of a group of double and triple female agents, each more devious than the next. The world had never seen women this evil or cold-blooded before. All Russian mafia in their former lives, each of these women were highly-trained killers. Each also came with layers of deceit and backstories so deep that no one knew precisely who they were or how many double, maybe triple-agents belonged to this all-female, subversive, intelligence group.

The majority of their work dealt with greed in one form or another. Whether their payment came in rubles, pounds, yen, or dollars, they weren't picky. Diamonds worked, as would the plutonium in those ICBM warheads. Bottom line, they worked for the highest bidder, which was seldom Mother Russia. Next question seemed obvious. Did they own these missiles? Had they sold them to Oz? Worse, how many more ICBMs did the Matryoshka's have, or were these their first?

Didn't matter. Julio snugged the buttstock of his rifle into his shoulder, put his eye to his scope, and zeroed in on what facial features he could make out. Yes. Definitely female. He could tell by their eyes as well as the shapes of their bodies. Their balaclavas made more specific identification impossible.

One gave a hand signal upward to the hovering Sikorsky. Within seconds, an aluminum, rectangular box was lowered. Had to be made of lead if they planned to remove the isotope.

Sure looked like it—until the box touched down and one of the Dolls jerked the lid open and pulled out a—

Dulce Madre de Dios! Automatically, Julio crossed himself with a heartfelt Father, Son, and Holy Ghost. He'd worked with enough Marine Corps Forward Air Controllers while active duty to recognize an LLDR, aka the formidable Lightweight Laser Designator Rangefinder.

The woman with the device flipped the legs of the LLDR's tripod open and leaned into the viewfinder. The Dolls weren't here to save the warheads. They were here to laser paint them before they retreated to a safe distance. Once painted, precise target information would be relayed to a strike aircraft overhead. Which had to be close enough in order to drop non-guided munitions to blow all three missiles. Problem was that a nuclear detonation this large would annihilate the nearby village where all those poor people had just gone. Pepe and his father would be evaporated. Possibly a good chunk of Minas Gerais, as well.

Julio swallowed past the hard lump lodged firmly in his throat. It no longer mattered who these assassins worked for. His mission was clear. He would not stand by and let the Matryoshkas murder the thousands of innocent people caught within these warheads' strike zone.

More focused now than ever before, he settled into the work he knew and loved best. Yes, loved. Saving innocent lives was what he'd been made for. It was time to do what he'd been created to do. Save the world.

Chapter Nineteen

"Sir, we've got company straight ahead," the Blackhawk's pilot advised Charlie Brown.

"We know who and how many?"

"Negative on the count, but Air Force reports a luxury class helo holding at our LZ. Could be sightseers. Could be media."

Charlie nodded, then clapped his pilot's shoulder. "No worries. We'll fast rope in and stay out of sight. No one will ever know we've been there. Drop us as close to the edge of the pit as you can. Then radio Dooley, tell him we may encounter enemy combatants." He waved Hazelton toward the open door. "Looks like we're going in hot. I'll touchdown first. You ready?"

"Always," she answered, her equipment loaded on her back and her hands already gloved for the drop. Charlie packed the larger equipment, as well as his usual ammo and weapons. He'd already climbed out and onto the helo's skid. But that was Charlie. Always ready to go.

Meg bit her tongue to keep from answering. Yes, she was ready, too, just wasn't the expert her Ranger friend wanted at his side. Damn this stroke for reducing her to an invisible woman and a burden.

The helo aimed toward the bluffs overlooking the São Francisco River, which would put them about two clicks from the gravel pit. Charlie and Hazelton would have to hump through the trees and brush to rendezvous with whoever had beaten them to the warheads. This could go bad in so many ways.

Meg's heart skipped a beat as the gravel pit came into view below. Sliding her hand along her waistband, Meg let the feel of cold steel hidden at her back soothe her nerves. She wasn't helpless, and she would do what was needed. Even if it meant disobeying orders. She wasn't GI anymore. Charlie needed to remember that.

The pilot broke in with, "Sir, I've got incoming communication from—"

He never finished. Like Meg would have, Charlie had already stepped off the helo's skid and was sliding down the heavy-duty rope to ground zero. Hazelton quickly followed his lead. Damn, but she'd stepped into space with the same degree of confidence as he had. Who was she, besides the UK's best nuclear engineer? Meg wanted to know Hazelton's backstory. She certainly handled herself like a Ranger.

"Damn it," the pilot cussed into his mic. "Captain Dooley will have your ass for this."

CB came back with, "No can do, Hotrod. He's too late to the party. I was already one step into thin air when you picked up his comm. Keep your ears on. Got a bad feeling about this one." Charlie was now headed due east toward the cloud of smoke with Hazelton, straight into danger.

"Christ," Hotrod muttered. "We've got company. I'm picking up chatter. There's more activity straight ahead."

"At the pit?" Meg asked.

He nodded grimly, then relayed that intel to Charlie.

"Copy that. We're almost there. Will get back to you when we engage." Typical Charlie Brown. All ego. He planned to take on whoever was out there all by himself.

In minutes, the helo was skids to the ground in a wide clearing overlooking the river gorge, its huge rotors powering down. Meg's heart had lodged high in her throat. Charlie and Hazelton were now in a race to get to the ICBMs before anyone else did. Would they get there in time? And if they did, would they survive what sounded like two enemy forces also intent on acquiring those nukes?

Her hands felt the adrenaline first. Soon, the entire left side of her body was trembling as hard as her fingers. Damn that stroke for turning her into an old woman with palsy. She moved to the chopper door, gripping the frame to keep her hands still, and peering across the clearing toward the pit. Searching for Pepe.

Praying for Julio. Charlie might even need backup support. Damned straight.

Just that fast, her trembling ceased. She'd entered that twilight zone where a trained soldier's system automatically converted to high alert and higher awareness. It was almost mystical when it happened, when she became one with the universe. Her nostrils flared to inhale every passing message written in the breeze. Every pheromone. Every wayward molecule of sweat, tobacco, cordite, or the odd alcoholic hint of some idiot's aftershave.

Her vision narrowed on the most direct route that would get her swiftly to Charlie should things go bad. Through the winding stand of trees. Around the upright columns of granite beyond those trees. Along the high ledge above the river.

Her ears tuned to far-off footfalls of boots and the steady rumbling hum of vehicles' wheels and motors. There were soldiers in the forest between her and the pit, moving stealthily over animal trails, through shrubbery and dry crackling twigs, branches. She'd have to avoid them for as long as it took to get to Charlie.

Knowing full well that Hotrod was watching, Meg drew her pistol from the back of her waistband and asked, "You got something more lethal than my Beretta on this chopper?"

"You're not going out there, ma'am," he intoned solemnly. Out of his seat now, he blocked her way forward, his muscled arms crossed over his chest in that stereotypical, *'I'm the boss,'* alpha male stance that her brothers had often tried on her. Dressed in OD fatigues that matched CB's, he did make an imposing sight hiding behind those dark glasses. But why, oh, why, did men even think intimidation would keep a smart woman in line?

Hotrod wouldn't hit her. He wasn't that big of an ass. And nine times out of ten, women were not only smarter than the tough guys bossing them around, they were better snipers and more thorough strategists. They followed through, and they got things done. At least, as much as they'd been allowed to in the all-boy black-ops clubs of military service. Were there female Navy SEALs? Maybe not yet, but that didn't mean there wouldn't be. Soon, damn it.

Now Meg was cussing like she used to in the Army. Well, so be it. This was serious shit, and she'd had enough of men thinking they knew better than she did. Sucking in a deep breath, she told Hotrod, "You are not the boss of me, and I wasn't made to keep the home fires burning, bucko. Either come with me or stay the hell out of my way. But I'm going. I've got a mission to defend."

"Bucko?" His lips pursed. It was hard to know what he was thinking behind the dark lenses of his Aviators, but he seemed to be channeling Tom Cruise. Only Hotrod was at least a foot taller than that short stack of blustering ego.

Determined to make a difference, Meg stuck the Glock back into her belt and grabbed the gear bag

Charlie had left for her off the floor. It felt heavy enough. Hurriedly, she unzipped the top and could have cried. Damn him, he'd known about her Glock. He'd packed extra mags and plenty .45 caliber ammo. Her very own sat phone. Water. First-aid kit. Protein bars. He'd thought of everything, even a clean change of underwear, a scarlet red leather thong. The dog. She could've kissed him.

The thought that she might never see him alive again, hurried her need to leave. Meg stared Mr. Top Gun down. She tried one last time. "Please get out of my way, Hotrod. I have to do this, and you know it."

"Boss is gonna be pissed."

"Only if he's still alive to get pissed."

Bowing her head, Meg closed her eyes and tuned her ears to the sounds from beyond the fading whump of the helo's rotors. Only bird calls and monkey chatter. Then—

BOOM!

Finally. Hotrod reacted like she wanted. Two compact assault rifles appeared out of nowhere. Holy shit, were those MK18s, the Navy's latest answer to close-quarter combat? Why yes, they were. She latched onto the lethal baby he'd handed her. Short commando barrel. No optics, just a smooth unblemished track that proved this weapon was meant for up-close and personal work.

She swallowed hard, not believing her good luck.

Hotrod shoved another bag into her. "Standard ammo won't work with these rifles. You'll need this."

She lifted the flap and peered inside. Sweet! Instead of a bag full of 5.56 cartridges, she was looking at boxes of ammo specifically designed for the assault rifle.

"You ready?" Hotrod asked at the door, a tactical vest dangling off his fingertips. He already wore tactical gear.

"You bet," she replied as she rested her new baby on the helo seat and shrugged into the armor-plated protective gear. Shouldering both bags, she lifted the submachine gun and nodded. "Let's roll, bucko."

Hotrod hit the ground running, but tossed over his shoulder, "Please don't call me that. One handle's enough, Patton."

That made her smile. *Patton? Me?* "Is that my handle?" she asked, already panting and sweating like a dog as she forced herself to keep up with his long-legged pace.

"You're bossy enough. Move out!"

Chapter Twenty

Julio set off another remote charge. Then another. He'd spotted the infiltrators sneaking up on the Matryoshkas, first at the lip of the gravel pit, then when a group of around twenty men headed down the trailhead leading to ground zero. Had to be one of Oz's main competitors, because there were dozens of soldiers this time, and they'd brought substantial firepower. All were dressed in the uniform of the day: camouflaged pants bloused into leather boots, matching shirts. Like the Crips and Bloods, these gangsters seemed to prefer specific colors. Oz might have liked red, but these yahoos wore gold berets accompanied by gold bandanas at their neck. Might as well have had targets painted on their foreheads. The gold made them easy to spot, easier to kill.

All were equipped with the weaponry that drug lords the world over chose, AK-47s or its equivalents. Jeeps and ATVs rumbled up to the edge of the pit, each bristling with fifty caliber machine guns, all ready for war.

Swallowing past his dry throat, Julio brought his detonator up and remotely set off the explosives fore and aft of the marching group on the trail. Men screamed. Others jumped off the trail and tumbled down the steep walls. Still others folded where they'd stood, killed by the blast.

Julio set off another charge, this one up top along the edge. He'd planned well. Three Jeeps and the truck with the AK exploded where they'd stopped. More screaming. More dead enemies.

Alert now and running for their lives, the Russian agents below were urgently signaling their helo for immediate lift-off. Which was plain not going to happen.

Julio ducked his eye back to his scope, his breathing steady and his head back in the game. Ending Oz's frenemies would have to wait. The immediate threat to Brazil—the Matryoshka Dolls—came first. In less time than it took to detonate those initial four charges, he targeted the Sikorsky's aft gas tank in his crosshairs. The two women were halfway up the rope by then, their exfil quickened by the helo's mechanical winch. Another woman in black stood at the open side door, waving them upward, waiting to haul them inside.

Normally, Julio would've felt bad neutralizing women. Not these gals. They were killers, plain and simple. Mercenaries with no conscience or heart and responsible for heinous, brutal crimes.

One shot. That was all it took to drop the big Sikorsky out of the sky. Only Julio hadn't aimed for the gas tank. Instead, he'd targeted the pilot. With a single shot through the side door and into the cockpit, he hit the back of the pilot's helmet. Julio knew he'd been successful when the person at the controls leaned forward, and the helo aimed bubble first into the flaming pit. With an enormous *OOOMPF*, the dying aircraft's rotors tilted and slashed everything in its path. Gravel, dirt, and debris. Eventually, the steady pounding impact tore the bird apart. Those deadly rotors zinged through the air like samurai swords. One final explosion blasted the helo into fragments.

By then, Julio was taking fire. It was time to move. He cast one last look at the Sikorsky to make sure he'd ended that threat. As expected, both agents were nowhere to be seen. He did catch the fireworks show when the helo impacted right where they'd been standing, though. Again there would be no bodies, and Julio was okay with that.

Moving faster now, he stepped back into his world of shadows and death. But something was terribly off. He could feel it in his gut and in the air. At the back of his neck. Like someone had him in their crosshairs. He knew damned well that more than just these opportunistic assassins were out there. If Russians had made it this far inside Brazil, any other country could be there as well. Which would spell all-out civil war if they weren't apprehended.

He heard it then. The rapid fire of a machine gun, but not coming from that armed group near the pit. *Madre de Dios, who else is here?*

Fast-tracking toward the sound, he couldn't believe his eyes. Charlie Brown. Some woman. Both dressed in some kind of space suits without helmets. Had to be nuclear hazmat suits.

Quickly, but covertly, Julio worked his way around the lip of the gravel pit. By then, he knew he was up against an organized army, and CB had walked into the middle of it. He must've thought he was outflanking the group that had headed into the pit. That was when the second contingent trapped him and his companion. When the vehicles blew, he and his companion found themselves caught in a wicked crossfire. The only thing keeping them alive was the trunk of the massive fallen tree they'd taken cover behind. Thankfully, Julio had the higher ground.

Methodically, he began a war of attrition, a war of one. History had proven many times over that well-placed snipers could change the course of battles. Firing and reloading, he worked with precision and skill, intent on turning the tide, saving CB and his lady friend. Julio picked off the men between him and CB first, then started on the group on CB's far side.

Again and again, all while taking enough flack that would worry most men, Julio worked steadfastly and surely. At last, CB was able to lift his head and safely return fire. He hadn't yet spotted Julio, but that was the way sniping was meant to be.

Those soldiers working their way around the other side of the pit were the problem. Too soon, they'd be at the site where Julio had hastily concealed his munitions dump. And he was running low. Only had a dozen mags left. He hated to blow his stockpile, but soon there'd be no choice.

Julio fingered the detonator that would end their advance. Interestingly, those men suddenly fell back, and began firing into the trees. Someone out there had a mini-gun and was laying down suppressive fire. *Gracias a Dios.* It was about time.

Whoever was coming, they were fierce and steady. Reminded Julio of a quote he'd come across on an online sniper forum he frequented: *"From a place you cannot see, comes a sound you will not hear."* He never knew who'd said it originally, but it was spot on in the dark world of covert operators. And right now, the person no one could see was gradually turning the tide. Just like Julio had done.

Someone yelled over a bullhorn then, and every last one of the opposing forces turned tail. As quickly as it had started, the shooting ceased. Julio flattened into the dirt and shrubs where he'd taken cover. He needed to stay out of sight until he knew who he was up against. Might just have been Mayor Velasquez and his people come back to save him. Julio wouldn't put anything past Susana. She knew where that stockpiled ammo was, and she'd have no problem fighting alongside men.

Like Meg...

Damn. His mind circled back to her every chance it could.

"That you, Hotrod?" Charlie yelled over the roaring inferno caused by the helo's demise below.

"You're a fuckin' genius, Gregor!" some gruff sounding male bellowed back.

"Yeah, well, it's Charlie Brown to you, asshole." Charlie stood then and dusted the seat of his pants.

So did the woman with him. He put a hand on her shoulder and bent down to look into her face. Whatever he'd asked her, she brushed it off and jerked a large bag up from the ground. Whoever she was, the woman definitely had attitude.

But who'd engaged the soldiers near the stockpile? Julio wanted to know. Stealthily, he eased onto his knees, but just as he did, a sharp stab of pain radiated up his right thigh. Damn it. He collapsed to his belly with a quiet groan. He'd been hit, and this time, he was really bleeding. He hadn't felt the round when it tagged him, only the blood leaking out of his body and soaking into his pants.

Firefights were like that. They got surreal quickly. Too quickly. Once adrenaline spiked, it created a buzz in a guy's head, a feeling of fierce masculinity, and an unreal sense of invincibility. Sensory overload was real, and it was dangerous. A warrior in the middle of making lightning-fast split decisions could only handle so much. Fog of war was real. Insignificant bruises and wounds often went unfelt and unnoticed until battles ended and brains kicked back online. That was how heroes were made and also how they died. More men and friends than Julio could count had saved their teams at the expense of themselves, all because of Mother Nature's miracle drug called adrenaline.

"You're bleeding!" a familiar voice cried out.

Meg? She was here? And holding a mini-submachine gun?

Time stopped. Julio didn't want her to see him like this, on his belly and bleeding. Too many generations of proud, Spanish-male machismo ran deep. "It's just a scratch," he told her like the idiot he was.

"It's not a scratch," she breathed, dropping to her knees at his side, her big, beautiful green eyes luminous with tears. "Oh, my God, Julio. You poor thing. You've been shot. Twice! Let me look at you."

His breath caught. She was crying—for him. No one had ever cried for him before. Not Bianca. Not his parents. Not Paloma. Her brand of sisterly love had always been competitive, push-and-shove, rough. If he'd gotten hurt or banged up back when they were little kids, she'd been more inclined to punch and tease, to tell her older brother to man up and stop whining.

But the light reflected in Meg's eyes was pure panic and fear. Pain. She was hurting for him.

Some guy in fatigues loomed larger than life behind her, a matching mini-gun in his gloved hands and a tactical headset strapped over his bare head. Military haircut. Dark as sin five o'clock shadow. Sharp black eyes. He looked like he hadn't slept in a while, either. His chin ducked into his shoulder as he cut out, "Man down," into his mic.

Had to be Charlie's wingman, Hotrod.

"Corpsmen already in transit," a voice from the *Iwo Jima* replied over the radio Velcroed to Hotrod's beefy shoulder. As they should. Hotrod was obviously another operator. He would've called for backup the instant he'd known Charlie was taking fire.

By then Meg's hands were gently mapping Julio's chest, his arm and his thigh. His face. She blinked back big shiny tears, hiding her fear, but she couldn't disguise the tender way she handled him. Or the way her face glowed with—concern. Couldn't be love. Julio was not that kind of lucky.

Groaning from the sheer pleasure of her touch, he closed his eyes and leaned his cheek into her palm, wishing he could finally rest. It'd be heaven to hold her. Kiss her. Take all night making love to her. Sleep for a week with her tucked naked in bed beside him, with him tucked inside of her. But why the hell had Charlie brought her along with him? Pushing to his side, Julio captured her roving hands before he lost his mind from the sensual pleasure of them.

"Those killers will be back," he told her as he lifted slowly to his elbows. "We need to move now."

"Not until I wrap a tourniquet around your thigh," Meg insisted as she leveled him onto his back. "I won't let you bleed to death, Julio. I've got you. You're safe with me."

He had to blink back more tears then, his lashes working overtime to stop the flow before it got away from him. He was safe? With her? If she only knew what those words did to him, she'd stop comforting him. Because Julio had never been safe, not once in his poverty-stricken life. Most certainly not once he'd joined the Navy and deployed, though, to be honest, things had settled down for him then. Until Domingo Zapata raised his ugly, tattooed head and destroyed everything.

Hotrod sent back one curt nod, his stance alert, his gaze constantly parsing the landscape for enemy combatants. "Understood, Agent Juarez, but Meg's right. You need a tourniquet now, then sickbay on that carrier. Only problem is we need to disarm the warheads before we leave. That's why Doc Hazelton's here. She's a nuclear engineer from the UK's Proliferation and Nuclear Policy Institute. She's the best there is and can do it. So lay your ass back down and let Meg do her thing."

The woman with Charlie could disarm a nuke? Good to know. "They're Russian ICBMs."

Hotrod's head bobbed. "Understood, Juarez. The United Kingdom and Washington have been tracking those warheads for months. You know how this fire started? Did an explosion create this fuckin' mess?"

"It's how I ended Orlando Zapata," Julio admitted humbly.

Meg had unbuckled his belt by then, making his body think of other, more pleasant scenarios than bleeding to death. It was hard to focus. "Oz brought the Russians and their ICBMs here," he explained. "He was entertaining them, roasting a wild pig. Celebrating and drinking. When he stepped between his fuel pumps and the barrel of my rifle—"

"You ended Zapata?" Hotrod's head canted. Skepticism colored his tone. His voice went hard, as if he thought Julio were lying.

"Julio fired the shot that ended Oz," Meg inserted with attitude, her fingers busily working Julio's belt under his thigh, then tightening it.

What he wouldn't give to close his eyes and be in bed with her.

"I was here," she continued, her voice radiating certainty. "I saw the whole thing. Charlie and I were over by the cabin when it happened. I thought Charlie had fired too soon and ruined my rocket attack, but it was Agent Juarez who'd fired. With one shot, he ended Oz and that stupid barbeque. Then, Julio fought off the soldiers Oz had hidden in the tunnel. Single-handed." She pointed to the smoking depression in the stone wall below. "There used to be two tunnels there, but I couldn't let Julio hold them off alone, so I fired another rocket and ended those suckers before they could kill him."

She was the person behind the well-placed rocket attack that had saved his life? Julio hadn't realized that until then. "You saved me," he told her sincerely.

Meg's slender fingers intertwined with his. She blinked those gorgeous green eyes down at him. "You are an idiot," she said in her tough, tender way. "Walking straight into those assholes like you did. Did you ever once think about me while you were strutting to your death? Shit, Julio. You scared the hell out of me. What else could I do but fire that rocket and save your life? You were throwing it away!"

"Why are you here?" He had to know.

Her brows furrowed and her forehead wrinkled. "To find you and Pepe. We think he ran away to find Oz and kill him."

That jumpstarted Julio's heart. Once again, he shoved up to his elbows. "Pepe is safe, Meg. I saw him. He was here. Oz had him working in the tunnel with everyone else. His name is Pepe Velasquez. His father is Rafael, the village mayor. They were both working in the same tunnel but didn't realize it until I showed."

"Really?" she nearly squealed. "You saved Pepe? And his father?"

Julio nodded, so damned proud of Meg for the way she adored every last one of her kids. "Yes. They've gone home now, but they took as much of Oz's weaponry with them as they could carry. They will be able to protect themselves now."

"Oh, good!" Meg cranked that belt extra tight, then secured the end through the buckle—just before she leaned over and her mouth melted all over Julio's.

He would've growled at the severe pain radiating up his right thigh and into his groin that extra tight tourniquet caused— if not for the honeyed-taste of her sweet tongue in his throat. If not for the way her hands clutched his head in a tender life-saving vise, her thumbs caressing his cheekbones and her tears dripping into his face. No woman had ever cried for him. Each drop felt like a blessing.

At that moment, the randy boy in his pants decided there was no pain too big that it couldn't rise to attention. Damned adrenaline turned even the most conscientious operator—and Julio prided himself on being that guy—into a mindless, horny bastard.

Hotrod clapped his hands sharply, just once, for attention. "You mean to tell me that you nailed two targets with one bloody shot, Juarez? You shot a no-kidding, once in a lifetime two-fer? No shit?"

Closing his eyes against the out-of-control need raging through his body like a wildfire, Julio shrugged like what he'd done was no big deal. "Oz had to die," he managed to say, though his voice was uncommonly deep and hoarse all of a sudden. "So did his friends. I just did my job."

Meg shook her head at him, her gaze incredibly soft. "Your job was to come back to me alive, tough guy. Did you forget?"

"No. I remember." Julio gave her that one. He had made a promise, hadn't he?

A big, wide grin cracked Hotrod's face. "Way to go, Juarez!" he declared as he leaned over and high-fived Julio. "Always heard of guys making shots like that.

Never met anyone who'd done it, though. Good on you!"

"Sir," he murmured, trying desperately to cover the bulge straining like a beast beneath his zipper with a casually placed hand. So what if it still held his rifle? There wasn't any other way he could be discreet. "I don't mean to interfere with your mission, but those soldiers will be back, and they'll bring reinforcements. You may not have enough time to diffuse the warheads before they return."

Hotrod's gaze cut to the pit below where Charlie Brown and Doctor Hazelton now had one ICBM panel open. "Got to," he growled, then leaned into his mic and asked, "Any idea how long this'll take, Jorgensen? Agent Juarez says those guys will be back, and you two are sitting pretty for an ambush."

A terse "Leave us the fuck alone!" came back loud and clear over Hotrod's earpiece.

"Then step on it. I'm just one guy up here, and no other cavalry's coming to save your ornery ass this time."

Julio exhaled a steadying breath, his nervous system fully aware of his wounds now. "I will help. I stockpiled Oz's ammo. It's nearby, and there are trees around it that'll give us the upper hand when the soldiers return. It's possible we can hold them off until those warheads are disarmed."

Meg's head bobbed. "Can you believe everything he had? It was like a Wal-Mart-sized ammo dump down there." She turned to Hotrod then. "And what's this 'just one guy' crap? Seems to me you had some help routing those creeps before. And you..." She turned on Julio. "You can't climb trees. You're injured. You need rest."

Hotrod swallowed hard, the cords in his neck tight. "Great. Three snipers against a fuckin' army. You two do know we can only fire one round at a time, don't you?" He made that sound like they were stupid. Which they probably were. Three against an army? Not smart.

"But we can delay them," Julio replied evenly. He'd been involved in enough dead-end causes in his life to know there was always the chance of something breaking loose in the middle of mayhem. No outcome was ever set in stone. Anything could happen, even in the worst of times. Which brought that foolish plan of walking into the Pacific to please his dead wife back to mind. If he'd done that, he wouldn't have met Dominic. Or Meg. Or the cocky guy with her.

Something about Hotrod irked Julio. He knew this man from somewhere else. Julio recognized him. Almost. Hotrod was one of those faces. His manner of speech, the inflection in his voice, was familiar. Julio just didn't have time to study the wheres or hows in the middle of yet another battle.

He wiped a quick hand over his brow. First, Oz. Then, those sixteen outlaws. The Dolls. Another band of guerilla fighters, all in the space of twenty-four hours. Or less. Not to mention backpacking all that weaponry out of the pit. Jesus, he was past the point of total exhaustion, moving into that brain-numbing twilight zone where he lost mental acuity and focus. Where he could get himself and everyone with him—dead.

Whatever happened next, it had to go down fast. Before he did.

Julio turned to Meg. "Thank you for caring for me, but I've been hurt worse before, and we have a job we must finish now. Let's give the doctor as much time as we can. That is why we were made. That is why we are here."

To prove he was still mobile, he climbed awkwardly to his feet without assistance. *Madre de Dios!* It hurt, but he gritted his teeth and breathed through it, blinking back the pain. Meg didn't need to see that.

Hotrod lifted his chin at Julio even as Meg leaned into his uninjured arm, voicing her unspoken solidarity with him. *Dios!* But that sweet, simple contact nearly did Julio in. She seemed to fit tucked into his side like she was. His good arm ached to curl around her shoulders, to pull her more tightly against his other side. But a display like that would send the wrong message. Meg was all woman. She'd think they stood a chance in hell of surviving, when he doubted they'd live to see another sunrise. Those soldiers would be back, and when they came, they'd bring more vehicles and more firepower. It was unfortunate she was here. Julio truly regretted that. But time was wasting.

Hotrod waved Julio forward. "Fine. Move out, then. Take us to your camp. At least we can get to higher ground before those bastards show."

Julio nodded. There was nothing else to say. Hotrod's unspoken message was quite clear.

And then, we'll die trying...

Chapter Twenty-One

Julio pulled Meg up into the highest branches with him, and into their sniper hide. Which was nice, since climbing trees was officially off her list of talents. With every step up, it took longer to balance. Several times, her left foot slipped because she couldn't tell if it was, in fact, where she meant it to be. Her leg was numb from the knee down. She'd overworked it.

But the way up was hard on Julio, too. He never complained but she could read the signs. By the time they were high enough up in the tree, he was drenched in sweat. His black shirt had to be holding in heat. He'd undone several buttons, but she wished he'd strip it off to cool himself.

Water was in short supply. Yet he'd been smart enough to accept her extra bottle when she gave it to him. If anything, she was one big fat liability, and she knew it. But she could still shoot, and she still had her weapon. Thank God, Pepe was safe. That and finding

Julio, buoyed her flagging spirits. She couldn't wait to tell Marta and Craig, the kids, Fernando and Joseph about Pepe and Julio.

Once she straddled the thick branch overlooking the gravel pit, she hurriedly opened both gear bags and spread out the remaining ammo and magazines she'd hauled up top with her, laying them out on the wide surface of the branch. She needed everything within reach for easy access.

Julio handed the half-empty bottle back.

"Keep it. I've still got some left in mine."

"Muchas gracias," he murmured.

She hated that she couldn't help him more, and that she was the reason for his depleted condition. But despite his injuries, Julio was still busy pulling the heavier crates of launchers and rockets up into the tree. Firing a couple rockets in the right direction could end this war before it started. That'd be nice.

But it could also get Meg and her buddies killed. Once a rocket launched, it waved the same red flag as a bullet when fired. Both led straight back to the point of origination, and the person who'd fired them instantly became a target. These trees weren't made of stone, and this was no castle. There was no moat full of alligators to keep bad guys away. It would only take one shot to give their location away and hellfire would rain down on them.

But this foolhardy plan was never about living forever, only about buying time so Charlie and Hazelton could safely disarm those nukes. Charlie always bragged he was living on borrowed time. He had to know fireworks were about to go off over his head, maybe through it. That was the luck of a covert operator.

Her gaze automatically zeroed on Julio. She'd wrapped his injured thigh and bicep as much as she could, given their dire, less-than-sanitary circumstance. Both still needed a thorough cleansing, stitches for sure. Yet he acted like he felt no pain. As if he were numb. Maybe he was.

It amazed her to know that he lived with this level of stress in his job. Like a man with a death wish, he'd intentionally put himself in harm's way. She'd seen him do it. He'd walked straight into that confrontation with Oz's soldiers, didn't even hesitate. Not once. He'd spat in Death's red-as-sin, bloodshot eye, and he did stuff like this for his country and humanity. For her and her kids. For people he didn't even know. But why?

What made men like him who they were? For that matter, how had he become a man of honor, valiant and self-sacrificing, in this infatuated, entitled, bombastic, selfie-world where others whined that their cushy life in Mommy's basement wasn't fair? That someone else should pay the college debt they'd signed up for. That hospitals and colleges, healthcare and education, should be free, free, free for everyone. That working for a living and making something of yourself was soooooo hard.

Well, duh. Big babies.

She'd worked with men like Julio all of her career, and they never ceased to amaze her. There were still patriots and heroes in the world. One only had to stand up, grow a pair, and be counted with them.

At last, he balanced the crates he'd just pulled up, between two broad, sturdy branches at his left. Deftly, he reached into one crate and withdrew six launchers. Six warheads came next.

"These are for you," he said, quietly handing them over. "Load the launchers now. You won't have time to reload after you fire your first shot. Make every strike count. Discard the expended launchers quickly. Don't fall out of the tree."

"Got it," she assured him.

Hotrod had set up his sniper hide in the neighboring tree. Despite the heavy growth of large, leathery leaves, Meg had only to look to her right to see that he'd also spread an extensive arsenal on the broad branch he straddled. Another crate of launchers and one of warheads rested at his back.

It was nearly time to strike. Hotrod had just touched base with Charlie. Hazelton had deactivated one of the missiles. Two to go. Meg hoped for a miracle.

The plan was simple: surprise whichever dirtbag showed first. Fire three rockets at the same time into the advancing soldiers. Create chaos. Aim to kill. Destroy all armored vehicles. End enough enemy combatants to slow the flow. Give Hazelton as much time as possible to disarm the ICBMs. Then drop to the ground and run like hell to the stand of trees nearer the trail that led into the pit. While Charlie and Hazelton had been working steadfastly below, Julio and Hotrod had stored more LAWs, weapons, and ammo in those trees. That was where they'd make their last stand.

Meg had no illusions. Men would die here today. Maybe women, too. This was their Alamo, their last stand. If they did nothing more than save the United States from an unprovoked nuclear attack, so be it. At least her kids were safe. Hopefully, American kids would be just as safe by the time this was over.

She shook her head, fighting off the dread that scuttled up her spine like a swarm of spiders every time she let herself think too long or too hard. She was a liability. Her fingers felt stiff as she fastened the strap that held her to the tree, then loaded the launchers into the bag at her feet where she could easily reach it. She had no business thinking she was Wonder Woman.

"Anything can happen," Julio murmured, his forehead glistening with sweat, his dark eyes bright and wise.

She nodded, but she also knew statistics. The odds of them surviving this confrontation were damned near nil. Whoever this usurper of Oz's mighty kingdom was, he had a large army and a lot of nerve. Plus, he now had something to fight for. Acquiring those ICBMs was enough reason to start a war. If he returned with tanks and cannons, they were done for.

Three against an army of hundreds was, at best, a foolish plan to even pray for. Make that, two men and half a woman. Yet there they were, Julio, her, and Hotrod, prepared to do the impossible. Meg prayed with every breath she had for strength to endure, to not fall out of this tree. That her aim would be true. That the tingling sensation in her fingertips would go away.

Uncapping her bottle of water, she took a quick sip, then tucked it back into her empty bag. Despite the oppressive humidity caught between these closely intertwined branches and the tree's thick leaves, her mouth was bone dry.

She licked her lips. "I know, Julio, but just in case something hap—"

His index finger came up to his lips and his head canted, demanding silence. "Don't jinx us before we start. I've been in worse situations. Trust me, Meg, and have faith in yourself."

Yeah, that. Easier said than done. He wasn't the weak link here. "I had a stroke, remember? I'm not—"

That waggling finger cut her short again. "Believe," he told her sternly. "Believe what you are doing is right and good. Believe you are strong and just. That you are the right hand of God. That he will always send His archangels in your time of greatest need. Then, you will prevail."

"Is that what you do? You pray for... angels?" She never would've guessed a hard warrior like him believed in such things.

"Always. He knows where I am, and what I'm doing, even now. I may not be His perfect Son, but he is still my perfect Father."

Whoa. A shiver raced through Meg's entire body at the ease with which Julio had just declared his astoundingly Christian beliefs. She should've known. He'd uttered *'Madre Dios'* often enough. "So you think you're what? A crusader? A white knight? An apostle?"

Julio shook his head even as he looped another loaded holster to the broken branch at his side. Man, these trees were alive with weaponry. "I'm just a messenger," he replied, his voice as emotionless as ever.

She had to ask. "What happened to you to make you so—"

"Cold?"

"No. Not cold." The last thing this man could ever be was cold. "Remote. You look at me with fire in your sexy brown eyes, but then you shut it down, and all you offer me is—"

"Shhhhh. They're back."

Oh, damn. Meg swallowed hard. Julio was right. Armed, dangerous men dressed in cammies were filtering through the trees as silent as vipers near the trailhead. The majority of them appeared to be waiting on the chubby guy wearing an olive-green beret and sitting in a Jeep in the deep shadows.

"Who's the guy in that Jeep?" Meg whispered as she stood, anchored herself into her harness, and shouldered her first launcher. After strapping the other end of her harness onto an overhead branch, she'd lined the bags of weaponry at her feet. She was as ready as she could ever be.

"Not sure," Julio replied just as quietly. He was on his feet and his LAW was ready to fire as well. "Hotrod?"

"Never seen him before," Hotrod muttered. "Asshat's packing two Desert Eagle 50s, though."

That he was. The Israel Military Industries' Desert Eagle 50, known for its gas-operated reload mechanism, weighed in at a solid four and a half pounds *without ammo*. Which made it one of the heaviest handguns on the market. Load that baby up with fifty caliber ammunition, and you'd better have a pair of big, strong hands and a bigger set of balls if you intended to use it.

The kinetic energy in its recoil alone was like taking a full-on body slam from the rear hooves of a pissed-off mule. A guy could literally knock himself out if he didn't handle this monstrous handgun with extreme care. Meg knew a couple operators who packed one, mostly for the shock and awe effect the handgun created in military circles. It definitely had a cult following.

"I'll take Asshat," Hotrod said. "You guys handle both flanks. Ready?"

"Yes, sir. I'll take right," Meg replied evenly. "My right, not Asshat's right."

"Understood," Julio muttered, the LAW already balanced on his shoulder, his eye to the reticule. "I'll take Asshat's right, my left."

With that perfectly clear, Meg took careful aim at the group of soldiers holding at Asshat's left, waiting on Hotrod's command. The moment he said, "Go," she pressed her launcher's trigger bar and sent a rocket straight into the army at Asshat's left.

Like hers, Julio's and Hotrod's rockets were both direct hits. Hotrod's blew Asshat and his ride away in a fireball that belched out sideways and engulfed the men standing closest to him. Julio's rocket did its fair share of damage, as did Meg's. Those three initial shots had pretty much decimated the core of Asshat's ranks.

Discarding the spent launcher as quickly as she could, Meg followed the first rocket with another. Then another. Furiously, she reloaded and fired until the rim above the trail was nothing but a smoking field of ash, twisted carnage, and burning debris.

Shaking like a leaf, she reached for another rocket, only to realize she'd used all six. She blinked at Julio. "You got any rockets left? I'm out."

He shook his head. "We've used all we had. Breathe, Meg. You did good, but if you don't breathe, you're going to faint and fall out of the tree."

"I am not," she argued, but yeah. Wow. Holy shit. H-h-hot damn. The adrenaline spike surging through her compromised system was worse than any she'd experienced before, maybe because of her stroke. She was dizzy, but she'd never admit it. Not until she had to.

Oh, damn. Maybe she had to. Dizzying exhaustion had crept up on her, dropping her chin to her chest, making it harder to catch her breath. A wave of tiny black dots swarmed her peripheral vision, and... Shit. She was going to faint. In front of Julio and Hotrod. Not good, not good, not good. Not now, damn it!

Sucking in quick, hard breaths and fighting to stay upright, she dropped her backside to the branch and straddled it like a horse, wishing it had a long mane to tangle her between her quivering thighs. A rope would work. Julio's callused hands. An—y—thing.

Fighting a rolling wave of nausea that came out of nowhere, she swallowed hard and focused on the rough, rugged texture of the branch to keep from losing her cookies. Stinging sweat trickled over her brows and filtered into her eyes. In less than seconds, she'd morphed from Wonder Woman with an attitude into timid shaking-in-her boots Chicken Little, afraid the sky was falling. It didn't get any more embarrassing than this.

Because she didn't dare take her eyes off the tree trunk for fear she'd pass out, she didn't see Julio move in behind her until he'd reached one arm around her and pressed her back firmly to his front.

"D-don't touch me," she murmured, bile creeping up her throat at the unexpected shift in perspective. Man, she'd never seen trees dance like the forest was now. Bobbing. Back and forth. Up close, then weaving forward and—

It had to stop. Shivering, she sucked in a shallow breath and closed her eyes.

"I've got you," Julio said simply. His thighs clamped around her ass, his arms two iron shackles around her arms and torso. "Relax, Meg. You're hyperventilating. Slow and easy wins the race."

Her entire body was a quivering mass of jelly by then. No pectin. All juice. There was no way he could hold onto her much longer. Her spine had gone weak and untrustworthy. Her limbs weren't rubber, more like limp spaghetti noodles. Her mind was all over the place. Sludge. The last forty-eight hours had finally caught up with her. Meg was afraid, very soon, she would ruin everything by proving, without a doubt, that she—the only woman in this tree—was the weakest link.

Hotrod's voice came quietly from his tree. "You see anyone moving over there?"

"Too much smoke," Julio answered. "Do you see any life across from us, Meg?"

She had to open her eyes and lift her chin then. A wave of dizziness hit. There was nothing beyond the blurry leaves of their tree. Even they had suddenly turned from vivid green to oily gray. "N-n-no. Did we get them all?" *Please, say yes, so I can close my eyes again.*

"We did," Julio murmured in her ear, his breath warm and low. His body solid and hard and... Any other time, she would have used that male weakness of his to her advantage. But she'd just had one very long day, and the adrenaline still coursing through her system had taken its toll.

The steady warmth coming off Julio was Meg's undoing. His sweat commingled with hers, and his strong warm breaths with her short panting bursts. One second, she was determined to shove off, scramble back onto her feet, laugh at her moment of weakness, and dive right back into action.

But the next? Those pesky black dots invaded every last space between those ugly gray leaves. Like the worst kind of black magic, the leaves pixilated into mist. She couldn't breathe.

Trusting Julio's hold with her last conscious breath, Meg lost the war. She had no choice. She let go.

Chapter Twenty-Two

Finally, Julio had the woman he cared for, limp, but back in his arms where he wanted her. He was sure Meg had merely fainted from the heat and lack of sleep. She hadn't been hit because they hadn't been shot at. And she wasn't bleeding. Only sweating. Like him, she'd been on the run for too many hours. They needed more than a few stolen moments of downtime to recuperate. But more than sleep, Julio desperately needed what he held now. The slight, warm weight of her body against his chest. The scent of her skin in his nose. Her trusting him enough to have passed out.

Like a greedy child at Christmas, he lifted her up from where she'd straddled the branch, and settled her crossways, her legs together, her rump on his thighs. With just that simple protective act of caring for his woman again, his lonely heart took wing. Memories of having once been a faithful, loving husband rolled over him. His eyes blurred with the sudden tenderness leaking out of his soul.

He'd thought he'd found true love before with Bianca. Now he questioned everything about their whirlwind marriage, their short engagement, but mostly, her faithlessness when he'd deployed. Her insistence they have a baby right away, even with their lousy debt ratio.

Everything back then had happened so fast. Too fast. He'd been charmed by the blonde beauty who'd fallen for him. Him, the humble son of Mexican jewelry thieves. He hadn't told her about his parents, though. That was his first sin. He should've been honest. He should've made certain Bianca knew exactly what she was getting into before they'd eloped and tied the knot. But he'd been a naïve younger man back then. A fool. He'd truly believed love would conquer all. Turned out, love held no such magic.

She discovered that lie herself when she'd Googled him and found headlines and mugshots instead of headshots on social networks. But hindsight only provided clarity, not forgiveness. No. He could see now that the diamonds she'd loved and the few plastic surgeries she'd convinced him she needed, were his penance for that starry-eyed error.

But Meg was everything Bianca was not. Tough. Sweet. A fighter and lover rolled into one. It'd been so long since he'd held an honest woman, much less one so fierce and sweet. With Meg safely ensconced in the crook of his injured arm, he ran his free hand over her head and righted her bandana, keeping her head covered. She'd been shy about her shorn hair. He wouldn't betray her now.

"Damn, she's a pistol. She finally pass out?" Hotrod asked quietly.

"Yes," Julio answered, glancing over his shoulder at his *compadre*. "Are you sure we ended the attack? So soon? I thought it'd take longer."

Hotrod held a sturdy pair of binocs to his eyes, gazing across the pit. "I'm as surprised as you. Thought Asshat would've brought a bigger army with him. Guess not. Either he was an idiot or we're just that good."

But being *just that good* wasn't good enough for Julio. They needed boots on the ground, someone to walk over there and visually confirm their suspicions. Julio just didn't want to let Meg go. She'd gone still and silent. Without that bulky sarape, he could see her chest barely lift with every breath. He wanted to hold her until she woke, then taste her lips again. Her neck. Her breasts. And straddling this wide-as-a-horse tree branch with a hard-on was—hard.

The slightest buzz vibrated from Hotrod's tree, then "Thank fuck!" he exclaimed into his sat phone. "Good to hear your shitty voice, CB. Yeah. Can do. You bet. Give me five. Look to the south. We'll be there." Then to Julio he asked, "Wake her up. We're moving."

Julio shook his head. "She's not going anywhere. I'll stay here until she comes to."

"Yeah, okay. See if you can get her to drink something once she snaps out of it. I'll hook up with our mighty leader. Be ready to travel when I get back. Here. Catch." He tossed his binocs across the distance between the trees. "Keep frosty, Juarez. You see anyone on my six, you end him, hear?"

Julio caught the binocs one-handed. "Copy that. Don't die," he said, like he needed another pair of binocs or to be told to keep his head on a swivel.

"Don't plan to," Hotrod replied, as, with a growly, "Hmmpf," he slid off the branch and stuck a three-point landing below. From the ground, he looked up at Julio, offered a quick two-fingered salute, then fast-tracked into the forest.

Meg whimpered, bringing Julio's attention back around. What a breathtaking sight. Lush lashes curled at the tops of her pale cheeks, fluttering like butterfly wings as she awoke. Her green eyes widened when she realized where she was and who had hold of her. Both her hands went instantly to her head, her lips pinched with regret while she searched for her bandana.

"Your cover is secure, Corporal Duncan," he told her quickly.

She blinked up at him. Her fingertips fluttered over her bandana as her cheeks flushed pink. "I... I... Thank you. I passed out?"

He'd missed his chance to kiss her. "We are both very tired. A body can only go so long without rest before it shuts down."

"But you weren't the one who fainted, were you? No, it had to be me." Exasperation edged her tone, but she made no effort to move. "We didn't lose because of me, did we?"

He wanted to smile. "No, ma'am."

"Oh, good. Did we win? We must have. I don't hear gunshots."

"Yes, we won. We did what we set out to do. We gave Doctor Hazelton time to do her job, and we couldn't have done it without you. Every rocket you fired was a direct hit. Charlie and Doctor Hazelton already have the radioactive isotopes safely stored. They're climbing out of the pit right now. Hotrod just left to join them. Once we get back to the Blackhawk, we'll be home free."

A contented breath sighed out of her. *"Dulce Madre de Dios!"*

For the first time in what felt like forever, Julio felt a genuine smile pinching his cheeks. His stiff lips nearly curved. "Are you mocking me, Senorita?"

She grinned up at him, her eyes bright, full of mischief, life, and sass again. "I never mock, Special Agent Juarez. I incorporate. If I like what I hear, I adopt and adapt. I make what I like mine. Sayings and prayers. Curse words, too. So watch out."

Mine. Out of everything she'd said, that one word stood out like a shining star. A tiny burst of hope bubbled up inside Julio's chest. What would it be like to belong to Meg? To be hers? Only hers. To come home to her smiling face at night. To finally rest in her arms at the end of secret, deadly missions.

Like an idiot, his mouth asked, "Does that include people?"

Her tongue made a quick pass over her bottom lip, and for the first time in his successful, covert career, Julio faltered. He couldn't stop himself. His strong sense of duty took a backseat to the desire her wet lips had just created. One more kiss. That was all he wanted. What harm could a single, stolen kiss do?

He caught himself before that desire took hold and ruled him. This wasn't the right time to become intimately acquainted. Definitely not the right place. Team members were still in danger, and duty always came first.

Not waiting for her answer to his leading question, Julio broke the tender connection before he made a bigger fool of himself. Lifting the binocs to his eyes, he tracked Hotrod's steady progress to the edge of the gravel pit. Still a burning conflagration, Julio couldn't see Charlie or Doctor Hazelton through the smoke until they were nearly at the top.

Once there, Charlie said something to Hazelton. She nodded, and they removed their headcovers. He set the large metal case he'd carried on the ground at her feet, then he and Hotrod took a side trip into the trees, through the wreckage of the usurper's army.

The stink of the battleground carried across the pit to Julio. Burning diesel. Melted human flesh. Other unpleasant smells. Two shots rang out, then two more.

Julio recognized them for what they were. Double-taps. Charlie and Hotrod were finishing the job, ending surviving belligerents before they ended them or called reinforcements.

Julio lowered the binocs and rolled his shoulder, more to ease the tension radiating up his back than because of his wounds. They needed to be tended to soon, but for now, he was mobile and he had Meg. Everything else could wait.

"What are you doing?" Meg asked. Still cradled in that same arm, she looked up at him with so much trust.

It was hard to answer. "Making sure Charlie and Hotrod are safe," he said, his voice hoarse.

"You're always doing that, aren't you? Always watching over people. Protecting others."

He exhaled through his nostrils and swallowed hard, fighting his body's response to her nearness. "It's what I do."

"You have a gift, Julio," she corrected softly. "You care about everyone. Even little kids."

Well, yeah. Especially little kids. Old people. Sick people. Dogs. Cats. *Madre de Dios*. Even that red bird with a broken wing he'd found one wintry day when he'd been back East. He'd nursed that little guy for weeks until it grew strong enough. Then, one warm spring morning, he'd set it free. The delicate splash of color flew away without a single chirp of thanks. And that was okay. The joy was in knowing that scarlet creature had lived despite his fumbling fat fingers. The cardinal was still warbling its life away out there in the wild. It might be just another bird to most people, but to him it had been a miracle.

Now wanting to encourage this intimate conversation, Julio went back to the binocs, watching Charlie, Hotrod, and Hazelton. His rifle sat loose and ready in the crook of the tree, in case his friends needed an assist.

The men were out of the trees and talking with Hazelton now. Leaning over, Charlie lifted the metal case and handed it to Hotrod. Must be the isotopes. Without a headset or commlink, Julio had no way to know for certain what it was or what was being said.

The meeting looked amicable enough. Hotrod nodded his chin toward the tree where Julio still held Meg. Charlie's shoulders turned until he faced them. The big guy waved, then cupped both hands to his mouth and yelled, but he was too far away. Julio couldn't understand what he'd said. He was too focused on the feminine weight relaxed against him. His time was running out. It was now or never.

He set the binocs on Meg's lap. "Meg, I—"

As usual, she was one step ahead of him. The second he gazed down and into her eyes, she cupped his grimy chin in both hands and ordered, "Kiss me, Julio. Before they get back. Just do it, damn it."

Another smile almost curled his lips. They seemed to be doing that more and more. With her permission, he tipped forward and took her mouth in what started gently, but ended in fiery, pulsing need. Her lips were so soft and delectably smooth and silky. Like cream. He couldn't help himself. He'd been hungry so long.

This woman was a different sort of female than the one he'd married. Strong and sure of herself, Meg took control of the kiss instead of lying limp in his arms. Twisting her body until they were chest to chest, she wrapped her fingers around his skull and pulled him deeper into her warm, wet mouth.

At the seductive slide and taste of her tongue, out of control passion spiked. A raging firestorm lit up his veins. Julio's spine stiffened, and suddenly, there wasn't enough oxygen in the world. What he needed to live and to be a complete man again was right here, lying in his arms. Meg was his next breath. The rest of his life. Maybe even all of his heart. He couldn't lose her, not this time. He needed this woman, in his future and in his bed.

Julio knew it then. He was not the man he'd been before. The shadows were no longer good enough. The curse of the long dark night he'd been trapped in had been broken, and Meg was the one who'd lifted that evil spell. He'd been a fool to walk into the Pacific.

Drawing in a belly full of air, Julio wanted more out of whatever time on earth he had left. He wanted that intangible *more* with Meg. Now, damn it.

Her mouth was so willing, her lips beyond sweet and intrinsically satisfying. When she moaned into his mouth, he angled his injured arm beneath her neck, lifting her against him. Breathing her in. Holding her closer. Molding her warm, willing body to his. What he wanted was close, intimate, sweaty contact. He craved it like a man lost in the desert craved water. Had to have it.

But for now... The torn flesh and muscle in his bicep reminded him he'd better not expect too much, too soon. But she'd acquiesced so willingly, arching into him and moaning into his mouth. Against his tongue. How could he resist?

Julio was lost in a firestorm of sensual sensation, each whimper and moan more tantalizing than the last. It was enough to distract the strongest man. But old habits died hard, and he refused to relinquish all control. As difficult as it was, he owed Charlie Brown, Doctor Hazelton, and Hotrod due diligence. He was their eyes in the sky. He had their six. He couldn't fail them any more than he could fail Meg.

Tearing his mouth away from the lovely temptation in his arms, he breathed heavily into Meg's face. "Please understand. I can't do this. It's not right. I must finish my job."

"I know, I know," she murmured sweetly, the green stars in her eyes bright and warm. Willing. "We both have jobs to do, but the first chance I get..." Lifting up, she melted her mouth to his, and Julio was lost once more. He couldn't stop kissing this woman. She was oxygen. His breath. His life.

Abruptly, she tore herself away, gasped, then growled a breathy, "We have got to quit this. Now. Before Charlie and Hotrod show up. Do you have any idea what they'll say if they see us kissing?"

Julio cupped her jaw and bumped his forehead to hers. He most certainly knew how men talked. "They'll say I'm a very lucky man. But the first chance you get—"

"I'm going to mug the hell out of you, Juarez. Count on it." She grinned, the sparkle in her eyes so full of wonder and real, no-kidding zest for life.

His facial muscles did that painfully, pleasant thing again. He could feel it. On his lips and cheeks. Even at the corners of his eyes. Inside his eyes. It came like a soft wave from deep inside his heart. He couldn't remember the last time he'd done this, but he was actually smiling. All because Meg had made everything wrong in his life, right again. Just seeing her made life worth living. Despite her handicap, genuine hope sparkled in her smile. It was in her eyes, too, themselves the color of life and living and, damn it. He was still here, wasn't he? He was alive. Yes, he'd lost the people he'd loved most, but his heart still pounded, his blood still heated, and his lungs still worked. He could breathe!

The time of grieving *had* to end, because—if it didn't—if he never let the sorrows of his past go—they would kill him. He had to relinquish the pain of losing Tomas and his anger at Bianca's selfishness. He had to, or those negative emotions would destroy him.

Oddly, he suspected that his walking into the Pacific to kill himself might have pleased Bianca. She would've wanted something dramatic like that. She would've relished the attention of being a sailor's widow. She'd always expected much from others but offered little in return. He had no doubt that his total sacrifice would've pleased her.

But Tomas? Julio knew in his heart that his son had truly and purely adored his father. That as tiny as he'd been when he'd passed, Tomas was in a better place now. Bianca had never been really happy anywhere. No doubt she was still as miserable as ever.

A bird on some nearby branch chose that precise moment to sing its warbling song. The brightest, clearest novena that Julio had ever heard burst out of the unseen bird's throat. It was nothing less than an innocent, ordinary creature's magnificent glory to God in the highest. A trumpet could not have formed more perfect, clarion notes. The music rang sweet and pure, straight up into the heavens. It touched his heart.

And Julio knew. Wherever heaven was, Tomas was there, and he was running with other children, squealing and dancing and playing and singing and... *Dios!* Tears Julio had never let fall, welled in his eyes now. Only these tears didn't blind him. Instead, they let him see.

Quietly, he choked back the pain of losing his child again. His baby! His son! Yet as he choked, the pure love of Tomas echoed through that little bird's song— straight to him.

Yes. Glory to God in the highest for giving that perfect child to me. Sucking in a cleansing breathe, Julio let his past go. His chest and belly expanded with the hope of a brand-new day. Because God had sent an angel to Julio, and that angel was Tomas. He wouldn't want his father to waste away in sorrow. From the day he'd been born, Tomas had loved Julio as only a child could—with all his little boy heart. He'd been the single bright light in a life Julio now realized had been bleak and unforgiving. Tomas would want his father to be just as happy as he was now.

Meg's sweet palm was at Julio's jaw again, cupping him as he wept. He was making a fool of himself, yet Julio couldn't stop. The floodgates had opened. With every tear that fell, a piece of heartache washed away. Meg was the answer he'd needed all along. She'd helped him remember, and she'd showed him what he'd professed he'd known all along. But hadn't truly understood. Life, no matter how hard or difficult, was still worth living.

Blinking hard, he bowed his chin to his chest. There Meg lay, like a queen in his arms, her soft emerald eyes glowing with emotion. He saw sadness there, but he also saw compassion and trust, discipline and honor. He saw a warrior who had just fought at his side, one who'd given all she had to give. One who would've fallen to her death, tumbling out of this tree, rather than let him, Hotrod, or Charlie down.

Pursing his lips, Julio blew the regret he'd carried in his heart for too damned long, away. He let it go. All of it. The grief. The guilt. The agony. At long last, he just breathed. It was time. Tomas would want his father to do that. Julio did, too. Because Julio finally understood.

Life was a gift.

Chapter Twenty-Three

"Hey. You're actually smiling," Meg crooned, her fingers still on Julio's strong chin and her eyes as blurry as his. Something monumental had just taken place. She could feel it; she just didn't understand precisely what it was. But this stoic man was smiling and crying at the same time. Not blubbering, but those were definitely tears caught like tiny diamonds in his thick, black lashes. Better yet, he wasn't doing anything to hold them back. It looked like some dam inside of him had finally broken, and he was letting go.

But then Charlie spoiled it. "Hello up there! You-hoo! Lovebirds!" he bellowed up at them from below. "You gonna build a nest and lay eggs, or you ready to get the hell out of here?"

Julio dashed a quick, rough hand over his face, took in a great big breath that made his belly expand, and replied loudly, "On our way, sir."

Meg, on the other hand, couldn't help herself. "Don't call him sir, Julio. It'll go straight to his big, fat head." Then she twisted around and yelled, "Very funny, CB. Give it a rest. I need a minute. I passed out, or didn't Hotrod tell you?"

"Course, I know you fainted, you big wuss. But we need to keep moving. Can't keep Captain waiting!"

"Dooley's not going anywhere, not without that plutonium!"

To heck with him and his high-tech aircraft carrier. Whatever was happening with Julio was just as important. Maybe more so. Meg didn't want to move, or she'd lose this once-in-a-lifetime connection with him. The big tough guy was actually grinning at her through his teary, red eyes. Darned if those smiling lips hadn't turned him into the handsomest man she'd ever seen. For the first time since she'd met Julio, she noticed his lashes. Sinfully thick with tiny, silver teardrops matted to them, they drew her into his dark chocolate eyes, like a helpless moth to a flame.

She ached to comfort this particular warrior in all the ways a woman could. He'd seemed so lonely and sad. Until now.

"He's right. We should hurry," Julio agreed, his voice hoarse, though he had yet to take his hands off Meg.

She nodded, her gaze caught in his stare. With effort, she forced herself to take in the rest of his masculine face. The angular jaw. The regal arc of his dark brown brows and the double crease between them. Tanned and nearly bronze, he had the look and physique of a noble conquistador. His Spanish lineage added elegance to his stocky, muscular frame. His nose was straight as a knife blade. Sporting a rugged scuff now, his top lip was thin, accented with a perfect Cupid's bow. But that bottom lip... Lickable. The urge to suck those lips, maybe bite them, took her mind back to their first kiss.

"He, umm..." she murmured breathlessly. "Charlie, umm... he already has the isotopes, right?"

Julio pulled her upper torso closer, his large palm like a dinner plate between her shoulder blades. "He does. Just like I have you."

Oh, those lucky isotopes.

This man had it all. Body. Muscles. Brains. The alpha predator cunning that made him lethal to breathy women who fainted like damsels in distress. Something crackled between them. Lust. Heat. Need thickened the already humid air around them. Between them. Something magical was happening.

"Y-y-you do?" she stuttered, afraid to breathe.

"Yes. I do," he replied without a trace of doubt.

That did it. Something in his tone tossed a can full of gasoline over the roaring fire in her gut. Her breasts grew heavy and she was pretty sure the tips of her nipples had just turned to rock. He sounded so certain, as if there were no doubt who was the dominant variable in this equation. He considered her his. She could tell. But Meg was no pushover. Until her crazy heart seemed to have a mind of its own, the way it hopped, skipped, and triple-somersaulted inside her chest and—oh, what the hell? She threw caution to the wind and crashed her mouth into his, kissing the holy bejesus out of him. So much for him being dominant. He should've grabbed the chance before she had.

"For God's sake, what's keeping you, Juarez?" Charlie shrieked, effectively ruining the sensual moment.

Julio didn't seem to hear him. His fingers smoothed up the back of Meg's neck, heading toward her skull. Cradling her head. Just as she lifted a hand to anchor her bandana, his hand lifted, then settled over that annoying scrap of cloth she desperately needed, anchoring it for her. *Awww.* Her heart melted at his thoughtful gesture. Somehow, he knew what that bandana meant to her.

She'd tossed it away that one time, only to succumb to all the wondering glances of ensigns, petty officers, and LTs onboard the carrier. Like a proud, silly duck, she'd scrounged up another bandana. But Julio honestly cared what was important for her. And somehow, knowing that, turned the bandana into—nothing. It wasn't important. Not really. Anyone with a brain could see she had no hair.

Breathing hard now, Meg gave into his mouth and tongue. The forest, even the tree they were sitting in, faded away. In all the whole wide world, there was only Julio Juarez and her.

She slanted her head, granting him more access to her mouth. Their tongues made love and he reached under her shirt, cupping her breast, flicking a fingertip through her very practical bra and making her nipple stand up. Meg moaned, wishing they were anywhere but in a tree with Charlie Brown standing under it!

There was so much to love about this man. The feel of his warm, smooth skin under her palms. The sculptured curves and muscular ridges of his back. The tenderness with which he returned her passion. His wet kisses. Arching forward, she filled his palm with more of her generous breast, needing his mouth on that diamond hard tip. If only he could. Would!

Breathing hard, he groaned.

That all-male sound was very nearly Meg's undoing.

Until Charlie bellowed, "Jesus Fuckin' Christ! Do I have to come up there? Is she that weak she can't get her fat ass out of that tree, Juarez?"

Julio broke the kiss then, but he was still so close that Meg went cross-eyed. His smile was back. "Charlie's a moron," he whispered. "You don't have a fat ass. It's perfect."

He squeezed her breast, lighting the invisible length of det cord between her pesky nipple and her core, like that sensation stalled her need to devour him on the spot? Meg stifled even as her most feminine muscles clenched at his touch. She was as substantial as melted butter in his hands.

He winked, then said, "Soon, Meg Duncan. We will be together soon."

She could only nod and mumble, "Ah huh."

He turned back into an efficient operator then, swiftly lifting her into a sitting position as he gathered their gear. Meg found herself once more cocooned between his thighs, her back to his very rigid front. This man wanted her and she wanted him. She would've helped pack what was left of the ammo and weaponry if his cock hadn't pressed hard and temptingly lethal against the extreme small of her back. The way his body moved confidently around hers was a heady thrill. She wanted to lean back into him, just absorb him into her soul. Never let him out of her sight.

But Julio was a man of his word. He finished packing before she came to her senses. "I can carry you," he said when she hadn't made a move.

That snapped her out of her daydream. "Umm, no. I'm a little slow, but I'm, umm capable. Let's not keep our fearless leader waiting."

It took her a minute to get in the best position to climb down. Julio held onto her elbow until she'd backed off the branch and caught her footing on the next branch down. By then, he'd shouldered all the gear, but for once, Meg didn't protest. She couldn't deny that her left side had grown weaker during this marathon day. The last thing she needed was to pass out again and have to be carried fireman style across any of these guys' shoulders. Charlie'd love that.

Hell, no.

When she was close enough to ground level, she jumped the rest of the way and stuck a three-point landing just to prove her point. Okay, so she wobbled a titch on impact, and that three-point turned into four. But she'd done it, by hell, and she'd done it on her own.

Lifting to her feet, she shot Charlie her best evil-eye. The gloves came off. "You're an ass. So what if I passed out? I've been on my feet for—" She honestly couldn't remember how many days she'd gone without sleep. "A long damned time! And my ass is not big."

"Figures you'd argue about the size of your butt instead of what's most important," he shot back at her, grinning like a jerk. There was a definite twinkle in his eye when Julio landed behind her. Charlie gave Julio an appraising once over. "You coming with us, Juarez, or do you still have *work* to finish here?" Innuendo laced his question.

Meg turned on Julio then. In the frenetic pace of getting here in time to save his life, then fighting those bad guys who wanted the ICBMs, she'd lost track of precisely who he worked for and why he'd come to Brazil. Like Charlie had said, it surely wasn't for her. Julio belonged to a United States Senator. He was Sullivan's man. Not hers. Of course, he was leaving. Oz was dead. The warheads were safe. Why would Julio hang around?

Without breaking eye contact with her, he took a deep breath and told Charlie, "One job ends, another begins. When will you make land?"

"The carrier? Not for another month or two. Captain's on maneuvers now that Venezuela's falling apart. But Hotrod can fly anywhere you need to go. Just say the word," he jerked his thumb over his shoulder like a hitchhiker, "and you're outta here."

Dazed, Meg took a step toward Julio even as her heart sank. Oh, crap. He needed to report to his boss. He might even have to do that in person. He was leaving. Of course. He had to. It took all her willpower not to run into his arms and kiss him. Tell him she cared. That she'd be lost without him. That she didn't want him to leave. Not now when they were just beginning to know each other.

But she was not a whiny, sniveling woman who cried when she didn't get her way. She'd seen firsthand the difference between a wife or girlfriend who truly loved her man and those shallow, selfish bimbos who lied, cheated, and destroyed their men's morale soon after they deployed. Too many Dear John letters had left solid, confident warriors shattered when they'd needed their loved ones' support the most. She refused to be like those airheaded women.

Trying her darnedest to keep her trepidation from showing, she faced Julio head-on. If he had to leave, then so be it. She'd be faithful to him no matter how long his next job took. Or the next. She would wait, and she'd keep him supplied with care packages and letters, texts, or whatever he needed while he was gone. Meg wanted to say those things out loud, so he'd know what to expect. But did he seriously want to spend time with a banged-up, hairless, gimpy woman?

His gaze never strayed. What was he waiting for? More sarcasm from Charlie?

Meg ran her tongue over her bottom lip. Despite the moist, tropical heat, her lips were always dry. Lifting a finger, she scratched the length of her nose. Finally, she summoned enough saliva to actually make her throat work. "I need to get back to my kids," she said, giving him a way out.

Deliberately and slowly, his head rotated from side to side. "No, Meg. Your kids are in good hands, or you wouldn't have left them. You need downtime. R and R. You're not *Wonder Woman*."

No, what I need is you.

Charlie snorted. "Gawd, I don't have time for this shit. Let's roll, people."

Julio stretched his arm to her, her gear bag dangling off his fingers. "Think you can carry this now?"

She nodded, taking hold of the strap, but he didn't let go. Instead, he used it to tug her into his comfort zone, right where she ached to be. Yet she held back from nestling into the steel traps of his arms. He might not welcome displays of public affection. It would break her heart if he pushed her away.

"I can't promise you forever, Meg," he murmured under his breath, his sharp eyes on Charlie's, Hotrod's, and Hazelton's backs as they began the hike to the helo. "But I'd like to explore what's happening between us. That is, if you feel the same way I do."

Her head bobbed. "I do. Yes. B-b-but don't you have to check in or something? Won't you have to leave?" Darn! She couldn't stop stuttering!

"Yes, I need to speak with Senator Sullivan as soon as possible." Julio released the bag, nodding for her to follow the others. He fell into step at her side. "But it's customary for operators to take time off after extensive operations, especially prolonged engagements. I'll contact Sullivan as soon as we're aboard. I'm sure he'll understand. The problem then will be privacy."

That sounded like he meant to stay with her. Meg hip-checked Julio, she was so relieved. But he didn't budge like she'd expected. When she bounced off that manly hip, she nearly tripped over her feet. Julio caught her before she biffed it. Man, this guy was solid, and she was falling for him.

"Leave that to me, Agent Juarez," she replied, her voice rough, and her heart climbing back up into her throat. "I know a guy."

Julio cocked his head at her, his dark eyes smoldering. He was one scrumptious, capable, delectable warrior, walking with her, not with the guys up ahead. Not even trying to keep up with Charlie or Hotrod. Julio had purposefully hung back to walk with her.

The gravel pit with its cacophony of still roaring flames, pops, and soaring whistles, along with those hellish smells, was behind them. Hotrod was ahead, leading the way with Hazelton and Charlie on his six. The Blackhawk would soon come into view. Meg hurried as fast as she could, needing to get back on the helo and aboard ship before she bowled Julio over and had her way with him.

"Will I have to kill him?" he asked as they walked, the slightest smile curling his lower lip. "That guy you know?"

"Oh, my gosh, no. Not Lucas, I mean Corpsman Giacomo. He's watching over Dom. Just wait until you see that little boy. He's remembered how to smile, and he's being treated, and he's in good hands, and..." And she was babbling. Embarrassed, she finished with, "But you need to rest, too. If you're like me, you can't remember the last time you slept. Right?"

A shadow passed behind his eyes. "True, but I have a feeling sleep will be welcome this time."

She wasn't sure what that meant, but the fact that he meant to stay with her, even for a little while, sent crazy little sparks wiggling up her spine into her bare scalp. Goosebumps prickled her shoulders. Meg simply... Could. Not. Wait!

Chapter Twenty-Four

"So I heard," Sullivan groused. "Next time, keep your damned sat phone on your person, and I won't have to rely on some Army Ranger for intel. Been trying to reach you for days."

"There was no other choice, sir. Meg Duncan needed it to contact the Nightstalker pilot. Giving her my phone was instrumental in saving those children."

"Yeah, I know." Sullivan wasn't happy. "Sergeant Jorgensen filled me in. How are she and the kids? Anything I need to know?"

"Just the usual. One child has tuberculosis and lower GI parasites. He's being treated successfully. They're all undernourished due to their captivity, but they're eating better now, and the crew here has taken them and their caretakers to heart. They're all happy."

"You're sure Zapata's dead?"

"Yes," Julio answered without hesitation. "The fuel he stockpiled ensured his and most of his army's demise."

"That when Jorgensen came to your assist?"

"And Meg. He sniped several soldiers, but she's the one who launched a rocket into the tunnel where the last of Oz's soldiers were holed up, guarding his gold. To be honest, I had my hands full. I was worried. There were many more guards in the tunnel than I expected. Without her help, I might not be alive."

"But you took two hits, is that correct?"

It figured Charlie'd told Sullivan that. "They're nothing, sir. Both near misses. Never slowed me down."

"Where?"

Julio swallowed hard, not wanting to admit he'd been shot. "My arm. My thigh."

"But you've been treated..." Sullivan let the implied threat behind those four innocuous sounding words hang.

Refusing needed medical care was a sure-fire way to get kicked off the SOBs. Sullivan didn't waste his time on snowflakes or ego-maniacs. "Yes, sir. Meg applied first-aid the second she arrived on scene. Then the Corpsmen cleaned and sutured both scratches as soon as we boarded. I'm still able."

"Scratches, my ass. So, she fired the rocket that saved your life, huh? Hmmm..." Sullivan paused. "Not the way Jorgensen tells it. The after-action report he filed with his CO, clearly attributes his fast thinking and expert shooting to catching Oz's men in that crossfire. He said you were outmanned and outgunned when he showed. That without his expertise, you'd be dead."

Which was only partially true. But totally expected. Julio'd pegged Charlie at first sight. Sergeant Jorgensen was one of those hard-charging soldiers who took credit for his team's success. Probably carved notches on his bedpost, too. It was unfair that he'd slighted Meg, though. One of these days, Jorgensen's fabrications would catch up with him. Just not today.

"I wouldn't disagree," Julio replied. "I was the SOB on site. I'd let his observation stand."

Which meant it was better this way. Let CB hog the credit. The last thing any SOB operator needed was to be outed in an official report.

"But he lied," Sullivan growled. "Not only on his written report, but on a secure line to me and Captain Dooley. The son of a bitch lied to both of us."

Julio exhaled a full measured breath. "The system forces hard-chargers like Jorgensen to lie, sir. Once he'd sent his written version to his CO, he had to stand by it, especially with Dooley present. What does it matter? I don't want recognition. Neither do you."

"Copy that. Just wanted the straight dope, not some fabricated bullshit." A full growl came over the line.

"But what Jorgensen didn't know, sir. What he had no way to report..." Julio swallowed hard at what he still had to tell Sullivan. "I took a chopper down before he arrived. The Matryoshka Dolls, sir. They came to detonate the missiles. Had a Lightweight Laser Designator Rangefinder. I saw it. You may want to check with your Air Force friends. See if they can pin down who or what country's aircraft was in geosynchronous orbit over Brazil during the past twenty-four hours."

Dead silence rang in Julio's ear.

"I took out the pilot and brought the bird down," he assured his boss. "All aboard were neutralized. Brazil is safe."

"Holy sssssshit!" Sullivan hissed. "Sec Def needs to know this."

Julio nodded, though his boss couldn't see him. The Matryoshka Dolls were not to be underestimated. They'd successfully infiltrated and robbed Bern, Switzerland's famed electronic banking system, Suisse One. They'd gotten away with billions, then spat in the elite establishment's face by robbing actual francs from inside Suisse One's allegedly, one-hundred percent, secure vault.

Had to have been an inside job. But which one of the Dolls was brazen enough to accomplish the actual theft? Who was the mastermind behind the intricately coordinated plan that allowed, not only a daytime break-in, but the highly publicized robbery? To this day, no one knew who'd duped Suisse One, or who'd leaked the story of their supreme banking failure to the world's major media outlets. That the Dolls were now involved in black market treasures like plutonium, spelled a world of hurt, not only for Brazil, but for every civilized country on earth.

"So... Meg, huh? She as good at keeping her mouth shut as you are?" Sullivan drawled.

"She knows this matter is classified, eyes-only, yes, sir."

"She had top-secret clearance while she was in the Army, you know."

Julio had nothing to say to that. He hadn't known, but he hadn't asked, either. One day on the run with Meg Duncan had not made him an expert on the subject. He'd need many days with her for that honor. Perhaps a lifetime. Which was probably why his big mouth blurted out, "Requesting two weeks leave, sir."

"Granted. Where will you be in case Sec Def needs you?"

That was a good question. Meg had mentioned Texas, but that might only be where her family lived, not her. Julio had once called Naval Air Station San Diego home, but since he'd lost Bianca and Tomas, he'd avoided going back. Couldn't bear the lonely California nights. But there was that out-of-the-way island off Costa Rica. A tiny, private island, it lay directly east of the sleepy coastal village, Puerto Veijo de Talamanca. The trees should've grown back by now.

"Costa Rica," he replied evenly.

It was on that island Julio had ended the bloody reign of Mitchell Franks with a righteous kill. The mastermind behind several ugly murders and a long streak of brutal chaos, Franks had used Domingo

Zapata like a tool to infiltrate three South American cartel bosses' organizations. Zapata had spied on them, while Franks let them think they were in charge. Instead, he'd used them the same as he'd used everyone he'd ever met—like puppets. Only that time, his puppets were powerful killers.

He'd successfully infiltrated the Northwest state of Oregon's upper political echelon by befriending then-governor, Mick Tennyson. Acting as Tennyson's wife's personal assistant, Franks murdered her while on an alleged 'business' cruise. Julio didn't know for sure, and he'd never ask Suede or Chance, but he suspected Franks and Suede's mother had been lovers. Julio also believed Franks had done something to Suede, that he'd hurt her during the time he'd lived in the governor's mansion. That was what Franks did best. He'd hurt, used, and disposed of every life he'd touched, all because he'd aspired to be President of the United States.

Until Julio blew him and his South American buddies, drug lords Viktor Patrone and Benny Garcia, back to hell. Julio knew for a fact that Franks' million-dollar home on the island was gone, because he was the man who'd detonated the bomb that destroyed it. But...

¡Ay, caramba! That was also the day he'd nearly suffered a massive heart attack when, of all the people in the world! Chance's woman, Suede Tennyson, had sashayed up the beach toward Franks' home—in a barely-there bikini. He knew now that she'd gone after Franks to avenge her mother's death, and Julio didn't

blame Suede for that. He would've done the same if Franks had killed his mother. But Suede's timing couldn't have been worse. Julio had already planted the explosives under Franks' house by then. *Gracias a Dios,* the Sin boys dropped anchor within the hour of her arrival.

But it was Viktor Patrone who'd ended the traitor Franks' worthless life, once Patrone realized how badly he'd been deceived. In turn, the Sin Boys had rescued Suede, then ended Patrone and Garcia.

Once Chance and his brothers were a safe distance from the island, Julio had detonated the explosives. The Sin Boys hadn't known he was there until then, and Julio had only stayed to make certain that nothing of Mitchell Franks or his diabolical friends remained. Not one finger. Not one toe. No evidence, no crime, right? And without evidence, no charge of incursion on foreign soil.

Someday, Julio might have to tell President Adams about that unsanctioned foray into Costa Rica. Perhaps. But maybe not. The brotherhood of Sullivan's SOBs was by far the most solid family Julio had ever belonged to. He would gladly die before betraying his brothers and sisters. All of them. He was faithful. To. The. End.

"Consider it granted," Sullivan replied. "But stay in touch this time, will you?"

"Yes, sir. I will," Julio promised.

Sullivan disconnected, and at last, Julio let a belly full of angst go. It was time to track Meg down.

Chapter Twenty-Five

Meg lay on the bed in a darkened private room just off sickbay, with Dominic snuggled under her chin. She loved this little boy so much. True, she loved all her kids, and each was unique in their own sweet way. But Dom was different. Perhaps because he'd always been so fragile, and he'd captured her heart the moment she'd laid eyes on him. For now, he was actually breathing easy. Better yet, his dark brown eyes when he'd first snuggled in with Meg, had been bright with the pure light of childish joy. That alone was worth celebrating.

For the first time, Dominic looked like a boy with a future, instead of a bag of sticks without hope. All because of Corpsman Giacomo's loving care. Lucas had not only spent the entire night in sickbay monitoring Dom, but he'd given Dom his first teddy bear. Now named Little Luke, the teddy bear's black button eyes stared out from under Dom's chin. He hadn't let go of the toy since Big Luke had put it in Dom's hands.

And Dom had called Meg Mum again, just before he'd melted his body into hers and dozed off. If Mum wasn't a heart-meltingly beautiful word, nothing was. With Luke's permission, she'd been allowed to remove Dom from sickbay and rest here, but only for tonight. He'd have to go back to the sickbay bed first thing in the morning to begin another series of tests.

But tonight, he was all Meg's. With his cheek still resting on her bicep, she faced her tiny warrior, her eyes glimmering with the storm of emotions welling inside her heart. Of all her children, he'd be the hardest to leave. So she didn't plan to. Every child deserved a mother, and Julio was right. Her littlest sweetheart had chosen her, so she'd chosen him. She planned to adopt Dom.

The other room Luke had secured for her, with Captain Dooley's permission, was a private stateroom instead of shared quarters with multiple berths, like the one Marta and Craig now shared with the other children. Meg's other room was nothing fancy. If anything, it was a bigger version of where she lay now. Utilitarian. Orderly. Designed for the bare minimum. But it would afford her more privacy. She planned to move Dom there as soon as he was strong enough. Thankfully, Luke understood that Dom needed time alone with Meg.

Surprisingly, at the last second, Fernando and Joseph had opted not to leave Brazil. Which made sense, since they were the ones who started the orphanage to begin with. They'd said their goodbyes at the helo. Meg didn't know where they were now.

The dimmest light slanted through the door she'd left cracked open, leaving just enough light for what she needed to tell Dom. "I'm honored you chose me, sweetheart." She placed one little kiss in the middle of his forehead. "I promise to be the best Mum ever. You're my son now, Dominic."

She realized then she had no idea what his last name was. There had to be a way to find out, but she knew better. The sad truth behind the orphans of Brazil was that too many of the littlest ones had been abandoned before they were old enough to remember their parents or their names. Some, before they were able to talk. Or walk.

The door opened wider behind her then, spilling a bright shaft of hallway light across the foot of the narrow bed. Hurriedly, Meg swiped a hand over her face. Luke didn't need to witness her breakdown. But when a warm palm settled on her hip, she glanced over her shoulder, ready to bite Charlie's head off for being his usual proprietary, selfish self. Luke wouldn't take that kind of liberty, and Charlie had no business touching her like that.

But it was Julio standing over her, his hand cupping her hipbone. Not Luke or Charlie.

"Hey," he said softly, his gaze dark as he took in the scene. "Looks like your little guy's doing better now that you're back."

She loved Julio's *'your little guy.'* At least, she hoped Dom would soon legally be hers. "He is. He's not feverish, and Luke removed the IV for tonight. He still needs someone to keep a close watch on him, so I—"

"You want to be that person," Julio ended for her, his tone soft and even, as if he'd just stated an obvious fact, not the opening volley of an argument like she'd get from Charlie.

Swallowing hard, Meg nodded, not wanting to have to choose between him and Dom. Wanting them both so much that her heart squeezed at the thought of giving either of them up. "I'm going to adopt him as soon as I can."

Instead of grumping or sighing as if his world had just ended like other guys would have, Julio smiled down at her. "He already calls you Mum. Might as well make it official, but..."

But what? Here it comes. He's no different than any other guy. He'll make me choose. He'll be just like Charlie... Yet even as Meg panicked, her heart told her to settle down. Julio loved the little guy in her arms. She'd witnessed his tender side the second she'd handed Dom into his safekeeping that first day. Julio didn't have it in him to be cruel to any child.

"But what?" she breathed.

"But where are Marta and Craig tonight? Are they still on board? Who's watching the other kids?"

That made Meg smile. "Marta and Craig are with everyone else in guest quarters. You should see them, Julio. That place looks like they've been having one continual party. Everyone on this ship has been so good to us. Why do you ask?"

He canted his head. "Do you think they'd mind watching Dom tonight, too?"

"Are you leaving?"

He licked his bottom lip. "No, ma'am. But this ship isn't due back to Naval Station Norfolk for a couple months. We could fly everyone out first thing tomorrow morning, but Dom can't be moved until he's stronger. I talked with your friend, and Luke has already made arrangements with the children's hospital in Norfolk, Virginia, to take Dom until he's stronger. Luke will arrange for an ambulance to meet you two at the pier whenever you arrive."

What does that have to do with Marta and Craig watching Dom? "Not you?" Meg could've slapped herself for blurting that question. Of course Julio wouldn't stay long enough to accompany her to any hospital. Black ops guys didn't hang around, remember?

He shifted his hips. "I'd like to."

What did that mean? Was he waiting for an invitation? Was that why he wanted Marta and Craig to take care of Dom? She couldn't ask fast enough, "Then would you stay in Norfolk with us?"

That gentle, sad smile again. "Yes, ma'am," he said, bowing his head once in affirmation. "I'd be honored to stay with you and Dominic."

Her heart jumped into her throat at the way his voice had just dropped an octave, from conversational into a panty-melting rumble. Baritone always made her knees weak. Had to be the badass vibes radiating off this guy. Did Julio even know what he was doing to her? Did he care?

"But then you'd leave me?" Why, oh why, did everything out of her mouth sound needy?

Julio lowered his backside to the edge of the bed. Meg eased her arm out from under Dom and shifted upright to make room for him. Dom never budged. Poor boy was tired. Healing was hard work.

When Julio turned his square shoulders to Meg, he looked so damned handsome. He'd changed into soft, worn jeans, probably his one and only spare pair. The collar of his gray Henley was unbuttoned, revealing the sparest glimpse of chest hairs. Black, crisp hairs Meg wanted to sift her fingers through, when and if, they ever had a chance to walk through the rigid valley between his pecs. Either his shirt was too tight, or his chest was just that magnificent. Julio didn't have man-boobs. Everything about him was chiseled granite. Solid.

His gaze dropped to the floor. "I didn't plan to fall in love," he stated quietly. "The first time. With Bianca. My wife."

Hope wheezed out of Meg's heart like air out of a flat tire. She'd never actually asked Julio if he was married. Damn it. She should have.

"She's deceased now," he went on to say, his tone soft and low. "I'd applied and was accepted into BUD/S when everything started. I was three days into

Hell Week. The San Diego police called my OIC to tell me Domingo Zapata had kidnapped Bianca and our baby son. Tomas had just turned one. I'd bought him one of those big, red, plastic trikes. His legs couldn't reach the pedals yet, but you should've seen..." Abruptly, Julio stopped talking.

"Oh, honey," Meg breathed, leaning toward him, her hands gripping his sturdy forearms like manacles. "Domingo is so much worse than his brother."

"It took me years," he told the floor, "but I finally found them. I got my *familia* back."

Every word out of his mouth was breaking her heart. "Years? Bianca and Tomas were Domingo's prisoners for years? Oh, God. I am so, so sorry. How despicable. How awful." More like unfathomable. Domingo was known for torturing women, men, children, even dogs and cats. He was a monster. A devil.

"Yes. it was. But then I found them. I brought them both back home. Just when I thought we were going to make it. That we'd all be okay. We were living in California again. Point Loma. In the newer, better house she had to have." His shoulders lifted as if he'd accepted every whim and wish Bianca had demanded of him. As if it were no big deal.

Meg held her breath, sensing how this sad story would end. It'd be better if Julio had been married and cheating on the woman he loved, but losing his *familia* to Domingo Zapata? Unimaginable.

Julio turned back to the child beside Meg. His hand flattened to the center of Dom's back. It rested there while the little guy breathed, but Julio still wasn't making eye contact.

"She wanted to go for a walk that day. Said the ocean always gave her hope. She asked me to go with her, but Tomas had cried all night, and he was sick. I couldn't take him with me and I couldn't leave him. I chose my son," Julio murmured ever so softly. He seemed to only have eyes for the sleeping boy beneath his wide, manly palm.

Whatever emotion he was dealing with, Julio certainly kept it under control. But Meg couldn't hold back her tears. This man had suffered the worst loss imaginable. He'd lost everything! He needed to relinquish that rigid sense of control and gnash his teeth and swear at God! He needed to cry. God would understand. Any father would.

"A Navy SEAL pulled her ashore, but she was already gone," Julio whispered. "The minute she'd walked out our back door, she'd cut her forearms from wrist to elbow. Her blood was on the trail down to the beach. She'd already known what she meant to do when she asked me to go with her. She also knew that I'd stay with Tomas. She never meant to come back to us, Meg. Only to leave."

The already tight muscles in Julio's neck tensed as he forced a swallow, and Meg would've given anything if he'd only turn his face and look at her. But it was enough that he kept talking and saying her name. He needed her to know his sad story, and that was something.

"But Tomas was never the same," Julio whispered, his voice so soft Meg could barely hear him. "He didn't remember me. He never called me Daddy again. I realize now that my wife deserted him while they were in Domingo's prison. For a long time, I chose to believe she did that thinking Tomas would be better off without her. But with my counselor's help, I've come to understand the truth instead of what I wanted to see. I know now that Bianca deserted Tomas long before they were kidnapped. I suspect she might've unintentionally encouraged Zapata's attention without knowing what kind of man he was. How dangerous. She'd always flirted with tough guys covered in tattoos and riding Harleys. That's the only thing that makes sense."

That *'unintentionally encouraged Zapata's attention'* comment was overly kind of Julio. He might not realize it, but he was still making excuses for his selfish wife. A mother who deserted her one and only child? Meg found that abhorrently despicable. Bianca wasn't a mother. She was an entitled brat who hadn't cared about the man who'd adored her or her son.

Julio drew in a slow, deep breath. "They must've met somewhere in San Diego. Maybe on Coronado or one of the piers, I don't know. There are many tourist traps in Navy towns. So much temptation. I suspect that was how and when he discovered my Colombian heritage, too. Bianca must have told him everything about me. Years ago, my father came to Mexico from Colombia. He fell in love with my mom and..."

Julio's shoulder lifted, a sure sign Meg recognized for what it was. Another secret. Another heartache behind his seemingly indifferent body language.

"Domingo worked for a drug cartel boss back then. Viktor Patrone. Patrone needed someone to infiltrate his competition, a Columbian cartel. That was why Zapata kidnapped my family, to force me to work for Patrone. I never understood how he found me until I finally sought counseling. I look Mexican, don't I?"

"You are beautiful to me," she told him honestly. *So, so beautiful, I could cry just looking at you.* Thank God he'd been smart enough to seek counseling. Meg's entire body ached to hold this man. To comfort him somehow, some way. But his eyes were so dark and so, so sad. He still refused to look at her.

His shoulders lifted as if she'd only told him it was a sunny day, but his big, warm hand remained in the middle of Dom's back. So much like a father's hand. Tender, yet callused and hard. But soft as a lamb. Kind. Loving. Protective. Goosebumps shivered up Meg's arms. Julio would make the best father.

"But nothing I did mattered," he murmured, his eyes once again on the floor. "Tomas died shortly after Bianca... left. They called it failure to thrive. He just stopped breathing one night. The thing is, I've been alone for years, but I'd like to get to know you better, Meg. That's why I asked about Marta and Craig. There's a deserted island off the coast of Costa Rica. If we can get away, I was hoping we could get better acquainted. But I'll understand if you'd rather—"

"Oh, stop!" Meg launched herself into his arms. "Kiss me, damn it, Julio. Right now, before you break my heart!" *Because you already have.*

She couldn't wait for an answer. He had to know how she felt. She'd certainly mugged him enough. Counting on those other impetuous kisses, she planted her mouth over his and swallowed his doubt. Growling, because she needed him to know how much she cared and that she'd been attracted to him since the moment she'd laid eyes on him, Meg took what she wanted from that kiss. And how she wanted him! He needed to know she was not Bianca! And Bianca was a fool if she'd played around with Domingo Zapata—a murderer!—instead of the hero waiting at home for her. In her bed! What kind of woman does that?!

Determined to block that terrible pain from forever freezing this warrior's wonderful, but broken heart, Meg smoothed her fingers up over the bandage on his bicep on her way to the back of his strong, muscular, but very stubborn neck.

When at last, he canted his head, she opened her mouth wider for him, loving the sweet, slick taste of his tongue on hers as he took over the dance she'd started. Wanting him with every pounding beat of her heart, she devoured him, aching to banish the bottomless sadness that had held him in its grip for too long. To help him forget, if just for a few seconds.

Breathing hard now, she mapped the smooth ridges down his back, while her other hand slipped around his side to cup his hip. He'd taken possession of her head, his fingers firm on her jawline, his thumbs gently stroking her dripping wet cheeks. Yes, she was bawling like a baby, but he'd suffered so much. What woman couldn't see that?

Bianca, that's who. There was an old saying. One woman's garbage was another woman's treasure. Well, Meg knew a treasure when she saw one. And Julio was her heart's most fervent desire.

He certainly knew how to kiss. With every stroke and slide of his tongue against hers, her back arched, as if it had a mind of its own. She'd never realized the sensations inside her mouth were mirrored so vividly at her core. As if his mouth was touching her—there. Loving her... Melting her...

Oh, hell. Why hold back any feelings? Any words? Julio needed to know. "Captain Dooley put me up in a private room," she mumbled around Julio's skilled tongue and lips. "Take me there." *Right. Damned. Now.*

She felt Julio's warm, manly lips curl into a smile against her mouth. Finally! She'd made him smile, and just knowing he'd let her into his heart, sent another heated jolt to her core. Her back arched into him for more, and how on earth did that work? Was pleasing him the key? Was comforting him? Meg intended to find out.

After a few more licks, growls, and nibbles, she pulled back from his strong, domineering mouth and murmured, "Did you hear me? I have another room, Agent Juarez, and it's private, and..." A growl burst out of her heart. "I can't wait to get you naked in that bed!"

A truly radiant grin broke over her. Like a sunrise, it bathed everything.

"So," he breathed into her mouth. "Does that mean the island's out?"

"Ooo," she groaned. A deserted island would certainly be romantic, but her mind was already lost in an ocean of sensation. The heated caress of his breath over her face. His freshly showered, masculine scent in her nose. His large, capable, work-roughened hands mapping her shoulder blades, neck, and the back of her head, all while making sure her bandana stayed put. His sweet, kindly heart beating through his entire body. Every last part of Julio had combined to turn her legs to jelly and her brain to mush. It was too hard to think, much less form a coherent answer. *What was the question?*

Meg groaned again, as suddenly, her backside was off the bed and she found herself up in Julio's arms, against that magnificent chest. Right over his heart.

"Where to?" he asked, his voice gone husky and gravelly deep.

"Turn left once we hit the hall, then down the first set of stairs, through two bulkheads, down another flight of stairs, through one more hatch, then back up a flight. But be quiet."

He grinned down at her. "Can you walk?"

"Of course! Put me down." Heaven knew she couldn't be seen being carried. She'd never live that down, especially if Charlie spotted her. But when Julio let her slide down his delectable body... When Meg inhaled whatever shower gel he'd showered with... Her legs melted.

If not for Julio's cat-like reflexes, she would've been on her knees. Which may not have been such a bad idea, now that she thought about it. That would've put her face at his zipper level. But no, no, no. Not here and not with Dom sleeping nearby. No. Just no. She might be a titch overheated, but she was not that kind of mother.

"Where are we going?" Julio reminded her, his eyes gleaming.

Oh yeah. That. She cast one last look back at her boy. "First, I'm going to page Marta and Craig to come take Dom. That will make them happy. They already wanted to keep him with the other kids tonight."

"For the rest of the night," Julio corrected.

Meg grinned up at him. "You are so on!"

Chapter Twenty-Six

They made it to Meg's private room without encountering any Army Rangers along their convoluted way. But once Julio closed the door and turned the key in the lock, he only had eyes for his woman. Meg had all but pulled him inside this room. He wasn't carrying on board, per Navy rules, so he had no holster or weapons to worry about. He'd safely stored his gear bag full of ammo with the quartermaster. Which made getting undressed easier. Quicker.

He helped her unbutton his shirt, then toed out of his boots while she undid his belt. He held stock still when she slid her hands over his ass until his pants pooled over his feet. He kicked them aside, then unbuttoned her blouse. Unzipped her jeans. Peeled everything off but her underclothes and her protective bandana.

They hadn't turned any lights on, but he wished he'd thought to do that now. He needed to see the amazing woman rubbing her breasts against his chest and running her fingers through his hair and into his scalp. He closed his eyes at the tender explosions sounding off in his heart. If she only knew what this stolen moment meant to him. How long he'd needed what she was giving him freely. A woman's touch meant so damned much. It nearly unmanned him.

"Lights," he managed to say before things got too far out of control. By then, he was down to his socks and jockeys. She was in her bra and panties, and damn it, yes. He wanted to see her. All of her.

"Well, umm, okay," she murmured shyly. "I guess. If you have to."

"I want to see your eyes, Meg."

He could hear her hand smoothing over the wall behind them until a soft *click* sounded. The lamps on both nightstands flashed on and—

His heart nearly stopped. Standing in front of him was a goddess, a full-breasted, wide-hipped goddess with creamy skin beneath the skimpy underwear she still had on. Her eyes were a mellow emerald, hazy and dark. Her lids were heavy. Her lips were swollen and still shiny wet from his mouth. A soft pink blush dusted the crests of her cheeks. Those lush, thick lashes blinking up at him tugged at his heart. It'd mean so much if she trusted him enough to lose that bandana. To let him see all of her, not just her very sexy body. But her whole heart.

She was, after all, nearly naked already. Yet he understood. That little scrap of cloth on her head wasn't about modesty. It was about trust, and trust didn't come on command. It had to be earned. When she was ready, she'd know how deeply he already cared about her. He could wait.

But what did she see in a guy like him? Julio ran a quick hand over his head, perplexed. He had no idea.

Just that fast, her brows slammed together, and her hands slapped onto her hips. That amazingly brash, don't-make-me-ask-you-twice glare zeroed in on him. "What's wrong?"

"Nothing," he hedged.

To prove how right everything was, Julio stepped into her, wrapped her inside his arms, and pulled her body flush against his. Nothing that was about to happen next could ever be wrong. In fact, for the first time in his life, the world felt right. His doubt faded the moment he realized he had to trust this woman if he wanted her to trust him. Was there any doubt? Okay then. He could do that.

"Strip," he ordered as he grabbed his pants up off the floor and searched his wallet for the condom he wasn't sure he still carried. A man with no dreams didn't hang onto things he had no intention of using. Damn. No condom. Even if he'd found one, it would've been too old to rely on. He let his pants fall.

With a wink, Meg reached behind her back and undid her bra. It flew over her head. But he stopped her just before she bent forward to remove her panties.

He had to. She was far too obedient, and the sight of her bare breasts swaying free and heavy... hot-damned erotic. Every milligram of blood in his brain fled south. Every muscle in his body went rigid and ready for action. But this wasn't about speed. At all. It might not even happen, if he couldn't locate some protection pretty soon. Like an hour ago. Damn it. He should've planned ahead!

"Not yet," he breathed raggedly, his breath coming in short hard bursts and his heart pounding like a drum. Couldn't she hear it? He sure could. What he couldn't do was tear his gaze from the plump, pillowy, creamy-white breasts and the pebbled nipples jutting out at him. Or the delightfully deep valley squeezed between them. His mouth watered even as his throat went dry. So much beautiful, soft-as-silk skin. He shouldn't have told Meg to strip, but who knew she'd be so eager to please him? So damned heartbreakingly beautiful? "F-first things first—"

"You looking for this?" A square foil packet glimmered between her fingertips.

"Yes," he admitted hoarsely. "You came prepared?"

Her shoulders lifted. "Not usually, but with you, I was sure hopeful."

Without another word, he had her back in his arms. His greedy mouth descended to her breast and nipple in wanton hunger. Once again, Meg arched, this time backward. In doing so, she pushed that succulent breast between his lips and into his mouth. Cocking his head, he opened wider, needing to lick and taste, nibble and suckle everything that was Meg.

Hollowing his cheeks, he worked that succulent tip until he drew a ragged moan out of her. Easing back, he breathed on that wet morsel. Goosebumps blossomed over her bare skin, and the tiniest spark ignited at his tailbone. Julio was too far smitten with the panting woman in his arms to hold back now. With his mouth actively engaged in doing what it did best— eating—he backed Meg to the edge of the bed, then gathered her against him and laid her carefully down.

She relaxed onto the pristine, white pillow with a sigh, wearing just that bandana and her panties. But what a sight. This dreamy-eyed woman staring up at him with stars in her big, bright eyes took his breath.

Julio knelt reverently between her legs, his arms alongside her head and his heart in his throat. Gently, he tugged her final thin silken line of resistance to the side. Just as he'd suspected. She was a redhead.

It was then the magic happened. With one quick swipe of her hand, her bandana was gone, tossed to who knew where. Only the panties remained, and they weren't going to stop Julio. The sight of her shorn head and those beautiful eyes full of vivid green trust, elicited a powerful surge of gotta-have-her-right-damned-now.

Sliding his fingers under the elastic waistband of his boxers, he scraped them off and tossed them aside. Exposing himself to what could very well be the same feminine disappointment he'd known with his wife, he waited. He knew his body had been built for labor, not beauty. He was not a good-looking man. Had never strived to be more than what he was. One didn't grow up in the harsh deserts of Mexico without a few bumps and bruises along the way. Without a few fistfights. His nose was too big and his fingers too stubby. He was plain, but dependable. A burro. Never a thoroughbred. Slow and steady like an armored desert tortoise. He got the hardest jobs done without flair or panache.

But the stars in Meg's eyes were real. He knew the moment she wrapped one hand around him and pumped, stroking him from root to tip, that she truly wanted him. All of him. Not just his Navy paycheck. Then she made it better. Tearing that foil packet with her teeth, she gloved him. Those beautiful green eyes never once blinked or looked away. It pleased him to know that Meg cared about protection, too. Not only for herself, but for that unborn child in her future. That it would be planned for and conceived somewhere besides in a borrowed Navy rack.

The wondrous, greedy glitter he saw there, combined with the seductive way she licked her lips, fanned the spark at the end of Julio's spine into a roaring inferno. Passion for this woman's heart, for her soul, gripped him now.

For the first time in years, Julio became a man on the best of missions. Breathing hard, he locked gazes with Meg, needing her permission before he went any farther. It'd been too long since he'd been with a woman, but now, the Juarez train had left the station and was barreling down the track. Straight for her.

"What are you waiting for?" she growled up at him, her face lit with a heavenly grace that seemed to glow from every pore. She made it better when she crooked her legs around his waist and opened wider, her heels digging into the cheeks of his ass.

Blinded by her enthusiasm, Julio barely managed to slide one leg-hole of her panties aside as he thrust into her willing depths. There was no feeling in his world like the heated acceptance of this brave, loving woman. Nothing. Ever.

She hadn't let go of him once since she'd gloved him. With every stroke of her fingertips over his shoulders and up into his scalp, she claimed him. Wanted him. The welcoming clench of Meg's most intimate muscles were deliciously soft, all-encompassing, and warm. When they gripped him like a vise, his eyes rolled back in his head, as finally...

He was home.

He'd thought he'd found true love once before, but he knew better now. This wasn't just passive acceptance of womanly duty. Not the way Meg lifted her hips and bucked into him as hard as he was crashing into her. Not the way she purred like a cat, rubbing her hands over his back and her nipples against his chest. Moaning with every quick, slick slamming together. Planting hot, wet kisses up his neck and licking his nipple. Growling, "more." Giving him the best gift a man could hope for. Meg was giving all of herself to him, from the top of her beautiful shorn head to the tips of her talented toes, now locked behind his back, to her heels still digging into his ass. Driving him higher. And higher.

Out of his mind and caught up in the tenderest storm of emotion, Julio took her mouth savagely, needing the taste of her on his tongue right damned now, while he filled her body again and again. The steady give and take quickly pushed them both over the edge.

She came first, but the moment her body stiffened around him... The moment she moaned, "Julio. I'm... I'm coming... Yesssssss!"

Dulce Madre de Dios! The world beyond the bed disappeared into shattering strobe lights. Lightning! He couldn't thrust hard enough. Deep enough. At last, his body let go with a heated bath of all he had to give this woman. His life. His devotion. All his love and every single second of the rest of his life belonged to the brash, bossy lady panting in his arms.

Sweat trickled down his back as he burrowed his face into the crook of her neck, breathing the sweet scent of her skin into his soul where he wished she'd want to stay forever. Did he dare hope for happily-ever-after? That was only how fairytales ended, yet they weren't real.

Julio swallowed hard, waiting for Meg to say something, anything but, "Get off me."

At last, she blew out a tremendous sigh. Her entire body shuddered, then tightened under what Julio knew was an exceptionally gratifying feminine aftershock. He could tell by the way her growl resonated through his sensitized body. How she'd just made him thrum with more need. Instantly, his lips curled into a proud smile. He'd given that to her.

Women had the best orgasms. They didn't end at the moment of release like a man's did. Long after the initial fireworks their overheated, miraculously seductive bodies produced were over, lesser mini-orgasms still rippled through them, elongating their pleasure.

Elongating him as well.

Mission accomplished.

Lifting his head, he took a chance that she'd enjoyed sex with him as much as he had with her. He kissed the end of her nose and looked down into those clear emerald pools. Only now, those pools brimmed over with heartfelt emotion. Tiny tears streamed down her temples. He would've asked if he'd hurt her, but the sheer depth of love shining back at him caught him short.

"That..." she breathed into his face, cupping his jaw between her hands. "That...was... the first time... Oh, my heck! That was the first orgasm I've ever had, and I've never felt so, so..." She squeezed her eyes shut, her bottom lip quivering. "You made me feel beautiful again, Julio. Me. A bald woman who can't stand up straight most days, much less walk straight. Did you know that? You wanted me, and I wanted you, and... and..." A ragged, squeak shuddered out of her.

"You are beautiful," he told her as he eased a hand beneath her head, loving the prickle of every short hair in his palm. "You're brave and daring." He let his gaze stray between the lovely breasts mashed against his chest. "You're the most beautiful woman I've ever known."

"You're just saying that." Her hand went to her bare head. "I'm bald, and men like women with long, gorgeous, blonde hair, not stubby crewcuts, which even that, I still don't have. I'm not very feminine or beautiful even with long hair. I'm bossy and—"

That earned her a surging thrust of his hips. "Trust me," he said quietly, never more sure of anything. "You're all woman. I would know."

The wary shadow that darkened her features fell away. "But you see me. You really see *me*, who I am, and what I need to do with my life, don't you?"

He nodded. "I hope so. But where is all this insecurity coming from? How can you not see how amazing you are?"

Her lips puckered into an adorable pout. This was Meg at her most vulnerable. "Because..." Another un-Meg-like whine. "Because... H-he left me, Julio. He never even said goodbye. He... he just left. The day I had my stroke. In the ER. He walked away and he never came back."

"Who?"

"T-Ted. My, my h-h-husband."

Damn. Julio hadn't known Meg was married. "You have a husband?" *Why didn't you tell me?*

"Had," she told him. "Divorced him before our first anniversary. The jerk."

Relief flooded Julio. Divorce was good. He didn't tangle with married women. Not that he'd ever had an offer. He hadn't. It was just a good rule. A rule he'd never had to exercise. Ever. Bianca had made sure of that.

"I'll tell you a secret," he murmured, running his palm over Meg's elegant, bare head. "I was worried, too."

Her eyes widened. "About what?"

He adored the stark disbelief in her tone. His shoulders lifted at what he was about to reveal. "I'm not a handsome man. You can do better."

She blinked. "Are you kidding me? Why would I want to? Who the hell told you that?"

Julio would never tell how many times Bianca had denigrated him. The truth he'd lived with had become clearer to him now that he'd found Meg. Bianca had been an abusive woman. Throughout their marriage, he'd been nothing but her faithful dog. A whipping boy. He'd taken her verbal assault because he'd loved her, and he'd prayed that someday, she'd love him, too. But now he knew better. Bianca had loved herself even more than her only child.

"You weren't any more happily married than I was, were you?" Meg asked, her fingers tracing his collarbone.

Pride kept Julio from speaking evil of his wife. He was not a backstabbing gossip. "It is best to let the past go," he offered evenly. "Someday, I might tell you a story, but for now..." He thrust his hips forward. "Let's focus on what we have here.

The sexiest smile curled her lips. "I like what we have here, *mi amigo*. I like it a lot. Please... Let's do what we just did again. Maybe a couple more times?"

A grin nearly broke his face then. Yes, broke, because he hadn't smiled that hard in so long. His cheeks felt cracked at the same time they felt soothed by joy. He was exposed and vulnerable, yet reborn at the same time. This genuine, giving woman made him stronger. Meg was the second chance he'd been searching for.

"Gracias," he whispered to God and to Meg, to every one of the guardian angels watching over him. His mother. His ornery maternal grandmother. Even sweet, innocent Tomas. They'd always been there. They were all that had kept him going these last dismal years, and now, they had led him to Meg.

The sassy woman with her legs spread beneath him whispered seductively, "You're welcome."

That did it. Taking a deep breath, Julio angled his head and kissed the unrepentant angel in his arms. He tasted mint and Meg, his favorite combination.

With a heavy sigh into his mouth, she wrapped both arms around his neck and cocked her elbows behind his head. Her fingers raked carefully over his scalp. "Have you ever thought about letting your hair grow?"

"Me?" His gaze instantly fell to the crest of her shorn head. "I will if you will," he murmured, his voice uncommonly deep and rough.

"It's red, in case you didn't already know. Chestnut, really."

"I know," he purred. "I looked."

The sexiest blush blossomed up Meg's neck and over her cheeks. Everything with the world according to Julio was good again. He'd lived through several levels of Hell, but now he'd found heaven inside Meg's strong, determined arms. Inside her generous, loving heart. Against her ample breasts. Despite her limitations, she'd still become the most selfless woman he'd ever known, one who had courageously devoted her life to protecting motherless children.

It was too soon and too fast, but Julio knew he was falling in love. That was his downfall with Bianca, falling too soon. Giving his heart away too quickly, before he'd truly understood the woman he'd thought he'd loved. But this time was different. For starters, Meg loved children, not rocks. She had a heart of gold. Real gold. The kind that paved the streets of heaven. Not fool's gold, the kind that lined pockets of greedy men and women on earth.

Her magnificent breasts heaved against him with a satisfied sigh, but all the talk had relaxed him. He pulled out, not giving their protection a chance to fail. Pinching the neck of the condom tightly, he asked, "How many of these do you have?"

Growling, she cupped his head between her hands again and grinned like a naughty little girl. "I bought a whole box! They were on sale at NEX, and I bought new clothes for my kids, some for me, too."

Her enthusiasm made him smile. An aircraft carrier was a floating city, complete with Navy Exchange stores, where sailors or military veterans could grab haircuts, Starbucks coffees, as well as shop for clothing, shoes, souvenirs, even flowers when available.

"By the time I get back from the head," he told her, "I want you out of those panties and ready for more."

She giggled. "Hurry back!"

Julio shoved off the bed and padded across the small berth to the head. He loved the tinkling notes of music within her laugh. Even that was freely given, like sunshine. Like rain. His eyes were finally open. He was seeing a whole new world, and it was beautiful. It was Meg.

Chapter Twenty-Seven

Meg rolled onto her side, waiting breathlessly while Julio was washing his hands in the head. She'd never been so daring with a man before. Not once in all her years. But he liked her, maybe even loved her. How wonderful was that? To have come all the way to Brazil on a wing and a prayer, depressed and thinking the best of life was behind her, only to find that the moment she'd arrived at the orphanage, her poor-me, pity-party vanished. And then Julio came along.

Working for the few children whom Oz hadn't yet kidnapped, had altered Meg's American-sized perspective in a huge way. There she'd been, by the world's standards, a privileged American in a strange land. She'd been feeling sorry for herself, when back home, she'd had more than all the orphans put together. A roof over her head. Nutritious food on her table three times a day. Entertainment at her fingertips. Heat during chilly winters, air conditioning in summer. Affordable medical care when she needed it. Best of all, big brothers who watched out for her and parents who adored her. Now, here was Julio, the force behind the change this time.

She loved looking at him. He hadn't shut the door, and that naked gorgeous male physique was on display. He was comfortable with his nudity, and that made her comfortable with hers. He hadn't said anything, but she'd seen the glint of approval in the corner of his eye when she'd tossed her bandana and bared her entire head. He might not know it, but his protectiveness about that inconsequential scrap of fabric was what had convinced her that she didn't need it. Julio didn't seem to see her handicap. Instead, he'd looked through it to the real Meg Duncan from the very start.

She'd been vain to hide behind a bandana, to even think that others couldn't tell she'd lost her hair. Vain and prideful. What was hair anyway? None of her kids worried about not having it. Why had she?

Julio was at the doorway to the head now, easily gripping the jamb above him, his gorgeous, sinewy arms raised and a quiet smile on his lips. His shoulders filled that doorway, his muscular thighs, too. A tattoo covered his right pec. Lots of words she couldn't read from the bed.

"What's your ink say?"

A pinch quirked his lips. "Ave Maria."

She cocked her head. "It's a prayer? Come here. I want to see it. The lettering is beautiful."

Lowering his arms, Julio walked to her, his body loose and his hips rolling.

Meg lifted to her knees at the edge of the bed, melting with every sensual step he took. Finally close enough, she read the prayer out loud. Hail Mary had been inked in large baroque lettering, in English, the other words in much smaller script. But so damned beautiful, her eyes watered reading it. Two stars to the left of his right nipple completed the overwhelmingly beautiful artwork. Amen was scrolled beside them, finishing the prayer.

By then, she couldn't hold back any longer. Leaning forward, she pressed her lips to the warm skin at the centerline between his muscular pecs and ran her tongue up to the hollow of his neck. Tasting the salty side of him. Worshipping him.

It was then her fingers skated over the bandage on his arm. She'd almost forgotten. Not once had he drawn attention to his wounds. He should have. Dropping back on her legs, she tugged the bedsheet up and covered her chest. "We should've been more careful. You've been shot. Twice. You're still healing."

His arms dropped and his handsome smile deepened. "I like that you care about me, Meg, but trust me. I've been hurt worse. These scratches are nothing."

"Prove it. Show me your scars, and I'll show you mine."

He raked her with a smoldering once over. "I'd rather you show me something else."

A full-on body wiggle shivered up Meg's spine at his words. Julio was not a small man in any way. He almost looked intimidating. But not to Meg. To her, he was her male, and she was his female. Together, they were unstoppable.

Tossing the bedsheet aside, she eased off the bed to her feet, her nakedness on display for the man she'd known less than a week. Not even four full days. If he wanted to look, she wanted him to see every last bit of her.

His gaze never left her face.

She took a step into him, her eyes locked on his, but wondering what a competent, capable undercover operator like Julio saw in a downhome country girl with a limp and a saggy face. True, the facial features on her left side were at their worst when she was tired, and when she'd overdone it. The remaining paralysis made her look as if she were always scowling.

Yet Julio didn't seem to see it. That was adoration shining on his proud face. Couldn't be love. You had to know someone a long time before you fell in love. Didn't you?

With one more step, Meg was in Julio's arms, and he was in hers. Breathlessly, she leaned her head under his chin against his chest. She let her fingers roam over the smooth muscles on his back, then down the taut ridges of his ribcage under his arm. Then up again over his chest and through those few crisp, black hairs dusting his pecs. Her index finger lingered on the flattened disc of his nipple beside the tattooed stars, gently strumming while her body turned liquid.

Sex between a man and a woman was a dance of total opposites. His body had been created to be hard and unbreakable, yet hers was made to be soft and to bend to his. To accept the magnificent steel rod pressed hot and ready to her belly. To bear his babies.

The thought of making a baby with Julio stole whatever common sense Meg had come into this dance with. She didn't want this feeling with Julio to be a one-time fling. She just wasn't made that way. The words whispered out of her even as she rubbed her nose against his neck. Man, he smelled good. "I think I'm falling in love with you, Agent Juarez."

He captured her chin in one hand and forced her to look up at him. "And that makes you cry?"

Meg shook her head. "No. It's not like that, but I gave my heart away too soon last time, and I'm afraid I'm doing it again, and stupid people who keep making the same mistakes over and over again are insane, and I'm not an easy lay, and another thing—"

He dipped his head and covered her mouth, swallowing the rest of what was working up to be a much longer run-on sentence. His tongue swept the last of her doubt away. This was possession, clear and simple. The muscles in Julio's arms bulged under her touch as he ended the kiss. Without any effort, he lifted her off the floor and against him. Laying her gently back on the bed, he stuck one knee into the mattress at her side and leaned that magnificently muscled body over her.

Threading her fingers over his scalp, Meg absorbed the fierce kiss, her tongue tangling with his in the frantic slip and slide of passion. One minute she'd been feeling sorry for herself—again—but now she couldn't give her body over to his exquisite lovemaking fast enough. There was so much of him to love. To lick and kiss and—

God, I do love this man, she thought. *It'll destroy me if he leaves, too. I'll die, I know I will.*

That didn't stop her hands from mapping down his muscular body to his hips, then around his back to his ass. With a taut, fit cheek in each palm, she bucked against his hips, inviting Julio inside. Needing all the raw masculinity overwhelming her with every guttural grunt and groan.

He took things exquisitely slower this time, making love to her mouth while, at the same time, he pumped long and slow push-ups over her. Into her. Leisurely letting her feel every ridge and satiny inch. Spearing her with uncanny skill that hit all the erogenous zones, over and over again. Warming her up. Rocking into her body the same way he had already rocked her world. With the skill of a sniper with his finger on the trigger. Only this time, the trigger was that tight, tiny knot at the apex of her thighs. He knew precisely what his fingertip was doing. With every flick and scrape of his thumbnail, her body tensed. Until...

"Julio," she moaned, her mouth still full and her heart opened wide for the breaking. For that was what this was. The only way he could ever break her was if she gave all. So, Meg did. She was under his spell now. Blinded by waves of intense sensation coursing over and through her, she gave her whole heart to the warrior pumping into her. No matter what happened next, she needed this connection. This man. This now.

He tipped his head away from her then. "Come for me, Meg," he breathed into her face, his breath hot. "Don't ever hold back. You need this. I know you do. So do I. Let go. Please, baby. Come for me."

"Wrong," she moaned, her eyes closed as the tsunami within her commenced its build up. "I need you. Only you. This is just icing..."

Her core clenched, gripping Julio. Her legs stiffened as her entire body became a loaded spring, pulled tight. So tight. To the point of breaking, tight. Until—

Julio thrust extra deep and hard and growled, "Pure love needs no words, only action to prove it exists. Talk is cheap. You already know I love you, Meg."

"Yessss..." With those words, white-hot lightning struck, lifting Meg's ass off the mattress. Their bodies exploded together. What a time to tell her. W-w-wow. What a gloriously wonderful time to fall—

"God!" she cried out, her fingernails now dug into Julio's taut backside. "I'm coming..." By then she was growling as hard as he was. They sounded like lions mating instead of a civilized man and woman. But this coming was completely feral and raw, as elemental as sex could be.

"Good," he purred gruffly. "Come, my sweet baby. Give it all to me. All of you. Please. Make me whole again."

Yes! Yes, yes, yes! Consider it done.

The thing that had begun with a sweet, feathery kiss, ended in a whirl of crazy, wild, life-giving fireworks. Mother Nature had packed so much shared pleasure into just a few sweaty seconds of heavy breathing, but this explosive coming was worth the pleasure of the ride. While the crest of her sexual tsunami tipped over and curled into itself, into her, Meg held onto the solid wall of humble male muscle surrounding her. Filling her. She hadn't noticed until then that Julio's big hands were cupping her ass again, lifting her off the mattress while he pistoned into her.

"I... I can't," she told him as, with every stroke, that sensual wave began another breathtaking climb. "It's too, too much, Julio. Too soon." She still hadn't settled from her last orgasm. How could she handle another? Her throat had gone raspy and dry. But her core wasn't. Julio made sure of that.

"There is no such thing as too much love," he whispered, his lips soft and wet at her temple. The tip of his tongue ran around the curl of her ear. "Love is all there is, Meg. Come again. With me. Let's be one."

Oh, God, she was doing it again. Not that she meant to. It was just happening, without her having made the decision or doing anything more than holding onto this man. Her man. With every seductive stroke of Julio's clever fingertips, with every moist nibble and every tender kiss, the sweetest tension built within Meg's heated body until... his love swept over her once more.

She closed her eyes and gasped at the powerful connection. His knees were between her thighs, his masculine scent in her nose, and the coarse brush of his chest hairs over her ultra-sensitized nipples... Everything that was Julio combined to fill her now. The whorl of his fingerprints on the skin covering her plump ass. The heat of his breath. *This, oh God! This!*

At last, the last sparks of fireworks fell to earth, and Meg fell with them, back into Julio's arms. She would never be the same again.

His forehead came to rest on hers. "I meant every word. I love you, Meg."

She couldn't help that tears filled her eyes. "I hear you," she whispered. "But I loved you first, and you know it."

That made him smile. "Are you always competitive? Even now? While we're here in your bed and naked together? Do you always have to be right? After we've just made the sweetest, tenderest love to each other?"

Meg shrugged. What did them being naked have to do with anything? "I'm not competitive. I'm right."

Man, when Julio smiled, when he truly let his light shine forth, he was a different guy all together. So damned handsome. She ran her palm along his shaven cheek, petting him like the dangerous jungle cat she knew he was. If there were apex predators in the world of men, Julio was that beast. Better yet, he was a happy beast, and he was all hers.

He leaned his forehead to hers. "Yes, you are right. But women are blessed with gifts men do not have. Intuition, for one. Homemaking skills, for another."

"Excuse me?" she asked, not sure she'd heard right. "Homemaking skills? I think you've got the wrong girl if you think for one minute that I'm just going to—"

He pressed a firm finger over her ranting lips to shut her up. "But this time I am right," he murmured, his deep brown eyes gone dark and dreamy. "It is only women like you who can truly make a house a home. That is what I meant to say. Only women can make a baby, too."

Oh. That. Something swelled inside her ribcage. By then Julio's legs were slack between hers, and she couldn't keep her hands off him. His body weighed hers down, but it was the most comfortable crush she'd ever felt. "It takes two to make a baby and raise a child," she whispered, so in love with this brave man that she could cry. "A mom and a dad. Lovers."

The pink tip of his tongue kissed the middle of his bottom lip. "Two is a very good number. So is three, when that third is a baby. But women also have the power to lead a man by his nose, to make him do things he would not usually do."

She egged him on. "Like what?"

"Like learn to play guitar."

There was so much she didn't know about this guy. "You play?"

He shook his head. "No, but I would learn. That way I could compose love songs for you."

"And sing them, too?"

His smile deepened into a grin. "Probably not. I am only good in the shower."

"You're on," she crowed. "This place comes with a nice big shower. I wanna hear you sing. Let's go."

He kissed her then. Thoroughly. Deeply.

But she knew what he was doing. Julio was trying to distract her.

Silly man. Distraction only worked with kids. Not with a woman who very much wanted this particular man to sing her a love song.

Chapter Twenty-Eight

So... There he was. In the shower. Making a fool of himself. Singing a love song. Badly. A small foil package waited patiently in the soap tray. But Julio loved the way Meg's eyes roved over every inch of his naked body. She'd told him to pick the song while she lathered up billows of sudsy body wash in her hands, then proceeded to smooth those billows over his chest and belly, until... Yeah. She knew how to work him and how to get her way. Because with every slick glide of her fingers, she'd won him over bit by bit, and soapy inch by inch. He'd given up and started singing.

"Love Me Tender" had never sounded so raspy, yet so perfect. Meg Duncan was as good as sunshine. As if he'd been a dying plant, she'd brought him back to life. Made him truly want to live again. Once again, the fiery blood of his Spanish heritage coursed through his veins. He was awakened to the beauty around him. The beauty in his shower. Err, her shower.

For the first time in his life, Julio knew true love. He knew what it was to be a man again. A lover. God willing, perhaps a husband, too. It seemed the perfect way for what he felt for Meg to end. Not with closure, but with his ring on her finger and the promise of forever.

While she worked his manhood, he fell madly in love. At last, he captured her nimble fingers and lifted them to his mouth. He suckled her index finger first, then the next. And the next, whirling his tongue over each slender digit until her eyes were bright with lust.

He was seeing a different side to Meg. With the right stimulation, this saint of a woman had turned into an energetic wildcat who knew what she wanted and wasn't afraid to tell him. He loved that she had no problem being naked with him. None at all. Even her bare head didn't seem to bother her anymore. She seemed at peace with the lush curves of her all-female body, the fullness of her breasts, the dip of her slender waist, and the flare of her hips. He was at peace with those feminine attributes, too. Very much so. In fact, he preferred the plush weight of Meg to the anorexic bodies the media held up as preferred models of womanhood. A woman shouldn't have to starve herself to please anyone, and a man worth having would never demand such a thing of the woman he loved.

It was then that Meg joined in, singing with him. Laughing with him. And Julio was falling hard. But man, what a ride. If this was true love, he was in it to win it. To the end. And for once, this ending would not be bitter. It would be better. Best. Because however it came, it would be with Meg.

Instead of wasting away, she'd turned her brokenness into beauty and strength. She could've chosen to spend her life moaning and groaning, becoming nasty and petty and bitter. Instead, she'd decided to become better, and she'd made it look easy.

"Turn around," his bossy shower partner ordered, making a circle in the air with her soapy finger. "Step out of the spray. I need to wash your back. Are those bandages still dry?"

Putting his palms to the tiled wall opposite the shower nozzle, Julio nodded. "Of course. They're waterproof."

She gave his ass a gentle smack. "You planned to get me into this shower all along, didn't you?"

"Like you and your condoms, I just hoped," he replied, lifting his shoulders in mock innocence. Of course he'd planned to get her naked. Showering together was an added bonus.

Instead of scrubbing his back, Meg leaned into it, plastering all those soapy womanly attributes against his spine and backside. Making his skin slippery. Starting a fire. Reaching her arms around him, she let her fingers flutter over his chest, then dived down his belly to his cock.

He groaned as she handled him with unabashed shyness. Her fingers were strong where they needed to be strong, then soft as feathers where he needed to be handled more gently. Still humming what would forever be his favorite love song, she stroked him to standing attention.

He did not want to come like this, not in her hand. But she was driving him to the edge of his restraint. The song hummed through him. With her pressed against him, all he could feel were the diamond-hard tips of her nipples. His mouth watered. Lust roared through his veins, pulsing with desire. If he lived to be a hundred, Julio knew he could never make enough love to her. With her.

Crazy with need, he turned into her and slipped his hands down her back to cup her ass. Her breath hitched and those dark green, sultry, come-hither eyes widened. Her pupils were big, black, and dilated, reflecting desire back at him. Her breaths came fast and hard.

When her arms wrapped around his neck, he lifted her off her feet and wrapped those beautiful long legs around his waist.

"You're so, so bad," she murmured thickly, even as her hips arched into his. "Wait a second. Where'd that condom go?"

Julio lifted the foil packet from the soap tray and gave it to her.

"You're so, so perfect," he told her sincerely. Everything that came out of her mouth was sweet and generous. Not once had she belittled him. She might be direct and, okay, yes, she was bossy. But Meg loved him. He could feel the warmth of it wrapping around him. He could see the honesty in her eyes. *Dios!* He wanted to wallow in it. To never leave this shower stall.

Meg used her teeth to open the packet. Maneuvering her lithe hand between their bellies, she gloved him, then impaled herself on him. To the hilt.

He closed his eyes at the pleasure suffusing every inch of his body. Then she surprised him once more when she sealed the deal with an urgent thrust. Nature kicked in then. His stance widened, and he began to piston into her, lifting her up, and then letting her glide back down. The shower sprayed over them like a warm baptism, drenching and cleaning them at the same time. Joining them. Making them one body with two pounding hearts.

He kissed her with all his heart and as much of his soul as he had left to give. Licking his way from her lips down her neck, he bowed his head to her breasts and filled his mouth, tonguing that hard tip until she groaned. He knew she was coming. Her body stiffened and her legs clamped around him like vises. She used his body for leverage, pushing the heels of her hands against his chest while she slammed her core into him again and again and...

He saw stars. Novas. An entire universe. A brand-new world. One that belonged only to him and Meg.

Thoroughly sated, and his legs shaking, Julio held on until Meg joined him seconds later, growling his name when she bit his shoulder. That little bit of pain turned into sublime male satisfaction. This woman, this wild, brave, amazing woman, had marked him.

Like the alpha female he'd known she was from the start, she'd claimed him. Even now, her fingernails were dug into the cheeks of his ass. For sure he'd find marks there, too. Moon-shaped marks he wished would never, ever fade.

This was what he'd been searching for all his miserable existence. To belong to someone. To be valued and needed, not for his rank or paycheck, but for who he was inside his skin. For what was in his heart.

Julio bowed his forehead to her shoulder, the shower spray now lukewarm. Yet even as his manhood shrunk out of Meg's body... Even as she slipped down his belly until her feet settled once more to the floor, his heart was full.

Cupping her jaw, he lifted her face to his and kissed her swollen lips, licked them, then kissed them again. He didn't deserve this woman, but Julio knew he'd spend the rest of his life serving her. Worshipping her. Loving her.

Chapter Twenty-Nine

"Why not Antigua? It's civilized," Hotrod asked pointedly.

Meg looked at Julio for that answer. They were on deck next to Hotrod's Blackhawk. It was just after sun-up, and a strong easterly wind had blown in. The helo's rotors vibrated under the assault, but Hotrod had assured them the weather was no problem. He was in his jumpsuit at the cockpit's open door, and ready to go, his helmet dangling from the strap in his hand. The reflective lenses of his Aviators bounced Meg's reflection back at her. It'd be nice to see his eyes for a change, but he always wore some kind of protective eye cover. If not his darkened helmet lens, then the Aviators. If she could ever make actual eye contact, she was sure she could convince him to get this show on the road before Charlie showed up and spoiled everything. He had a knack for doing that.

Julio stood beside Meg, his hands loose at his sides and his gear bag at his feet. Dressed in a new pair of denim jeans instead of his customary black get-up, he was as ready as Meg to get off the carrier. He was wearing dark glasses too, along with his work boots, and the leather bomber jacket he'd purchased at NEX. But the plain white, sexy-as-hell t-shirt beneath that jacket had to be two sizes too small the way it stretched over his wide chest. The way it delineated the sheer power in those muscular pecs.

Meg had no idea ordinary cotton fabric could turn a man into a sexy beast. But it surely had. Her fingers itched to get under that shirt, maybe rip it off. Standing beside him was pure torture when her mind was still back in bed, where he'd gotten acquainted with every bare inch of her body. It still thrummed from what he'd done to and with her in their morning shower. Which she'd adored. She wanted to return the favor.

Julio had a way of never making her think twice. With him, she was beautiful again. He'd turned her back into herself instead of the Doubting Thomas she'd been since her stroke. Who was she to argue? If he thought she was gorgeous, then she was. To prove her newly found femininity, she'd left her bandana behind. Refused to hide behind it ever again. Didn't even know where it was. Eventually, her hair would grow back, but if it didn't? She no longer cared. Julio loved her just the way she was. He'd told her so, and that was good enough.

But damn, this sturdy hero beside her looked like a bad-boy biker with an attitude behind those Ray-Bans. Yup, they definitely needed more space and a heck of a lot more time to themselves. He had a couple weeks off and it'd be months before the carrier docked. It was now or never.

But Hotrod was right. Antigua would make a cozy retreat. Southeast of Puerto Rico, its deep harbor accommodated even the largest cruise ships. Surely, she and Julio could recharge their batteries there instead of some burned-out island.

"Too many people," Julio replied, his voice as even and emotionless as ever.

She'd quickly come to understand that he was a different man behind closed doors than he was in public. Her man's pride ran deep, and she respected that. There would be no public displays of affection once they'd stepped outside her room.

Which made her smile. The only reason they'd even come up for air was they'd gotten hungry. Aircraft carriers might come with deluxe accommodations, but not room service. Not that she and Julio had checked to see if there was any such thing. She didn't need to be the subject of any scuttlebutt that would surely follow her calling the galley for an order of eggs and ham.

Hotrod's chest heaved with a long-suffering sigh. "I'd rather take you somewhere stateside, not drop you two on some deserted, undeveloped island off Costa Rica. I'm not a damned taxi."

"Stateside will do, kind sir," Dr. Barbara Hazelton chirped, her British accent as classy as ever. The breeze caught her very lovely blonde hair, making her look like a college girl instead of Britain's leading nuclear engineer. Wearing white slacks and a pink silk blouse beneath what had to be a London Fog trench coat, she smiled like a movie star on the set.

What was it about that blasted accent that turned every male head on deck? Like Julio's. Meg wanted to reach out and slap the back of that man's hard head, but she'd never embarrass him like that. Unless he continued staring at this blonde bombshell. His eyes had gone scary dark. What on earth did he see in Hazelton that he hadn't seen in Meg?

Irritated now, and surprised at how defensive she'd become over some woman she'd barely met, Meg cleared her throat, determined to make her point. "Sorry, Doc, but we were up top first, and we're not going states—"

"But we could," Julio interrupted, his tone still even, his jaw set, and his damned focus still on Hazelton.

Meg could've been on fire and he probably wouldn't have noticed. She cocked her head and sent him a "What the hell?" ice glare, even as Hazelton offered a pert, "Cheerio, then. Let's be off. If you're sure?"

Oh, that was rich. Pull the sweet damsel in distress card. Bat your long, thick eyelashes, which are probably fake. Purse those full, red, and no doubt, botoxed lips. Damn you.

Meg wanted to slap the smirk off Hazelton's face. And Hotrod! For the love of god! All he'd offered Meg was a curt, "Morning, ma'am," when she'd showed up bright and early. But Hazelton had earned one of his mega-watt grins? For what?

Julio was the one who'd suggested they get away for a couple days, not Meg. And Charlie had all but promised Hotrod could and would take them anywhere they needed to go. Yet Julio and Hotrod had both up and changed their weak little male minds because this blonde bimbo showed up and said jump?

"Island first," Meg told Hazelton in her best Corporal's voice. "Then you can go wherever you want." *Back to England would be nice.*

But Hotrod was already shaking his head. "No can do, Duncan." *Now I'm Duncan, not even ma'am?* "Doctor Hazelton's mission takes precedence over everything else on this ship. Your little vacay will have to wait."

She opened her mouth to argue this was most certainly not a vacation, but Julio intervened. "Which was why I agreed to go along with Doctor Hazelton. Stateside is better than nothing."

He was going with Hotrod and Hazelton? "Since when?"

"Since she said she needed to go stateside." Julio's broad shoulders lifted like this betrayal was no big deal. He'd taken his Ray-Bans off and tucked the stem into his t-shirt's neckline. His dark chocolate eyes were too damned bright, and still fixed on Hazelton. Not on Meg where they should've been. The ass!

While her blood boiled, Meg held her tongue. Hazelton on the other hand, had no trouble directing the four sailors behind her where and how to stow her four, small, metal crates, most likely the plutonium and her equipment, on board the Blackhawk. "Do be extra careful, boys," she piped up. "Strap them nice and tight. One slip and who knows what might happen. Why, we could be responsible for another Godzilla."

That, and the annoying patronizing way she talked down to them as if they were mere boys, earned her a hearty round of male chuckles. But it also bought those crates extra-special handling. The young men she'd enlisted to help couldn't seem to do enough. One even saluted before he winked and walked away. Yet not a one of them had said a word to Meg.

Once they were gone, Hazelton turned that creamy complexion on Julio, her blue eyes suddenly warm and her tongue sliding suggestively over her lush bottom lip. "But I really do hate to abscond with your ride. Please, my good man," she said to Hotrod. "May Agent Juarez ride with me? There is so much I need to ask him, and it'll save me having to cross over the pond again."

"Yes, ma'am," Hotrod replied easily, gesturing Julio forward. "Up front with me, Juarez. Looks like you're co-pilot this trip."

And I'm chopped liver.

Julio took two steps forward. Away from Meg. The ass!

"Wait a minute," she ground out, once again feeling decrepit, forgotten, unwanted, and cast aside. And damned pissed that she'd given her heart and her body to this... this man who was leaving her! Were there any guys on earth worth the skin they were wrapped in? Sure didn't seem like it, and now she was on the verge of tears! So angry, she wanted to stamp her feet. *Damn, damn, damn!*

Julio glanced over his shoulder and—finally—his gaze connected with hers. "Hold up," he told Hotrod who was busy fastening Hazelton's harness, the poor helpless thing! For a smart woman with a PhD, she sure acted stupid this morning.

Julio hurried back to Meg like a heat-seeking missile. About. Damned. Time! At least he wasn't afraid to take hold of her forearms when he got to her, not like that was as good as a hug. But it was better than nothing.

Meg cast her gaze across the deck to the Pri-fly, short for the primary flight control tower where the ship's Air Boss monitored incoming and outgoing aircraft, including this Blackhawk. She didn't want Julio to see the betrayal she felt in her eyes, but yeah. There he was, about to go off with the first blonde he came across, leaving the hairless wonder behind. Meg ran a quick hand over her scalp. Of all the days to decide to brave the world and declare that hair did not make the woman. It sure as hell did. She wanted her stupid bandana back!

Julio tipped her chin up with two fingers and made her look at him "Hey," he breathed. "You're upset. I can tell."

"You think?" snapped out of her. She pursed her lips, then froze her heart. *Not going to cry, damn it! Not in front of that... that woman!*

His face mellowed into... No. That was not love! It couldn't be. He was going off with another woman and leaving her behind, and it just couldn't be love shining in his beautiful, dark chocolate eyes! Not this time. Damn him for making her fall for him.

"Meg," he said softly, pulling her forward and into his chest and—at last! His strong arms circled her like the lover she'd thought he was. Like the man he'd been for the last twenty-four hours. Like he cared! "I don't want to leave, but I have to go. I can feel it. All is not as it seems. Stay strong. I will come back to you."

Damned if her bottom lip didn't quiver like the wimpy woman she wasn't. "You've said that before, bucko," she replied, meaning to sound tough, but whining instead. Damn these tears!

He cocked his head then closed the distance with purpose. There, in front of God and every sailor on deck, Special Agent Julio Juarez, Sullivan's best man, planted a kiss on Meg's mouth that boiled her blood in all the best ways. Okay, so she was crying by then and making a royal fool of herself, but she clung to him anyway. And he clung to her, one arm crooked around her neck, the other on the small of her back while he swallowed her insecurities, every last one of them.

"I love you, Meg Duncan. Surely you believe that after all the love we've made. As God is my witness, I love you so, so much." he breathed into her mouth. "Only you. Wait for me?"

And there it was, the promise she'd made to never turn into a whining military wife, or one of those selfish women who operated on the *'love the one you're with'* concept. The cheaters. The liars. Yeah. Them.

Swallowing hard, Meg bucked up and nodded at the man who was her one true love. Her love for this incredible man was squeezing out of her eyes. Like their day in bed, she gave Julio what he asked for before he left.

"Of course, I'll wait for you. What'd you think? That I'll kiss someone else the second you turn your back? I'm no pansy-assed bimbo." *Like Hazelton. And Bianca!* "But you'd better be careful out there, Juarez." Meg stabbed her finger into that stone wall of a chest. "You'd better come back to me." Blinking hard, she bit her bottom lip. Instead of coming across strong and fearless, she'd ended her rant in a voice so squeaky, she was ashamed of herself. But watching him walk away was harder this time. He was taking her heart with him. It hurt!

"Oh, Meg. Not Megan. Sure as heck not Nutmeg. Just my beautiful, beautiful Meg." Julio shook his head softly, his already warm eyes lit with the tenderest glint. "Baby, you have no idea how I wish I'd met you a long, long time ago."

That endearment and all that it meant, that his sweet Tomas might still be alive if they'd met each other sooner, was her undoing. Stifling the damned sob climbing up her throat, Meg curled back into Julio's magnificent arms, and hid her face in his shirtsleeve.

"I can't let you go," she sobbed, "and I'm sorry I'm acting like an idiot, but I love you, Julio. I... I need you." Yup. She'd officially morphed into a crybaby.

He kissed her once more, luxuriously slow this time. His lips were warm and soft. They caressed hers with deliberate tenderness, as if he were pouring all his heart into her mouth. Into her heart. He groaned when at last, he broke the kiss and rasped, "You can't possibly understand how much hearing you say that means. After all these years..." He blew out a sigh. "I never thought I'd find anyone like you. I lost hope and my way. I gave up."

"Well, I'm here, and I'm not going anywhere. You be careful, okay?" she asked earnestly, trailing her fingertips down the thick veins on his muscular bicep to lock fingers with him. "Don't court death like you did in that gravel pit that night. Take cover when someone's shooting at you. For God's sake, Julio, you belong to me."

Nodding somberly, he stepped back. "My heart beats only for you," he murmured. "Watch the skies. This shouldn't take long."

Famous last words.

Chapter Thirty

Julio climbed aboard with zero enthusiasm. For the first time in his career, his chosen vocation had asked too much. He'd never before felt so torn nor this inadequate. He'd been shot twice only days ago. Physically, he was compromised, and he needed more downtime to heal. But stepping out of the lush warmth he'd found inside Meg's arms, and walking away from her, so soon after making love with her, was by far the hardest thing he'd ever done. He'd finally found a measure of peace in the storm that had been his life. Yet once again, duty called. He was leaving his one shining star and his only safe harbor. Didn't seem fair and it didn't feel right. Yet there he was, locked into always doing the honorable thing, simply because that was what Navy SEALs, even those who rang out, did.

Hotrod had already strapped into the pilot's seat and put on his helmet. While he talked back and forth with the tower, requesting weather reports and updates, Julio strapped into the co-pilot's seat and pulled on the only helmet left in the cockpit. The steady thwack-thwack-thwack of rotors revving overhead diminished once he secured his com-link, then diminished more as he tightened the helmet strap under his chin.

He'd never ridden up front in a Blackhawk cockpit before, much less been privy to pilot/control tower chatter. Without a doubt, this MH-60M was a dynamic workhorse. Its usual crew consisted of pilot, co-pilot, two crew chiefs or two door gunners, but Hotrod had come alone this time. It could carry an even dozen troops, their equipment, and it sported an external sling for heavy equipment. Maximum internal payload came in at a solid twenty-six thousand pounds. External payload, Julio wasn't quite sure. He'd seen a Blackhawk hover with precise skill at the edge of a mountain cliff, one skid on solid dirt, the other in the wind, as its crew retrieved Army casualties while in the middle of a firefight. It'd been one helluva daring rescue, and Julio fully believed Blackhawk pilots worked miracles. Yet here he was. Taking up space.

This helo's four main rotor blades and three aft tail rotors were powered by the two growling YT706-GE-700 engines overhead that could push its air speed to a maximum one hundred fifty knots.

Julio had once been on board a Blackhawk during aerial refueling. Talk about a thrill. But mostly, he'd served as door gunner on more lethal versions of this same bird. Some MH-60Ms were outfitted to support medium assault armament, such as miniguns, cannons, Gatling guns, air-to-air stingers, and AGM-114 Hellfire anti-tank missiles. Navy snipers usually dangled off helicopter skids or out helicopter doors. They fast-roped down to hot targets, and, occasionally, rode as mere passengers instead of harbingers of death. But never as co-pilot.

As he settled back, he took in the night-vision-compatible digital cockpit array of LCD displays. Instead of fuel, temperature, and the typical automobile-type gauges he'd expected, Julio was looking at streams of full-color flight and mission data, a moving map, health, and sensor data.

He leaned forward to glean as much information as he could about the condition of this helo before dust-off. Crew and engine alerts showed steady, but there was so much information to absorb. Forward-looking infrared video. Radio. Navigation data. Other data streams he didn't fully understand. But all this technology was controlled by the full alphanumeric keyboard like he used back home? Breathtaking. This rugged aircraft was straight out of science fiction.

Julio knew these birds were also equipped with infrared jamming devices, as well as laser detection systems, chaff and flare cannons. Covertly, he made a quick sign of the cross, thankful he wasn't expected to pilot this bird. All he had to do was sit tight and enjoy the ride. *Gracias Dios!*

Well... that wasn't all Julio had to do. He hadn't volunteered to accompany Hotrod for nothing.

Something about the British woman sitting in the rigid rear seats had irked Julio from the get-go, so much that he'd asked Sullivan to verify Hazelton's credentials. Only Sullivan hadn't yet gotten back with anything substantial, only that, yes, she was the UK's top nuclear engineer. Yet Julio knew damned well Hazelton was not who she pretended to be. So here he was, either an idiot for leaving the woman he loved behind, or playing hero again.

Julio sucked in a belly full of air once the skids tipped forward, then leveled off as it lifted up and hovered momentarily above the flight deck. Once airborne, when the Blackhawk headed north into the wind at breakneck speed, Julio let that breath go.

He sat in silence for a while, but they were moving too fast. Soon he'd lose his chance to question Hazelton. He had to act now. He turned to Hotrod. "Where are we going, Chief?"

Hotrod's lips were pursed tight. "Naval Air Station Key West, Florida."

"How long before we land?"

"An hour or two. Just set her on cruise control." Without taking his eyes off the helo's flight deck displays, Hotrod pressed his right hand against his chest. His fingers curled into an S, then his index finger and thumb made an O. American Sign Language. Hotrod had just sent Julio a covert SOS.

But cruise control? Really?

"You ever been there before?" Julio asked conversationally while he signed, "What's wrong?"

Hotrod turned to face Julio and flashed a toothy smile. "You know it, Bro. I grew up in Miami." When he faced forward, he tucked his right hand back into his chest and signed, "Doc is not what you think."

Just as Julio suspected. Hotrod had picked up on the same vibe Julio had. "Must've been nice," he said while he signed, "You got a plan?"

"Best childhood a kid could ask for," Hotrod continued easily, his right hand on the stick while he looked over his shoulder and told Doctor Hazelton, "Make sure you're strapped in, ma'am. Things are going to get bump—"

He never finished. One second, he was bright-eyed and cocky. The next, he'd slumped forward in his harness, a tiny dart stuck in the side of his neck.

Julio snapped around, his pistol instantly on Hazelton, his harness already undone. "Don't move," he ordered the fierce woman now pointing that damned tranquilizer pistol at him. At least, he hoped that was a tranq in Hotrod's neck.

"Or what?" Hazelton snapped, aiming squarely at Julio's chest where she couldn't miss. "You'll shoot me? Go ahead. See how long this helicopter stays in the air with a dead stick."

She must not have heard the cruise control comment.

He'd turned fully in his seat by then, his boots in the aisle and positioned to leap into action, his target close and his mission clear. "You're a Doll. A spy. A Matryoshka gangster."

Her lip lifted with a sneer as the polished British charm she'd exuded disappeared into cold-blooded ice. "You want to make small talk, Agent Juarez? Now? While your buddy dies? Do you have any idea what I have in this weapon?"

Weapon, not gun. She was former military.

"Don't care," he answered bluntly as the helo veered gradually to the right and farther out to sea. "Drop that pistol or I drop you. You're not taking the plutonium."

With the slightest turn of her wrist, her weapon was once again on Hotrod. "Are you sure about that? One hit only knocks a guy his size out for an hour or so. But two hits..." She tsked. "Special K is a killer at that strength, Juarez, and this little baby holds four darts. You sure you want your buddy's death on your conscience?"

He wasn't falling for that. Without hesitation, Julio fired twice. Once, to end the conversation. Twice, to make sure Hazelton knew she'd been shot despite the tactical armor he was certain he wore. He didn't need her dead. Only out of commission. In seconds, she was restrained. Still breathing, but talking gibberish.

"Jesus Bloody Ch-Ch-Christ," she hissed, now on her knees with her wrists cuffed behind her, and drooling face-first into the molded seat. She'd dropped the tranquilizer pistol, but her body was mostly on the floor. "You... sh-sh-shot me?"

There was no need to answer that stupid question. Of course, he'd shot her. He was just surprised she was still coherent enough to talk after being hit twice at close range. By his Beretta M9, no less. She might've been using tranq darts, but Julio's nine-millimeter should've knocked her out. That must be some tactical vest she was wearing.

Hurriedly, Julio scrambled to secure her weapon. Emptying the chamber of its loaded mini-syringe, he carefully extracted the other two darts, then stuffed them into an overhead compartment. He settled her pistol at the small of his back. Meanwhile, the bird was slowly losing altitude. Spinning in wide, out of control circles, they were going down. Guess that cruise control didn't last very long.

Hotrod flopped sideways out of his seat, held only by his harness. His helmeted head lolled on his shoulder. Still out cold. Not good.

Swiftly, Julio pushed Hazelton prone to the floor, face up, then patted her down to make sure there were no more hidden surprises behind that trench coat. Just as he'd suspected. The coat had hidden the set of sleek, ultra-modern, state-of-the-art tactical plates he found beneath her blouse. This was why he hadn't wanted Meg on this bird.

Julio loosened the ties to Hazelton's plates. When he log-rolled her to slide the plates out from under her, he went stock still. He'd found a small, rectangular device taped between her shoulder blades. A satellite messenger device. And it was broadcasting.

Hazelton moaned when Julio ripped the tape holding the device off her skin. Too bad.

Since satellite messenger devices relied on global satellite networks instead of cell coverage and the limited reach of cell towers, they worked worldwide. Some models allowed GPS navigation and communication options, including two-way texting. But more importantly, they tracked the wearer's exact location, which meant that someone knew precisely where Doctor Hazelton was right now. Fortunately, they had no way to know she was out of commission.

Quickly, he activated the screen to reveal Hazelton's last text. The time sent display showed that she'd communicated with someone just before takeoff.

Her text read: *I have what you want.*

Unknown contact: *How many will be with you?*

Hazelton: *Two men. Don't worry. They'll be out of commission by the time you show.*

Unknown contact: *Are you sure?*

Hazelton: *Trust me. I've taken down better men than these. They won't cause any trouble.*

Unknown contact: *Where can we meet?*

Hazelton: *The usual. Are you nearby?*

Unknown contact: *Always.*

Hazelton: *My boss wants payment this time.*

Unknown contact: *We're on our way.*

Julio swallowed hard. That comment, instead of an answer to Hazelton's question, spelled trouble. Unknown contact had been waiting somewhere nearby, possibly for days. They'd known where she was all this time, even during retrieval of the plutonium. And now, they were on *their* way.

Hazelton lifted her head just high enough to look at Julio. She wasn't nearly so put together now, not with her blue eyes crossed, her hair askew, and a thin string of drool sliding off her bottom lip. "You... you know h-h-how to f-f-fly this b-b-b-bird?"

Julio wasn't in the mood to answer. This *b-b-b-bird* was now going down fast.

Unlocking the side door, he slid it open and let the wind into the helo. The cool slap in the face and the smell of saltwater in his nose filled Julio with purpose again. He remembered who he was. One of Sullivan's best and the man who loved Meg Duncan.

Cocking one arm back, his pistol still in his other hand, he fast-balled Hazelton's GPS locator out of the helo and into the ocean. Let Unknown contact track that. Next, he tossed the empty syringes, but kept the unused ones, not that he expected she'd left any fingerprints on them. Most likely, she didn't have any if she was who he suspected.

Stalking back to where Hazelton lay on the floor, Julio lifted her into one of the passenger seats and buckled her in. She was unconscious by then, not going anywhere. He checked on the four small cases she'd brought with her. For a second, he debated tossing them overboard too, but didn't. Recovery would prove too risky, and there was always a chance foreign powers might reach them first.

He retested the straps holding Hazelton's cargo in place. Satisfied they weren't going anywhere, Julio hurried up front. Back in the cockpit, he loosened

Hotrod's harness and transferred him quickly into co-pilot position. Julio strapped him in and made sure he was breathing. Hotrod's face was flushed and his breaths were coming in short pants, but other than that, he appeared none worse for wear. He'd be okay.

The helo's rotors had now pitched forward, sending them into a dive that, if steep enough, would slam them cockpit first into the Atlantic. But they hadn't pitched that far forward yet, and swimming was plain not in the cards today.

Julio strapped himself in as pilot and quickly checked what displays and readouts he could read. Current cruising speed wasn't even close to this bird's top speed of two hundred miles per hour. He hoped that was a good thing. The SilentKnight multimode radar display was flashing terrain-following and terrain-avoiding data faster than he could make sense of it. There was no way he could fly this bird.

His heart pounding now, Julio adjusted his mic and dialed ground control at Fort Campbell, Kentucky, on the helo's radio. He desperately needed simple, user-friendly instructions on how to fly and land this technical bird. He got Army Air Traffic Control Specialist, Jaxon Buttars, on the first ring.

After listening to Julio's brief explanation as to what had happened with Hotrod, Jaxon said in one of those calmly, professional voices all air controllers used, "Sure wish I was smart enough to talk you through this, Agent Juarez. But I'll be frank. You're in a tough spot, and I'm no helicopter pilot. You need help. Hold please."

"You want me to hold?" Julio barked. "While I'm in a Blackhawk about to crash?"

"Yes, sir. That's exactly what I want you to do. I'm gonna contact Warrant Officer Duncan. He's one of our best pilots. He'll know what to do. Won't take me long. Promise. Just need to make that call. Please hold."

Shit! Now Julio was listening to dead air and sweating. And cussing. A good case of anxiety set in, but not for him. For Meg. He'd told her he'd be back, and he didn't want to let her down. He'd already done that. There was no way he'd disappoint her again.

A click sounded in his helmet's headset as another, more mature sounding voice came online with, "Chief Warrant Officer Trevor Duncan at your service, Special Agent Juarez. Sorry to meet under these conditions. I understand you're piloting Hotrod's helo, is that right?"

Julio couldn't believe his ears. "Trevor Duncan? Meg's brother?"

"Yes, sir, I am, but let's hold off the chitchat until you are skids on the ground, shall we?"

"Copy that," Julio breathed. "Yes, sir, Hotrod's incapacitated, shot with a tranq dart, but he's alive and breathing. Just... Help me not kill him, sir."

"Exactly what I intend to do, Agent Juarez. Now sit tight and listen very carefully to everything I say, then do precisely what I tell you. Lucky for you, Hotrod was recently selected to fly the one and only experimental Blackhawk in the fleet. The baby you're piloting is one of a kind. I'm sure you know by now she's got cruise control of a sort. You'll find out just how experimental that bird is real soon. For now, keep sharp. Don't panic. There's a toggle switch to the left of your airspeed readout, beside the main flight deck. Do you see it? The needle should be standing at zero. That'd be the vertical needle, sir, not the horizontal. Let me know when you've located it."

That was easy enough. "Got it." But cruise control? Julio had thought Hotrod was kidding about that. What else?

"Good. In a couple minutes, I'll need you to toggle that switch to the left and take your hands off the stick at the same time. Both needles will be horizontal at that time. Once I'm in control, do not touch anything, understood? Can you do that for me?"

Julio nodded, his throat still bone-dry at the ramifications of killing everyone on board.

"Can't hear you, sir," Meg's older brother said crisply. "I need audio confirmation. Please say again."

Julio spoke up this time. "Yes, yes, sir, I'll do whatever you need me to do."

Trevor's voice switched back into conversational then. "You do know the bird you're flying is a highly specialized version of Sikorsky's S-60, don't you? Agent Juarez, you ought to be proud of yourself. You're one of the few and the elite now. Not everyone can fly a Blackhawk, but these particular babies are exclusive to the Night Stalker mission. No other spec ops group has them. And Hotrod's bird is the only Blackhawk with remote capability."

"Understood," Julio responded. But he wasn't flying anything. Not really. Which made him wonder if Hotrod had ever been flying this helo?

A quiet chuckle vibrated in his ear. "I don't think you really understand, Agent Juarez. I said remote, as in remote-control. Once I give the order, and after you comply, I'll be flying that bird. Not you."

The helo's frame started shaking then, and they were going down in a lazy death spiral, cockpit first. Whitecaps on the Atlantic frothed cold and gray below, and it looked like Julio was going to get that watery grave after all. Didn't seem fair, dying when he'd finally found someone to live for. Sweat trickled into his eyes. It'd sure be nice if Duncan gave the order to toggle that switch now.

"You still with me?" Duncan asked, his tone just as calm as before. The man had some of that Atlantic ice water in his veins.

"I am," Julio answered tightly, wanting to believe that Duncan knew what he was doing. But it wasn't Chief Duncan heading into the Atlantic, was it?

Plenty of muffled chatter came over the connection from Fort Campbell's traffic control tower, but nothing Julio heard sounded remotely conclusive. Nothing gave him any sense that this disaster would end well. There was too much argument, too many voices.

Dulce Madre de Dios! This was hair-raising. Staring Death in the eye. Relying on someone he'd never met before. Trusting. Wishing he could hold Meg one more time before he died. Trying to breathe. Scared for the first time in his life that this might be the real end.

It seemed like forever, but was most likely only a minute or two, when Duncan's deep baritone came back with, "Please toggle that switch now, Agent Juarez, and remove your hands from all controls. From now on, do not touch anything but the suicide strap over your head or your ass if you want to kiss it goodbye. Please keep your arms and legs inside the vehicle at all times. I'm in control now."

"Yes, sir. Toggling now," Julio said as he leaned forward and toggled that switch. Just as he grabbed the webbed strap overhead, the bird lurched and—*Dios!*—dived. Then accelerated! This was Duncan helping? Felt more like an extreme roller coaster ride on its way down.

"Jesus," Trevor hissed, his tone not so convincing anymore. "This bird's bucking like one of my daddy's wild mustangs."

Did he think that was funny? The thought had no more than entered Julio's mind, when the helo shuddered and picked up another couple knots of air speed. Straight down. Julio checked velocity. The Blackhawk had now reached maximum air speed, and they were in a breath-sucking death spiral, instead of fighting against it. The Atlantic was coming up way too fast. Impact had to be mere seconds away.

The helo started spinning again. Julio couldn't keep track of how many revolutions the bird made as it plummeted to its death. Instinctively, he leaned back into his seat. Like that few inches would make any difference when this bird hit water.

Trevor growled a hearty, "You son of a bitch, Hotrod! What'd you do to this helo? Where's your Goddamned rotor brake?"

That didn't sound good. Expecting death any second now, Julio closed his eyes. Meg's beautiful smile flashed to mind. The sparkling glint in her green eyes would forever remind him of sunshine breaking through the canopy of the forests of Minas Gerais.

"I'm sorry I let you down," he whispered. "I'll always love you." But he asked her older brother, "You're flying this bird by remote c-c-control?"

"Trying to, Goddamn it," Trevor replied tersely. Sounded like he might be sweating as much as Julio was.

There was no sense talking. Julio gritted his teeth and held onto the suicide belt for dear life. Fragments of his past flashed before his eyes. The day he'd rescued Bianca and Tomas. He had saved them, and he'd done all a husband and father could humanly do to ensure they lived. That they'd died was not on his head. It never had been. Bianca had made the choice to kill herself, and Tomas had died simply because he'd lived too long in Hell. A tender child simply didn't have the inner strength to overcome what a monster like Domingo and a mother like Bianca had done to him.

But Meg would cry herself sick if he died today. At this speed, the chopper would surely break apart upon impact. His body might never be found. She'd be devastated. Heartsick. After living through What's-His-Name's rejection, the ex whose name Julio could not for the life of him remember, and after suffering a life-changing stroke, Meg, more than anyone, deserved a happy ending. Julio didn't want her to waste the rest of her life wondering what happened to him. Whether he'd survived the crash, or whether he was living somewhere else, with someone else. Or if he'd forgotten her and the love they'd made. As if he could ever forget those sweet moments.

Tears brimmed, but he blinked them away. More than anything, Julio wanted to be the man who put stars back in her eyes. He wanted to see her face light up when some doctor or nurse on some future day put Julio's baby in Meg's hands. He wanted to watch her cry tears of happiness, not sorrow. *Madre de Dios!* He wanted to give her hope. The life she should've had. Julio knew it then beyond all doubt. His life had always been important. His life *was* dear. Very dear. He wanted to live! With Meg. *God, please. Let me live! I promise to be a better man!*

"You still there?" Trevor asked suddenly.

Julio blurted, "I'm deeply in love with your sister, Chief Duncan. I can't—don't—want to live without Meg. I love her. Please... keep us alive."

A rumbling, "Hmmmmm..." came back to Julio as the bird leveled out at what had to be the very last second before impact. Trevor Duncan had cut it damned close. The helo's skids turned into skis as they skimmed rough ocean waves for a few frightening seconds. At last, the bird leveled off into an abrupt, shuddering hover.

"*Gracias, Padre Celestial,*" Julio breathed, his heart pounding up his throat, possibly out the top of his head, too. *Thank you, Heavenly Father.*

"You're welcome," Trevor Duncan growled, "but I'm not God, and Chief's a better handle for me. Don't want to ever step on the Big Guy Upstairs' toes, you know. So... You love my sister, huh? Precisely how on earth do you know Meg? Did you serve with her? Are you Army?"

Julio bowed his head to his chest, thankful the Blackhawks heads-up display didn't include live video. Thankful there was no way Trevor could see him crying like a baby. Sucking in a deep gut-full of I'm-still-alive, he told Meg's big brother, "No, sir. Former Navy. I work for Senator Sullivan. When your sister requested an assist for the orphans she served, I helped them get away from Orlando Zapata. You might've heard of him."

"Yeah, I know the bastard," Trevor growled. "But he's dead? You ended that son-of-a-bitch. You're sure?"

"Yes," Julio replied, still breathing hard and finding it hard to believe he was alive. "I'm sure he's dead. Check your satellite feeds over Minas Gerais, Brazil, for the last couple days. You'll see smoke from his gravel pit. The Zapatas' reign of terror is over. Oz is dead, and Domingo's incarcerated in America's most secure federal prison."

"No shit? Dom's doing time up north, in the Arctic Circle penitentiary?"

Dom. Dom. Dom...

"Y-y-yesss," Julio stuttered as his mind went cold, like someone had just walked on his grave. Why did the nickname that Domingo Zapata shared with the sweetest little orphan in the world, make the tiny hairs on the back of Julio's neck stand up? Why had his throat gone even drier than it had been just micro-seconds earlier when he'd been staring Death down?

No. Not only no, but hell no! It wasn't possible. There was no way a child as pure and innocent as Dominic could ever share DNA with Domingo Zapata. Absolutely not. Never!

"Where he will die," Julio offered weakly, even as his heart screamed, *'Dominic is not Domingo's son. He couldn't be. Could he? No. Just no. God wouldn't be that cruel.'*

Yet even as Julio railed against the sheer happenstance of a fate so vile, he knew now why Meg had found Dominic tossed out of Oz's mine and lying on a garbage heap. God might not be that cruel, but Orlando Zapata had been. It was the law of the jungle, a heinous, bloodletting ritual that military conquerors the world over had practiced for eons.

Burn thy enemy at the stake for all the world to see.

Pillage his treasury so all the world would know.

Salt his fields.

Rape, defile, and murder his women, daughters, and concubines.

Hunt every last one of his children, bastards, every living relative, to the ends of the earth. Torture them to death. Leave no trace that enemy had ever existed. Or ruled. Or breathed.

Spread the word of his demise, near and far.

Declare yourself better, greater, and grander.

Build monuments over his.

Rewrite history.

God knew the ancient Egyptians had certainly done enough of that. As were certain Americans even now, in these modern, supposedly enlightened times, rewriting history to match their political agendas. Leaving legacies of lies and whitewashed half-truths for future generations.

A heathen warrior the likes of Orlando would've surely applied that same fate to any niece or nephew who might—someday—have become his formidable adversaries. Talk about a dysfunctional family. The Zapata brothers had crafted dysfunction into an art. It was in their blood. Could it also be in Dominic's?

"There's an island a couple clicks due north," Trevor said as the helo lifted just high enough out of the waves and accelerated on a much more orderly course. "I'll get you there, but it'll be up to you to stay out of trouble. Can you do that?"

"Yes, sir," Julio replied, his mind numb, still on the boy he now believed was, in fact, Domingo's son. God, where was Dominic's mother? Julio needed to find her. Or did he? Was that unlucky woman even alive?

Within minutes, the Blackhawk hovered over a narrow stretch of sand in the middle of nowhere. Surrounded by ocean, Julio didn't know where they were, and for some reason, the navigation maps were offline. Maybe because Trevor was at the controls.

"This little gem is only here because of the last hurricane," Trevor said.

Gem? Looked more like a soggy sandbar. Julio kept his opinion to himself.

"Brazil is still off your port. Sun'll be setting soon, so if you plan on exploring, get it done as quick as you can."

Explore? There was nothing to see out the helo's windows except a narrow neck of two, maybe three miles of sand, and a spindly palm tree at the opposite end that could only be a couple years old. It was that little. And scraggly.

"Yes, sir," Julio breathed as he cast a glance over his shoulder at Hazelton. She'd been tossed around a little, but her harness had kept her upright. Mostly. Hotrod was in the same state of disarray. Julio cringed at what Hotrod might say when he came to. Blackhawk pilots had formidable egos. He wouldn't take being so quickly neutralized well.

Trevor set the helo down quite gently, considering he did it from Kentucky. "There. Sit tight, Juarez. Help's already in transit to your location. We've been tracking your transponder signals since the moment you called. ETA in two hours, maybe less. See if Hotrod packed any protein bars in that bird. Wouldn't be surprised if you find a bottle of rum. He prefers dark Jamaican. Course, he thinks he's a pirate, too."

Julio jolted back to his current dilemma. "Chief, is this bird equipped with blue force tracking capability?" Blue force tracking was the US military's GPS-enabled capability to locate friendlies and hostiles in the field.

"You bet. Look up and you'll see several monitors attached to ceiling rails. They're labeled. Should be easy to figure out which one's blue force, even for a Navy guy. All you have to do is turn it on. Why? Who are you expecting? Trouble?"

Julio swallowed hard. Chief Duncan might hold the highest security clearance, but Julio didn't know that for sure. He wouldn't break protocol by revealing the whereabouts of missing plutonium. "Thank you, sir, but I'm not at liberty to say. Please contact Senator Sullivan at your earliest convenience. Tell him where I am, and what you know. He'll explain."

"Copy that," Trevor asked without questioning. "Watch the sky, Juarez. We'll be bringing the rain. And, oh, by the way... If you truly love my sister like you said you did when you thought you were dying, you'd better make dammed sure you live. She'll kick my ass if you don't."

"Yessss," Julio hissed, smiling through his teeth. "I intend to."

Chapter Thirty-One

Meg sought refuge in the tight, cramped quarters where Marta and Craig had arranged a giant slumber party the night before. Not that every night since they'd boarded the carrier hadn't been a similar party. Meg had yet to hear from Captain Dooley as to Julio and Hotrod's current location, their final destination, or if they were already on their way back. Her nerves were strung tight. She'd always hated waiting. It wasn't in her nature. She was a woman of action, not sitting around worrying. Hearth fires, bah!

Just after Hotrod and Julio left, Corpsman Giacomo had stopped by with a paper plate full of Rice Krispie treats he'd made for the kids. That was sweet. Corpsman Shaw came with him, with a bag of simple toys for the kids. While all those things were more than generous, they also filled these tight quarters and created more chaos than Meg could deal with. She'd lived in tents the past year, in the wide-open remote

Highlands of Minas Gerais, where a person could breathe. She had cabin fever now. Yet ditching responsibility wasn't an option.

Dom was still in sickbay, but even without Pepe, Meg still had Maria, Joachim, Phillipe, Pedro, and the littlest ones, Trino, Mikel, and Frederick, all boys. Seven children were not much trouble. Not since Marta and Craig had taken on the majority of childcare. But Meg missed the Alcaldo brothers. Fernando and Joseph had always been so quiet. She wondered what they were doing. Maybe starting another orphanage? The Highlands of Minas Gerais could surely use one. Especially since Julio had freed all the enslaved villagers. Surely some adults had died in Oz's mines. Had they left children behind? Who would take care of those parentless kids now?

Meg licked her lips. Life shouldn't have to be so hard. But it was. Trevor once told her this life was only a test, and that death was like birth, just another doorway to further enlightenment. She didn't know how he'd gotten so wise, but she hoped he was right.

Because if he was, then Dom had passed through one heck of a doorway. After his brush with death, he seemed to enjoy being the center of attention now. Some kind person had turned three plastic hangars and a handful of inflated rubber gloves into a mobile of funny-faced animals that hung over his railed bed. Someone else, had to have been a female sailor, gifted Dom with a plush homemade, Minky, dimple-dotted quilt. Fringed with soft suede, it consisted of golden squares full of cartoon monkeys, bears, and lions.

Dom loved it. It had become what American boys and girls called *his blankie*. He whined if it wasn't nearby, and Meg loved the sound of that little boy's whine! He was finally acting like a normal kid. She couldn't wait until he pitched a genuine temper tantrum and shrieked his guts out. That'd be spectacular!

The little guy also had a collection of three Navy ballcaps and one round, white, cloth sailor cap, all presents from doting sailors. He still slept most of the day, but his cheeks were actually filling out a little and his color had improved. Not by much, but Meg could tell he felt better. His eyes were brighter, and if she had anything to say about it, he would live a long, happy life.

If only she knew where Julio was and what he was up to, everything would be perfect.

"Time for a walk about," Craig declared all of a sudden in boisterous Portuguese. He slapped both hands to his chest. "Come on, kiddies. Let's see what else there is to see on this big, old boat."

A delighted squeal burst out of Maria. "It's a ship, Mr. Brunner! Captain says boats are little and ships are" —she stretched hers arms as far apart as she could— "really big."

Craig tapped his forehead with his fingers and rolled his eyes as if he'd forgotten. "By golly, I did it again, didn't I?"

"You did!" several children squealed along with Maria. "You did! You did! You forget. You always call a ship a boat!"

Meg smiled at the gentle way Craig had spun them up while he slid into his jacket. He was one of a kind, always willing to shepherd this little flock while the women cooked, cleaned up, or cleared out the clutter.

"Good idea," practical Marta said, now on her feet and hurrying to get everyone dressed for the windy weather currently lashing the deck. "Hurry now, children. Dress warm and don't forget your jackets!" As if they would ever forget the Navy jackets and silver lapel pins Captain Dooley himself had personally gifted each child. "Be sure to keep your heads down once you are up top, and don't forget to hold tightly onto each other. We wouldn't want anyone to blow away, would we? Maria, you hold Trino's hand. Joachim, take Michel. No? Okay then, Pedro, take Michel's hand, and Joachim, you hang onto Phillipe and Freddie."

"I not Fweddie," sweet little Frederick whined. "Me is Fwedwick."

"Oh, I'm so sorry!" she exclaimed even as one eyebrow arched with a titch of impatience. "I'll be sure to remember next time, okay, Frederick?"

He beamed up at her, his eyes bright. It looked like Marta had an admirer. A two-foot-tall admirer, but a fan nonetheless.

"The wind's not that bad, Mother," Craig reminded her. "Just a brisk breeze and a little rain. These kids are strong. Don't worry so much. We'll be fine."

"But the runway might be slippery, and they're so small," she blustered.

The kids squealed. "It's not a runway. It's a deck!"

Now Marta rolled her eyes. "Never mind. These children don't need to catch colds. Mind them well, husband."

He shot her a toothy grin. "Always, my dear wife. Now, for the love of God and all that is holy, get out of our way and let us go for our walk on the..." He paused, cupped a hand to his ear, and...

"Deck!" his seven miniature charges squealed, even little Frederick who had a good grip on Joachim.

Meg had slipped into her jacket by then and was diligently shepherding the children into the hall. At the next bulkhead, Captain Dooley intercepted them.

"May I speak with you in private, ma'am?" he asked her.

She looked over her shoulder to Craig.

"Ah, go on," he said as he waved her away. "Me and the little ones'll be fine. We're going to have fun, aren't we, darlings?"

"And I'm helping!" eight-year-old Maria piped up, her cheeks flushed with excitement and her eyes bright as she pulled toddler Trino along as fast as his short legs could go.

"That you are," Craig replied. "Everyone! Hold hands now. Follow me, my little blue ducklings. We are off on an adventure!"

Meg smiled as Craig strode past Captain Dooley, the children chattering like little magpies at his heels. Craig was one in a million. Like Julio. She could see him doing the exact same thing and with just as much gusto. Her chest expanded with a heartfelt sigh. Man, she loved that guy.

"Yes?" she said as she turned back to the ship's captain.

Dooley was not the only O-6 grade officer on this carrier, but it had become quickly apparent to Meg that his men and women held him in high regard. He was their captain. Corpsman Giacomo never mentioned him without passing along some hidden compliment or praise.

Dooley stood straight as an arrow at well over six feet. At first glance, he was just another guy, but one look into those piercing hazel eyes, and a person knew different. This was a powerful, intelligent man who commanded one of America's most magnificent displays of national strength and pride, a multi-million-dollar floating city, equipped with the most technologically advanced, state of the art war-fighters.

Dressed sharply in his khaki-colored captain's work uniform and jacket, he bowed his head to her in quick acknowledgment of respect. The beige turtleneck collar under his work shirt belied the practicality of the man, while the high and tight cut beneath his Captain's cap demanded respect.

"We've received word about Hotrod and Agent Juarez from Fort Campbell," he said without his customary courteous preamble.

She canted her head at information that didn't make sense. Why had Julio gone to Kentucky? Was that where Doctor Hazelton demanded they go? Or was he already on another mission? Her heart skipped a beat. "And?"

Captain Dooley's hazel eyes softened. "There's been an accident aboard the Blackhawk, ma'am. All on board are safe and accounted for. As far as we know, everyone's in decent condition."

"Decent?" she asked. "What...? How...? Were they attacked?"

"Yes and no." He took firm hold of her wrist then, steering her through another bulkhead and farther away from where her children lived. Farther from Craig and Marta. "Senator Sullivan asked me to secure you for the duration of our voyage."

"Senator Sullivan? Secure m-me? Why? I have work to do. Kids to care for. I can't... Oh, my God. Are you taking me to the brig?"

He tossed her a half-smile at that. "No, ma'am, but I am placing you under armed guard for the duration of this exercise. Would you mind spending the rest of your time on board in sickbay? I know a little boy who thinks you're his mother. In fact, he's been calling for you today."

"How do you know what's going on in sickbay?"

That half-smile again. "It's a captain's job to know what his crew and passengers need. Trust me. Dominic needs you now."

But Meg needed something, too. "What happened to Hotrod and Agent Juarez? Are they safe?"

"You mean Julio?"

She nodded vigorously, afraid if she said anything more, she'd reveal too much.

"Yes, they're both safe. The Blackhawk is damaged, so they're spending the evening on an island off the coast of northern Brazil. But rest easy. Rescue is in transit, and, if all goes as planned, Hotrod and Juarez won't be there long. As you know, Julio works for Senator Sullivan. That makes him a high-value target, and, knowing what we know now, that makes you a target as well."

Me? A target?

Dooley nodded at the two young men standing at attention and sporting rifles outside sickbay. Navy military police were called Masters-at-Arms. Both were young and wore the same khaki working uniform as their captain, except for the cloth badges affixed above the name tapes on the right side of their shirts. Both second class petty officers, they looked too young to be armed like they were. Yet Meg could tell by the strict way they addressed their captain they were serious professionals.

"But... Wait!" Locking her knees, she stymied forward progression, which brought Dooley's stern gaze back to her.

"Yes, ma'am?"

"Why am I a high-value target? Who's out to get me? I'm just a foreign aid-worker."

His lips pinched. "Because you're connected to Agent Juarez. Don't deny it. I noticed the connection the second you two landed on my deck. This is just a precaution, because if I noticed it, someone else might have noticed it, too."

Well, that was disconcerting. She nodded, aware just how discerning Captain Dooley was. She hadn't even really noticed him until now. She and Julio were closer now than they'd been that first day they'd landed. Could Dooley tell that, too? "So?"

Instead of answering, he segued to, "What do you know about Matryoshka Dolls?"

"Nesting dolls? Umm, I've got a couple sets. My brothers have been all over the world. They're always bringing knick-knacks back for me." Why was that worthless trivia important?

"Not those kinds of dolls," Dooley grumbled, as, once more, he ushered her along and into sickbay. Nodding at the armed guards, he sealed the door behind him and shut them out. "I meant the subversive, all-female mafia out of Kazakhstan, formerly a Soviet republic, now home base for the bratva."

Meg swallowed hard. Every military member knew the various terrorist groups around the world, including the exceedingly wealthy *bratva*, aka the notoriously brutal Russian mafia, also known as Solntsevskaya. The bratva controlled much of the crime, not only in Russia, but in the Ukraine, Denmark, Netherlands, Czech Republic, the UK, France, Spain, Africa, Australia, and too many other countries. They'd recently arrived in New York City, and had immediately sent their soldiers into the streets to attack NYC police officers and other first responders.

But Matryoshka Dolls? They must be new. "I've never heard of those kinds of dolls before."

Dooley motioned her to the recliner positioned alongside Dom, who was sound asleep. Oddly, Corpsmen Giacomo and Shaw were missing. There was no one else in sickbay but Meg and the captain.

He pulled up a rolling, swivel stool and straddled it, facing her. "I understand you held top-secret clearance while you served in the Army."

She nodded. "Yes, I handled some intelligence. Very little, though. Mostly I was back-up for Lieutenant Underwood. He was the official intel guy."

"Well, you're not in the Army now, and that clearance no longer applies. But Senator Sullivan authorized me to read you in and share what little we know." Dooley flicked his fingertips against his pant leg, as if ridding himself of an invisible piece of lint. "We believe Doctor Hazelton is an undercover agent working for the Matryoshkas. She's recently been to Smolensk, as well as Minsk, both hotbeds of Matryoshka activity. While her legal name in the United Kingdom is Barbara Hazelton, we now know there is no Barbara Hazelton, at least not a thirty-four-year-old blonde who lives in London. The real Barbara Hazelton died on Rhode Island in 1979. The woman with Agent Juarez and Walker is Eva Bell. Yet even that name is misleading. Her parents were Russian immigrants who immigrated to England in the early nineties. Her real name, the name she was given at birth, was Eva Prostakov. Do you know what sleeper agents are?"

"Of course. They're spies, operatives living in targeted foreign countries, some as young children. Their parents are the actual agents, but they indoctrinate their kids to perform as double-agents, too. On the outside, these families appear normal. But inside, they're assassins waiting for orders to strike."

"Exactly. Eva Bell's parents were two such Russian immigrants, Elena and Sacha Prostakov. Soon after they arrived in England, they applied for citizenship, denounced their Russian citizenship, and changed their last name to Bell. They'd brought one daughter with them when they arrived, four-year-old Eva. For thirteen years, they lived in Aldershot, southwest of London. When she turned seventeen, Eva came to America for her engineering degree, then returned to England to work for the UK's Proliferation and Nuclear Policy Institute."

"And now she's on the helo with Julio and Hotrod."

His lips pinched. "Exactly."

Meg took hold of Dom's limp little hand, thankful for the small comfort touching him offered. She could barely swallow. "Is she still alive?"

"Yes. She's been neutralized for now, unfortunately, not until after she tried to kill Hotrod. According to Sullivan, once they're retrieved and off that island, Agent Juarez has been charged to immediately return her to FBI Headquarters in Washington, D.C."

"I see." Well, that figured. There went Meg's plans for Julio's return party. Darn Senator Sullivan and darn that liar, Hazelton. "But the FBI? Not CIA?"

Dooley shook his head. "No. Sorry, there's more."

God, what else?

Drawing in a deep breath that did nothing to calm her nerves, he said, "Someone sabotaged the Blackhawk that went down near Buckingham Palace last week. Thirteen Green Berets were killed. All evidence points to that saboteur being Hotrod. The Bureau is assisting in that investigation."

Meg shook her head vehemently. "Was he even there?"

"No, but a SEAL like him wouldn't need to be, would he?"

"He's a former SEAL? Uh uh. Not Hotrod. He's Army, a Nightstalker pilot. He wouldn't do such a thing. Who told you that?"

Dooley's lips pursed. "His Navy record. What else?"

"I don't believe that. He can't be Navy."

"Why not?"

"Because..." She blinked, no longer sure what she knew.

He cocked his head. "Be very careful what you say next, Miss Duncan. We're not in the States, and anything you say can and will be used against you. Not by me, though. You can trust me. Just don't talk about this with anyone else. This is top-secret. You never know who's listening."

A shiver raced up her spine. "I won't."

"Good. So, tell me. Have you known Hotrod long enough that you're willing to put your reputation, possibly your life, on the line to save his?" Dooley sat there expectantly waiting, his hazel eyes so sharp they seemed to be boring holes in her skull.

"I just met him," she qualified, "but Hotrod seems so... legitimate. So honest. He helped Julio and me destroy the army that was trying to steal the plutonium from Hazelton, err, Eva Bell, and Charlie Brown, umm, err, Gregor Jorgensen." Man, it was getting hard to keep track of everyone.

"Go on."

Meg explained how she, Julio, and Hotrod had hidden high in the trees where they could easily launch rockets across the pit into the invading soldiers. How she'd gotten sick, and how Hotrod had taken the initiative to leave the cover of those trees, approach the warzone, make sure it was clear, then coordinate a safe exfil back to the Blackhawk. He'd looked so good. So brave. How could a man like him be guilty of sabotage? Not that he wasn't qualified to do such a thing, but, no. Meg shook her head. She couldn't imagine such a thing. Not Hotrod.

"So, in your limited experience with a man you've worked with *once*" —Dooley emphasized that word to belittle her— "you're willing to vouch for a man like Walker Judge?"

"Who?"

"Hotrod's real name is Walker Judge, ma'am. He's the disavowed Navy SEAL currently convicted of murdering his commanding officer in San Diego. There's a nation-wide manhunt to locate him. The bastard's on the FBI's most wanted top ten, and he had the nerve to show up on my Goddamned ship."

Meg sat back in her seat with a breathy, "He's what?" American news didn't often reach the forests in the Highlands of Minas Gerais. Not that a story about a disavowed Navy SEAL would've meant anything to her if it had. She'd been too busy caring for her kids to worry about the outside world's problems.

Dooley nodded, but no satisfaction glimmered in his hazel eyes. He looked down at the floor. Shook his head. Then lifted his chin and looked into Meg's face again. "That's right. Somehow, Walker learned how to fly a Blackhawk, and he's impersonating a Nightstalker pilot. Or, worst-case scenario, some stupid flyboy aided and abetted him. But now, he's put me and my ship at risk. You see, I've worked with the man before. I should've recognized him the moment he landed, but I didn't. Not that he introduced himself like he damned well should've, or stuck around much while I was on deck. I've worked with the son-of-a-bitch on more ops than I care to mention. Some I can't talk about. And I still didn't recognize him."

"So, you're telling me Julio is stranded out there with a Russian spy and a murderer? Oh, and that Walker Judge is not only guilty of murdering his CO, but sabotaging another Blackhawk that caused the deaths of thirteen Green Berets? Anything else? Treason, maybe?" This whole story seemed so bizarre.

His eyes turned from golden hazel to a deadly dark brown. "No, ma'am. I'm telling you Julio now has one helluva warrior at his six. Least he will have, as soon as Walker wakes up."

That sounded a lot like pride. "Wait a minute. What?"

"Unfortunately, Hazelton got off a shot that tranquilized Walker. Ketamine. But as God is my witness, Walker never sabotaged that helo in London, and he didn't kill his CO either. Don't ask me how I know. I just do."

Chapter Thirty-Two

Hotrod came to with amazing alacrity. One minute he was out cold, his head leaned against the interior wall beside the co-pilot's seat, right where Julio had left him. The next, he'd jerked out of his harness, was up on his feet and grinning, as steady as if he'd never been knocked out or belly up.

"Where?" he bit out as, quickly and with practiced precision, he took in the fact that his bird was now landed and Hazelton was cuffed. As well as both closed side doors and the faint light glimmering behind the pilot seat from a single overhead bulb.

"Off the northern coast of Brazil, *Chief,*" Julio replied easily.

He'd remembered where he knew Hotrod from, just wished Hotrod had told him up-front who he was instead of finding out the hard way. He'd gone through Hotrod's wallet, checking for anything that might identify a medical condition, just in case. What Julio found was Hotrod's California driver's license and his real name. Walker Judge. As in Navy SEAL Lieutenant Walker Judge from SEAL Team 18, the fugitive on the run. Which was why Julio taunted him with that Chief designation now. "I'd tell you more, but then I'd have to kill you. Unless there's something you want to tell me first."

"I didn't do it," Walker growled as he ran a quick hand over his head and through what little hair was there. The man didn't look anything like the SEALs Julio had worked with. He was too neat. Too tucked in and too proper. Too good. If anything, he looked like a bright, shiny candidate for OTS. *Officer Training School.*

Julio was sitting opposite the spy formerly known as Barbara Hazelton. Slowly, not wanting to startle a man with Walker's specific skill set, he leaned forward and put both palms flat on his knees. He knew Walker's story. Who didn't? It'd been all over the news for months. After a bungled trial where the Navy's own Naval Criminal Investigation Service had coerced contrived confessions out of Judge's girlfriend, her neighbor, then two pansy-assed sailors who'd served with Walker, the Navy convicted him without evidence, of murdering his commanding officer with his bare hands.

Not that he wasn't strong enough or trained specifically to do something like that. Julio was certain Walker most certainly could. That was what SEALs did, what they were trained to do. But this particular

Navy prosecutor had gone out of his way to indict Walker when all evidence had proved otherwise. Julio had read the full brief and every last word of trial transcripts. The politically-minded prosecutor had willfully ignored valid witnesses and had continually overturned evidence that would have proved, without a shadow of doubt, that Judge hadn't been at the scene of the crime. In fact, not once had he stepped foot inside or gone near Commander Goff's residence where the murder had taken place. Ever.

His CO wasn't known for cozy gatherings at his lavish home on Ocean Beach, much less a get together that had ever included an invite for Walker. It was common knowledge among the teams that Goff and Walker had never seen eye-to-eye. So what? That happened when alpha males worked together. They'd argued, yes, but not once had anyone come forward with proof or evidence that Walker had ever been violent with Goff. Nada. Zip.

Never mind that the prosecutor's office had willfully wiretapped Judge's attorney's office and home phones, or that NCIS had intercepted Walker's attorney's legal assistant's emails. In the end, the political powers that commandeered the Navy got what they'd wanted. They'd stripped Walker of his Trident and sentenced him to fifty years hard time in Leavenworth. They ruined his life. His girlfriend dumped him a week after the verdict came out, during a less than spectacular interview with TMZ, during which she claimed he couldn't perform. Every last word she spewed sounded like spiteful revenge porn to Julio.

Interestingly, Walker had been shackled, cuffed, and bound for Leavenworth, Kansas, when the two Navy guards transporting him contracted a bad case of food poisoning. It occurred during a refueling stop between the rental car agency and Leavenworth. No, really. The van they'd rented ran out of gas in the middle of flat-as-hell Nowhere, Kansas. The bug they'd contracted turned out to be E Coli. Julio wondered how and precisely where they'd picked that up. He also wondered why the rental agency hadn't topped off the tank of their rental vehicle before they'd signed it out.

So many things didn't add up. But the truth was that Walker Judge, a highly trained, highly decorated Navy SEAL had simply walked away from the rest stop while his guards were knelt over, too busy worshipping their private porcelain gods. Which made it extremely interesting that Walker had deliberately come to Brazil now to assist Senator Sullivan. That he worked out of Fort Campbell, Kentucky, as an Army Nightstalker pilot, no less. Those were both highly visible military occupations. Surely someone, somewhere, had questioned his identity, his qualifications, or worse, recognized him. Had the world gone bat shit crazy? Or was Walker just that good at this undercover business?

Since Julio thrived in the same dog-eat-dog black ops world, he had to admit that Walker had an oblique way of gliding through most crowds without drawing attention to himself. That was because he kept his head down and didn't make eye contact. Despite the fact that he was a reasonably good-looking man, he dressed in plain, every day clothing or uniforms that matched the service members working around him. He blended in, never stood out. Seemed to have no ego. Like a man with a bounty on his head.

"Let me guess," Julio said without a hint of sarcasm. "You work for Sullivan, too."

There went Walker's hand again. Scraping over his head and through his military cut, light brown hair. Down the back of his taut, shaven neck. The wrinkles etched deep on his forehead gave him away. Every action he took now revealed a man poised to run. Or fight. His shoulders were slanted, his fists positioned to strike, and his boots were primed for quick retreat. Unfortunately, there was no way off this narrow strip of sand.

"Can we talk? Somewhere else?" he asked, nodding that big chin of his at Hazelton.

Julio nodded to the side window. "It's not a very big sandbox. We'll have to be quick. I'm expecting visitors."

For the first time, Walker noticed the blip on the blue force monitor. "Who are you waiting for?"

"Not them, but I'm afraid *they* are waiting for me. And now you. It's good you woke up."

Walker's sharp blue eyes scrolled past Julio to the still unconscious woman sprawled across the aisle, her head tipped back, her mouth open and snoring. Not a pretty sight. But hey, she'd had a lot of dental work done. Julio was fairly certain she'd had a nose job, too.

"What'd you give her?"

"A shot of her own medicine, after a double-tap from my nine-millimeter."

"God damn, she's a tough broad. You shot her and she's still alive?"

Julio shrugged. "It was me or her. I won. But she was also wearing tactical armor. I took it off in case she comes to and decides to die fighting."

"Thank God. What'd she hit me with?"

"Horse tranq." Julio pulled the two remaining cartridges of Ketamine out of his jacket pocket. "The same thing I also gave her."

"You suspected her then, too?"

"From the moment I met her, yes. She has certain tells." Julio glanced at Hazelton. "She licks her top lip when she lies. Like a snake. She wrinkles her nose. I'm certain she wears glasses when she's not on a job."

"Where's her piece?"

"Her tranquilizer pistol is in the Atlantic along with her tactical plates. But these" —he gave Walker one of the hypos— "I kept. You should keep it in a safe place. We may yet need it."

Walker nodded as he tucked the hypo inside his jacket pocket. "Where's the plutonium?"

Julio shrugged. "As far as I know, in the four crates she brought on board."

"Did you check? Are you sure?"

"No, I've been a little busy making certain we didn't land in the ocean. You're welcome to check."

Walker shook that suggestion off. "Nah. I don't care. Not like anyone would believe me. My word's worthless."

As hard as that was to hear, Julio agreed. Walker's word wouldn't stand up in a court of law, not since he'd escaped his guards on his way to Leavenworth. But none of what happened in the past mattered now. To make sure Hazelton was still out cold, Julio double-checked her cuffs, then thumbed one of her eyelids up and open. The whites of her eyes were red, and her pupils were dilated, nearly all black. Only when he was certain Hazelton wasn't going anywhere, did he follow Walker Judge outside.

Sliding the helo's door closed behind him, Julio stepped far enough from the helo that Hazelton couldn't hear them if she was, somehow, not as unconscious as she looked. He wouldn't put anything past her.

The wind had died down, and the sun had set an hour ago. There were no stars or moon in the sky, and the only light within miles was the dim overhead lamp in the helo. But this conversation had better be quick. The sub, or whatever that GPS blip was, was less than ten miles off shore. Julio had no way of knowing whether they were the Matryoshka Dolls, some poor fisherman who'd gotten lost, or if those Dolls had a man in a skiff headed his way.

"It was a set-up," Walker bit out. "God damn, I'm tired of running, but they won't let me be!"

"How can you be working for the Army if you're a convicted felon? Why are you even here?"

"Your buddy Sullivan. He knows people. He made it happen. And I'm here for the same reason you are. To assist Meg Duncan. Sullivan had to work a lot of damage control once she reached out for her buddy, Charlie Brown, and involved Army Rangers. Which is why he activated me, to keep a lid on CB. But I'm not worried about CB. He and I go way back. Until now, I've been flying mostly reconnaissance, easy-ins and easy-outs. Hot exfils. You know what I'm talking about."

Julio nodded. "The kind where no one cares or notices who's flying the helo, as long as they get in and out without being shot down. No one questions the man behind a helmet. But the press is laying for you. Surely someone has identified you. People talk."

"Yeah, well, you know as well as I do the best place to hide is in plain sight. I changed my name, and Sullivan inserted me at Fort Campbell with the Nightstalkers. Who'd ever think to look for me there? So what if I *look*" —he bracketed that word with air quotes— "like somebody else? Everyone's got a doppelgänger. People ask. They tell me I look just like, well, me. But so far I've been able to laugh it off and go on with what I'm doing."

"You also wear dark glasses. Helmets with visors. You cut your hair. You shaved."

"Yeah. That." Walker ran that same hand over his head yet again. Here in the dark, he radiated enough angst to power a small country. He looked thinner than Julio remembered. Now that he wasn't hiding behind dark glasses, the black circles under his eyes were more prominent. He licked his lips. This guy was running on empty. It showed. "To be honest, this was supposed to be my last job. Charlie knows how to pilot a Blackhawk. He's been training. He would've brought Meg and you back, but when we got wind of Hazelton's con—"

"Are you positive you can trust him?"

Walker nodded. "Charlie makes three. Only others are Sullivan and you."

"Captain Dooley doesn't know?"

"Not yet."

"You were going to stay in Brazil, weren't you? You weren't going back to the States."

Another nod. Another sweep of his palm over his head, his frustration boiling over. "The plan was for Charlie to fly back and tell everyone he'd recognized me, that we fought, that I tried to kill him, but he killed me first. But when he saw the size of that fire, the plan changed. He radioed me while I was back at the helo with Meg. Thought it'd be more final if everyone believed I went down in that fire, that I'd been burned alive. He figured a gruesome death would make NCIS happy, that they'd stop looking for me. I can't live like this anymore, Juarez. I served my country with honor for twenty Goddamned years. Don't you get it? I'm not going to prison for something I didn't do!"

"I do get it, Walker. I do," Julio replied quietly. "But you need to know that you're not alone, Chief. There are many of us military and former military who are on your side. We believe you. Many patriotic civilians believe in you, too. We never trusted the press. They're all liars spewing political propaganda that will eventually destroy our country and every good man who stands for it. They're out for nothing but greed and power."

"Great," Walker hissed. "All that adoration and a quarter won't buy me a fuckin' cup of coffee, much less keep me out of Leavenworth."

"But you have no familia? No one who'd cry for you if they thought you'd died?"

Walker shook his head. "I wouldn't have gone along with this cop-out if I did."

That was beyond sad. It was tragic, and it made Julio's decision easy. "Then we will prove they're liars. Eventually, we'll find a way to clear your name. We'll set you free. But Hazelton wasn't running a con, Walker. She's part of a subversive Russian mob known as the Matryoshka Dolls. She stole the plutonium for them. Most likely, she has a buyer, and I believe that buyer is headed to this island right now. Chief Warrant Officer Trevor Duncan has sent assistance, but they're late. They were supposed to have been here thirty minutes ago."

"Who?" Walker's head nearly canted onto his shoulder. "Trevor's on his way? He's coming here? Great! God, I mean, shit! That's the best news I've heard all year!" His cocky smile was back. "Trevor's always late. Trust me, if he said he'd send help, then he's on his way. He'll be here."

"That would be nice," Julio admitted even as he drew both pistols, his gaze now intent on the dark, roiling surf beyond Walker. Without making eye contact, he tossed one handgun, grip first, to his only ally. "Because we have company, *amigo.*"

Chapter Thirty-Three

Meg was alone in her private quarter. Earlier, she'd left sleepy Dom with Corpsman Giacomo when he'd finally been allowed back into sickbay. Guess not even the captain of the ship could keep med tech's away from their patients for long. Luke had been kind and attentive as he'd checked Dom's vitals, then asked Dom what he'd wanted for dinner. Luke had also asked questions, but Meg hadn't felt like making small-talk. So she'd retreated to where she'd spent the night with Julio. Unfortunately, he wasn't here now, and she needed him. He'd know what to do.

Blindsided by the fact that Hotrod was really Navy SEAL Walker Judge, she still wasn't certain why Dooley had confided in her. Searching for that answer, and because she'd lost touch with current events across the world during the past year, Meg signed onto her room's laptop and went online. She'd spent the last two hours researching Walker Judge, reading everything she could find on his short trial, his lawyer's lengthy brief, even Judge's request for an Inspector General investigation into Commander Goff's life and death.

Navy SEAL, check.

Various commendations and medals, wow, check.

Nearly twenty years serving his country, check.

No wife. Both parents deceased. No sisters. One brother KIA three years ago in Yemen. Check and triple-check.

Reading the details of that KIA stabbed Meg's heart. She couldn't imagine one of her brothers being killed in action, or getting that kind of notification. His brother's death had to have been tough on Walker. Yet everything she found pointed to an honorable man following in the footsteps of his father, grandfather, and great-grandfather. His brother had also been Navy. It was very apparent that Walker had always known what he wanted to do with his life.

According to his lawyer's brief on the trial, he had an exemplary service record, which Meg had already substantiated. Yet Navy brass had consistently ignored that record and the medals for heroism, above and beyond the call of duty, that they themselves had awarded him. The JAG prosecutor had blatantly disregarded Walker's constitutional right to a fair trial. NCIS, through well-timed, albeit illegal, leaks to dishonest reporters, tried him in the public eye. Even the men and women selected as peers in his jury, had been hand-picked by Navy brass.

So unfair.

The more she read, the more unanswered questions Meg had, and the more she believed something was fundamentally wrong with the top echelon in the Navy. Not only that, but not once had Meg gotten any off-color, quirky vibes from Hotrod, err, Walker Judge. True, she'd just met him a couple days ago, but after growing up with four belligerent brothers, she was usually a good judge of male character.

Walker Judge was the real deal and a hardened warrior. He was like Julio and Trevor. He could've been that face on Navy recruiting posters. Walker fit the profile. He was one of those rare breeds that ran into trouble, not away from it. He was a warrior for good, a bulwark against evil. So what if he liked to rough-house and had gotten into a few brawls over his career? Wasn't that what Navy SEALs did? Even if it wasn't, Meg didn't care. She'd liked Walker the moment she'd met him.

The problem seemed to lie within the military's criminal justice system. The UCMJ, Uniform Code of Military Justice, was uniquely different from its brother, the civilian justice system. UCMJ had its own body of laws, and military tribunals were supposed to interpret, enforce, and protect those laws. They were supposed to be impartial and fair. They were supposed to be founded on truth.

Yet Meg knew all about those sanctimonious military tribunals. If some pompous general or admiral wanted a lower-ranking lackey in Leavenworth—*wham, bam, yes, sir, it's done.* Good men and women didn't stand a chance against the butt-kissing and rule-bending that went on behind closed Navy and Army doors these days. Not unless they were wealthy and could afford good lawyers. Even then, those lawyers had better watch their backs. God help anyone who didn't kiss the right ass in this highly-charged political climate.

But now, a head pounding case of eye-strain had set in. Meg couldn't see straight. She needed a break.

Pushing away from the desk, she turned the swivel chair around and smiled at the unmade bed across the room. Luscious memories of being with Julio in that bed warmed her now. There in the dark, she welcomed them. Her shoulders lifted. She shivered remembering the way he'd nuzzled her neck and kissed her fingertips. Her lips. His mouth had been warm, wet, and seductive. Yet always gentle. Even as driven as he'd been when they'd first lost control together, he'd never been rough or selfish. He'd made certain she'd been pleasured first. She was pretty sure he'd made her purr like a cat, too.

He'd been so careful, almost reverent in their lovemaking. That alone was a new sensation, being treated with love. Over and over, he'd proved to her with his body that there were still trustworthy, humble men in the world. With every beat of her heart, Meg believed in Julio. She trusted him to come back to her. He'd promised. But he wasn't returning tonight, that much was sure. Not if he and Walker were stuck on some island with a busted helo and that snake, Hazelton.

"I knew she wasn't who she said she was," Meg told the empty bed. That almost made her smile. Those two, tough, macho guys had been brought low by a blonde bimbo with long legs. Meg wished she were a fly on the wall inside the Blackhawk. They had to be embarrassed.

But what was Julio doing now? Was he thinking of her? Was he remembering their night and day of passion, sex, and a couple gloriously fun, romantic showers? Her ex, Ted Jeurgen, had always rushed to shower after they'd made love. He'd been a clean-freak. Which explained why he'd deserted Meg in her hour of need. God knew stroke patients were too messy for a man with OCD issues. At least that was what Meg believed. It was never that Ted didn't love her. He'd just loved himself more. Even that didn't hurt like it used to. She'd moved past worrying what she'd done wrong with Ted. At last, she was healing. Letting go.

Because Julio was most definitely—Not. Ted. And he knew things about her partially-paralyzed body that Meg hadn't expected. Like where his fingertips could draw the most delicious shivers out of her. Like when to ease back and just hold onto her while she exploded into stars. Like how to balance his weight and hers while he pumped into her in the shower. Like how to smile...

That man had the most beautiful smile. It lit up his entire face, and it smoothed away the sadness in his eyes. All those rugged angles softened. She loved making him smile.

Between his dark eyes, dark hair, and those breathtaking lips, she didn't know which part of Julio she liked best. There were so many choices. His wide chest, sprinkled with just enough hair to tickle her fingertips when she smoothed her palms over his pecs. The way he licked his lips, and the salacious gleam in his eyes when she'd undressed in front of him. The sound of him groaning in her ear, murmuring his 'I love yous.' The spicy, clean scent of his skin. The feel of his ridges and muscles. That scratchy five o'clock shadow. Those splendid washboard abs that led straight to her idea of heaven on earth.

Meg shook her head, amazed at how her life had changed. When she'd left Texas a year ago, she'd been depressed and looking for one last fight. She'd been down, feeling useless, and totally absorbed in her own problems. She'd thought she'd needed to prove herself, that she could still be a warrior. A tough girl. Like brash, take-no-back-talk Corporal Duncan.

Now that she looked over the past year, it was easier to see how much she'd been like Ted. Self-absorbed. Focused on all the wrong things. But now she was different, all because she'd found another family to love. In finding those orphans, she'd also found her real self. Better yet, she'd found the best reason for living—for someone else.

Meg pulled to her feet and walked to the bed. Sighing, she sank into the blankets and pillows that still smelled like Julio. She wrapped her arms around herself, imagining he was hugging her. When he came back, she'd be waiting. Maybe not here on the *Iwo Jima*, but somewhere.

She promised.

Chapter Thirty-Four

Silently, Julio climbed into the Blackhawk and flipped off the single overhead light while Walker made himself useful. Since Julio hadn't disarmed him, Walker had already handed Julio's pistol back. He didn't need it, not since he still carried two SIG pistols, a seven-inch blade sheathed on the holster low on his right thigh, along with a compact Ruger with a laser-scope on that same holster.

The man had transformed from an anxious fugitive from justice, into a skilled and lethal operator. He'd pulled a modified, bolt-action SOCOM MK-13 rifle out of an overhead compartment. With practiced ease, he checked the chamber, popped the tremendous scope cover, and said, "I don't suppose you kept your lazy ass busy while I was out cold."

"Had to do something, Sleeping Beauty," Julio replied evenly, pocketing two more mags for his Beretta. A flare gun in case Trevor finally showed. An

Ontario MK 3, six-inch, stainless steel blade, aka Navy SEAL standard issue knife. "Couldn't take a nap. You snore like a pig."

Walker ignored the dig as he handed another SOCOM MK-13 rifle to Julio. "Don't suppose that something included fireworks."

Without making eye contact, Julio accepted the heavy sniper rifle with a shrug. "I thought our visitors would deserve a warm welcome," he said as he checked the weapon's chamber, sighted the scope to make sure its laser was active, then slung its strap over one shoulder. This weapon was similar to the rifle Chris Kyle had used, minus a few modifications. It would do.

Still digging for something far back in the overhead compartment, Walker muttered, "I'll take the north end of this sandbox. You didn't set any explosives there, did you?"

"Not yet, but take cover behind the tree. It's skinny but so are you. It'll work while I draw the Dolls in. Hope you aren't squeamish about shooting women." Julio slapped a full mag into the pistol that would go into his left holster. Later. For now it rested in his right gloved palm.

"Not if they're shooting at me." Walker jerked a tightly-packed black backpack out of the compartment. "Or if they're decked out in suicide vests. Always hated bitches who hide behind kids."

"Or when they rigged their babies with explosives." At the angst that reality recalled, Julio turned to face his friend. "Be safe. America needs men like you."

That earned him a grunt. By then, both men were geared up and ready. Walker slung the backpack over one shoulder and reached out a hand. "Been good working with you, Juarez."

That sounded a lot like goodbye. Julio took hold of Walker, but instead of shaking his gloved hand, he jerked Walker into a man-hug and slapped his back. "I meant what I said, *amigo*. America needs you. Don't let her down, and don't give up just because of a few assholes. We'll fight to the death for this plutonium now, then we'll fight harder to clear your name."

Walker didn't reply. Just grunted again as if nothing could save him. The political war he'd been caught up in had worn him down. Julio worried Walker might use this confrontation to do something stupid. Like die. Which made Walker the same as him the day he'd been willing to walk into the Pacific to please his dead wife. It made him stupid, but Julio understood. A man often did stupid things when faced with no reason to live. No way forward. Nothing but fighting a corrupt military system ahead.

Back then Julio had been as low as he'd ever been. He'd honestly believed he had nothing to live for. Somewhere in his mind he'd thought death by drowning would've pleased Bianca. She'd finally be happy with him. But in truth, Bianca had never loved him or Tomas as much as she'd loved herself. Julio knew it now that he'd met Meg.

Like sweet Dom, Meg had rescued him, a man who'd seen war and the world and who should not have needed rescuing. A man who should've known better. Unlike Bianca, who'd had everything handed to her throughout her life, Meg had less than nothing the day she'd marched into OZ Metallurgy Mining, Inc., to get her kids back. Yet she'd gone despite a serious impairment. She'd risked her life to save theirs, and she'd done the impossible. She'd spat in Orlando Zapata's ugly face, and she'd saved her children.

Meg Duncan was simply, utterly, the epitome of love. Because love, true, pure love, put others first and kept people alive. It reached out with sacrifice, and it pulled the lost and lonely wanderer away from the mesmerizing edge of self-destruction by serving them, instead of denigrating them. It made excuses for their sins and weaknesses, their failures. It offered hope instead of demanding compliance. Instead of demanding anything. All love wanted was what was best for others. It encouraged, not disparaged. It made little boys smile and grown men beat their chests and growl back at the heartless world, "I'm still here! And I will win! Not you!"

So, Julio didn't release Walker's hand when Walker shoved away from the personal contact like most guys. They were both wearing gloves. They were both hardened warriors who would soon take lives in the name of their country. But first and foremost, they were brothers.

"I will not let you die," Julio said, his grip firm and unyielding. Not willing to let Walker just pass through his life like a ship with no anchor. "Brothers fight for each other, and I promise. I will fight for you."

Walker finally lifted his chin and stared back. Better yet, he blinked. "I believe you," he replied, his voice strong and convincingly hard.

For the first time, Julio was peering into ice-blue eyes tinged with the bleak shadow of men who fully believed they were alone in the world. Who'd seen too much, done too much, and yet who still had a war to fight. To win. But Julio also saw the lie lurking there. Walker wasn't fooling him.

"I cannot save you if you won't accept my help, *amigo*."

Walker gave him his chin and broke contact. "I don't need saving, Juarez. Let's get this done, then you can psycho-analyze me all you fuckin' want on our way back to the carrier, or wherever the hell we're going." Reaching back into that overhead, he pulled out a couple NVGs. Night vision goggles. "Here. You'll need one of these."

But they were too late. A bullet splattered against the bullet-proof window, spider-webbing the clear shield. Walker jerked the opposite door open and was gone without another word. Julio secured the night vision goggles on his forehead, then unsnapped Hazelton's harness and let her drop to the floor. The dose of Special K in those hypos had obviously been intended to subdue a heavier man instead of a conniving, willowy woman. She'd be safer on the floor.

Sliding the door facing the direction of the gunshot open, Julio dropped to one knee, and activated the NVGs. Even the smallest hint of warm bodies now turned lime-green. The surf was dotted with blobs of lime-green, a dozen or so creeping on their hands and knees toward the Blackhawk like sneaky ninjas. All were armed with rifles or spear guns on their backs. All were also in black diving suits, their diving masks on top of their heads, and crouched low, as if they thought they were invisible.

Not anymore.

Tucking the sniper rifle into his shoulder, Julio laid down a burst of suppressive fire between him and the beach to cover Walker's retreat. The night was dark, but the three closest ninjas went down. The rest were now lime-green tinted zombies, still crawling forward but on their bellies now. Ducked behind the helo's open side door for cover, he watched for the length of a heartbeat as answering gunfire peppered the helo. Luckily, Blackhawks were armor-plated, bottom and sides. Doors too.

"Put your weapons down!" Julio yelled once the thunderous assault ended.

A harsh but definitely feminine voice came back to him. "Do you think we're stupid?"

Well, yeah. That had crossed his mind. Had to be the Dolls. Definite Russian accent. Definite alpha-bitch attitude.

Again, he twisted his upper torso into view and peppered the sand and surf, fully aware that the door at his rear was still open and unguarded. But trusting Walker to have his back. That was what brothers did.

He'd no more than entertained that sure knowledge, when a shot rang out and a single black diving-suit clad body fell through the door in question. The handgun in her hand fell out onto the sand while what was left of her landed inside the helo with a gurgling, "Ooomph!"

Extending one boot, Julio shoved the dead body out. He looked up just in time to see another shadow hunched low and creeping toward the helo from the same direction. He would've turned completely around, altered the angle of his aim to protect himself, and ended this assassin, too. But like before, a shot rang out and that Doll also went down.

Julio left the door open in case things got too hot and Walker returned.

Returning his attention to the other side of the helo, the side where he'd strafed the beach, he didn't care if these invaders were Dolls or not. They'd started the war. He meant to end it. With Walker on his six, he could.

Lowering his barrel, he sent another pulverizing spray at anyone stupid enough to be still on their hands and knees in the surf. One, two, then three and four more lime-green assassins succumbed in the water. But, as expected, a couple dark shadows had gotten in too close. They attacked from his left and right while he was still firing, his eye to his scope, and his peripheral off-line. Their arms and upper bodies appeared too quickly through the door.

One jerked his rifle as if she thought to simply pull it out of his hands. Not so. The barrel was hot, and diving gloves were not heat-resistant. That idiot cursed, but let go and backed off, shaking her hand as if that would slow the pain of third-degree burns.

The other brandished a long blade. He almost felt sorry for her when she took too long lifting the blade over her head. That was all the invitation Walker needed. Another shot vibrated through space and time. She arched backward, then folded to her knees with a drawn-out hiss of death. The blade must've been heavy. The top of it dug into the sand behind her, pulling her backward as she fell.

Several more Dolls succumbed while Walker cleared the shore, picking these overconfident females off, one by one. They still didn't seem to realize they were being targeted from somewhere other than inside the helo.

Julio punched the last shadow standing, the one with burned hands, in the throat. She went down hard, but he needed this one alive. Switching hands, he set his rifle aside and unholstered one of his Berettas. Tipping his upper body forward and out of the helo, he grabbed onto the assassin with the burned hand. She pitched a fit, and it took a full minute of wrestling to drag her inside. But in the end, she was no match for him. All it took was squeezing that burned hand and her stiffened knees went slack. She cried out a string of Russian curses.

Not like Julio cared. Swiftly, he jerked her inside and beyond the reach of her girlfriends. It took one solid whack with his pistol grip to her forehead, and that was that. She sagged face first to the floor. Good enough. Keeping an eye beyond the surf where these assassins had landed, he tugged another set of cuffs out of his jacket pocket and secured her to one leg of the metal bench seat once and for all. That put her far enough from Hazelton that they couldn't assist each other's escape if they happened to wake up too soon, which he doubted.

"If you move, I will kill you," he promised the sleeping murderers. "Please, senoritas. Try me."

It would've been better if he'd had a way to communicate with Walker. Julio would know what Walker was looking at then, and how many other Dolls he'd taken out besides those nearest the helo. Or if he'd been injured, was down, and needed help. The not knowing always worried Julio.

With two Dolls now subdued inside the helo, he stepped out into the night and onto the wet, packed sand, needing to see who was left. The several shapes sprawled in the foamy surf were definitely dead bodies. That two Dolls had gotten close enough to come at him from behind was disconcerting.

How many of these Russian assassins were there, and how had they gotten to shore? There were no RHIBs, *Rigid Hull Inflatable Boats,* bobbing beyond the never-ending breakers, that Julio could see. No chuffing whine of outboard motors came to him on the wind. Not anything. Which made him think submarine. Which made sense. A sub could've certainly lingered anywhere along the Brazilian coastline, close enough to have monitored Hazelton.

He stilled, relying on his years of training and experience to detect the slightest sound, even the rub of a body against sand. The quiet murmured command to kill. Another onslaught of ninja warriors—or worse. The screaming whine of surface-to-air missiles. The flash of rocket-propelled grenades.

But the only sounds that came to Julio were the ever-present crash of waves eating away at this sandbar, and then—*Gracias Dios!*—the far-off thwack-thwack-thwack of heavy-duty rotor blades. That had better be Chief Warrant Officer Trevor Duncan.

Still on high-alert and poised to defend himself from all sides, Julio secured the Blackhawk. He'd just closed both doors when a lightning bright spotlight stabbed through the darkness off shore and zeroed in on him.

A loudspeaker boomed. "That you, Agent Juarez? Permission to land."

He waved at the helo, sending a thumbs-up.

In seconds, the noisy rotors were kicking up dust, dirt, and stinging sand. Several geared-up, large-bodied guys fast-roped down to the beach, each sticking wicked three-point landings. Like sumo wrestlers, their hefty bodies landed in positions to action. While the helo banked sharply, circling the minute island in a tight spiral that grew larger with every blistering pass, two of the Rangers, or whoever they were, busied themselves searching the bodies in the surf and looking for others.

The third jogged straight for Julio. NVGs always made a warrior look like something out of a science fiction movie. Julio was surprised when this guy shoved his goggles up and revealed features similar to Meg's.

"Chief Duncan," he said, one gloved hand extended.

Duncan caught Julio's hand in what he undoubtedly meant to be a finger-crushing grip. It was always the same between warriors. The first man who flinched lost the time-honored battle of one-upmanship. "You must be Agent Juarez. I see you couldn't wait to get this party started."

"I had help," Julio replied, not blinking and matching that handshake with equal power.

"So I understand. Where is that son of a bitch Hotrod?" Duncan asked as he released his hold on Julio and looked past him to the helo. "Shit. Looks like you've been in a war."

"She's a little scraped," Julio admitted, looking over his shoulder, expecting Walker to materialize any minute now. Where was he? Couldn't he see that all was secure and that help had arrived? "Hotrod's undercover on the far end of this sandbar. I suspect he's hunkered down behind our one and only palm tree."

"You call that a tree?" Duncan waved one of the men who'd fast-roped down with him over. He gave curt instructions to get the two females inside ready for transport, then radioed the helo still circling above, and ordered it to prepare to take on four more passengers.

While Julio waited on Duncan, a sickening cramp clenched the pit of his stomach. "Excuse me, sir, but I'll be right back."

"I'll go with you," Duncan said, his tone as steady as if he did these kinds of exfils every day. Which he might. He was a Nightstalker.

With his Berettas still in hand, Julio set a quick pace to that scraggly tree, only to find nothing but expended brass shells littering the sand beneath it. No sign of Walker. Swallowing hard, he cast a searching stare back the way he and Duncan had just come. The helo rested at the opposite end of the island. Nothing lay between the tree and that bird. No way could Walker have gotten off this sandbar.

"Thought you said he was here?" Duncan asked, the blade of his hand pressed to his forehead as he stared at the waves rolling in.

Julio bit his bottom lip, no longer sure of anything where Walker was concerned. At last Julio found what he'd been searching for, a pair of boot prints in the wet sand, leading to the surf. Walker had done it again. He'd escaped.

Julio turned on Duncan. "Hotrod isn't who you think he is, Chief. He's really former Navy SEAL, Walker Judge."

Duncan's face turned to stone. "That bastard? You're shitting me."

Julio nodded, worried for the man somewhere out there on the volatile Atlantic Ocean. Where sharks, poisonous jellyfish, and other predators lurked. Worse, Walker was alone. That all by itself hurt Julio's heart. He could write a book on solitude.

"We need to send a team after him," Julio said to the black night.

"Not on my watch," Duncan muttered. "If Walker thinks he can make it to land without gear or brains, let him fuckin' try. Dumb bastard. Who gives a shit?"

"I do," Julio answered honestly. "Something is very wrong with the charges against him, and I believe him, Chief. Every person deserves a chance to prove his innocence. He needs our help. You have to go after him."

"No, I don't. For Christ's sake, read the news. That murderer's had more than his share of second chances. Now, are you staying, or are you coming with me? Because if you're smart, you'll get your ass on board. Decide now. We leave in five."

Like that was a choice? "Yes, sir," Julio replied, too tired to argue. *Like it or not,* "I'll be on that helo."

"Smart move," Duncan hissed. Yet as he turned and marched away, Julio could've sworn he murmured something that sounded a lot like, "You go, Hotrod. Give 'em hell."

Chapter Thirty-Five

Two days after Meg's conversation with Captain Dooley, Dom started eating on his own. Applesauce and pudding first. Then soup and toast. Weak tea. Rice and bananas. Luke suggested fresh air might help him recuperate quicker.

So that morning, Meg and her two armed guards were back in sickbay. While they took position in the hall, she dressed Dom in the new jeans, undershirt, and Navy t-shirt she'd bought him. Socks and cowboy boots, so small and cute that they brought tears to her eyes, completed his first set of real clothes, not castoffs. His Navy jacket and ballcap finished him off, and Dom was a new boy, ready to go up top. He still looked like one of those sickly Saint Jude's kids with his big dark eyes and nearly hairless head. But to Meg, he was her miracle baby. He looked just like her.

"Mum!" he squealed, pointing to where Marta, Craig, and the rest of the kids were now standing at sickbay's open door.

"You're ready to run like the wind, aren't you?" Meg asked him even as she bundled him in his favorite quilt. "But not yet." This boy had been through Hell. She wasn't going to let anything happen to him. If that meant carrying him until he was one hundred percent cured, she intended to do that.

"Look!" Maria cried. "He's smilin'!"

"Ah, baby, he smiles all the time now," Craig replied. "You just haven't seen him lately, but wait until we get up top. He's going to love seeing the ocean and this big b-b-b-b...ship!"

"He can walk with me," Maria declared, a determined glint in her pretty brown eyes.

"Maybe later," Meg said as she handed Dom over to Marta. "He's still got an IV line and the bag that goes with it, honey. How about Marta and Craig carry him until that's gone, so you won't have to worry about it?"

"Okay," Maria agreed easily. "But then, it's my turn, 'kay?"

Craig ruffled the short hair on her head. "You got it, princess. Let's head out." He winked at Meg. "See you when we're done with our adventure."

"Come on," Maria whined, pulling Craig's hand to get him moving out the door. "I want to go up top."

Meg smiled at those Navy words coming out of that little girl. Yet the upcoming pain of waving goodbye stabbed Meg's heart. God, she loved these kids. How could she ignore the possibility they still might have parents who cared and were looking for them? How could she find those parents for them? They deserved that much. So did their families. There had to be a way. She needed to contact a Brazilian adoption agency. They'd know.

"You kids go ahead," she said as brightly as she could. "Make sure Dom has ear protection. Keep warm!"

"Mum!" Dom squealed, wriggling out of Marta's grip, his hands stretched for Meg to take him.

Man, this was hard. She forced a grin. "Hey, big boy. Don't you want to see the flight deck? There are lots of jets up there."

His nose scrunched. Poor kid probably didn't know what a jet was. "Mum!" he squealed again, still reaching for her. The panic in his eyes was breaking her heart.

Instead of taking him from Marta, Meg leaned forward, kissed his forehead, and told him. "Hurry back, sweetheart. I love you. Be good!"

Marta turned her back, effectively creating a wall between Meg and Dom. But sweet little Dom pitched a fit, bucking and kicking, screaming and arching his back to get back into Meg's hands. He had become everything Meg hoped for. A regular boy.

She couldn't do it. Choking on a sob, she took Dom back, and pressed his thrumming little body to her heart. So this was what separation anxiety felt like. *Shit. It felt like shit!*

She held him close, blinking to keep her tears from falling. That would only make the other kids sad, then they'd all be bawling. But, God. Who would've thought she could love another woman's child as hard as she loved this little lost boy? But she did. To lose Dom now, to have to put him into Brazil's foster care system—would kill Meg.

"It's okay, baby," she murmured into the top of his head. "I'm not going anywhere. I just can't go up with you this time, okay? Go with Marta and Craig. When you've seen all the jets and you're tired, come back, and I'll be right here. Promise, sweetheart." She kissed the top of his Navy cap. "I'll be waiting for you. You're my baby, and I'm your..." She paused, her heart breaking at the uncertain path ahead of her.

Sure enough. Dom sucked up a shuddering breath and whispered, "Mum."

"Yes, Dominic," she told him sincerely, wishing it were so. "I'm your Mum." *For now.*

God help me find a way to be just that. Dom's Mum. Please don't let me break his heart.

She waved goodbye and watched her babies leave. They were no sooner in the hall when one of her guards shut the sickbay door and closed her in. Again. That was the catch to this fun adventure. Meg couldn't go with Dom. She wasn't allowed up on deck, not with some invisible assassin lurking in the Atlantic to kill her. It sounded crazy, but Dooley was adamant. Even if the kids were flown to American or back to Brazil, she wasn't going with them. Only Marta and Craig. Meg was under protective order. Talk about unfair.

Now that the children were eating better, and Luke had thoroughly assessed them, they were all happy and smiling. Craig and Marta had kept them entertained and busy from day one, had even started them back on their studies. Then along came Ensign Shaw. He'd proven to be quite the artist. He'd gifted them with sets of watercolors, modeling clay, and then spent hours showing them how to paint and otherwise play. The deck was no place for children, but since so many of the sailors aboard had taken them into their hearts, the children always had plenty of exercise. Sometimes in the onboard gym. Sometimes playing hopscotch in the halls.

But now that time was coming to an end. Meg could feel it. Everything Ensigns Giacomo and Shaw did seemed directed at getting Dom healthy enough to travel. Not that Meg minded, she just hadn't wanted the kids to leave before Julio returned. He needed to say his goodbyes, too. He loved these kids. She knew he did.

Captain Dooley hadn't gotten back to her with further news on Julio or Hotrod, err, Walker Judge, except to tell her they were both off the island, and Julio had gone onto Fort Campbell, then Washington, DC, with his two prisoners. It seemed he'd acquired another one of those Matryoshka Dolls on whatever island he'd been stuck on. How that happened, Meg had no idea. But it figured. Julio seemed destined for covert life.

But worse, she had no way to contact him except through Captain Dooley. Meg didn't feel right asking. The captain of an aircraft carrier was an important, busy man. She didn't want to bother him.

Meg felt off-balance, as if everything and everyone was moving on without her. Especially now that she'd had time to ask Dooley about the possibility of securing humanitarian protection for the children. Not only did they not meet the requirements for humanitarian protection under the *Hague Convention on Protection of Children and Co-operation in Respect of Intercountry Adoption*, but national Brazilians were given first priority when it came to adoptions. It didn't matter that they'd been kidnapped by Zapata, or that she, a United States citizen had rescued them. Neither did their orphan status.

Meg would not only have to prove that each of her children had no extended family, but that no other Brazilian citizens wanted them. Which was difficult, since these orphans hadn't come with much history or backstory, much less official paperwork, like birth certificates or shot records like kids in America. They hadn't come with anything. In most cases they were starved little rescues when they'd been found. Joseph and Fernando had simply gathered these babies up on their daily patrols through the local villages and provided safe refuge. They had no way to know who the kids belonged to, who had deserted them, or what

disaster had stolen them from their families. If any.
Joseph and Fernando had just stepped in where others
had not, and rescued kids who'd needed rescuing.
They'd saved these children's lives, but even that didn't
matter.

As for Dom? While it was extraordinarily rare for a
United States citizen to be allowed to adopt a healthy
Brazilian child, special needs children were another
category. That was where Dom fit. But once again, Meg
could adopt him only after she'd satisfactorily proved
he had no family. That no one wanted him. Which was
sad, because he deserved to be wanted. All of her kids
did. But really. Everyone in the village had known
about the orphanage. If anyone knew who these kids
belonged to, wouldn't they have come forward? At
least notified those relatives?

To top that off, Brazil's adoption laws demanded
that prospective foreign adoptive parents live in Brazil
with the prospective adoptive child thirty days prior to
adoption. Which was not going to happen. Even if she
could somehow prove that Dom was indeed, an orphan
without any family who wanted him, she was confined
to one of the best aircraft carriers for the next two
months.

Damn it.

Chapter Thirty-Six

"She's what?" Julio asked, choking at how terribly wrong this interview had gone. He couldn't believe his ears. After he'd hit Fort Campbell just long enough to connect with an outgoing helo bound for Washington, DC, he'd landed at Reagan National Airport. There FBI agents hustled him and the two Dolls across the Potomac River to FBI Headquarters. Now he was seated in a posh interview room that didn't include two-way mirrors, or a metal table with posts for cuffs and shackles. Or the alleged murderer, Doctor Barbara Hazelton.

"You heard right," Senator Sullivan said. Seated across from him on a similar white leather couch, McQueen looked like he hadn't slept any more than Julio had.

"She tried to kill Hotrod, sir," Julio asserted, the flaming injustice of this latest twist beyond his comprehension.

"Not so. She knows how to fly that Blackhawk," FBI Agent in Charge, Stan Millard stated. "She's certified and she would've landed it safely and escaped once you two were neutralized. You're the one who put Hotrod in danger." His head rotated from Julio to McQueen. "Speaking of your buddy, where is he?"

Julio didn't wait for Sullivan to answer. "You tell me," he replied, returning stare for stare, but damned sure not going to out his brother. "You're the one running double-agents, not us."

"Professional courtesy, Millard," McQueen bit out. "We wouldn't be here today if you'd been straight with me the first time I called."

"What the fuck were you doing sending men into Minas Gerais?" Millard snapped.

McQueen's palms hit his knees as he lifted to his feet, walked to Millard's desk, and looked down at the agent. "You need to remember who you're talking to, Agent Millard" —McQueen didn't even bat an eye— "Where is Director Strong this morning? Get him in here."

Millard had the grace to blink in the face of a true predator with actual political power at his fingertips. "My apologies, sir. Yes. Yes, of course." He straightened some things on his polished oak desk. Things Julio couldn't see beyond Millard's flamboyantly large nameplate. Things that probably didn't amount to a hill of beans, but made him look and feel important. "You have to understand, Senator. This operation has been three years in the making.

Until this avoidable mistake" —he shot an accusing glare at Julio— "the Bureau had everything under control."

McQueen crossed his arms in that quintessential I-don't-give-a-shit stance that he did so well. "No you didn't, not if it unraveled this quickly. I'm done speaking to you, son. Get Zachary in here. Now."

Millard's eyes shifted to the door, but he was smart enough to say, "Yes, sir."

Not everyone could command the director of a federal agency. But Sullivan could.

Jumping to his feet, Millard still had to crane his neck to look up at the senator when he scurried out of the office. But there was small comfort in that show of submission. Doctor Hazelton, who Julio had just been told was an FBI double-agent working inside the United Kingdom for the United States government, was still going free, along with her Matryoshka Doll girlfriend. As usual, the man with boots on the ground was the last to know.

It took thirty long minutes before Director Strong cracked the door open. At least as tall as Sullivan, and just as silver-haired, he wasn't alone. No. That would've been too easy. A bedraggled Barbara Hazelton, wearing shackles, cuffs, and an orange jumpsuit, shuffled in at his side.

"Senator," Strong said with a curt nod at Sullivan as he shut and locked the door behind him. "Agent Juarez. Good to see you again. What's it been, two years?"

"Twenty-one months, sir," Julio replied as he nodded back at one of the most powerful men in America. Twenty-one months since he'd rescued his wife and son. Eighteen months since Bianca walked into the sea. Eleven months since Tomas passed away in his sleep. In Julio's arms. Foolish anniversaries to remember. Harder ones to forget.

Director Strong had sent an operator into Brazil to assist Julio the day he'd gone into Domingo Zapata's lair to retrieve Bianca and Tomas. Agent Persia Coltrane, one damned brave woman and a fine undercover operator. She'd already been working inside Zapata's small circle of guerillas. She'd set the fire that had caused enough distraction and allowed Julio to get his family out of Zapata's bunkers.

"My apologies for what you've been through, Julio. Perhaps this will help." Zachary Strong directed Hazelton to the wooden chair alongside Millard's desk. Dropping to one knee, he undid her shackles first, then her cuffs. "Anything I can get you, ma'am? A good stiff drink? Coffee?"

Once freed, she rolled her shoulders, then eased back into the chair with a sigh. Interestingly, the woman sported bruised and bloodied knuckles, a black eye, and a fat, shiny lip. She looked like she'd been in one hell of a fistfight since Julio had last seen her. "Thanks, Zachary. A glass of water would be nice. Sure feels good to be out of that cell and away from that bitch," she said in her perfect British accent.

"You bet," he replied as he filched a bottled water from Millard's private refrigerator behind his office door and handed it to her. "These gentlemen deserve the truth, Eva. Tell them."

Hazelton graciously accepted the bottle, uncapped it, and took a long swallow before she shook her hair over her shoulders and turned back into the savvy woman Julio knew. "Yes, I suppose they do. But this stays between you fellows and me. Understand?"

"They've both got more clearance than you," Strong muttered. "Just tell them."

That seemed to surprise her. "Senator Sullivan. Agent Juarez." She took a deep breath. "I'm sorry I misled you, but I am the best nuclear engineer in the world. Unfortunately, I'm also a double-agent working for Director Strong inside the Matryoshka Dolls. My real name is Eva Bell."

"That's why the black eye and bruises," Julio said. "You had to keep your cover."

Her bloody cracked lips pursed before she winced and rubbed a fingertip lightly over them. That shine had to be antiseptic salve. "Ouch. Yes. The other Doll you captured is Anastasia Zoytova, and the second she came to, she accused me of betraying her. It became necessary to prove my worth. Inside the Dolls, that means you fight to the death. Unfortunately, your men" —she sent a withering glare at Director Strong— "stopped me before I could strangle her. Now that she's still alive, she'll accuse me again. She's got more clout than me. You do realize there'll be repercussions, don't you?"

He shrugged. "Which you'll have no trouble overcoming."

"Damned straight," she bit out as the back of her knuckles came up to her tender lips like a prizefighter's.

"Quit stalling," Strong urged.

Eva tipped forward, her battered fingers clenched between her knees. "It's like this. My parents migrated from Russia to England when I was just a little girl. I have no recollection that far back, but I do know they were then, and still are, Russian spies. They were sent to create an alibi and a sleeper cell. I was their first agent. By the time I turned seven, I knew how to kill an adult male with drugs, razors, wires, knives, and a multitude of pharmaceutical products. Not that I had actually done it, but I'd watched enough training films, and I'd practiced. I was capable. I also knew how to plant explosives. Easy for me, because who would've suspected a child? Especially an adorable, blond, little waif with a proper British accent and bright blue eyes?"

She blinked her bright blues at Senator Sullivan.

"And?" he growled, unimpressed with her battered, but still uniquely feminine, charms.

She took the rebuke like a pro. "My father gave me my first real mission a month before my seventeenth birthday. I was supposed to kill FBI Agent Bullock. On personal leave in London, he'd been seeing the sights and was supposed to be at Trafalgar Square with his wife and three-year-old daughter that day. I remember the sky was overcast. A thick fog had rolled into the city. Covered everything. You could lick the smell of the Thames off your lips. There were pigeons and tourists everywhere. Traffic. Always traffic. Buses. The smell of diesel smoke..." Her voice trailed away.

Eva faltered. But just for a split second. Rolling her shoulder, she faced Julio head on. "I couldn't do it, Agent Juarez. I. Just. Couldn't."

"You wear glasses," he told her.

Her head canted as if he'd surprised her. "Yes. I hate contacts. Why do you ask?"

For the first time since he'd met her, this woman wasn't lying.

"I believe you," he replied evenly.

"Ah," she murmured. "I gave myself away, didn't I? Damn. I'll have to be more careful. What am I doing wrong?"

He wasn't about to share what he knew about her tells. "Why couldn't you kill Agent Bullock?"

An unintended pout pinched her lips, not suggestive, but thoughtful. As if she were remembering. "I was supposed to slip a miniature explosive into one pocket of his trench coat, then walk away. The bomb was powerful enough to kill him and anyone within a hundred feet of him. I'd practiced sneaking up on my parents and planting it, then strangers in the streets, doing this exact same drill. Not with real explosives, just with typed cards with BOOM written on them. It was easy enough to get close to him. I was proud of my sleight of hand skills. I could've done it."

Julio stared at her. Eva seemed to be trying to convince herself.

Lifting that plastic bottle, she took another sip of water. "But I was nervous when I approached my very first target. Of course. You know how it is when you're expected to kill someone. I didn't know Agent Bullock. Didn't know he had a family, either. But none of that mattered until... until I saw him."

Somehow this conversation had narrowed down to just Julio and Eva.

"He was a handsome, tall man with short, red hair, blue eyes, and freckles. He wore an Irish tweed cap, a gray woolen trench coat, white shirt, and pressed black slacks. Every sound and sight became ultra-important. Every person. Every selfie being taken and every accent in the crowd. I didn't want to miss a thing. All five senses were on overload, zeroed on my mission. I swear, I could smell the tacos from *Tortilla Charing Cross* a block away. I was three, maybe two feet from Bullock, so close, I could smell his aftershave and his wife's hairspray. The starch in his crisp white shirt. I almost had him, but... but then" —she took another deep breath— "he lifted his little girl up high and put her on his shoulders. Perfect opportunity, right? His coat wasn't buttoned. God, the stupid gray thing flapped in the damp, foggy breeze. Nearly slapped me in the face, I was that close. He never would've felt my hand in his pocket. I could've gotten away with it. But... but..."

Julio waited while she ran both hands over her face, then dragged her fingers through her hair, combing it straight back before she dropped her hands into her lap. "What stopped me was the pure, childish adoration on the face of his three-year-old daughter. Do you believe that? Something so inconsequential as a child. A tiny little girl. A kid. But God, she was perfect. Tiny like Tinkerbell. I think he called her Lizzie. Curly blonde hair. Bright blue eyes—just like mine. The voice of an angel, soft and pure. Joyful. He'd lifted Lizzie onto his shoulders, so she could climb onto one of the famous Landseer Lions. And you know what? He told her to stay still and not fall. Which she did. Lizzie was grinning so hard, but she said to him, as cute as a bug, 'Come on up, Daddy. I won't let you fall.' Can you believe that? She thought she could keep him safe on that stone lion?"

Brushing a hand over his eyes to clear the tears sparkling at the corners, Julio nodded. All he could see was Tomas' baby face, smiling up at him from his crib. Kids were generous and gracious like that. They wanted nothing more than to help their moms and dads. They wanted to be good. Like Tomas. Like Eva Bell when she'd been a child. She'd just wanted to please her parents. Which was why she was here today.

She continued, her voice hoarser and her accent now flat. "Well, before I knew it, he'd jumped up there with her, then tugged his wife up too, and I'd lost my chance. Once he and his wife joined her, Lizzie squealed and clapped her hands. His wife ooooh'd and ahhhh'd at the view. Agent Bullock lifted that little girl of his back onto his shoulders, where she had an even better view. By then she so excited, she was smacking the top of his head. She was so beautiful, and her dad was so proud. Even with her hitting his head, he grinned like a fool. A happy, blinking fool. For a moment there, I couldn't remember why I was there. I wanted to run."

Coughing into her hand, Eva broke eye contact. "The thing is," she ground out, talking to the floor now.

Julio didn't blame her. Confessions were difficult. Repentance was harder.

"That little girl was seeing Trafalgar Square from the height of a princess, instead of a mere commoner. And... and the man I'd been sent to kill... to murder... The man my parents said was evil and wicked just because he worked for the United States of America... That handsome red-haired man who was so obviously in love with his blond, blue-eyed wife and his pretty little daughter..."

Eva swallowed hard. Her head snapped up and her eyes locked onto Julio. Her hand flattened over her heart. "Don't you get it? I was looking at the life I could've had, Julio. It was like I was seeing me for the first time. That little girl should have been me!"

"What did you do?" he asked quietly.

Again her fingertips raked through her hair. "I... I saw it all then, Agent Juarez. The lies. The life I should've had. What the love of a real father looks like. I saw an American family who adored each other. Honestly..." She blew out a deep sigh. "That little girl looked just like me, only she had stars in her eyes. But me? I had a fuckin' mission in mine. My need to please my parents and the mother country I'd never set foot inside, ended that day. It dissolved in the fog and mist on Trafalgar Square. I. Could. Not. Do. It."

"Your parents couldn't have been pleased when you failed," he murmured, sure this retelling was just as hard on Eva as it was on him.

"You've got that right," she scoffed. "Oh, sure, they forgave me since that was my first foray into the clandestine world of sleeper agents. After they beat me. Both my mother and father took turns for a week. With belts and whips. Rubber hoses. I was no princess. I was just a tool. A seventeen-year-old tool they'd honed to do a job for them. A disgusting, cold-blooded job." Her lips pursed. "After that, they kept me under lock and key until I was re-indoctrinated, reformed, and submissive. Longest damned weeks of my life. But that was when I knew I had to leave if I was going to live. Hell, after being punished so severely for being too weak to kill a man... make that hundreds of innocent tourists, including that sweet little girl..."

She closed her eyes at what she'd nearly done. "What would they have done to me if I'd blown up the wrong guy? I was seventeen, for God's sake. It could've happened."

"The same thing they will do to you if they ever catch you," he replied.

Eva leaned toward him, her blue eyes gone hard. "Which is why I need to go back down there and murder Anastasia before she wakes up. That's my only way back into the Dolls without raising suspicion. I have to follow their code, not mine, or I'll never bring one of those bitches to justice."

Strong shook his head. "Not happening. Killing her will only make you look complicit with the Bureau. As if we'd known what you were supposed to do, that we allowed you to commit murder just to keep your cover. Every criminal in the world knows the FBI doesn't allow inmates to murder each other. You had your chance and you took it. We intervened like we should have. Anastasia's nose is broken and you might've cracked her larynx. She's being seen by our doctor. What more do you want? We stopped you. Blame it on us."

"I want to finish the job you gave me," Eva growled.

"And you will," Director Strong leveled back at her. "Trust me. The guys downstairs forced you two women apart, just like they should have. Our ROEs only authenticated your cover. Play it like Anastasia's the betrayer. Let her explain why she was dumb enough to get caught. Or was that part of her plan? Get caught, then point the finger at you and cry betrayer? What's her weakness? Dig into her. Find out how to neutralize her without killing her."

The bright blue darkened in Eva's eyes. "That might work."

"Are we through here?" Sullivan asked tiredly. "I've got shit to do and this isn't it."

Strong rolled his eyes. "Sorry I was late to the fight, McQueen," he said as he stuck his hand at Sullivan. "Always good to see you, but let's just do dinner next time."

Sullivan slapped a handshake into Strong's open palm. "Will do. Let's hit the trail, Julio."

Julio lifted to his feet, his eyes on Eva. "You can do this, but only if you believe."

That brought her head up. "Is that what kept you going? Keeps you going? Believing?"

He nodded. "Yes." *And I pray. And now I love Meg.* "I can help if you want."

She grunted at that. "Not inside the Dolls, you can't. Trust me. This mob is an all-girl thing."

"A mean girl thing," he corrected, concerned that there was more tenderness inside this cocky lioness than even she knew. That could get her killed.

"You're damned straight," she shot back at him. "Take care of that pretty foreign-aid-worker. She loves you, ya know?"

Julio nodded before he had time to think how Sullivan might take that news. But he might as well know. Julio loved Meg. But now he cared what happened to Eva Bell as well.

"Here," he said, working his wallet out of his back pocket. Handing her his business card, he said, "I will come if you call."

Stretching forward, she took the card, glanced at it, then tossed it to the floor. "No thanks, Juarez. I don't need your help, but that Navy SEAL does. He's the one in trouble, not me."

So, she knew about Hotrod, aka Walker Judge. Wasn't that interesting?

Julio followed Senator Sullivan into the hall. "Has that helo already returned to Kentucky?"

Sullivan grunted. "So... You and Duncan, huh?"

That he didn't respond to Hotrod's disappearance was even more interesting.

"Yes, sir," Julio admitted openly.

"Thought you were headed to Costa Rica?"

"We have unfinished business with the orphans. They need to be placed somewhere safe. I need to get back to the *Iwo Jima*."

Sullivan ran a hand over his silvery head. "Shit. I sure hate to tell you, but there's been an escape."

Julio knew before Sullivan said another word. "Domingo Zapata? But how?" That far north federal prison was supposedly the most secure on the planet.

"Some idiot guard tried to bully him. Walked straight into his cell. Got in his face and challenged him to fight, the dumbass."

"Let me guess. That man is dead now."

A muscle twitched in Sullivan's jaw. "Not only dead, but damned near beheaded. Domingo had him on his back in seconds, then cut his throat before security could get to them. Grabbed his keys and—"

Julio looked south. "And now he's headed home."

Of course Domingo had cut the fool's throat. The Zapata brothers were both narcissists and schizophrenics with delusional, psychotic skills that surpassed normal people's comprehension. Domingo had simply, somehow, made a weapon, then bided his time and waited for a testosterone-fueled guard, some egotistical moron who knew better than everyone else, to challenge him. Why had that guard ever thought he could bully a born killer?

"That's what we suspect. But it'll take time for him to get from the northern part of Alaska to South America. He's got to survive the Arctic freeze first."

Julio knew better. "If you believe that, you don't know Domingo Zapata, sir. I need to leave. I need to get back to that carrier as quickly as you can get me there."

Sullivan nodded. "I was hoping you'd consider tracking him, but you're right. Protecting Duncan and those orphans is more critical. Come to my office. I'll work the details."

Chapter Thirty-Seven

Okay, so she shouldn't have convinced Marta to trade places with her. She shouldn't have lied to Captain Dooley, either. But when the call came from the Brazilian mainland, demanding the return of all under-age Brazilian citizens, including Dominic, Meg had no choice. Dooley had agreed to return her children on one condition: that Marta and Craig be allowed to continue as their caregivers.

In the end, this was actually the perfect outcome. Meg needed to contact a Brazilian adoption agency. She could do that as soon as she landed. After she filled out their required paperwork, and by the time they'd searched their official records and proved once and for all that Dom was truly without family, her thirty days in-country requirement would be satisfied. Dom would be hers, and she would finally be his real Mum.

Meg kissed the top of his sleepy head as the Blackhawk lifted up from the deck. At the moment, all of her kids were buckled in and harnessed. All wore their spiffy new Navy jackets, also helmets that included ear protection. All were also chewing on strips of red licorice, courtesy of Lucas Giacomo. Meg was going to miss the men and women of the carrier. They were all heroes in her book.

But this was why she'd overdressed in multiple layers, then covered those layers with Marta's blouse, long skirt, and topped the disguise off with her Navy jacket. To fool all those kind sailors, and to get back to Brazil with her children. They needed her more than she needed protection. Whoever was supposedly out there gunning for her must not realize she'd been trained by the US Army. Weren't they in for a surprise?

Meg almost felt bad for those two brave Navy guards outside her room. Captain Dooley wouldn't be happy when Marta walked out of that room—again—instead of Meg. Shit would definitely hit the fan. But Marta was smart. She knew she was supposed to keep out of sight at least until tomorrow morning. By then, Meg, Craig, and the kids would be back in Minas Gerais. At least, that was the plan.

Man, the smell of the wild, gray Atlantic ocean was a beautiful thing. It filled Meg with energy at some primal level. Made her want to dig into parenthood with all she had. Made her believe she could do the impossible. What had Julio said? *Believe what you are doing is right and good. Believe you are strong and just. That you are the right hand of God. That he will always send His archangels in your time of greatest need. Then, you will prevail.*

Meg focused on doing just that. What she was doing was right and good certainly best for Dominic. She knew she wouldn't be able to adopt all her children. Life just didn't work out that way. She might not be as strong as Julio, either, certainly not right-hand-of-God strong. But she was strong enough. And she would prevail, no doubt about that. Hopefully—*cross my fingers and hope to die*—ultimately, she and Dom would be related by the time this adventure was over.

Was she fooling herself? Had she counted all her chickens before they'd hatched? Did she have her cart before her horse? Yes, yes, and oh, hell yes. But she'd lived through enough crap in her life to believe in the magic of Karma. Dominic would always be hers, one way or the other. If not legally, then by heart. Convinced she could do anything, she cast a silent but fervent prayer to the saintly woman Julio revered enough to wear her prayer on his chest. *'Madre de Dios! Please help me.'*

Then she snuggled in for the noisy ride over the Atlantic. Before long the green ocean known as the Amazon rainforest lay below, its massive canopies rippling like waves in the brisk wind. A storm was headed inland, but for now, there was only a steady easterly wind. Which suited her just fine. With a wind at their back, this helo was making good time. Her secret was safe.

Soon this helo would bank southward, and before long, Meg and her kids would be back in Minas Gerais. They weren't being delivered to the Highlands, though. Which was good as that poor excuse of an orphanage had seen its last days. Their destination today was a landing strip north of the beautiful city of Ouro Preto, the center of the richest mining district in Brazil.

Lucky for Meg, there was an outreach office in Ouro Preto for the Brazilian National Adoption Agency. She'd checked. Finally, everything was going her way.

*****

Julio loosened his grip on the overhead strap. Had to. His gloved fingers were numb.

Senator Sullivan had ordered another Blackhawk, this one out of Andrews Air Force Base, Maryland, to get him into Brazil as swiftly and as legally as possible. His assignment: Apprehend and end Domingo Zapata with extreme prejudice.

The Nightstalker pilot this time around was Sergeant Ronald Churchill. An interesting name that brought to mind a damned brash United States President who'd challenged the liars of the world back in the nineties like a gun-slinging cowboy, combined with the upper crust of Britain's finest. Ronald Reagan and Winston Churchill. Two rock-solid heroes, they'd made the world a better place during their times. Julio missed men of character and strength like those two lions. The only men who compared to them these days were covert giants like Senator Sullivan and a cocky former Marine living in Alexandria, Virginia. Alex Stewart.

While still working for President Adams, Julio had joined forces with Stewart during the operation that had ended another bastard with royal blood in his veins, Basheer Bagani. Until that mission, Julio had never worked for a man so intense. Even McQueen Sullivan couldn't compare to the single-minded, attack trained Devil Dog, Alex Stewart.

How Julio wished Stewart were going into Brazil with him. It'd be nice to have someone trustworthy and capable on his six again. Someone who said what he meant and meant what he said. For the first time in years, Julio wanted a like-minded warrior at his side. He'd been an island of one too long. Sullivan needed to change his ROEs. Sending single assassins on missions to clean up the world's messes might be expedient, but each lethal assignment was mentally exhausting and the solitude behind each kill was hard on the man behind the scope.

Turning his focus back to the scenery out the window, Julio was suddenly tired of being all he could be. He wanted back into the lush, warm comfort of Meg's arms. Funny how sex worked. But while he'd filled her with his body, she'd filled him with her heart. She'd given him a soft place to land and a reason to want to live again. He didn't want to lose those precious commodities. Because they weren't just things; they were treasures he'd searched for all his life.

For now, this bird flew like a rocket. With Brazil's permission this time, they'd already breached the country's airspace and were over the rainforest, headed south to Minas Gerais where the older Zapata brother was most likely headed. His forbidding hole-in-the-rock complex of concrete bunkers, tunnels, and barriers, lay directly west of his brother's original mine, OZ Metallurgy Mining, Inc. Not that the Zapata brothers were close. They weren't. Had never been. Not even as boys. Not unless you called their numerous attempts at killing each other, close. Close calls, maybe, but not close in the way Julio was with the Sinclair brothers. Or Walker Judge.

The only good thing about this unexpected mission was knowing Meg was still aboard the carrier, and that Sullivan had ordered Dooley to place her into protective custody. She was safe.

But Julio worried for tiny Dominic. He had no way of knowing who that child's father was, but he suspected Domingo Zapata. Which meant Dom had most likely been conceived through rape. Possibly brutal rape. That was Zapata's way. Nothing Domingo had ever done hadn't ended in blood and death. He wasn't one to seek out ladies, unless they were ladies of the night. Or sex slaves.

That made more sense. The animal called Domingo had kept a harem of battered women at his bunker. Julio had seen them during his escape with Bianca and

Tomas. There was no telling which woman had fallen for his lies, and had possibly, hopefully, for her sake, died after giving birth to his bastard son. Zapata would've killed her, otherwise. That was how he'd dealt with his women. Once he was done with them, he cut their throats. Unless this time, one of them had actually charmed him enough into letting them live long enough to bear his child.

Fate's damned icy-cold fingertip slithered up Julio's spine again.

Bianca had also been in that bunker, and she'd been there long enough to have submitted to Domingo's ugly demands. What was worse, she certainly could've charmed him, especially if she'd known him from San Diego. Or if she'd supplied the information he'd needed to acquire a Navy SEAL, which Julio had been working his guts out to become back then.

Was that even possible? Could Bianca, the beautiful blonde woman Julio had once loved, be Dominic's mother? Had she betrayed her husband, then her baby son, to please a black-hearted killer the likes of Domingo Zapata? Wasn't that a mind fuck of off-the-chart proportions?

Julio crossed himself, instantly repentant for the filthy word he'd thought. But more because of the sins he suspected his wife had committed. Against him. Against Tomas. Worse, she would've been with Zapata while she'd left Tomas alone. A toddler, left alone to defend himself against an animal. Crying himself to sleep. Crying for his father.

¡Santa Madre de Dios! Cold, hard anguish ripped through Julio's soul at all his son had suffered. For what?! To please a killer? To save herself? Deserting sweet little Tomas was bad enough, but the more Julio remembered, the more that scenario fit. Bianca hadn't been housed with Tomas in the concrete, windowless cell when he'd located his son.

His throat went dry at that tender recollection. Tomas hadn't even cried when Julio had picked him up. He hadn't remembered his father. Only Zapata. The monster behind Julio's son's nightmares.

Agent Coltrane was the one who'd led Julio to Bianca's cell at the opposite end of the bunker. It all came back to Julio. Bianca's room had still been one of concrete, but it had been clean and warm, had windows with curtains. A real bed. A lamp. A rocking chair. Simple amenities that no other rooms had.

She'd looked up when he'd called for her to come to him. So surprised. Shocked even. But she'd covered that initial glance with a full body slam and a feverish kiss that had, at the time, felt authentic. Yet not once had she sought to comfort or hold her frightened son, the boy gathered under Julio's arm. Not one fuckin' time. He'd chalked it up to post-traumatic stress then, but now...

Rage burned like volcanic lava in his gut. Had she ever loved him? His head shook automatically. No. He knew that now. Bianca had only ever loved herself. And possibly...

¡Maldita sea cada Zapata que haya vivido! Yes, him. The cold-blooded murderer, Domingo Zapata. The man who'd treated Julio's son the same way Orlando had treated Domingo's. Like trash.

Julio ran a hand over his hard, shorn head, pissed at himself for being the dumbest burro, as in ass, on the planet. For not seeing the real woman he'd married for what she'd been all along. For forever believing Bianca was a lady of grace when she was nothing but a conniving, convincing liar. She'd deserted her child. His child! For a Goddamned rapist!

Julio crossed himself again, seeking forgiveness for using the Lord's name in vain, and for what he intended to do once he caught up with Domingo. Had Bianca borne Zapata a son? Was Dominic that child? Was that why'd she'd walked into the ocean? Out of despair? Because Julio had stolen her from her one true love, when he'd thought he'd been rescuing her? Because she'd quite possibly loved Domingo's son more than she'd loved Julio's son?

It seemed far-fetched. Too far-fetched. And yet the truth remained. Bianca had deserted Tomas. That much Julio knew for sure. He'd seen it with his own eyes. After all Julio had done to save her, after he'd risked his life going into Domingo's lair to rescue her and Tomas, she'd killed herself anyway. Because she'd chosen to love a killer over a hardworking, honorable man.

Tears choked him as he sat there alone, staring at Brazil below, but seeing nothing. God, he was tired. He wanted Meg. Needed Meg. Desperately wanted to hold Dominic's pure little boy body again. Needed to see that little guy's smile and to know he was safe. To smell the top of his head. To kiss that head like he'd wanted to kiss Tomas. Again and again. Only those two angels in his life could ease this burden he carried.

Yet even as the bird flew him to his destiny, Julio knew. It was time to talk with Agent Coltrane. It was time to know everything she hadn't told him.

Chapter Thirty-Eight

Touchdown! Meg could've squealed with delight when the helo's skids landed at a private airport outside Ouro Preto.

"We're back!" Craig sing-songed cheerily to the kids.

Maria clapped. They were all as excited as Meg. She just hadn't expected the welcoming committee lined up just outside the only hangar on the strip. Stuffy and officially dressed in business suits, they looked like...

"Who are those men?" Meg asked to be sure.

Craig shrugged, but the Navy pilot spoke right up. "They're from the local Council of Guardianship, Brazil's version of child protective services, ma'am. They're here to ensure these kids are adoptable and that they get placed in proper care."

"But Captain Dooley said Marta and me—"

The pilot interrupted Craig with, "Yes, but you're not Marta and Craig Brunner, are you?"

Oh, shit. Dooley knew. He must've discovered Marta.

Meg's heart crashed to the floor. She clutched sleeping Dom to her heart. "But Dooley knows I'm going to adopt as many of these kids as I can."

The pilot nodded. "And these people are here to facilitate that process, ma'am. Trust Dooley. He's on your side."

Didn't feel like it.

One of those official-looking men marched straightway toward the helo. Dressed in a gray linen suit, white dress shirt, and shiny black dress shoes, he ducked under the still spinning rotors, but reached the door just as Dooley's pilot kicked the latch, slid it open, and called, "Ola!"

"Ola," the man returned grumpily.

Meg just sat there, unprepared for whatever might happen next. This was supposed to have been a trip home. She hadn't geared up like she normally would have. There was no Beretta in her back holster. No ammo in her gear bag. Only animal crackers, wet wipes, and—hope.

The man peered inside as he counted, "Uma. Dois. Três..." like some unfeeling, ignorant Portuguese robot. No smiles for the kids. No treats to make this separation go easier and no welcome home. Nothing. Tall and skinny with dark hair and bushy brows, he hadn't even introduced himself or looked one of these kids in the eye yet. He didn't care about them. Like so many people in the world today, he was just doing his job.

"No," Meg said, that thing in her neck called a spine as stiff as stegosaurus plates but quivering with rage. "This is not right," she declared, her grip firm around Dominic. "You can't just show up without announcement and take these kids like they're nothing. They're mine."

Like most Brazilian men who knew better than any female on earth, this guy dismissed her without even a second glance. Or one word of respect.

That pissed Meg off. She stood, her shoulders squared as she stepped between him and her kids. "I am officially adopting these children. All of them. That's the only reason I came back with them. You can't have them."

"Now, Meg..." Craig started to say.

She let him have it, too. "No, Craig! This is not going to happen. I don't just hand over my children to some guy who doesn't have the decency to treat me or them like people!" Then she turned on the pilot and ordered, "Get Dooley on the comm. Do it! He knows what I'm talking about. He's the one who made the deal with this... this jerk!"

The pilot actually obeyed, which did nothing to slow the panic attack creeping up Meg's hackles. These disinterested, uncaring guys actually meant to take her kids. Right now. Without so much as looking at them or treating them like the precious children they were. God, she was so—

BOOM!

Meg fell back into her seat at the same time Mr. Council of Guardianship's head exploded. My Hell! Someone had just shot him. The right side of his head was gone. Blood and brains and—

Craig slammed the door closed while the rest of the welcoming committee screamed and ran to the hangar for their lives. The cowards! They'd left these innocent children behind!

The pilot scrambled to get the helo off the ground. The rotors whined as they powered up. Another bullet spider-webbed the side window.

"Go, go, go!" Meg urged both pilot and helicopter.

Had to be Brazilian homegrown guerillas out there shooting, come to make a name for themselves by taking a US Navy helo down. That's what this was. A local militia takedown.

"Get this bird in the sky!" she shrieked at the pilot, who already had the rotors working overtime. "Faster!" she ordered as the skids hovered precarious inches above the ground. "The kids! We've got to save the kids!"

Another BOOM. Then another. The helo shuddered, then dropped back to the tarmac.

"Just lost the tail rotor," the pilot yelled over the crying children. "Weapons are in the overhead bins! Might want to arm yourselves."

But Meg was already in that overhead cabinet, frantically pulling out one of those MK18 assault rifles. Handing it to Craig, who looked damned perplexed there among all those frightened kids, she told him, "This is loaded. Aim to kill, Mr. Brunner. It's the only way you're going home to Marta."

She no more than touched the grip of the rifle she intended to claim, when the door crashed open. One uglier than hell, troll stood there, his rifle pointed inside at Craig, who instantly dropped his MK18 and raised both hands.

Oh. My. God! Meg wanted to kick his ass! He couldn't have looked more stupid and weak if he'd pointed at her and said, "She made me do it."

One massive black tattoo covered the guy at the door, from head to toe. Black crosses and swastikas. Strings of black sixes and chains. Symbols she'd never seen before. All over his bald head, face, neck, even, when he blinked, on his eyelids. Tattoos covered every inch, even the skin of his feet showing through his orange sandals. That was weird. Orange sandals. Who did that?!

He sneered at Craig, but he was obviously looking for something. Or someone. It couldn't be one of these children. But when his gaze landed on Dominic, now snuggled under Meg's chin with his skinny little legs wrapped around her like he was a monkey and she was his mama—which she damned well was—this creep's black eyes glittered. All black eyes. No sparkle and no white showed around his pupils.

A shiver rattled over Meg. This troll looked like the spawn of Satan. Or Satan himself.

"What do you want?" she asked like she had a right to question him, shaking as hard as she was. *Belligerence. Always lead with plenty of attitude and fuck 'em to hell belligerence,* Trevor had always said. *Never go down easy. Make 'em pay for every last inch.*

Instinctively, Meg turned her shoulder to this asshat at the door, blocking his view of Dominic. God, she wished Trevor were there now.

The ugly guy's face cracked. It wasn't so much a smile as a grin of cruel vulgarity. And Meg knew. This was him. Teeth sharpened to points. Enough ink that he looked black instead of Brazilian. He could only be Domingo Zapata. Orlando's brother. The older brother of the bastard Julio had killed. What was he doing here? Wasn't he supposed to be locked away in some Arctic prison for the rest of his life? *Oh, shit. Oh, shit!*

"You," he grunted, singling her out with the business end of the sub-compact machine gun in his hand. "Come. Now."

Oh, crap, Meg thought, but she said, *"Madre de Dios!"* Julio's words. For good luck or for God's intervention, she didn't know. Oh, heck. Just for the hell of it!

"I said come!" Domingo bellowed, frightening the kids even more. Maria buried her face in Craig's shirt, sobbing.

Backing away from the door, Meg eased sweet little Dominic off her hip and handed him over to Craig—

"No!" Zapata spat. "He comes with you. The boy comes. Now."

Trembling and scared witless, barely able to breathe, Meg nodded at the ugly man who would soon be her captor. "I'll go with you, but please, let this little boy stay," she begged, still determined Dominic stay with Craig. "He's all I have and—"

"All *you* have?" Domingo's dark eyes turning darker. Flatter. Continually scanning the airfield, it was obvious he knew he hadn't much time before help arrived. "He isn't yours, *cadela*," he spat.

Meg knew enough Portuguese to know he'd just called her slut. Well, two could play that game. "How would you know he's not mine, you ass?" He would make her pay for this. She knew it, but she wouldn't go easy.

Just when she thought Zapata couldn't get uglier, he did. All that atrocious ink turned his features into a demonic mask. "Because he is my son! My boy! Now come. You and him. Quick! Or I kill all these *crianças*." *All her children.*

Meg's heart fell. God, no. This monster was Dominic's father?

Julio! Where are you?

Chapter Thirty-Nine

Julio rolled the knots in his neck away and wiped the sweat on his forehead to keep it from running into his eyes. He'd arrived too late. Zapata had a ten-minute lead. He'd already disappeared into the forest north of Ouro Preto. With Meg and tiny Dom.

To make everything worse, Zapata knew Dom was his son. That was why he'd come, to get his boy. Craig told Julio that before he'd gathered the children back into the helo Julio had arrived on. Craig and the children were now headed back to the *Iwo Jima* in that helo, where they'd be safe. Someone would return for the damaged Blackhawk. For now, the pilot of the Blackhawk Meg had been on, Lieutenant Damien Cutler, had been left behind to guard the bird. The mayor of Ouro Preto had sent an army of police officers to assist. Julio hoped that would be enough.

This incident would surely create havoc for USA and Brazilian diplomatic relations, but Julio didn't care. To hell with Brazil's local Council of Guardianship, too. They'd done nothing to protect the children. Worse, Craig said they'd frightened the kids. Not that witnessing the esteemed Brazilian leader die, whom Julio now knew as the deceased, Jose Gutierrez, hadn't already scared everyone. But city officials should've known better and done more than send a handful of businessmen to do what an army should've done. These hills were thick with thieves and marauders. More should've been done to secure this runway, especially since the Brazilian government had known precisely where this Navy helo would land.

Diplomacy be damned. If Brazil cared so much, they should've done more to help their unwanted and motherless children to begin with. Maybe they wouldn't have so many then, and none of this would have had to happen.

The global failure to protect children galled Julio. He was angrier than he'd ever been. After he'd waved the chopper off, he'd begun walking northwest to that stone-cold bunker Zapata called home. That was most likely where Dominic had been born, and where Zapata stored more weapons and ammo. Where his cold-blooded gang of killers might still be waiting. And planning.

Well, let the motherfuckers plan. Let them think they had a chance of seeing another day! Didn't matter how many, didn't matter where or how. Julio's heart had turned cold at the hard and ugly chore ahead of him. But he would clean this rat's nest out, once and for all.

His language had deteriorated during the long flight back to Brazil. But he also knew God understood the heart of a warrior, that sometimes, it had to become stone in order to do what needed doing. In order to survive. Words would never be as important as steadfast hearts. As life. As rescuing the weak and innocent from animals like Zapata. Bottom fucking line: Zapata was going to die today. Every son of a bitch who stood with him, too.

Pissed to his core, Julio tracked Zapata as he'd tracked every other terrorist and low life he'd been ordered to target. Relentlessly. He had two goals in mind, murder and rescue. End the asshats. Save the only family Julio had. *¡Mi familia!* He couldn't lose this one, too. God couldn't be that cruel. He just couldn't.

"*¡Maldita sea, Dios!* It's happening again!" he railed at the creator of heaven and earth. *Damn it, God!* "Show me how to be a better man, how to be worthy of this woman and this precious son. Please. Show me the way. Hear my prayer. Be with me. Be my right hand. Give my feet wings and keep my heart strong."

Because that organ thumping like a beast inside his chest was breaking. Julio had come full circle, back to the worst days of his life. He couldn't fail again. He wouldn't!

As he had when he'd first arrived in Brazil, he wore a single gear bag strapped to his shoulder. That bag held a couple bottles of sports drink. Protein bars. His blow-out kit. Two extra shirts in case he'd need to cover any blood, or worse, when or if he came into contact with any villagers after the upcoming battle. There was no sense scaring the locals on his way out of the country.

That bag also carried plenty of ammo for the Berettas holstered under each arm, as well as for the Heckler and Koch MP7, aka room broom, hanging off his other shoulder. The modified, bolt-action SOCOM MK-13 rifle Walker Judge had given him, lay flat against his back, holstered for now. But loaded. Like every other weapon Julio packed.

His gear bag was damned heavy. The trail before him, heavier. But tracking was not as hard as he'd expected. Not with the continual bent and broken branches pointing his way forward. Showing him the way. Meg, even now with a child in her arms—hopefully still in her arms—and partial paralysis weighing her down, had left a trail of breadcrumbs.

Dios! He loved that woman. With hope in his heart for the first time all day, Julio broke into a steady jog. Forward. Ever forward. Zapata wouldn't be able to move as quickly through these trees, not with a woman determined to slow him down while carrying a child. Julio could overtake them. Make that, would. He'd get ahead of them. When Zapata arrived back at his hole-in-the-wall bunker, he'd be in for one helluva surprise.

*****

Man, this guy was intolerable at so many levels. Every question Meg asked had only earned her a grunt or stone-cold silence. For as short and squat as he was, Zapata was quick. And pushy. And rude!

He had no problem poking her with that damned pistol he'd pulled out of his rear holster, urging her to walk faster. Growling like a bear, other times snorting like a pig when she faltered and lost her footing. And spitting. Always spitting. Yet he wasn't chewing tobacco, at least not the kind she was familiar with. Whatever he kept stuffing in his cheek, it was black and nasty when it spewed out of his mouth. Looked as if he'd hocked up thick, black phlegm. The jerk took no precaution to keep her or Dominic from seeing it either. Just hocked it up while he walked, and spit it, sometimes into her path. Where she might slip and fall trying to avoid the mess. Keeping up with this creep was getting harder and harder to do. Gross!

"Please," she said, panting while poor Dom sweated against her. They hadn't been allowed one chance to catch their breaths, and Dom was frightened. He had yet to loosen his stranglehold around her neck, and his head, now hatless, kept bumping under her chin. Jolting her when she stumbled. Not that Meg minded. She was just winded, and her left side had grown weaker during this forced march. She didn't have a lot of strength or balance left.

"Please," she wheezed, trying again. "My boy, err, your son, needs to rest. You're scaring him and he's frightened. He needs a drink."

The asshat leading the charge up this bushy hill never slowed. Didn't even hesitate or acknowledge that he'd heard. Just kept going.

That did it. With a loud sigh, Meg dropped to her haunches and pulled the only bottle of water that Zapata the Troll had allowed her to grab, out of the flimsy bag flapping off her back. It'd sure be nice if there were more in that bag, but at least, Dom wouldn't go thirsty. Yet, anyway.

Casting an evil glare back at her, Zapata growled. "Walk, *cadela!*"

Again with the name calling.

"No," she told him right back. "Your son needs a break, and so do I. I've had a stroke, you idiot. I can't walk as fast or as long as you can, and neither can Dominic. We're taking a break, and then we'll walk and walk some more. Got it?" She tossed that at him with attitude.

With a grunt, the troll lowered his ass to the dirt uphill, glaring down at her like a damned black human-thundercloud. Grunting. Picking something black and disgusting from between his pointed fangs again. Still spitting.

Oh, sweet Jesus. Meg had heard that the Krahô Indians, one of Brazil's indigenous tribes, chewed some kind of psychedelic plants for their shaman rituals. Was that what he'd been chewing and spitting all this time? Or was this guy high on the cocaine produced from coca shrubs grown in this region? Was he hallucinating? On some other drugs? Or was he just plain cruel like Orlando?

He flicked his black-stained fingertips at her, his sneer as hate-filled and as lethal as the second she'd first laid eyes on him. Yup. Just plain cruel. She'd heard stories of Domingo's brutality, each worse than the last. This was going to be a long day.

Chapter Forty

At last. Julio slowed from full combat run into a steady trot. He was covered in sweat and every muscle cried for relief, but finally, he'd heard a noise that didn't belong in the woods. He froze, casting his senses out like a net into the trees and bushes ahead. Up into the green canopy. Cocking his head, he drew every last meaningless whisper of wind or birdsong to him.

Instead, an angry, "Holy shit!" came back loud and clear.

Then, a tearful, "I'll kill him! So help me, God, I'll kill him! Get me out of here!"

"Meg?" Julio asked quietly, as he approached that blessed, sweet, pissed-off voice from behind the tree where she must be tied.

"Julio?" she cried, when he cleared the shrubbery.

He couldn't believe what he saw. Meg wasn't tied. She was impaled. The twelve-inch blade stuck into her left shoulder, just below the collarbone, held her fast to that tree. Her hands and fingers were bleeding, as was the shoulder. Hot angry tears streamed down her red, red face.

Damn Zapata to hell! He'd smeared her poor face and head with her own blood. No doubt he'd painted himself with it, possibly Dominic, too. That was how Zapata worked. In blood.

"You're here," she cried, frantically. "Say something!"

Julio snapped out of his need to kill Zapata, and stepped into rescue Meg. But he didn't dare touch her or hold her. Not yet. Touching her would only hurt her, and that knife had to come out. Now. Before she bled to death. Her fingers and hands were already sliced and bleeding from her own attempts to save herself. He leaned his rifle against the tree.

"Please," she begged, her bottom lip quivering. "Don't j-j-just stand there. T-t-talk to me."

He nodded, not sure what to tell her that would make any difference. He decided on the truth. Taking firm hold of the knife's metal handle, already slippery with blood, Julio braced his other palm to the trunk over her head, and said, "I have to hurt you to save you, baby. Please, don't" —he jerked the blade out of her and tossed it aside— "scream."

She hissed, sucking in a giant breath, as he caught her. Her eyes rolled back in her head. Julio should've known Meg wouldn't scream. She was not most women. Somehow, she'd mentally prepared herself for this exact scenario. Or she was just that tough.

Crouching, he folded her wilting body onto his lap and pressed her head against his chest.

"That hurt," she whimpered as she leaned into him, her poor bloodied body racked with tremors and adrenaline. "Rescuing a person isn't supposed to feel that bad, you know. I think you did it wrong."

Jerking his gear bag off his shoulder, Julio grabbed his blow-out kit, surprised she was able to joke. Grabbing one of his extra t-shirts, he folded it, then pressed it hard to the hole in her shoulder.

She winced, but hissed, "He has Dominic. He's his father. Did you know?"

Julio worked intently on the gash below her collarbone. "I suspected. How long has he been gone?"

"Forever," she whispered, trembling like a leaf. "But really, maybe only five minutes before you showed."

That timeline agreed with what Julio saw as he tore open a good-sized packet of QuikClot with his teeth. The blood painted on Meg's face, neck, and head was fresh, still damp. Without warning her because he didn't want her to tense up, Julio applied a hefty dose of the stinging, antiseptic anticoagulant to her shoulder.

Again, she didn't scream, but she shuddered plenty, and he felt bad that he'd had to hurt her to help her. A pressure bandage came next, then he worked the same methodical examination on her fingers and palms. At last, he'd done all he could. Meg's shoulder, fingers, and hands were bandaged, and his first-aid supplies were depleted. He looked from where he sat to beyond the forest to where he needed to be.

"Don't even think it, Juarez. You are not leaving me behind. I'm going with you," she growled through clenched teeth.

He peered down into those startling bright, and very dangerous, emerald pools. "I know."

"Bastard said he'd send someone back. To stay put. That they'd come for me. The liar!"

Julio's head snapped up at that disquieting news. Liar, nothing. If Zapata sent anyone back, it wouldn't be to rescue the woman he'd pinned like a frog to a tree. Instantly, Julio's sharp eyes quartered the forest and shadows ahead. It had taken an hour at least, to get Meg ready to travel. A wicked man on the run could do a lot with that amount of time. Warn his *compadres*. Send his assassins back to finish Meg. *Kill his son*.

Tenderly, Julio eased Meg off his lap and set her back against the same tree trunk she'd been impaled on. He needed to see better and farther. Automatically, he tugged a pair of gloves out of his pocket and slid his hands into them. One gloved hand went for the Heckler and Koch MP7 on his shoulder. He handed that to Meg without tearing his eyes from the many ways a killer could come at her through the forest between Zapata's bunkers and here.

"Extra mags and ammo in my bag," Julio murmured, keeping his voice low and quiet. "Take what you need. Be ready."

"You think he'd send someone back to kill me? Not h-h-help me?"

Exactly. And if she'd been thinking straight, she would've known that. Julio nodded, his palm at his side, motioning her to be still.

He'd just spotted two men in camouflaged shirts and pants, make that three, walking toward where Julio and Meg crouched, chatting with each other, but carrying rifles like deer hunters on an all-day hunt might. Carelessly. Held at their sides, like luggage. Not paying attention as they should've been. Probably because they expected a defenseless woman still nailed to a tree, instead of the one now aiming her rifle in their direction.

"Is someone coming?" she whispered.

"Yes, but they're too far away. Stay low." *Please, for the love of God, stay low. Rest while you can. Let me handle this.* Julio didn't want to think what these bastards would've done to Meg if he hadn't shown. Pigs, even the two-legged kind, were straight-up cannibals.

He lifted to one knee alongside Meg, needing to be sure. Needing them to see him. Not her. He'd never been a fan of that military saying: *From a place you will not see... Comes a sound you will not hear.* Hell no. He wanted these guys to damned well know they were going to die, who was going to kill them, and why.

Crossing himself with both arms, his Berettas slipped easily from their opposing holsters into his palms.

At last, the killer on the far left froze and waved for his buddies behind him to halt. All forward action ceased as three pairs of cold, dead eyes zeroed in on Julio. Then Meg. Then the rifle in her hands.

He waited. They were close enough now. They knew. They saw. Now was the time to declare their innocence. Or die.

As expected, all three sprang to life with a roar. Like demonic conjoined triplets, they burst off the balls of their feet, firing their rifles on the run. Frightening, yes. Intended to shock and awe the inexperienced, maybe. But not smart.

Julio fired twice. Meg fired once. All three assholes fell, but then Meg fired again and kept firing. And firing. ON one knee now, she kept spraying their bodies with her room broom, her system on overload, until at last, Julio reached for the weapon and stilled her trigger finger.

"I... I... I..."

"You did fine," he assured her as he lifted the short stock up and out of her grip. "Thank you for having my six."

"Y-your s-s-six?" she hissed, her voice quavering and weak as she tipped back into the tree and planted both trembling hands at her sides. "I... I think I had your h-hundred, m-maybe your th-thousand. I c-c-couldn't s-s-stop."

"Works for me," he replied simply. She'd only done what he would've had to do. One shot might take a man down, but a double-tap made certain he stayed down.

So what if Meg had turned that single-tap into a dozen or twenty? Now, Julio didn't have to go out there and do it.

"I can w-w-walk," Meg told him, her voice still weak, but colored with her usual stubbornness.

He didn't want her to come with him. She was severely wounded, and to be honest, he'd been surprised how firmly she'd held that weapon with injured, bandaged fingers and hands. But there was no choice. He couldn't leave her here. "We don't have far to go. Tell me when you need to stop and rest."

As he spoke calmly and reasonably with her, he reached back into his bag and retrieved a bottled sports drink. Twisting the cap off, he put it in her trembling hands, then wrapped her fingers around the bottle to make sure she didn't drop it. Poor thing was on the verge of falling apart, not what he needed when he confronted Zapata.

Meg's smile was as weak as her voice, but she lifted that bottle and tipped her head back, downing half the drink before she set the bottle on her trembling kneecap. "Thanks. I only had enough water for Dom. But that's okay. I didn't mind."

But Julio did. Forced marches were hard on the strongest men, but for a woman to go without rehydration? In this heat? Unthinkable. Julio gave her just enough time to rest. Gave those well-touted electrolytes and water the minimum time to restore her energy, too.

But time was not on their side. By now, Zapata would've heard the gunfire. He was now forewarned and forearmed. Which spelled trouble for Dominic. Zapata was not known for kindness. Whatever he wanted that boy for had nothing to do with fatherly love.

Julio lifted to his feet, not sure how he could safely rescue the boy without further traumatization. Life shouldn't be this hard.

"I'm going with you," Meg said again. She set a hand to the ground beside her and rolled to one hip, shaky but determined to get back on her feet.

"Not yet," Julio told her patiently, his palm gentle on her shoulder.

With a huff, she leaned back against the tree trunk, a sorry, sad sight with all that blood smeared on her face and over her head.

Tugging his pack of wet-wipes out of a pants pocket, he handed them to Meg. Then, Julio took a tiny hypo from his blow-out kit. He only carried the one. "This is only a local, Meg. It won't last long, but it will kill the pain while we travel. Do you want it now, or would you rather wait until we take Zapata down? Until you have Dom back?"

"Later," she replied quickly. "I've got a son to rescue, and a man to kill. Hurry, Julio. Help me up, damn it. Let's do this."

Julio almost smiled. This woman meant to die to save a boy that wasn't even hers. An orphan. *Dios, I love her.*

Chapter Forty-One

Zapata was going to die. No ifs. No buts. No two ways about it. First, Meg meant to put one round through one of his thick, meaty legs. Didn't matter which, as long as it stopped him. Then, another through his cold black heart. That sucker was probably inked, too. Damn him to hell.

Not that she thought those shots would kill Domingo Zapata. God, she hated the name. It resembled Dominic's too much! But she was pretty sure Zapata didn't have a heart like Dominic did, not the way he'd jerked that frantic little boy out of her arms, then dropped him screaming and scared-to-death on his poor little backside. Zapata had to. That was the only way he could stab Meg to that tree where animals could've gotten at her. Panthers. Bears. The occasional harpy eagle. Even ants could've eaten her alive!

But the most heartrending part was that poor Dominic had watched the atrocity. He'd screamed, "Mum!" so many times that his cries actually hurt worse than being pinned to a freakin' tree. Zapata wasn't a man. He was a rabid dog, one that Meg meant to put down before he hurt her sweet little boy again. She couldn't wait to end the motherfucker!

Her blood boiled, and a frightening kind of rage energized every step forward. Since the moment she'd climbed unsteadily to her feet, she'd set the pace, and Julio had let her. Without any words, he walked at her side. Smart man. Because she was *not* leaving Brazil without that little boy. No way in hell. Dominic was going home to America with her. Today!

Until Julio's hand clamped onto her good arm. Ha! That was a joke. She had no good arms left. Only a deep-seated need to get her son back... No. Matter. What.

"Hold up," Julio cautioned in that deep, wise voice that got under her skin every time he used it.

Breathing hard and sweating like a hog, she slowed just enough to spare him a perturbed glance. He didn't look as weary as she felt, or as tired. But he was angry. It radiated off those tensed muscles up his neck and across his heaving chest. His eyes were darker black now, his jaw looked square and carved out of stone. The short stock rifle he carried swept continually from side to side, as if he expected another ambush. Smart man.

"What?" she asked, jerking out of his touch. Then instantly regretting it. Man, that sudden move hurt almost as bad as walking. Worse, the bleak shadow that passed through those dark eyes of his told Meg she'd hurt Julio's feelings by pulling away.

He shut that response down before she could apologize or explain how much this rescue mission meant. There was no *try* in this day, just *do, do, do,* damn it! Just save Dominic before his asshole father hurt him anymore. Just die trying if it came to that.

Still trudging at her side like a loyal dog, Julio asked quietly, "Have you been inside Zapata's bunkers? His cellblocks? His lair?"

"Nope, but I'm sure as fuck going in today." A warrior's need to curse Zapata back to Dante's seven levels of Hell filled Meg's soul. "Going to kick his ass, kill him, and take my kid," Meg growled with confidence. Then she thought to ask, "Have you?"

"Once." Julio replied. "It's built of concrete blocks. Fifteen-inch-thick, square, concrete blocks. Not hollow like the ones you find at Home Depot, but solid concrete. There are no windows in two of the three outbuildings. All have steel, barred doors that will be locked. The only way in is with the keys Zapata wears around his neck, or through the narrow openings beneath those doors, where water, food, or live rats are shoved in."

Meg swallowed hard. Still marching, never hesitating, but... "Live rats?"

Julio nodded grimly. "Sometimes snakes and spiders. Anything to torment his prisoners, the women and girls he keeps there."

Whoa. She hadn't expected those scenarios. But okay then. Neither rats, snakes, nor spiders would stop her from savng Dominic. But they did make her think. *Women and girls, huh?* "How do you want to do this? How many guards do you think he's got? Where should we hit first?"

Man, how she wished for one of those tank killing LAWs. Nothing could stop her then.

But why was anyone, man or woman, ever loyal to monsters like Zapata? Or Hitler? Or Lenin, Stalin, and Putin? That, she'd never understand. This had to be hell for Julio though, reliving the exact same scenario that had gone so wrong only two short years ago.

Meg shoved her feelings aside. This rescue would not end with suicide and failure to thrive. Never! Once she had Dominic back in her arms, she'd smuggle him into the States if she had to. She'd get him the best help she could find. He would live a long life. Zapata could go to hell!

Julio pulled her to an abrupt stop. Which did not help. Moving was better. Not moving made her instantly dizzy and tired. Made her want to drop to her ass and rest for a spell.

His sharp eyes noticed when she slapped a palm to the nearest tree trunk. It was either that or fall down. Instantly, he pulled another bottled drink out of his bag and pushed it into her hands. But to open it, she had to lean her back into the tree to balance. It still took too long fumbling the cap off. Turning it to break the seal took more strength than she had, and Meg knew she was on the verge of exhaustion. But she refused to fall back or hold off, not until she had Dom. Sleep and rest could wait. He couldn't.

"Are you sure about this?" Julio asked when she was finally able to take a sip.

Her hands shook even as she lifted that sixteen ounce bottle. And there she was, the weak link again. Shaking from shock, and, okay, wounded, damn it. Meg nodded her determination. "I'm not leaving without Dominic."

"Okay then." He jerked that bolt-action MK-13 up high into his shoulder. Nearly into his injured bicep. Meg remembered then. She wasn't the only one hurt here, yet Julio had never complained nor shirked his duty despite his wounds. And that pain in his heart from losing Tomas had to be killing him all over again. This had to feel like an instant replay of what he'd lived through when he'd rescued Tomas.

She stared into the trees, her heart broken for the man she loved, yet breaking all over again for the child she very well might lose today. She and Julio. If only she were made of stronger stuff.

"We go in fast and we shoot to kill," he told her sternly, the light in his eyes gone flat. His jaw set a fierce angle and his voice cold and hard. "Don't look for Zapata or his armed guards. I'll take care of them. Just locate Dominic. Don't save anyone else. Don't listen to anyone crying. Don't speak. Don't fall. If it's not Dominic, keep moving. Keep your eyes on the goal, Meg, not the obstacles."

That frightened her. "Who... who else is in there?"

Julio shook his head. "No one we can help. We're here for Dominic only. Don't forget him for one damned second. Waste anyone who gets between you and that boy, got it?"

Whoa. Julio had just morphed into one badassed warrior again. His black eyes were hard as flint, and she could swear his jaw had turned into an iron anvil. Each command came out clipped and final. Mean.

"L-let's do this," she replied with as much bravado as she could muster. "You lead. I'll follow."

Meg stuffed the nearly full bottle into her shirt. Dom would need it. He was the important one here, not her. Not anyone else. If she fell today, Julio would make sure Dom made it out of Brazil and was adopted by decent, kind people. Maybe even by him. That'd be nice. They needed each other.

Okay then. They were now within sight of a couple concrete structures that scared the bejesus out of her, they were so tall and wide and imposing. Didn't matter. She'd already reloaded her weapon. The flimsy bag Zapata had let her keep, now carried two full magazines, courtesy of Julio's masterful preparedness. It was time to shock the living hell out of Zapata and take back what he'd stolen. His son's life!

Chapter Forty-Two

Leading with his rifle, Julio stepped into the narrow dirt alley that ran between the two cellblocks at this end of Zapata's compound. There were no windows in either building to give Julio away, or allow a glimpse of who, if anyone, waited hopelessly beyond the concrete walls. No hope of hearing anyone call or cry out for help, either. The whole place was eerily quiet, which made Julio wonder if he'd guessed wrong. Was Zapata even here?

Straight ahead, the wall of the third concrete building loomed, creating a T-intersection and a decision point. The imposing, ten-foot-high wall of the third cellblock, the place where he'd found Bianca living in modest comfort while his son had languished, blocked the way forward.

With any other warrior at his side, Julio would've gone left while that operator went right. Together, they'd silently and efficiently put down whatever obstacles they encountered. They'd search the third cellblock for armed assassins, then meet at the firepit in front of Zapata's barren bunker. The place where he'd once lived and had committed unspeakable horrors. Rapes. Murders. Tortures. It was no home away from home. More like living Hell on earth.

But this time around that operator was Meg, and like it or not, she was compromised. Stubborn, but not able to stand long on her feet. She wasn't able or strong enough to fight as viciously as she might need to. Which meant they'd both have to turn right.

The only problem? They'd have to pass the one barred doorway. The last time Julio had done that, the cell had been crammed full of desperate, starving women and girls, some just toddlers. They'd reached out for him, and begged for help. Cried. Screamed hysterically for him not to leave them. Fortunately, Zapata had been out of Brazil back then, up north in the States hunting Suede Tennyson, now Suede Sinclair, Chance's wife. Zapata hadn't left his bunker or cellblocks properly protected.

After taking down what few guards there were, Julio had searched the cellblocks while FBI Agent Coltrane had handled the exfil for all those women and girls. But those voices and tears still haunted him. He'd faltered that day. Meg might falter today. Could she handle what she might see? What she might hear? All that begging? Those tears? Those tiny little children?

Julio crossed himself and whispered a quick Hail Mary to the Virgin to protect Meg.

Too soon, they were at the T-intersection. He ordered her to, "Stay on my six, Duncan. Eyes forward. Don't let anyone touch you." *Or stop you from reaching Dominic.*

She cupped his shoulder, the covert operator's hand signal for affirmative.

Okay then. With nerves strung tight, Julio glanced to his left to make sure it was clear, then turned right. Stealthily, he and Meg crept past the only barred door, and found it empty. Small comfort that.

Advancing along the concrete wall of the final cellblock toward Zapata's bunker, Julio froze. Meg hadn't yet seen what he had. He didn't want her to.

Yet Zapata had seen him. "You cannot hide, Agent Juarez," he called out, his voice raspy and gruff. Heartless. "Come out in the open, where I can see you. I have what you want. We both know that."

Julio stepped into the clearing between the cellblocks and Zapata, his rifle sight set on the bastard's forehead. But poor Dominic was huddled against the far wall of the round metal cage hanging above a stone firepit that, for now, was cold.

"Mum!" he called frantically once Meg cleared the final cellblock, his skinny arms stretching between the bars. His frantic calls turned to shuddering sobs of, "Mum! Mum! Mum!"

Instinctively, she took a step toward him. "Dom! No!"

"Stay," Julio ordered as he caught her by wounded shoulder.

Her breath hitched, but she obeyed and stopped in her tracks. Painfully alert now, he sensed others coming up behind him and Meg. Around them. Through the trees. Between the cell blocks Shadows with weapons and magazines being rammed home with sharp metallic clicks and slaps.

Meg's thigh bumped his. Then her bicep. She was scared.

But Julio never hesitated. He'd been in worse stand-offs before. "The boy goes with us," he growled. "Get him out of that cage. Now."

Zapata's square head canted fifteen degrees, as if seeing Meg surprised him. "You saved the woman. Why? Do you think to trade her? For my son? She is nothing to me," Zapata muttered, his voice as gravelly and cruel as ever. A smoker's voice. Gruff. Grating. Cold. His index finger lifted, pointing back and forth between Julio and himself. "This is between you and me. Not the hairless *cadela* who thought she could steal my son. She is nothing. But we have unfinished business, *meu querido irmão.*"

Little brother.

Julio gave the insult right back to him. *"Porcos vagabundos não têm irmãos, mas apenas um encontro com a Morte! E este é o meu único negócio pendente com você."*

Pigs do not have little brothers. Only a date with Death! That is my only unfinished business with you.

Zapata didn't answer, just stared at Meg, as the prickly sensation of more scopes zeroed in on Julio's head. They'd walked into an ambush. He'd have to be quick on the draw to save both Meg and Dominic. He'd have to be lucky if *they* were going to live. He didn't plan to, but Meg and Dom would.

Because this was what faithful husbands and fathers did. They died protecting their *familias*. In the grand scope of things, Julio now knew why he'd been born, and why he'd suffered throughout his life. Everything he'd endured and lived through, every heartbreak and funeral, had brought him to this single point in time. From the beginning, his life had been forfeit. The only reason for his birth then was to save Meg Duncan and the son she loved today.

So be it.

Relief flooded his soul as Julio's chest filled with sublime understanding. He'd never been more sure that the God he'd worshipped and prayed to all these sad, lonely years, had answered every one of his prayers. The divine decision had been made Julio had taken his first breath. God had always known who he was, that he would forever be His obedient son. At long last, there was comfort in understanding precisely Who had always been in charge. In knowing that God had never deserted him. That He was here, even at the end.

Julio's heartbeat calmed. The grip on his rifle had never felt more solid nor his mission so clear. At last, Zapata *would* die. Julio might also, but Meg and Dom would live to go home. Back to Texas. *Count on it.*

Once more worthy to be at Meg's side, Julio straightened. Peace filtered down from that far off heaven above, which had suddenly drawn near.

Until Meg roared like an Irish banshee, pivoted to her right, stuck her pointed elbow in Julio's side, and let her weapon roar. "Br-r-r-r-r-r-t!" Then another deafening, *"Br-r-r-r-r-r-t! Br-r-r-r-r-r-t! Br-r-r-r-r-r-t!"*

Bright, deadly laser bursts flashed from the business end of her Heckler and Koch. Pivoting in a tight semi-circle, with her back to him and swearing like a sailor, she lit that dark, shadowy clearing with magnificent sprays of focused lightning. Yet not a single predator fired back. Had they all overlooked her? Had she simply caught them by surprise?

Regardless, Julio fired, covering her. Only when he turned to his left did he catch the red, white, and blue of several God-blessed, forward assaulting flags on the arms of the camouflaged warriors who'd literally dropped out of heaven. That explained why Zapata's men weren't shooting back. They were caught in a crossfire between her and the fast-roping USA assault team that had just—in the nick of time—joined the fight.

By then, Julio's rifle was out of ammo. He switched to his Berettas, accurately picking off Zapata's bastards one by one. There was no escape. Zapata'd underestimated the power of God and of the woman at Julio's side. His men had gotten in too close, too fast.

They couldn't run from Meg or whoever those USA angels were.

In the midst of all that eardrum-shattering destruction, Julio saw Zapata's mouth open wide, no doubt bellowing orders no one could hear. Sneering like Satan, he jerked something out of his rear pocket and tossed it into the firepit. Instant flames burst to life.

Backing against the bars of what had become a deathtrap, poor little Dominic's mouth opened wide with an unheard, "Mum! Mum!"

Meg's weapon ceased firing, as she ran into Hell to save her boy. "No! No, no, no!"

Instinct took over, and before that team from Heaven—or Fort Campbell, Kentucky—mistook her for an enemy combatant, Julio followed her, covering her ass, while she closed the to Zapata.

With every step she took, he watched her intently, like a snake. His upper lip twisted into a wicked sneer. One black-inked hand lifted, the dark blade in his fingers balanced between his fingertips, ready to be thrown. This man rarely fired a gun, but he was damned good with knives.

Not. Today.

The Berettas that had saved Julio's life so many times in the past, now riddled Zapata's short, squat body. He jerked backwards. His shoulders pitched forward and his arms flopped, when each deadly round plowed into his thick chest and gut. God, the satisfaction.

Julio's aim was true; he didn't miss once. Yet Zapata still breathed. The initial impact had blown him flat against his bunker. With a hard thump, he'd hit the wall. But he hadn't dropped his blade, and Meg was now fumbling to free Dominic, shouting, "God, help me, Julio! Julio! Anyone!"

Frantically, she strained back on her heels, pulling the heavy metal cage aside and away from the fire. Flames hadn't yet reached it enough to have heated any bars. As long as she held the cage at that angle, poor Dominic was in no danger. But the woman didn't seem to understand that in rushing to save Dominic, she'd put herself in harm's way.

Frightened, Dominic punctuated every grasping reach for her with, "Mum! Mum! Mum!" He'd plastered himself to the side nearest Meg. His arms were stuck between the bars, clutching at her, demanding she hold him instead of the cage.

All Meg could see was her boy. She'd lost situational awareness. Zapata could and would still kill her.

Julio put himself between the woman and child he loved and the bastard he hated. Dominic didn't need to see what happened next. Neither did Meg.

Zapata had just sunk to his knees. But the son of a bitch's chest was still expanding. Because of Kevlar. The bastard had come to this fight prepared. *Fat lot of good, that.*

Because finally, the time had come. After too many years planning for this precise moment, Julio arm straightened as he zeroed down on the psychopath from Hell.

Zapata's ungodly black eyes glared up at Julio. Yet even wounded, with blood dripping out of his mouth, godawful hatred growled out of him. *"Vejo você no inferno um dia."*

I will see you in hell, this day.

Julio shook his head, the pistol in his right hand warm and sure—like an old friend. "I think not," he replied evenly and in the language of his chosen country. "When I die, I will go to my Father and my son."

Sudden awareness flashed like a flame come to life deep within Domingo's evil eyes. "Your son? He is dead?" An ugly smile lifted that sneer. "I killed your weak little bastard after all," he purred, lifting his knife. "That is good to know. Then go, *amigo*. Go to hell. Join your pitiful excuse for a man-child in—"

"I am not your friend!" Julio hissed at the man he hated with every fiber of his father's heart. "But this"—he aimed, and, with full intent and years of missing that perfect man-child, Julio put one round through Zapata's tattooed forehead— "is for Tomas! My son!"

Then, for insurance, a quick double-tap. "And this is for *your* son, Zapata. You are a fool. You lose. Everything. Now go to hell with your brother and never know peace."

Which was not all Domingo deserved, but which was all Julio could humanly do. True justice would still come to this wicked excuse of a man, but it would come at the hand of God. Julio turned back to the woman and the child he loved. He would never confess this sin, nor seek forgiveness for it. Ending Domingo's bloody reign was a most righteous kill. God damned well knew it.

"Julio, help me," Meg cried.

With a quick mental snap back to reality, he rejoined the battle, which had turned into clean-up now that Zapata was dead. Quartering the scene, Julio confirmed that none of Zapata's men's bodies so much as twitched. And those angels who'd fast-roped from heaven? None other than Special Agent Coltrane. She and the three hefty men with her were moving from body to body, securing the scene. Applying double-taps where needed, not first-aid.

Reaching down, Julio jerked Zapata's keys off his bloody neck and turned his attention to the tender little lamb bleating for his "Mum! Mum! Mum! Muuuuum!"

Wasn't that just like a son? To look past his father to the mother he adored?

Meg was still working at the hatch, but her bloody fingers were too slippery. Poor thing. Sweat glistened on her grimy forehead, and the knife wound in her shoulder was bleeding through her bandage. "I can't... Grrrr... Shit, Julio! I can't get him out!"

"Muuuuum!"

"Allow me, Mamita," Julio replied. But first, with one hand he reached over his shoulder and ripped his shirt over his head, then tossed it over the pit and smothered the fire. He wouldn't put it past Meg to burn herself saving Dom. God, this woman never quit. Not once had she hesitated in her zeal to save this boy. Her boy.

My boy.

Even now, Meg cast Julio a savage, "Help me, damn it!" that made him smile.

"Yes, ma'am," he replied, his chest swelling with pride and more love than he'd known was possible. This was what real mothers did. They fought for their children even when they were on their last legs, and Meg was barely holding on. Maybe he'd been wrong about that whole divine decision thing. Maybe he wasn't the one meant to die today. Maybe the man who'd had to die was the Julio he'd been before he'd met this amazing mother bear.

Her stubborn head bobbed. "Yeah, well, it's out now, Juarez. Hurry up! This cage is heavy!"

Silly, wonderful woman didn't seem to realize the fire was out.

Easing the heavy cage out of her trembling hands, Julio turned it until its hatch faced him. A single padlock was all that stood between Dominic and his weary Mum. "Are you ready to get out of there?" Julio asked, as he tried the smallest keys first.

Nodding vigorously, the sad boy bounced his tummy against the bars, tears streaming down his face. "Me Muma. Me M-m-mum."

"Then your Muma it is," Julio promised quietly, as he pulled the hatch open and angled Meg's son—never Zapata's!—head first and out between the bars.

The moment she had Dominic in her hands, Meg's butt hit the concrete. She started cooing and murmuring, calling him her brave little boy. Telling him she was so, so proud of him. That she loved him and would never, ever leave him.

If only Meg had been Tomas' mother. He would've lived.

"Oh, baby, baby, baby," she cried when Dominic broke down, sobbing into her chest. "You're safe, sweetheart. Promise. I'll never let you go. Ever. I love you too much to lose you again." Then, "Mmm, mmm, mmm," she murmured, as she covered his head and face with kisses.

Tears filled Julio's eyes, his heart broken at the sight of true and holy motherhood sitting cross-legged there on the ground with her hand extended to him. Covered in tears and sweat and blood, but smiling and at peace, all because of that sweet little guy snuggled under her chin. He couldn't help it; he turned away. Because those were the purest kind of kisses, and they were breaking his heart. Those were mother's kisses, the sweetest blessings a child could ask for. They were warm, moist stamps of love incarnate. What Tomas should've had every day of his short, tragic life.

Rage ignited deep in Julio's gut all over again. *God damn Bianca! God damn Zapata—!*

"Julio," Meg cried, her grimy, sweaty face dripping with tears. "Get your ass down here. I need you. Now. Come on! Sit with us. Please. Dom needs you, too."

Before he complied, Julio scanned the battlefield one last time. Coltrane and her men were efficient and quick. No one moved except them. Except Meg and Dominic.

Madre de Dios... How gloriously righteous motherhood glowed. How perfect. The light in her dewy green eyes shimmered like nothing else in the world. Certainly not like the weak light off stones or gems, wealth nor power. She was everything Julio had ever wanted in a woman. Like him, Meg knew *familia* was the only thing worth dying—and living—for.

Julio dropped to his knees in homage before this woman. This angel. With tears in his eyes, he gathered his new *familia* into his arms. He sheltered them, and, silently, he vowed to die for them.

His cheek landed on top of Meg's sweaty head, and relief shuddered out of her. But when one tiny, dirty hand reached up though the tears and tangled arms and latched onto Julio's ear, it was Dom who shattered what was left of Julio's warrior's heart. The sweet child held onto that ear until he'd wiggled out of Meg's arms and burrowed into Julio's.

As thin and fragile as he was, Julio worried he might hurt Dominic. But that little boy seemed to want what only Julio could offer—a father's embrace. Which Julio gave freely. As soon as his arms closed around Dom, the boy snuggled under Julio's chin, sobbing and hiccupping, seemingly inconsolable. But oh, so still. With each shuddering breath he calmed. One little hand flattened over Julio's sternum, those five fingers fluttering as if, somehow, Dominic knew he was finally safe.

Humbled, Julio smoothed a big, manly palm down the little man's back, giving Dominic the same comfort he'd once given Tomas. Pouring his heart into his second son.

Leaning back on her palms, Meg looked up at Julio, her emerald greens still brimming. "Told you he needed you, Daddy."

Dios! That word! The pain that always came with it ripped through Julio's gut like a lightning strike. But suddenly, as if someone had finally flipped a switch, the pain blossomed into comforting warmth instead of icy despair. He hadn't sunk into the sucking black hole of regret like he had before. Instead of wanting to die for all he'd lost, at last, Julio realized how much he'd found. He was free.

With a shudder, Julio took a deep, satisfying breath. He was going to be a father and husband. A daddy. As if this were a lesson he hadn't yet learned to the Lord's satisfaction, he bowed his lips to Dom's sweaty head and whispered, "Si, Padre. You are right. I do choose life. I will always choose life. Your life."

Meg ended his prayer with a reverent, "Amen."

Chapter Forty-Three

Meg held tight to Dominic. As if he'd known how weak she'd grown, Julio's bone-crushing hug hadn't eased since they'd settled aboard the chopper Dooley had sent to retrieve them.

Man, that Agent Coltrane was some kind of super-agent, the way she and her guys had dropped out of nowhere at the last second. Guess some Texas senator had jerked her chain the moment Domingo Zapata broke out of that *allegedly* secure federal prison. Coltrane must've dealt with Zapata before. Interesting.

Meg was ten kinds of exhausted and sore. After they'd rescued Dominic, Julio gave her that shot of pain-killer, and it helped. Then. All she'd needed was him and Dominic back in her hands. The Zapata brother's death-grip on the Highlands of Minas Gerais was over. Done. Pepe and his village would now live in peace, at least for as long as it lasted. But with every jolt and bump the helo made, streaks of fire radiated through the hole in her shoulder. She wasn't sure how much longer she could last.

Dominic was sound asleep with his thumb in his mouth, snoring into the hollow of her sweaty neck. Julio wasn't talking much, and Meg didn't blame him. He'd kiss the side of her head, and occasionally, her lips. She couldn't have heard him over the noise anyway. She hadn't been given a helmet with a commlink, not that she cared. She had nothing to say to anyone. Not yet. She needed more time to decompress and process what she'd done at Zapata's bunkers. Trevor was right. Killing, even in self-defense, took part of a person's soul. Yet she'd do it all again. Losing Dominic or Julio would've been worse.

This marathon day had to have been hard on Julio. Marching into Zapata's stronghold had certainly scared the bejesus out of Meg. She couldn't imagine what reliving Tomas' rescue, only to lose that precious boy months later, did to Julio. Talk about a nightmare.

Her entire left side had gone numb hours ago, and she had a killer migraine that worried the crap out of her. She'd had a similar headache the morning of her stroke. God wouldn't be that cruel, would He? She'd been humbled enough these last twenty-four hours, hadn't she? Why punish her now, when she had everything she'd ever wanted in her arms and wrapped around her?

'I'll go to church again. I'll be good,' she silently promised the Almighty. *'Heck, I'll be great, if only You'd let this small infraction slide. I shouldn't have*

deceived Captain Dooley. But don't punish me for loving this boy enough to die for him. And kill for him.'

Although none of what happened today was her fault. Well, except for dodging Dooley. That was *not* exactly smart, but Meg knew she'd do it again. Dominic had needed her when his bastard father showed up. The creep. Who could believe such a little lamb had come from the loins of that... that animal?

'So there,' she told the Lord with a hint of attitude. *'None of what happened today was my fault. If not for me, Dominic would've had to face Zapata all by himself. You should thank me for being gutsy enough to do stupid stuff once in a while. Although...'* She swallowed hard. *'That was probably Your idea all along, wasn't it? You needed someone to stand with Dominic in his time of need. You didn't want him to be alone, did You? So You... You picked me?'*

God didn't answer. Of course. Unlike Meg's, His ways were more subtle. Yet the notion that He'd chosen her for this awesome, awful mission humbled Meg. Tears sprang to her tired, bleary eyes. She could understand why God needed Julio. The man prayed to Him. Hell, he had the entire Hail Mary tattooed on his chest in reverence to the Holy Virgin. But Meg? She wasn't even physically strong. She was a defect and a burden and... Brazil might not let her adopt Dom. That worried her the most.

'God,' she prayed. *'I love this little boy. Please smooth the way for me to keep him. Please. I... I can't*

let him go. He needs me, and I love him. I'll be so, so good to him.'

Which made her think of Domingo Zapata and the Spanish hexes and curses he'd inked all over his ugly body. Even his face and his skull. *Ewww.* He and Julio were polar opposites, the darkly stained spawn of Hell fighting a guardian angel. One who had only ever fought for good, while the other murdered innocent women and children. The eternal dichotomy. Good versus evil.

The pain in her head throbbed and Meg turned away from Julio before he saw. *'And, oh yes, thank you for sending Julio to save me again. I don't know how he found us, but I know he believes in You. He told me so.'*

Like she had to tell Him that? Meg chalked up all this chatting with God nonsense to the throbbing pain in her head. She hadn't prayed this much in years, not since Julio showed up with his *Madre de Dios.*

Currently, the chopper was on its way back over the Atlantic to the *Iwo Jima* where she no doubt had a butt reaming coming. Well, bring it the hell on. She'd never apologize for risking her life to save this child—any child! But man, she was so, so tired. Dooley had better watch his step. She wouldn't go down easy.

It'd be really nice if she could just crawl into the bed and sleep for a week. Preferably with Julio in her arms and Dominic somewhere close by with his blankie. But she'd probably end up in the brig, and that was so wrong.

Julio tapped her helmet, so she had to look at him then. He cocked his head, a question she couldn't answer in his sharp eyes. She shouldn't have looked. Her heart was too full; her tears betrayed her. Meg found herself pulled onto Julio's lap and her head pressed against his shoulder, helmet and all, while she cried.

He started rocking, and her troubles faded away. Her head stopped hurting. She had what she wanted, Julio and Dominic. She only hoped she could keep them.

Once the helo landed, Julio took Dominic, then helped her climb onto the deck and steadied her until she had her balance. A wave of dizziness hit her anyway, and she latched onto Julio's wrist before she fell. Corpsman Giacomo must've seen. The next thing she knew, he'd draped a thick, warm blanket over her. Another corpsman showed up with a gurney, and by then, Meg was going down. In her zeal to save Dominic, she'd put aside the fact that she'd been pinned to a freakin' tree, and it was all catching up with her now.

And then, she was flat on her back with an oxygen mask over her face.

Julio leaned over her with a sleepy Dominic in his hands. "You're going to sickbay," he shouted over the noisy rotor slap of an incoming helo.

Like a spoiled brat, Meg cried, "But I want to stay with you."

The gentlest, sweetest light washed over his ruggedly handsome face. "You will," he promised before he leaned into her and kissed her forehead.

She gave back as good as she could, but exhaustion was calling her name. The trip to sickbay was a disjointed ride. Corpsman Giacomo wasn't smiling. Somewhere along the way, he'd started her on an IV drip. "Who did this to you?" he asked, his voice hard and tight.

"Domingo Zapata. He kinda stuck a knife in me and pinned me to a tree. You believe a guy would do that?"

"I'll kill him," Lucas snarled.

"Julio already did," Meg explained drowsily. "Then he saved my little boy, Dominic, and… and me." And that did it. The day had kicked Meg's butt. Again, she couldn't stop the tears.

"Don't let her kid you," Julio murmured as he materialized at her side from somewhere else in the room and intertwined his fingers with her. "This woman could've taken on the entire seventh fleet today. You should've seen her. Word to the wise, do not mess with Meg Duncan. She'll whup your ass."

Meg hadn't known he was there. She'd lost sight of him, but his words almost made her smile. Until Captain Dooley loomed over her and said, "You disobeyed a direct order, soldier."

"Yes," she whispered dreamily up at his stern face. "And I'd do it again."

That was the last thing she remembered. Until the next morning when she opened her eyes in the same bed she and Julio had made love in. Better yet, his warm, rugged body was pressed intimately against her back. She wiggled her bandaged toes and fingers, so damned thankful she hadn't had another stroke. God did work in mysterious ways.

Her head was resting on Julio's bicep. He'd wrapped his other arm around her shoulders, palming her breast like, well, like a man. He certainly had a hand full, and she was glad she could give him that. She'd been with him long enough to know he liked— make that adored, worshipped, and revered—her breasts. Her bandaged shoulder felt tight, but not as bad as she'd expected. Of course, she had yet to move much more than fingers and toes.

"You're awake," he breathed into the nape of her neck.

Meg sighed. "No, I'm pretty sure I've died and gone to heaven. How'd I get here?"

"Captain Dooley paced you I my custody. He said you were more trouble than you're worth."

"Hmmm. Guess that means I don't have armed guards anymore."

"No, ma'am. All threats are neutralized. You're good to go." She lifted up to let him ease his arm out from beneath her. Once on his knees, he pressed her flat to her back. "Did I hurt you?"

"You could never," she replied as she held out both arms to him. "Come here."

He obliged, aligning his muscular body over hers. Whoa. This man was ready for action, and suddenly, so was she.

"You scared the hell out of me," he said quietly, blinking down at her, his forearms alongside her head. "Back there, when you started shooting. That wasn't the plan."

"I didn't know we had a plan."

"We didn't. Not really. But when you screamed and ran straight at Zapata, I thought you were going to strangle him with your bare hands, if he didn't kill you first. What were you thinking?"

"That he was burning my baby." Speaking of which... Her heart triple somersaulted up her throat. "Where's Dominic?"

"Don't worry. He's with your buddies, the Lucas and Dan show."

Meg could've laughed if it wouldn't hurt her shoulder. "My buddies?"

Julio lowered his face to hers until they bumped noses. That was when she realized she had no clothes on. Neither did he. Expertly, he eased his wide, male body between her legs, and pressed a kiss to her forehead, then one to each eyelid. "Yes, your buddies. Everyone on this ship loves you, Meg. Some of them are trying to find a way to put you in for a medal of honor."

What a silly idea. "That isn't going to happen. I'm no hero. Heck, I'm not even military anymore."

"I know, but you give your love away like it's a free gift, and you went above and beyond what aid workers are supposed to do. You've drawn these people toward you. They love you, and they adore Dominic. He's become quite the celebrity. You should see the toys he's got now."

"Love *is* a free gift," she told Julio as her hands smoothed over his too-serious face. His freshly shaven chin and cheeks. His elegant black brows, knitted so tight. She ran a fingertip down the straight blade of his nose. "It's what makes the world go around, remember?"

And conversation stalled. Her core clenched, as he kissed his way down her body, far enough down that he had to ease back on his haunches to continue the downward trek.

What was this handsome man thinking?

Pausing over the nested curls at the apex of her thighs, Julio nuzzled where no man had ever nuzzled before. Gah! It was so damned erotic. Instinctively, she lifted her hips and arched into his mouth. Her greedy but poor bandaged fingers delved into his rich, thick hair, holding him in place as he licked and tasted. Growled and tongued until she was out of her mind and couldn't hold still anymore.

"Julio, I... Gah, I..."

The fireworks started slowly, then rippled up her spine and out the top of her head like one of those tank killer rockets. *God, oh God, oh God!* With just his mouth, he'd made her fly, explode, and... lightning. He'd created lightning. In her!

So good! So, so high! This incredible man worked wonders. Long after the lightning slowed, pleasure throbbed through her twitchy, happy body. All she could do was breathe through it until her heart settled back to normal sinus rhythm.

Tears filled her eyes. Meg honestly didn't know what she'd do without Julio in her life. He'd brought so much joy and compassion. Strength. He'd made her believe in herself again.

He looked up from his work, his mouth wet and his lips shining. And smiling. His eyes were uncommonly dark and bright. "More?" he asked, his voice as deep and humble as ever. He licked his lips, the tease.

"Yes, please," she whispered, her body and heart on fire for this man. "Only this time, come with me?" she asked. "Please. I don't want to fly without you, Julio. Ever again. If it's too soon, tell me to shut up, but you know I love you. I can't remember a time when I didn't."

He climbed back up her body, his shoulder blades rolling like a massive jungle cat's, and his chest brushing over her diamond-hard, sensitized nipples. Setting the flame. Teasing as he enticed. "I do know that."

Meg cupped the back of his head and pulled his face into her neck. She didn't know what she'd meant by that emotional rant, only that she needed him to be—the one. Her one and only. Forever. Did she dare ask him—*that?* Would he say yes, or would he pull back because that particular question was a man's prerogative, not a woman's? Would he be offended if she beat him to it?

She'd seen his reticence when she'd caught up with him the day he'd been shot. He hadn't wanted her to see him wounded. This was a proud Spanish male, which was partly why he gave back so much to his country. Which was also why she adored him. So much, that Meg closed her eyes and kissed the sweet spot under his ear.

Man, she loved this guy. So she held back. Julio was worth waiting for.

Epilogue

Children were messy. Noisy. Carefree. Sometimes smelly. And if lucky, they were rambunctious, maybe a little naughty, too. And healthy. At least, well on their way to being healthy. Simple things children everywhere deserved to be.

Dominic, the resident boy wonder, had finally achieved the age in his short life where he dared Julio and Meg at every turn. Did the expertly designed baby gate at the bottom of the staircase stop him from visiting his Mum while she worked in her upstairs office? Not on your life. He simply took hold of the railing while standing on the bottom step, then climbed the open staircase from the outside. Sometimes, he even chortled with every step he climbed, as if he were getting away with something. Which he was.

On the twelfth step, when his hard, little head bumped the front room ceiling, he ducked and scrambled between the uprights, then scampered into Meg's office, where he was not supposed to be. Dominic knew that, but he did it anyway.

Meg was the real culprit. Because not once had she refused this charming three-year-old when he appeared mischievously at her side. If anything, that warm motherly snuggle, hug, and kiss rewarded that headstrong boy.

Julio couldn't blame her, as once again, he unfastened the gate and climbed the staircase to retrieve his son for his much-needed afternoon nap. Dom was a good boy, and he was finally healthy enough to behave like a normal three-year-old. His daily FDC, his fixed dose of the four strongest TB drugs on the market, had recently been readjusted due to his increased weight and energy. The boy Julio had once thought was dying, smiled all the time now. He loved to climb, and he giggled like a little kid should. What's more, he was smart and rapidly learning English, as well as the Spanish and Portuguese Julio kept teaching him.

It was important a child remember his ethnicity. His heritage. Well, except for his father. Julio hoped Dom would forget that bastard and all that had happened in Brazil. He didn't plan to ever tell his son who his real father or mother were. Ever. Dom didn't need the curse of that foul parentage hovering over him the rest of his life, and Domingo and Bianca didn't deserve one second of this little guy's remembrance. They didn't deserve him at all. They had what they'd wanted most out of life—each other. In Hell. Good riddance.

It was now four months since Julio and Meg had adopted Dominic and brought him out of Brazil. Together, they'd bought a starter home on the outskirts of Big Springs, Texas, where her parents still lived. It was small, nothing like the grand house Bianca had insisted on in California. But this place was the one Meg wanted. It was home. Three bedrooms, a two-car garage, and a thirty-year mortgage.

While Meg managed her new business, a Texas state program to feed hungry school children, Julio managed Senator Sullivan's *Dia de Muertos Team* long distance, with an occasional hands-on visit to New Mexico. He'd hired two more special operators, Tripp Mendez and Mateo Navarro, to replace the men he'd lost. The former warrior was an Army Ranger, the latter a SEAL. Both were capable, steady operators and actively engaged back in Brazil at the moment. Julio had them checking on Mayor Rafael Velasquez and Pepe, as well as the other villagers who'd been enslaved. Tripp and Mateo's mission was more humanitarian than lethal, this time.

Rick Santiago had stayed on as advisor after Julio hit Senator Sullivan up about changing his Rules of Engagement. Sullivan agreed. Said one was, after all, a lonely number. That two was better, especially in the dark world of covert ops. Which meant Julio would still be part of a twosome when required. And that was okay. There was still evil in the world. As long as God needed him, he would go.

The moment Dom caught sight of Julio at Meg's office door, he scrambled onto her lap, grinning like the little charmer he'd become. "No, Daddy, no," he said adamantly, shaking his head back and forth while he ducked under Meg's chin, still keeping an eye on Julio. "Mum. I stay with Mum. Not you. No, no, no." Those big brown eyes of his sparkled. He knew which parent was the softie.

"Yes, yes, yes, son," Julio answered, his heart warmed by the tender scene. "You've had your medicine. You know it makes you sleepy. Mum can't work and hold you while you sleep, can she?" They'd had this discussion before.

Dom nodded just as adamantly as he'd shaken his head before. "Ah huh, she can. Mum can do anything."

There was that. But it'd sure help if Meg stopped grinning. Sitting there in her office chair with her laptop opened on her right, and her arms around the boy she adored, she positively glowed. There was no other word for it. Her hair had grown long enough she was finally able to curl it. The sun filtering through the blinds behind her cast a golden light on her, turning those chestnut curls into a halo. Motherhood looked good on Meg.

The doorbell rang. Julio cocked his head at her. "Why do I get the feeling you and the universe are working against me?"

She tipped her head back and laughed. "I would never! Go. See who wants to sell us solar panels this time. I'll put this tiny tyrant down for his nap. Then..." Her brows arched. "Maybe we can take a nap, too."

Julio winked. He loved afternoon naps with Meg.

"Aww," Dom whined. "Me wanna help."

Meg dropped a kiss into his head of dark curls. "Daddy's right. Nap now. Play later, kiddo."

Another "Aww." Another whine. Then a big wide yawn. Once his head finally hit his pillow, Dom would be out for the count. One just had to get him to that pillow.

Meg lifted to her feet, her hands on his tiny butt while he sagged against her. That damned obnoxious doorbell rang again. "Don't you have somewhere else to be?" she teased.

Julio honestly couldn't imagine where that might be. There was nowhere better than where he was now, standing here in the light of a good woman's—his woman's—grace. Loving her with every beat of his battered warrior's heart. Wanting to cup her smiling face between his palms and kiss her until she moaned.

"You are beautiful to me," he murmured like the sap he'd become these last few months.

Her smile widened as she came to a stop at the doorway he blocked. "And you are the best Daddy a little boy could ever ask for. Now give your father a kiss, young man."

Without hesitation, Dom tipped out of Meg's hands, puckered his lips, and leaned his shoulder into

Julio's chest. "Wub you, Daddy," he murmured as he planted a kiss on Julio's jaw.

Julio gave his son a quick hug and a kiss to his curly head. "And I love you, troublemaker. Now go to sleep. If you're good, we'll make milkshakes after dinner." Nutritionally fortified milkshakes, but Dom didn't need to know that.

"Okay," he sighed. "Night, night."

That crazy doorbell rang a third time!

"Wow, someone really wants to make a sale," Meg chuckled. "You, go. Tell whoever it is we're not buying, while I put this guy to bed."

Still complaining and yawning, Dom babbled a grumpy mixture of Portuguese, Spanish, and English. Meg was laughing from his bedroom when Julio headed back downstairs.

"I'm coming," he muttered. *"¡Ay, caramba!* Don't you people ever quit?"

Only it wasn't a salesman. It was FBI Special Agent Persia Coltrane standing there with one hand on her hip and tapping her toes while she waited. The second Julio opened the door, she tossed a handful of dark wavy mane over her shoulder and growled, "Jesus, Juarez, it's about time. It's hot today, damn it. Can I come in or do you want to do this out here where all your neighbors can hear what I have to say?"

Yup. As ruthless and brash as ever. That was Coltrane for you. All those neighbors amounted to the old farmer and his wife who live three miles down the road in one direction, and the young married couple who'd just moved into their brand-new home a mile in the other. The field of alfalfa behind Julio's and Meg's home didn't count.

He gestured Coltrane to enter, then ushered her past their toy-strewn, eclectically furnished living room to the kitchen he'd just tidied up after Dom's second breakfast. The dishwasher still hummed as he pulled a chair from the breakfast table. "Can I get you a cup of coffee, *mi amigo*?"

"Yes, please," she replied as she lowered into the proffered chair—Meg's chair—with a huff. "I like it black. You remember, don't you?"

"Of course." He'd remembered everything from their limited time together.

FBI Special Agent Persia Coltrane was the one-time-super-spy who'd been tucked deep inside Zapata's close-knit circle of bastards and degenerates. Back then, she'd worked for the CIA. Because of her mixed Hispanic heritage, her long dark hair, her bronzed olive skin, and her badass rep for getting the impossible done, she'd accomplished much during her two-year stint in Brazil.

Number one of those accomplishments was the day she'd slyly rigged an explosive within Zapata's personal bunker, then detonated it and created one helluva fire that masked Julio fast-roping from a stealth helo. Without her help, he wouldn't have known where Tomas or Bianca were in that maze of cellblocks. He would've wasted precious time. As it was, he'd stayed too long on the ground, and had nearly been apprehended by one of Zapata's guards.

Even that memory brought recrimination. Bianca had stalled leaving. She'd fussed that she wasn't prepared to simply up and leave. She'd risked his and Tomas' lives. Now, Julio knew why.

"You like it out here in the middle of Nowhere, USA?" Coltrane asked, her fingernails tapping a beat on the tabletop, as she perused the half-empty built-in china cabinet across from her. "I mean really. How's a big, badassed guy like you settle for all this—" her perfectly outlined, pink painted lips scrunched with disdain "—boredom?"

Filling two mugs to the brim, Julio had to smile. "One person's boredom is another's paradise."

Settling one mug on the placemat nearest Coltrane, he set the other at his place at the table and sank into the chair between Dom's highchair and Meg's. Where Coltrane was now sitting. He liked sitting between the people he loved most. These days, the simplest things brought him pleasure. Eating breakfast, lunch, and dinner with his *familia*. Cleaning up after them. Listening to Meg hum lullabies to his son. Making popcorn on movie night, or ice cream cones and milkshakes. All those ordinary, little, everyday things that never got old. Julio had learned the best lesson the hardest way. The truest treasure on earth was and forever would be—*familia*.

Coltrane took a healthy sip of coffee. "How's the kid?"

"Dominic is fine. Thank you for asking."

"He's..." She cleared her throat. "He's, umm, thriving?"

"Yes," Julio murmured, noticing the hesitation at her painful word choice. "This is his forever home now, and he knows it. He is happy. So are we."

"You two going to adopt him? I hear getting a healthy child out of Brazil is damned tough. Lots of regulations that don't favor us US citizens."

"Already did. Remember, *amigo*, we have an obnoxious United States Senator from Texas, on our side."

"Senator Sullivan? He worked this for you?"

"For me and Meg, *si*. But mostly, for Dominic."

McQueen Sullivan hadn't pulled any punches when it came time to stand up for Dominic and what was best for a sickly, three-year-old boy. He'd flown to Brazil and met with the current president. After that, Brazil's wise leader had made a grand public gesture, blaming the Zapata brothers for the strife in Minas Gerais. At the same time, he'd credited his National Guard with restoring law and order. Which worked for Sullivan and Julio. Julio had never cared about the politics behind grand gestures. By then, Meg had already filled out the overly redundant paperwork to adopt Dominic. They'd already been living in Ouro Preto with him to satisfy Brazil's thirty-day rule—just in case they got lucky and were allowed to adopt the son they already loved.

With one private word from Brazil's president, the country's National Adoption Agency suddenly became compliant. Very eager to please. At least eager to get them out of their country. They'd hurried Meg's paperwork through their convoluted system of checks, balances, and double-checks. Within days of Sullivan's meeting, Julio and Meg were back in the USA with Dominic.

Meg's other children still lived in Brazil, at the new, modernized orphanage with Craig and Marta, Fernando and Joseph. Several of the orphans relatives' had been located. Others had stepped forward to adopt. Sweet little Maria had a paternal grandmother who wanted her back. *Pronto!* Who knew?!

"Did you marry her?" Coltrane always had a lot of nerve.

"Not yet," Julio answered quietly. But the diamond he'd selected for Meg was paid for and sitting in his nightstand drawer. He just needed the right time to pop the question. Maybe soon.

Both his and Meg's wounds had healed. They were healthy and happy. Employed. Her paralysis had improved to the point where her confidence boomed. He just wanted to give her enough time to get to know him better. He wanted her to be sure. Her divorce had been brutal. How does one recover from betrayal like that? Unfortunately, Julio knew the answer. Hence his hesitation.

Coltrane blew out a gut-deep sigh. "I have what you asked for," she said as her empty mug hit the table.

"You're not going to like it. But you already know that, don't you?"

He met her sharp, shrewd gaze with a humble nod. "I have suspicions. That is all." He hadn't tasted his coffee yet. He could only handle so much bitterness in a day.

"Okay then. Here." She slid a portable hard-drive across the table. "That's as much as I can legally give you. It's not the redacted version. View it at your leisure, but don't say I didn't warn you."

He didn't touch the drive, just looked at the evidence that would convict or pardon Bianca once and for all. It was peculiar how a man's entire life came down to singular, defining, truth-or-dare moments like this. His heart kicked deep inside his chest at what facts he might soon learn. It was suddenly hard to breathe. His lungs seemed unable to fully expand. His chest hurt. A heart could only take so much betrayal before it burst. Did he really want to know what was on that drive?

Coltrane reached one arm across the table and took his fingers away from his mug. Curling them inside her palm, she said, "Your son was never alone, my friend. I was there, remember? During that long, hard year, I made friends in that hell-hole. Not every prisoner was a selfish bitch. Some were mothers who cried every night for their own lost babies. Some were little girls who couldn't bear to hear another child weep. There were good hearts trapped inside Zapata's zoo, Julio. Trust me. Your Tomas was not alone."

But his mother wasn't there for him, was she? The woman who should have sheltered him, didn't, did she? Instant tears flooded Julio's vision. There was no sense trying to hide them. He didn't need to lie to Coltrane. She'd been there. She knew.

"There's nothing I can say to ease your pain, *mi amigo*. Nothing, but that I am so Goddamned sorry for your loss," she murmured softly. Still leaning toward him. Still trying to make right the worst crime a child could suffer. "I've never been a mother. Probably never will be, but—" Coltrane inhaled a deep breath. "—I'm a damned good aunt. I sheltered those I could while I was there, especially the smallest. You have to know that Zapata's only interest in kids was using them for leverage. Once he got what he wanted, he left them alone."

Julio stared at the drive, afraid to ask. Afraid he already knew the answer. But asking anyway, "H-how soon?" He coughed into his free hand. Cleared his throat. Carried on. "How soon after Bianca arrived did she...? Was she...?" *Dios,* it was hard to speak the defiling words. Had Zapata needed any leverage to get Bianca into his bed. Or was that why she'd come to Brazil, to be with him? Then why had she dragged Tomas along with her? Just to hurt Tomas? Or to hurt Julio? The thought galled him that she'd spat on all he held dear and sacred. Like his marriage vows. His baby boy.

"Are you asking me how quickly she went with Domingo?"

He nodded, wiping a quick finger under his nose. Unable to speak.

Coltrane's voice dropped to a whisper. "She was usually at his side. She didn't argue with or fight him. Ever."

"Were..." *Dios!* This was unspeakably hard. "Were you there?"

Coltrane nodded. "The day he showed up with your wife and son in tow? Yes, I was there. He'd built a helicopter pad on top the one cellblock. I saw. I know."

There was so much more Julio wanted to ask, but even this small amount of information was breaking his heart. Tomas might not have suffered the atrocities as Julio had thought, but he'd still been deserted by the mother who should've had his back. Who should have loved him more than she'd loved herself. Who should've protected him above everyone else. But especially against—*him. Zapata. May he burn in Hell forever.*

Stifling his grief and his anger, and blinking hard, Julio lifted his gaze to the ceiling. Bianca had unmanned him from the beginning. Nothing she'd ever said had been true. Julio knew that now. Then she'd betrayed her son, the tiny helpless boy Julio would gladly have died a thousand times for.

And yet, right now, beyond this very kitchen, up on the second floor, Bianca's second child, Dominic, still breathed and, yes, giggled. He was safe and sound, no doubt drowsily listening to a bedtime story, while Meg—the Mum *he'd* chosen—snuggled him against her lush body. His little head was probably resting on her pillowy breasts while he sucked his thumb and pretended to read along. He did that now, comforting himself with his thumb, whenever he grew tired. Or when carb overload hit his still frail body.

Meg would speak softer and softer until he dropped off to sleep. Then she'd sit in that rocking chair, holding her little boy tightly, not relinquishing her quiet time with him any sooner than she had to. Not until Julio climbed back up those stairs and winked at her to join him.

She'd offer some silly protest then, but finally, she'd lay Dominic on his toddler bed. She'd cover him and make sure his blankie, that Minky, dimple-dotted quilt that he loved, was the first thing he saw when he woke. Julio would stand over their son with Meg. She'd have a sappy, motherly glow on her face, and she'd kiss Dominic one last time. Julio would kiss that tender little boy, too—his son—carefully, so as not to wake him. Then he'd kiss him again. Once just for Dominic. Once again for Tomas. Both of his boys.

There was no way to go back in time and correct Bianca's betrayals or ease Tomas' suffering. Life didn't work that way, and Karma was not that kind. But knowing that Dominic would never suffer as Tomas had... That he stood a good chance of beating tuberculosis, marching off to preschool in a couple years and kindergarten... Then grade school, high school, and college... Knowing that from now on, he'd always have a fierce mother and father bear at his back, ones who had and would march straight into Hell for their son... even before he'd legally been theirs to defend.

There was comfort in that sure knowledge. Julio swiped a hand across his eyes and swallowed hard. At last he could breathe. He had believed in his God and he had run the hard race. He had done all he could, and in the process, he'd saved Meg and Dominic. A couple times.

Coltrane squeezed his fingers, then released them as she shoved back in her chair.

"Oh. I didn't know we had company," Meg said from the kitchen door. "Am I interrupting? I can go back up to my—"

"Never," Julio growled as he cleared his throat again and beckoned her to come join him.

She came quickly to his side, but there were times when simple wifely contact wasn't enough. Julio tugged her onto his lap, circled her waist with both arms, and faced the friend he would always love for her self-sacrifice on behalf of his son. Like him, Coltrane had done as much as she could to protect Tomas. She would always be his *amigo*.

"Meg, meet FBI Special Agent Persia Coltrane. I've told you about her."

"It's so good to finally meet you, Meg Duncan," Coltrane replied as she shook Meg's hand. "Good work in Brazil."

"Likewise. Julio told me you helped him save Tomas. You looked out for Tomas, didn't you?"

"Yes, ma'am, I did." Coltrane's gaze shifted from Meg to Julio. "That's what we do, isn't it? We serve. Fidelity. Bravery. Integrity. Some of us still have it."

"Thank you," Meg replied as she leaned her head onto Julio's shoulder. "You're one in a million."

Coltrane shook that off, her dark hair flouncing off her shoulders. "No, ma'am, I'm not. You are. Take good care of my Vaquero. I'll see you around."

Julio scrubbed a hand over his face. *Madre de Dios! Not that.*

By then, Agent Coltrane was out the door and gone. But Meg was still in his arms, her head cocked up at him with curiosity, and her lips curled at the corners. *Here it comes...*

"Vaquero?" she asked, her eyes an extra-bright emerald. "As in a—"

"Yesssss," he hissed. "As in cowboy. It's just a tag, a handle. A nickname when I was Navy." One he'd never wanted and now, would never live down.

Meg's smile widened. "You mean all this time I've had a gunslinger on my six? Really? You're a no-kidding cowboy? Ooooh, I like that! What'd you do to earn that handle?"

The awe in her voice humbled and embarrassed Julio. He was nothing special. Just a guy doing what he could to make this tired old world safer for everyone, not just for the privileged few who could afford security systems, twelve-foot high walls, and bodyguards.

"I didn't get it because I was good with firearms." Though he was. "A vaquero is not a gunslinger. He's a keeper of flocks, sweetheart. Of sheep. I'm no angel." She ought to know that by now.

"Wanna know what my handle is?" Meg asked excitedly, a definite tease in her sassy tone.

Julio looked down into the sparkle of her eyes, thrilled that she'd let that annoying info byte slide, but not really caring what others called her. He lifted to his feet with her securely in his arms, shoved the chair out from behind him with the backs of his legs, and headed for the stairs again. "Mine," he whispered. "That's your handle. Only one you need."

"Well, yeah. Of course, but Hotrod gave me a handle the day we flew back into Brazil, and I'd never had one til then and—"

Julio came to a dead stop on the third step up. Tipping his head, he covered her mouth with his and swallowed her words. Handles weren't important, not in his current line of work, where too much information could get a guy or gal killed. Ghost might've been a better nickname for him, although now that he thought about it, with his hands all over Meg, Julio didn't feel like a ghost anymore. He'd materialized, been resurrected, and brought back to life because of her.

"Make love with me?" he asked, his feet back on track to their bedroom. One door down from Dom's.

"Yes," she breathed into the hollow of his neck, inciting him until he took the stairs two steps at a time.

They fell into bed together, his hands under her shirt, her hands under his. Undressing each other had always been half the treat, but when he got down to her silky red panties and matching bra, his breath wheezed out of him. Julio rolled Meg to her back and stilled her greedy fingers before she took hold of him where there would be no turning back.

The tenderness of this rare moment snuck up on him with all its maybes and what-ifs.

It was time.

Swallowing hard, Julio reached past Meg to his nightstand. Tugging the drawer open, he retrieved his gift, then closed the drawer so no elbows or knees would hit it. He put the small square box in the center of her chest, over her heart and right above those red, silk-encased, perfect breasts.

"This is for you," he whispered, his throat dry. "I've waited long enough. Maybe too long. But I wanted you to be sure—"

"Yes," she said. "I'm sure."

"But you went through so much with your first marriage, and I—"

"Stop talking. I'm sure."

"But really, Meg. This will last forever," he declared adamantly. "I believe in true love and commitment. Honesty. Until death do us part. Maybe I'm just a foolish romantic, but—"

She yawned. The woman he loved yawned! In the middle of his proposal!

"Am I boring you?"

Those naughty eyes grinned back at him. "Remember that time you told me that talk is cheap? Umm, let me think, I'm pretty sure you said..." Meg rolled her eyes, as her index finger landed on her pursed lips, tap, tap, tapping as if she were thinking. "Something about how pure love needs no words, only action to prove it exists. Yada, yada, yada, something, something, something."

That did sound familiar. "Yes, I said most of that. Without the smartassed yadas. But yeah. I remember."

Her arms slipped around his shoulders. Her hands came to rest at the nape of his neck as her long fingers danced up his scalp into his hair. He looked down at her bare body, totally smitten with her lush, gloriously beautiful breasts, now flattened like succulent pink pillows against his darkly tanned chest. Julio licked his lips, his heart thudding with an irregular hop, skip, and jump. He couldn't swallow. Didn't dare breathe. She had him right where she wanted him, and she knew it.

"I... ahh..." He forgot what he was going to say. Or if it was even his turn to talk. This woman drove him absolutely crazy.

She tugged him down to her face, her pretty eyes nearly crossed, she was that close-up and personal. Those sweeter-than-honey lips were wet and tempting.

"The thing is I don't need an expensive ring. I only need you. You're my hero. Every time I've needed someone at my side these last few months, you showed up. You were there for me. Out of the blue. I knew I loved you the first time I saw you. I've been dying to ask you to marry me, but now you've gone and asked me, and I said yes because you also said 'let's make love instead of talking'.

"You're not going to open it?" He'd shopped for weeks. The ring cost a small fortune, and he'd put a lot of thought and worry into it. Meg should at least look at it.

"Well, all right," she groused as she took the box into her hands and opened it. But then, she did it again. Instead of oooohing and ahhing over the size of that sparkly rock, Meg took the ring out of its velvet holder and set the box aside. He could tell she liked the ring. At least, she seemed to like the braided, rose gold band. The diamond, however, was pinched between her index finger and thumb like it was simply a handle or something.

He was having trouble swallowing and breathing again. He didn't want to ask. Maybe she wasn't a jewelry person like most women. After all, she had said yes. That should be enough. Shouldn't it? Still, he waited. Something was missing. He just didn't know what.

Until Meg peered up at him with tears in her eyes, blinking like a little girl as she lifted the band up to his nose. "You see," she squeaked, "the most important part of engagement and wedding rings is this right here. This band of gold or rose gold or whatever it is."

"Rose gold," he supplied quickly.

"Okay, rose gold then," she murmured, her brimming eyes on the band. "Most girls want diamonds and glitter, but me? See this band, how there's no end to it? How it goes around and around without a single seam?"

Closing one eye, she held it close to her other eye. "If you squint and look really hard, you'll see it's a piece of perfect workmanship, or machining, or however they made this ring. And, honest, the diamond's real pretty, Julio. But this band... This is the most important part, because diamonds fall out and get lost and settings break, but this circle of gold..."

There went that tongue again. "This circle holds everything together. It's made of one perfect piece of metal. It's just like our love, Julio. Never ending, like I hope our life together will be. Like... us. Forever and ever."

Julio felt the tears in his eyes about to fall. In his haste to do everything right, he'd forgotten the lesson of the stone. That those who loved stones more than their forever familia, lost everything in the end. He was a very stupid man.

Her slender fingers began trembling. She swallowed so hard he heard the gulp as her throat muscles worked. There was nothing more beautiful than the pure light of love in the emerald green jewels shining up at him. The pink tip of her tongue ran the length of her sweet bottom lip. Wetting it until it shone—for him. Making him hard—for her.

"I love you, Julio, with every piece of my ornery heart," she squeaked, her tears leaking into her temples now. The more she blinked, the faster that salty river flowed. "But I don't need diamonds and jewels, sweetheart. I only need you." She sniffed. "So, yes, I'll marry you, and I'll take especially good care of you and our sons and daughters, and however many babies you want to have with me. What more do you want?"

Gracias, dulce Madre de Dios! He should've known. Meg wasn't and never could be anything like What's-Her-Name. She had more heart and courage than most men and women he'd met. More fortitude and honor. But he'd been so caught up in the traditional mindset of proposing... He'd been so worried about things that didn't really matter—like rocks—that he'd lost sight of the brilliant woman he was marrying this time around. Like a true warrior, Meg was leading the way, and teaching him to let go of the ways of the past. Teaching him the way of the heart. Only heart. Not rocks.

When he could finally speak, Julio breathed, "Only you," into her mouth. "You're all I want and need."

Meg tipped her chin into his chest, her body quivering as she wrapped her arms around his neck and sobbed. "I do love the ring, Julio. It's very beautiful, and I will wear it proudly the rest of my life because you gave it to me. It scares me sometimes how much I love you, but it's true. I. Love. You."

With a sigh of repentance for having been an idiot, Julio let his body crush her to the mattress. Meg spread her legs and shifted her legs and feet around him, circling him with her entire body and soul.

Julio melted against her. Slowly, and with full intent, he tugged the red silk panties aside and sank into her, so thankful for the brave, courageous woman in his hands and in his heart. *Madre de Dios*, he'd been right the day he'd told her that pure love needed no words, only action to prove it existed. Talk was cheap, but this was real. This moment. This woman.

Not Megan. Sure as heck not Nutmeg. Just… Meg.

THE END

Preview King of Hearts

Deuces Wild, #1

I'm on my way.

Again.

Tucker Chase couldn't get to her house fast enough, but damn, he was tired of the on-again, off-again rollercoaster romance with Melissa McCormack, and the siren call of the temptress he wasn't man enough to resist. He was sick of her mixed signals, too. One minute pulling him in for another kiss, the next, pushing him back, not ready to move on. Why not? *He* was ready. Why'd she have to make everything so hard? Why couldn't she find that God-blessed closure she needed?

It was a stupid question, and he got it. Really, he did. A widow needed more time to move on than a divorced man, but how much more time? *To hell with closure.*

He punched the steering wheel of his black Dodge Challenger. He'd been playing this game for over a year, and during that year, he'd been uncharacteristically faithful. He hadn't once looked at another woman, which was not his style. He'd taken it slow with Melissa—also not his style. He'd romanced and dined the hell out of her, he'd bought her more roses than he'd ever bought his ex-wife in their short, explosive marriage, and he'd waited. Oh, how he'd waited.

But every single time he took things a little too far, every time he read her sexy body language and thought she was past regret and ready to give in to him, bam. She drew back and pulled away. Son-of-a-bitch but he was tired of the regret glimmering in her blue eyes. The shadow she seemed to nurse like a long-lost friend. The ghost of her dead husband.

Damn Brady McCormack for being such a stand-up guy. For being her hero. For getting shot to hell in Iraq and coming home a quadriplegic. For dying. And damn Melissa for still being eternally faithful to her first true love. How could a flesh-and-blood guy compete with a marble headstone in Arlington?

Tucker couldn't. He looked both ways before he crossed the busy intersection against the light. Damn it. Despite his intense heartache for Melissa, he wasn't angry with her for loving her husband. Not really. That was actually part of what drew Tucker to Melissa. Her loyalty. Her undying devotion. She was that once-in-a-lifetime, too-good-to-be-true, impossible dream girl.

From the get-go, she'd been a single ray of sunshine in his solitary world where warriors crossed paths with evil incarnate. She was that first breath of fresh spring air on a chilly March morning. If anything, he was jealous of Brady, and more than a little angry the guy went and got shot up so bad that he'd eventually died. Melissa deserved to be happy again. Tucker wanted to be that guy.

The car to his left blared a warning. He flipped the driver off, hit the gas, peeled rubber, and kept moving. There he was, half-crazy with needing Melissa and running red lights to get to her side before she changed her mind. Dodging slow traffic. And cursing all the way.

Melissa was not like other women. She was a one-man-and-one-man-only kind of gal, and he'd been caught in the same breathless grip ever since. One look into the liquid depths of her ocean blue eyes and he'd fallen like a punch-drunk sailor over his own big feet. Strength swelled in those shimmering windows to her soul, but other things lingered in the shadows. Sadness. Bravery. Her morals.

He cussed the early morning traffic on the Northern Virginia freeway. Tapping his fingernails on the stick shift, he forced a deep breath to calm his need for speed. The last thing he wanted was another ticket, and this souped-up pony would get it for him if he didn't rein it in and take it easy. Melissa wouldn't like *that*, either.

Sheesh. That woman!

For now, she lived in a singles-only condo west of Arlington, close to her family and her husband's family. That was another thing. Her parents were good Christians and nice people. Tucker had met them. He liked them, especially her mother. Camille had welcomed him with open arms, a hug and a big smile. But her father? All he'd done was scowl and grumble during Tucker's visit. It took extra patience to get through that night.

Then the McCormacks, Jed and Lois. Where to begin? Brady had been their only child, their pride and joy. When he'd died from complications due to his war injuries, Melissa became their world. If her own parents didn't dote on her, Jed and Lois surely did.

She was everyone's rock star. Tucker was just another groupie hanging around for an autograph. She meant the world to them. He was the proverbial bad boy they hoped she'd grow out of, get over, and leave in the dust when she moved onto someone more socially acceptable. So what if he had a reputation for being a notorious hard-ass around D.C.? What decent FBI agent didn't? They got the dirty jobs done, and they had a lot to be proud of, damn it.

He pulled onto Melissa's street and roared up to the security gate of her condo complex. "Hey," he said smoothly to the up-tight security guard. "I'm back."

"I see that. Slow it down. Five miles per hour, please." The stuffy guy raised the wrought-iron security gate, and Tucker made sure he didn't exceed the pathetically slow speed limit to her door. Melissa waited for him on the sidewalk and double damn if she didn't take his breath away like she always did.

He shoved the stick shift into park and let the sight of her wash over him. His heart swelled. As frustrated as she could make him, Melissa also made him proud. This woman was as strong as she was beautiful, as intelligent as she was kind. She also had a soft streak the size of Texas, and it ran clear to her soul.

He took time to drink in her voluptuous curves. There wasn't a hard line or edge to the woman. "Melissa," he called as he scrambled out of the Challenger, his heart in his throat like always.

But look at her. What man could resist? Blond long hair hung in spirals down her back and over her shoulders. Full breasts bounced beneath her pale-yellow top. As she walked toward him, curvy hips swayed with a provocative catch-me-if-you-can. Even her lush, sweet lips were turned up into a perfect bow of juicy temptation, the soft Virginia sun bright on her face. This woman had been created to drive him crazy, all lush curves from her plump hips to her full and very soft breasts. He would know. Second base was as far as he'd gotten. She just wouldn't give it up, no matter what he'd tried, and believe him—he'd tried.

"Tucker! Hi!" She smiled, full of vitality and happy to see him. Her fluffy Yorkie, Taz, bounced at her ankles. He looked happy to see Tucker, but what dog wasn't? Dogs were smart enough to recognize a good guy when they saw one.

Tucker closed the distance with long strides, wondering which of them was the bigger fool, her for leading him on or him for letting her. "You called?" he asked as she walked into his arms. He gathered her up, and closed his eyes, inhaling the feminine scent of green apples and vanilla musk. Maybe cinnamon. God, it was happening again. He wanted to rub her over his chest—and other places—just to keep her essence with him all the time. That was what he'd missed—this simple reminder that she really did belong to him. That they were made for each other. That he could be her hero, if she'd just let him in.

The battle for her heart never went away. It hadn't since he'd first seen her, and her scent only made it worse. There he was, as hard as a rock in all the wrong places and ready to try again.

Tilting her chin upward with his thumb, he looked into the sweetest face. Her lips blossomed with a genuine smile, and he succumbed to her invitation. He took her mouth with all the tender love in his heart, running his tongue over her lips and allowing her time to let him in. She always did, and Melissa knew how to kiss. She seemed to pour all of her womanly charm into that sensual contact. She fully engaged, her arms around his neck, her breasts pressed to his chest, and her teeth and tongue actively involved. Nipping. Tugging. Tasting him the same way he tasted her.

Like it or not, Tucker Chase was hooked like a great sea bass off the Atlantic coast. A man could get used to the sensual sweep of her tongue over his, the tango of mint and lipstick. The promise of that elusive more he'd been looking for. The way she sucked his lower lip into her mouth and nibbled. The soft murmurs of a satisfied woman he ached to satisfy even more. Yeah. She wanted him, and God knew he wanted her.

He let his hand sink to the small of her back, his fingertips splayed over the round plump cheek of her ass. He longed for the day she'd let him get a good grip, but he didn't dare tempt fate. Not today. She'd sounded anxious on the phone earlier. He needed to pay attention.

She eased away from his mouth and leaned her cheek to his chest, her head tucked under his chin. See, that was what turned him inside out. She wanted to be close, really close—just not as close as he wanted her to be. And yet she did. He could read it in her eyes, just before she'd push him away. She wanted him as much as he wanted her, but that noble Marine she'd married and buried stood in the way. Every time.

"It came," she said, a tremor of excitement in her tone. "It finally came. I've been selected."

He would've answered, but the seductively warm heat radiating from this woman's sexy body robbed him of all common sense. He cocked his head and waited for the rest of the story. What had come? She'd accused him of not listening enough, and he knew better than to open his big mouth, insert foot and admit it.

"I'm leaving next week. Remember?"

Tucker needed to see her face for sure then. He eased her back, his thumb under her chin to tip her gaze upward, just enough to read the answer in those lovely eyes. "You're what? Leaving to go where?"

"You didn't hear me, did you?" she asked, that look in her eyes again. *That* look. The one that showed up right before every shove-off and goodbye. "You weren't listening to me last week, were you?"

"I thought I was, babe," he admitted guiltily. "I really do try, but you're so intoxicating. I might have missed something."

The smile faded. *Here we go again.*

"You never listen, Tucker, and don't give me that 'babe' or 'I'm so intoxicating' stuff." She bobbed her head back and forth in a bad imitation of a swagger. "I need you to care about the things I care about. I need you to see me. Really see me."

There it was again, her palm square in the middle of his chest, enforcing her personal space. Like he didn't know what 'no' meant. He didn't mean to snort like he did, but holy shit. This woman drove him nuts ten ways to Sunday. "Where are you going, Melissa? Just spit it out and tell me."

"I've been accepted for a three-month mission with Doctors for Charity. I leave next Tuesday," she said quietly. "I've talked about this with you. It's important work. Tell me you remember."

He scrubbed a hand over his chin. Three months? She might as well have told him to drop dead because his heart sure felt like it had. What was he supposed to do while she gallivanted to the other side of the world on some humanitarian crusade with a bunch of horny doctors? Sit home and wait for her to decide to come back? Write letters? *Shit. Just shit.*

She took a step out of his arms, her eyes narrowed. "You honestly don't remember, do you?"

"Yeah, I remember." Kind of. She had been excited about something a month ago. Maybe he should've listened a little better. *Three months?* "When will you be back?"

Melissa rolled her shoulder, sending a cascade of golden silk flying, the curled ends cupping her breast the way he'd like to. "I just told you. Three months, Tucker. I'll be back the middle of February."

"February what?" He ran a hand over his head and down the back of his neck. That meant she'd be gone over Christmas. Holy hell. There'd be no joy in Whoville and less in his heart.

Melissa peered closer, her nose wrinkled. "What is that thing in your eye, *Tucker Chase*?"

Oh, oh. Her tone and use of his full name jerked him back in time to grade school and his ornery third grade teacher, the one who used to smack him to get his attention. He blinked, stalling. "It's nothing. Just an implant to help me see better. Don't worry about it."

She took a step closer and tipped his chin up, her brows joined in a deeply etched and sexy V. She squinted. "You've... you've got a contact? When did you get it? What's wrong with that eye?"

The implant was more than a contact lens. The state-of-the-art mechanized zoom lens was a futuristic FBI option that went along with his cochlear implant, only people weren't supposed to notice it. Especially not Melissa. *Damn.*

Tucker bowed his head, wishing she'd understand the advantage it gave him in the field but knowing that was unlikely. "It's not a contact. It's just an ocular implant, no big deal. It's cool. I can adjust it and... Thursday," he admitted, losing ground. *Two days ago.*

She cocked her head, challenging him. "You had eye surgery, and you didn't think to tell me?"

Shit. Just shit.

"You know..." She tugged Taz's bright pink leash, bringing the happy-go-lucky little guy to her side. "Maybe we need to take a time out, maybe figure out what's really going on between us."

"Are you breaking up with me?" he asked, a titch too sharply. Women just didn't do that. Not to him.

"Honestly, I don't know what I'm doing," she said sadly. "You don't let me into your life, Tucker. Like this implant. I should've been there with you when you had the surgery. For that matter, you should've talked this over with me before you took matters into your own hands. But you never do, do you? For heaven's sake, one minute you're hot, but the next—"

"Damn it, I'm always hot, Melissa. That's who I am. I'm hotheaded, and I'm hot-blooded, and I want you in every way a man can possibly want a woman. But you never give me the same signal twice!" He took one step away from her before he said anything that would get him into more trouble. "You let me hold you like a lover, but you're not one, are you?"

"Excuse me?" she asked, blinking as if she'd just been slapped.

That wasn't what he'd meant to say. True maybe, but not smart. He took a deep breath and tried again. "Babe, I'm sorry. You know I've got a big mouth, but I lo-lo-l—" *Oh shit*. He snapped his big mouth shut. He'd almost said it, the one word that wasn't in his playbook. Not anymore.

Of course she picked up on that little mistake. "Don't you dare tell me you love me now, Tucker. Don't. You. Dare." She stabbed her index finger into his chest, punctuating his mistake. "Love isn't a cheap pick-up line and it isn't a cure-all when you're too busy to listen. It's not a solves-all blurb for the few moments you're interested, either."

"But I am interested. All the time." *How could she not know that?*

"No, you're not." He loved the spark in her eyes when she got riled up. "Every time we're together, you've got your finger in your ear listening to that voice in your head, that FBI cochlear implant that keeps you up-to-date twenty-four-seven on everything else in the world but me. And now we'll have your bionic eyeball. We'll never have one uninterrupted moment alone, will we? You can't save the whole planet, Tucker. Have you ever once considered that? Do you always have to be the hero?"

He would've told her how stupid that question was—after all, who didn't know that SEALs were always the heroes—but his cell phone buzzed an incoming. Didn't it figure? At least HQ hadn't called the hotline this time. She'd be pissed if he stuck his finger in his ear to better listen to the latest calling-all-cars over her ranting. He'd never hear the end of that.

"Do you?" she asked again. Melissa closed her eyes and took a deep breath. Sweet little Taz whined. He wasn't happy either.

Tucker's heart kicked up a funny thump because he'd forgotten her question. His phone buzzed a second time. *Here we go again.*

She was absolutely right. He needed to take a timeout from his job once in a while, but something big was going down, maybe in D.C. His cell buzzed an incoming. He needed to respond to headquarters before everything blew up.

"Sorry," he mumbled, scooping his vibrating cell phone out of his pants pocket. Her lips pinched into a thin, tight line, but he answered anyway, one eye on her and not the bionic one. "Chase. What's up?"

"Trespassers on the White House grounds," the FBI switchboard informed. "They jumped the fence. Three of them. Wearing hoods. Possibly armed. Metro is engaged now. Requesting FBI backup."

"On my way," he replied, because that was what FBI agents always did. Like SEALs, they showed up every time and they did their job.

"See?" Melissa asked, her smile gone and the sunshine with it. "Each time we get together, this happens. You get some secret message. You take off because you have somewhere better to be. Someone else to save. Someone who isn't me. And to top it off, now you've got your office in your ear talking over anything I say. I'm tired of it, Tuck. You're exhausting. I'll see you in three months, but I want an answer then, and it better not be sex-related. Got it?"

Hmmm. Sex-related. He couldn't help but notice that her breasts heaved when she got her dander up. That her nipples peaked beneath that pale-yellow T-shirt. That her pretty face flushed with an enticing peach blush that probably matched her petal soft breasts. That she chewed her lower lip. That *he* wanted to chew her lower lip. His tongue slid against his teeth just thinking about the way she tasted. Honey with the sweet, salty hint of caramel apple and—

"Tucker," she growled, another splash of hot-damned sexy on his already hardened manhood. "Are you listening to me? Have you heard anything I said?"

He nodded, but the blood supply train to his brain had jumped tracks and headed south. "Yes. I heard you. Three months. Ninety days. Middle of February. Got it."

"And then what?"

He gave her what he thought she wanted to hear. "You'll be home."

Her lashes went down. She shook her head just enough to let him know he'd gotten it wrong again.

And Melissa walked away.

Thank you for reading Julio's story!

If you enjoyed this book, be sure to check out the other SOBs novels:

Angel, #1
Assassin, #2

Coming soon: *Damned, #4*

Irish Winters' flagship series:
In the Company of Snipers

Coming soon: *Walker, #21*

Other Irish Winters' novels:

King of Hearts, Deuces Wild
Joker Joker, Deuces Wild
One-Eyed Jack, Deuces Wild
Ace, Deuces Wild
Smoke, Hearts and Ashes
Ash, Hearts and Ashes

YOU ARE THE KEY TO THIS BOOK'S SUCCESS

Please tell other readers why you liked Julio and Meg's story by leaving an honest review at the retail site where you purchased it.

Recommend it to your friends. Lend it. Most of all, enjoy it!

The best way to keep up with my new releases, giveaways, and actionable intel is to sign up for my spam-free newsletter at IrishWinters.com.

About the Author

Irish Winters...

...is a best-selling author who, when she isn't writing, dabbles in poetry, grandchildren, and rarely (as in extremely rarely) the kitchen. More prone to be outdoors than in, she grew up the quintessential tomboy on a dairy farm in rural Wisconsin, spent her teen years in the Pacific Northwest, but calls the Wasatch Mountains of Northern Utah, home. For now.

She believes in making every day count for something, and follows the wise admonition of her mother to, "Look out the window and see something!"

Connect with Irish online:

On Facebook
www.facebook.com/IrishWintersAuthor/

On Twitter
www.twitter.com/irishwinters1

www. IrishWinters.com